The Cosmos of Destiny

A Novel By A.J. Mayers

A.J. Mayers

This is a work of fiction. Names, characters, businesses, organizations, places, events, and incidents are the product of the author's imagination or are used fictitiously. Any resemblance to actual persons, living or dead, or actual events is entirely coincidental.

To my late grandfather Miller for igniting that spark as I settled into my own destiny...

Contents

Chapter One:

The Noah's Ark Project

The President was pacing back and forth by his desk in the Oval Office of the White House. He kept absentmindedly adjusting his half-moon glasses and thumbing through his electronic tablet computer for news coverage on what was happening outside the White House lawn. The headlines he scrolled through on the touch screen did not comfort him. It seemed as though the entire country was reaching a pandemonium of epic proportions.

The President peered through the blinds, which had been shut, to look at the chaos ensuing outside. There were thousands of armed military personnel and secret service agents with guns and silver cross weapons called Disintegrators, which were being used for defensive purposes to keep the throngs of civilians at bay from barging over the fence of the White House. People were screaming, yelling obscenities, and carrying around picket signs. The overall consensus of the crowd was that they were extremely angry with the government.

There were three helicopters hovering above the White House with their weapons at the ready as well. One of them landed on the lawn and a man in a suit ran out of it escorted by a few secret service agents. The man ran up the steps to the entrance of the White House and was greeted by more secret service agents that conducted a pat check to make sure he was not carrying anything dangerous.

The man was then escorted in haste to the Oval Office to meet with the president. One of the agents in tow knocked on the Oval Office door and announced himself.

"President Williams...Landon Parker has arrived."

The agents stayed outside of the Oval Office and Landon walked in to greet President Williams.

"Will," Landon said, "are you ready for The Noah's Ark Project to take on full effect?"

"What other choice do we have?" President Williams said somberly.

"It's only been forty eight hours since the Times Square incident and at this rate, there will be no United States to call home. We're lucky we have weapons to keep the civilians out there at bay," Landon said. "I'm getting word of several riots breaking out across the country. People are turning on each other. This morning a church was burned down just outside D.C."

President Williams ran his hands through his light-blonde short buzzed hair. He peered outside the window again and sighed heavily.

"The project, sir, was always meant for a situation like this where there was a possibility for the end of days on Earth," Landon said.

"But we don't know that the world is ending. It's still revolving around the sun."

"The sun has been eclipsed by those dark shadows...the Dark Ones, as they are called," Landon said. "They have possessed some people already and are helping to add to the hysteria. There is no going back to the norm. Something like this was predicted in the Moonshadow files."

"No," President Williams corrected Landon. "The Elders told us we would become over populated and that population control would be the plan of action."

"But in case of an emergency," Landon said, "where our resources would run out or civilization would crumble, we would use the United States Square Aviator to transport a certain number of people and male and female species of animals. Noah's Ark."

"How can we pick who gets to live on?" President Williams said. "It's unfair."

3

"The brightest minds, individuals from the government, doctors, scientists, scholars," Landon said putting up a finger for each professional he named.

"And we will be put in a deep sleep for how long?" President Williams asked.

"That will be determined once the USSA is up in space and far away from Earth. It will head on a course to where Threa is," Landon said.

"Our visit cannot go unannounced to Threa's population," President Williams said. "We need to let Manuel know we are coming and we are bringing life to their world."

"First of all," Landon said, "We don't have access to a Communicator. The one that the Dark Ones used to call Threa has been destroyed. They came and took Shane at the Empire State Building and then saved us right before the building collapsed. It happened so fast, but I remember the white light and I saw Manuel. He didn't say anything to me, but he was in a hurry to leave. I don't think they will be coming back to save us. They taught us how to save ourselves with the Ark."

"That being said," President Williams added, "how can we just show up unannounced?"

"They used humans to keep their race alive by living among us," Landon said. "They owe us. Manuel worked with us once. He will have to understand."

"I think we should be diplomatic with their world and let them know we will be coming," President Williams said.

"Once again," Landon said, "We don't have a way to communicate with them."

President Williams smiled mysteriously at Landon and walked over to a cabinet behind his desk. He pulled out a brass key and inserted it in the keyhole. He then placed his eyes over two red dots that appeared on the cabinet when he turned the key. The cabinet swung open. Landon nearly fell off the edge of the President's desk that he was leaning on, in shock of what was revealed hidden safely in the cabinet.

"A Communicator!?" said a flabbergasted Landon. "How? I thought it was destroyed by the Dark Ones?"

"This," President Williams said, "has been passed down from president to president over the past two decades completely done privately without the NHR's knowledge. It was a promise made to Manuel when they left Threa several years ago."

"The presidents have been in contact with Threa?!" Landon asked gripping at his chest. "All…these…years?"

"Off and on. Not frequently, but just once in a while they would check in on us," President Williams said.

"So even after the Communicator that I had at my condo was stolen, you could not have come forward to help the Non-Human Relations agency?"

"Don't get your pants in a twist," President Williams said. "It works only one-way. Only they can contact us. We cannot contact them. I hoped they would somehow contact us during the time that the Eye Opener's threats became a damage to national security. Unfortunately they didn't call in."

"I'm pretty sure Shane would have been able to use it to call Threa!" Landon said almost shouting, which caused the Oval Office doors to swing open.

"Everything alright?" One of the secret service agents asked.

"Yes," President Williams said, blocking the silver cone Communicator from view. "Do you mind giving us some more time alone?"

The agents nodded and stepped back outside.

"We will take the cone with us," President Williams said. "I am positive that Manuel will reach out to us within the next couple of days. I'm not sure how long it takes their technology to reach us. What time will we board the helicopter?"

"Um," Landon said still trying to process what he had just learned. "We should leave in the next half hour or so. We need to transport to a battleship that's a few miles off the coast in the Atlantic Ocean. The USSA was not greatly damaged in the Dark

One attack, and now that we have it back in our possession, it is best that we don't let them take it over and use it against us like they did two days ago in Times Square. The USSA will pick us up on the battleship and then we will head to space."

"These are dark days," President Williams said. "These are dark and somber days."

"Without the sun, I'd have to agree with you on the dark part," Landon said. "What happened to the Moonshadow ranchers?"

"After the Humanoids from Threa showed up in their ship with their light, the Dark Ones retreated temporarily and we were able to gain control of the ship remotely from a military base," President Williams said.

"I see," Landon said while looking at his watch. "We should probably head out to the lawn now. The helicopter should be arriving shortly."

As soon as Landon finished his sentence, a group of secret service agents barged into the Oval office once more and announced the arrival of the helicopter.

President Williams drew the office blinds again and saw it hovering above outside. The helicopter was black and it blended well into the night sky making it seem almost invisible. At the gates of the White House, he could see a large crowd of angry civilians rioting. A group of secret service agents had situated themselves on the lawn by the gates with Disintegrators pointed at the crowd in more of a barricade and uniformed fashion.

"Do you think it wise that we have them armed with Disintegrators?" President Williams asked one of the agents.

"Sir," The agent said. "Bullets will not be as effective if the crowd begins to break through the gates. Once they witness the power of the Disintegrators, and how they turn solid mass into dust, it should deter them from wreaking havoc."

"The Eye Openers have created a mess for us," President Williams said.

"Anyone who was involved with the Eye Openers, has been arrested," Another agent said.

6

"It does not matter," President Williams said somberly. "The damage has already been done. Back in my Sector 7 days, many of the NHR agents spent hours in meetings developing new ways to keep peace and order. Secrecy was needed."

"The NHR was wiped out at Sector 8," Landon said. "That agency is no more. Kat—or whatever her name is. That Dark One queen is behind all this."

"We should go now," An agent said to the president.

President Williams and Landon were escorted out onto the lawn of the White House. When President Williams stepped onto the grass and into the spotlight from one of the several helicopters hovering above, there was a huge uproar from the crowd and they began to vigorously shake the fence.

A man in the crowd pulled out a gun and aimed it at President Williams. A secret service agent aimed his silver Disintegrator at the man without thinking about what would happen. Before the man could pull the trigger, he turned to dust, but not before the light hit through the White House's fence, leaving a large gap easy enough for people to fit through.

Within seconds, civilians began to climb through the gate. The agents began shooting anyone that crossed into the lawn. The dust remains of those shot began to pile up into heaps and the light kept making more gaps in the fence.

"You need to be careful where you shoot!" An agent could be heard yelling over the roar from the crowd. "They are about to break through…"

Eventually, the gaps that were caused by the Disintegrator misfires, made the fence so weak, that it buckled down with the pressure of the rioters. It was like a tidal wave that had hit the sand of a beach. Thousands of people were pouring onto the lawn with several of them trampling each other to get to the White House and both President Williams and Landon.

"Oh my God!" Landon gasped.

Both President Williams and Landon were unceremoniously pulled by the neckline of their blazers and practically dragged onto the black helicopter, which had just landed as soon as the fence broke. The helicopter's mission was to take them to the battleship where the USSA was stationed.

Once they were both in, the agents slammed the door and banged on the side of the helicopter to signal to the pilot to fly them out of there. Had they waited a few seconds longer, the civilians would have been able to climb onto the helicopter. Below them was a sea of angry faces staring up at them. Several of them began shooting at the helicopter they were in, but luckily it was made of a bulletproof material.

"I've never seen anything like this before," President Williams said. "It's like we are at war with each other now."

"They are at war with the government. You are the face of it. To them, we are the enemy," Landon said, and he pulled out a bottle of whiskey. "Care for some? It'll take off the edge."

"No thank you," President Williams said politely.

The scene below them on the White House grounds was mayhem. Fires started and more and more causalities resulted from either civilian gunshots or secret service Disintegrator blasts. In the end, the agents and officers were greatly out numbered and people ran into the White House and began breaking windows and vandalizing every inch of the house they could get their hands on. Fires started and slowly they could see the White House become engulfed in flames. The further they flew away from scene, the smaller the orange glow of the fire became.

"If we leave on this ship to space to wait for this to blow over, what do you expect we will come back to?" President Williams asked Landon.

"Well I did not work much on the project when I was in the Non-Human Relations agency at Sector 7, but the Moonshadow files did tell me a bit about how The Noah's Ark Project works."

"Enlighten me," President Williams said.

"Well, another branch of the government has picked several animal species and will have them housed in the battleship. They will be transported onto the USSA as well as several chosen humans. Us included. The ship will set out into space in a course towards Threa. We will all be put in a deep sleep as the ship travels to our destination. What we do when we arrive is anyone's guess. I suppose we will knock on the door or ring the doorbell of the Humanoids."

"How long will we be asleep?" President Williams asked.

"The ship has never been tested for space travel, but as it runs on energy created by Threa's natural resources, it could be about six months until we arrive, which is a break through because any kind of man-powered and manmade vessel, would never be able to accomplish such a task in a short time. Especially due to the distance."

"You call half a year short?" President Williams said sarcastically.

"If it was a ship made by us," Landon said. "It would take thousands of years to get to Threa."

"This astronomy stuff is not my forte," President Williams admitted.

"Mine neither," Landon said.

"This is an embarrassment," President Williams said, and tears began to form in his eyes. "I'll be remembered as the president that caused the end of a peaceful civilization."

"There may not be anyone left to remember you," Landon said. "Mankind will turn on itself. Survival of the fittest will take place. This is hell on Earth. The Eye Openers said the world would end and they caused this to happen."

"I wonder how the other countries across the world are handling this," President Williams said.

"Not well," The pilot flying the helicopter interrupted. "Sorry to eavesdrop Mr. President. Other countries are not allowing United States citizens to travel into their borders. It's as if every country is now fending for itself and closing itself off to outsiders. There's a lot of distrust."

President Williams sighed and then wiped the tears out from his eyes. He looked over at Landon.

9

"We both worked at Sector 7 a long time ago. I keep thinking back to that night we took Derek Conrad to photograph the alien ritual. Do you think things would have been different had we not let him into the secret of alien existence?"

"Well, the Dark Ones were still hiding on Earth," Landon said.

"Valid point," President Williams said. "I just feel like there was something about that night that caused all these wheels to set in motion. It caused Shane to be involved and drew attention from the NHR. A few of the NHR retired agents went rogue and created the Eye Openers, and now here we are fleeing the now destroyed White House on our way to an evacuation ship created because the Elders once said our world would become overpopulated and we would need to control the population."

Landon went into deep thought. He looked over at President Williams and spoke what was on his mind.

"How did the Elders know exactly? I mean think about it. How could they predict many of these events happening?"

"They have not come true," President Williams said. "We have not become overpopulated."

"The NHR was taking the precaution via the Moonshadow files and obviously the creation of the USSA, because they believed they were right," Landon said. "If anything set the gears turning, it was our early communication with the Elders and letting us borrow their technology for allowing them to secretly live among the Earth population and conduct tests. It was us that caused this mess. We all worked at Sector 7. Some of our colleagues worked at the very beginning stages of the NHR at Sector 1. We cannot blame one night with Derek Conrad for where we are today almost two decades later."

President Williams looked out of the window. It was starting to rain as they began to fly over the Atlantic Ocean on course to the military battleship where the USSA was docked.

"We should be arriving shortly," The pilot announced.

As the helicopter began to descend, a large looming object sitting in the water appeared. It was a naval base the size of three football fields. On top of it was a square-shaped aircraft called the United States Square Aviator. It had no windows, and was a dark, metallic gray color.

The helicopter landed on a helipad and a group of officers approached it holding several umbrellas.

"Mr. President," One of the officers yelled over the howling wind and sound of rain hitting the ship's deck. "We'll take you straight into the USSA. We've loaded all the species and their quarters have been sealed, contained, and they've been put into a deep sleep for travel."

"Are we missing any other key people that will be joining us on the journey?" President Williams asked.

"Unfortunately per Mr. Parker's request, we were unable to find Mr. Shane Baker, Mrs. Alice Hastings-Liffen, and Mr. and Mrs. Mike and Caroline Campbell," The officer said and gave Landon a solemn look. "They are nowhere to be located."

"I don't know what happened to them after the collapse of the Empire State Building," Landon said. "I know they had to have been saved by the ship from Threa like we were. I believe they may have taken Shane to Threa, but what about Alice, Mike, and Caroline?"

"Is it important for them to come with us?" President Williams asked as they were escorted right below the hovering USSA.

"They are close to Shane and know all about Threa and its life," Landon said matter-of-factly.

"Well we don't have much time," The officer said. "We've had talks with the United Nations, Mr. President, and there is chaos. Russia, in particular, is not happy. Rumors are swirling that they might launch a missile at this ship. They are outraged that we did not include any other countries as part of the Noah's Ark Project."

"How could we have?" President Williams said. "This project was built on a theory. Never did we imagine it could become reality."

"We fear other countries will turn on us," The officer said as they began to float up into the USSA from under it.

They arrived inside the craft and were instantly relieved of the cold weather. The environment was quiet and dry.

"This reminds me of a passage from the Moonshadow files," Landon said.

Landon felt his jacket pocket and realized that he no longer had the Moonshadow files as he had given them to Shane.

"Shane has them," Landon said. "I just remembered."

"Yeah, he showed it to me," President Williams replied. "What did you remember?

"World War Total," Landon said. "It's the aftermath of the Elder's teachings about what would happen to Earth if the world got wind of the truth. World War Total is what the name suggests. A total world war. A war on Earth within itself—of all people. It sounds like this is already starting to happen."

"It is," The officer said. "I'm officer Bradley Wells. I will also be acting captain of the USSA because of Stanley Holt's unfortunate death. He was head of the NHR, therefore making him captain of this ship, but I was asked by President Williams here to take the lead after the Eye Openers wiped out all active NHR agents."

"I still cannot believe that happened," President Williams said.

Without any warning, there was a loud explosion from outside of the USSA. Captain Wells touched a screen on the wall and it soon became transparent so they could see outside. The ship below them was on fire. The force of the blast caused the USSA to sway slightly in midair, but it was otherwise unaffected by what appeared to be an attack on the ship.

Crewmen were running off the side of the ship and jumping into the frigid ocean to avoid several more explosions that were occurring as the fire spread throughout the ship.

"What's going on?" Landon said in shock.

Captain Wells dialed a number on his cell and the person who answered him on the other line gave him bad news.

Captain Wells hung up on the caller, put his cell phone in his jacket pocket and gave President Williams a grave look.

"Russia did send a missile. The navy ship is sinking. We need to leave now."

"But we still need a few of my White House personnel that I have selected to join us," President Williams said. "I believe they'll be arriving shortly via helicopter."

"They will have nowhere to land," Captain Wells said. "A Russian submarine is lurking below and they are waiting to get a clear shot of the USSA, no doubt."

"This craft is impenetrable, though," Landon added.

"We need to go. NOW!" Captain Wells said, and they felt the ship vibrate as it began to fly up, high into the dark rain clouds. Through the window that appeared on the wall, they could see the ship below them sink.

All of a sudden a missile was shot out of the water and in the direction of the USSA. It hit the ship, but the USSA remained unscathed by the attack. It was made of material from Threa and could not be destroyed by a manmade missile. The missile imploded, causing the USSA to shake furiously.

"Thank goodness this craft is strong," President Williams said while clutching his chest.

"We are about to leave Earth's atmosphere," Captain Wells announced. "Gentlemen, follow me to the sleeping quarters. We have about fifty other individuals who have already begun their travel slumber. The ship is set on autopilot for the coordinates of Threa's location."

"Do we have to sleep now?" Landon asked.

"When you wake up, it will be as if no time has passed. It will be about six months until we arrive at Threa's coordinates. Happy dreams everyone."

Landon and President Williams followed Captain Wells to a very large room in the ship. Landon recognized the room as the one that Kat Twain and James Carter used to hold a meeting with the Moonshadow residents.

"What happened to the Moonshadow residents?" Landon asked remembering he was not even sure where Penny and Peter Mills could have ended up as well. They were on the observation deck of the Empire State Building when the Dark Ones attacked and a huge ball of white light saved them.

"Many of them died," Captain Wells said with a dark look in his eye. "They did not know how to adapt to the world outside the ranch. Alright, take a pod, and let's nap."

The large room they were in had several silver pods that were lined up near each other. Each one had a clear window and beneath that window was a sleeping person. Captain Wells opened three empty pods and gestured for President Williams and Landon to get into one.

Once they were nestled snuggly into their prospective pods, they each pressed a button on the pod's handle and it closed shut. A gas was dispersed from a nozzle inside the pod and both Landon and President Williams fell instantly asleep as the USSA made its way further and further away from Earth. Captain Wells' finger lingered on his button, but he did not press it.

Chapter Two:

The Key Hunt

The skies were a shade of bluish-grey. There was nothing but endless cumulus clouds that covered the entire sky. One could not see a patch of the atmosphere or the stars above. The days had looked the same for months now and many survivors had no idea what time of day it was. However, it was possible to tell if it was night or day because at night everything was pitch black with the exception of some sort of artificial light source or fire. During the day, the clouds covered the sun; however, it gave off a very faint light that illuminated the clouds grey. Every day looked as though a tumultuous storm was about to break, yet the clouds appeared calm. The weather outside was very cold because the sun's rays were blocked. It was currently summertime, but the temperature felt like winter.

Two individuals in large brown cloaks were walking through the rubble of a neighborhood. Many of the nice homes and apartment complexes were abandoned. Every single window of every home had been broken. Many lawns in the neighborhood were left to die, as there was no one around to keep them.

The two cloaked figures looked as if they were close to collapsing. They had been traveling for weeks to get to the exact neighborhood they had arrived at. One of them took a break from walking and sat on what was once a bus stop bench. The person took off her cloak and shivered when her face was exposed to the air.

She was a beautiful middle-aged Asian woman with long straight black hair, which looked unkempt as if it had not been washed in several days. She had dark shadows under her brown eyes and looked as if she was on the verge of tears.

The other cloaked figure took off his hood. He had short black hair, dark brown skin, and wore a pair of eyeglasses. One of his lenses was cracked. He put his arm around the woman and gave her a kiss on the cheek.

"We're almost there, Caroline," He said.

"I can't believe we made it this far," Caroline retorted. "Mike, I wish Landon was here with us. It is his condo, after all, that we are looking for."

"We were separated that night in New York City. I don't even know what happened to Mariette," Mike said. "But it is common knowledge that Landon was on board the USSA. He gets to be a part of a small group of people that will live on. His knowledge of everything that happened will be useful one day. Our race's survival depends on the project he is now a part of. We just have to hope that we can survive our home. Here."

"What if we can't find the spare key that we have been searching for in his condo?" Caroline said. "Our mail was intercepted and that NHR agent was able to find his address because of it. They took the Communicator from his house. And don't forget, Landon also spoke of the key in the letter and where he was hiding it."

"He also said it was a wedding gift for Alice in the letter," Mike replied. "I don't think an NHR agent would have really cared about its significance."

Caroline nodded in agreement and took a deep breath, "I never thought we would have made it back to L.A."

"I know," Mike said. "So many dead ends and so many borrowed cars later and here we are. A ghost town."

Caroline looked up at the sky and did a double take. For a second she thought she saw a black cloud of smoke peaking through the clouds, but the next second it was gone. She shivered at the thought and turned back to her husband.

"There's a gas station up ahead!" She said, sounding ecstatic for the first time in days.

"Let's go!" Mike urged, and they ran in the direction of the gas station.

All of the gas pumps had signs that said "No Service" on them. The gas station itself looked as though it had been the victim of looters. Several snack bags were littered on the ground from whoever had opened them to eat their contents. There were not very many food items left on the shelves. Mike managed to find a bag of salted peanuts, which he opened in haste to share with Caroline.

The freezer section left an awful smell that permeated the air. Any foods that were once frozen had thawed with the lack of electricity and spoiled. There were a few soda bottles left that were lukewarm, but that did not stop Mike and Caroline from opening them to quench their thirst.

Mike walked over to the cashier counter and nearly fell over backwards at the site of a dead man behind the register.

"Oh my God!" Caroline yelled when she saw what startled Mike. "How did he…"

"He was shot," Mike said covering his nose as the smell of death reached his nostrils. "There is a gun by his side. That must have been for self-defense. I'm guessing looters took him out."

"What has this world come to?" Caroline gasped.

"What world?" Mike asked. "Look around you, there's nothing left of it but death and ruins from the chaos that broke out because of the Eye Openers—Kat exposed the secrets of our country."

"You mean Sunev?" Caroline corrected Mike.

"Well, she was possessing that Kat woman's body when this all went down," Mike said. "Anyways, are there any more food items we can put in our bags?"

"I found some bags of pretzels," Caroline said picking them off the shelf and putting them in her travel bag.

Caroline headed to another section of the store and looked over to see that Mike was distracted. She put an item in her pocket and said, "I'm going to head to the restroom."

"It probably won't flush," Mike said. "Just thought I'd mention that."

"Doesn't matter," Caroline said and she went into the women's restroom.

Mike was going through the cash register and saw that the storeowner had been robbed as well. He found some cigarette lighters and put a few of them in his travel bag knowing that they would most likely come in handy. He even took the storeowner's gun and put it in the bag as well.

Mike picked up the store's telephone even though he knew there was no chance it would work. Once he confirmed that he was right, he slammed the phone back on its receiver in frustration.

Caroline came out of the bathroom looking flushed. Her cheeks were pink and she was sweating slightly.

"Girl issues," She sighed.

"Ah," Mike said wanting to change the subject. "Perhaps we should go. This store is mostly cleaned out. Landon's condo should be up the street."

"Right," Caroline said, and her eyes seemed unfocused and bothered.

They walked out of the gas station and onto the middle of the street where several cars had been left abandoned. Some cars looked as though they had been set on fire because they were charred black.

Up the road, they noticed a deer was walking aimlessly through the neighborhood. It was the first sign of life, besides themselves, that they had seen in a long time.

"It's so bizarre to see a living creature," Mike said. "That's a beautiful deer. Look at its antlers."

"And it saw us and ran off," Caroline groaned following the deer running over several yards to hide after seeing Mike and Caroline walking towards it.

Caroline kept absentmindedly rubbing her stomach. Mike passed her a bag of pretzels, which she took willingly and began to eat.

"The address to the condo is just up this next corner!" Mike said excitedly. "I cannot believe we finally made it."

They took a right on the road and stopped dead in their tracks at the site of a man with long black shaggy hair staring at them from up the street.

"Hello?" Mike called, and the man just stared at them expressionlessly.

"What's your name?" Caroline asked sounding slightly nervous.

The man began groaning and ran straight at Mike and Caroline.

"AAAH!" Caroline screamed and it echoed throughout the neighborhood.

Mike and Caroline turned on their heels and ran straight for the nearest house. They arrived on the porch and ran up to the door. Mike twisted the doorknob only to discover it was locked.

They made a run for a gate on the side of the home that led to the backyard. It was unlocked, so they opened it and went through and locked it from the other side. They could hear the man groaning and hissing as he neared the gate they went through.

"Let's see if we can find a place to hide," Caroline suggested.

They made their way to the backyard patio and found the back door to the home. The windows of it were already broken, so they squeezed their way in through one that led into the kitchen. Caroline fell onto the ground and brushed herself up. She reached for two knives that were on the countertop for self-defense.

"That's not a normal guy, is it?" She asked.

"I think he's possessed," Mike said.

They heard a crash coming from the backyard and without another glance they ran up the stairs of the house to the second floor.

They found the master bedroom and locked themselves inside, then hid inside a closet. When they opened the door to the closet, Caroline let out a small scream that was stifled by Mike's hand. On the ground was the decaying body of a woman. The smell hit their noses like a whip to skin. There was shuffling downstairs and a look of horror on Mike's face.

"He knows we are up here," Mike whispered as Caroline began to sob into his hands.

The man downstairs was knocking things over. There were crashing sounds of paintings falling and glass shattering. Very hard thuds were heard coming up the steps. The man was saying, "Come out and face me" in a very raspy hiss.

The doorknob of the master bedroom began to wiggle as he tried to open it from the other side. Caroline's heart began to beat fast and she was edging into a nervous breakdown.

Mike braced for the worst. He felt himself shiver as the air around them seemed to have dropped in temperature, yet the air conditioning was not working.

The door crashed opened and framed in the middle of the doorway was the man with long black shaggy hair. His eyes flashed from hazel to red then back to hazel. He had a very large menacing grin.

The man was closing in on the two when Mike pulled out his gun and covered Caroline's face. He pulled the trigger with his eyes closed and the next sound he heard after it fired was the sound of a body hitting the ground.

"Mike!" Caroline panicked. "Where did you get that gun?"

"The gas station," He answered. "It just saved our lives."

Caroline and Mike looked at the body of the man sprawled on the ground from his fall after the bullet came in contact with his chest. The body began to convulse and then out of his mouth, black smoke poured out and hovered over the body. It formed into a figure. The smoky figure had claw-like hands connected to two arms. There were no visible legs. They could only tell that it had a head because there were two red eyes glaring at them. The figure hissed at them and then it flew straight out of an open window and into the clouds where it disappeared.

"Those Dark Ones...," Mike said. "We cannot trust anyone that has survived since the day the world ended. The Dark

Ones could be manifesting inside any surviving humans. We could be next."

Mike and Caroline composed themselves. Mike put the gun back in his pocket and gestured for Caroline to follow him back downstairs. They looked through the pantry for any left over foods. They found a can of tuna and some stale crackers. They took them happily and left the house through the back onto the street.

"Will we ever be able to stop them?" Caroline asked.

"The Dark Ones?" Mike asked.

Caroline nodded.

"I don't know," Mike shrugged. "They've brought darkness here. There hasn't been sunlight in nearly half a year."

"Do we really think this key will open up something to help save us?" Caroline asked.

"I would hope so," Mike said. "There's something special behind that door. What it is, I do not know. All I know is we have no other plan and we chose to not go on the project Landon is now a part of. We chose to stay here at home to attempt to survive."

"It's the dark days now," Caroline said. "I feel almost foolish for not taking the route Landon did. Even if it is risky."

"We made a promise to find this key," Mike said. "Shane— wherever he is—would have wanted us to."

"We don't know if he is still alive," Caroline said. "Last thing I remember was the Empire State Building collapsing beneath our feet. I don't know how we survived."

Mike and Caroline continued their journey to the destination in which they had been traveling for weeks to get to. They arrived at a luxury high-rise condominium in the downtown area of Los Angeles. There was a newspaper stand just outside of the main entrance. Mike opened it and pulled out the copy of the Los Angeles Times.

The date on it was from January, which was six months back. It was currently mid June. The headline on the front-page read "President Williams to announce a breakthrough new technology tonight!"

"After that night," Mike said somberly, "everything changed."

"What I would give to be able to read a newspaper again or go online and surf the web. Or even have a cell phone," Caroline said brushing fresh tears out of her eyes.

The windows to the glass door of the condo's main entrance had been shattered so it was easy for Mike and Caroline to enter through it.

"Be careful," Mike warned Caroline. "You don't want to get cut on the broken glass."

They were in the lobby of the condo. A large chandelier was lying on the ground in pieces. It had once hung magnificently from the ceiling.

"He's in apartment 315," Caroline said. "We should take the stairs to the third floor. I doubt there is any electricity left in this city."

"I haven't seen a working streetlight in ages," Mike said.

"Maybe we should search some of the units for food," Caroline said while touching her stomach.

"That's a good idea," Mike agreed. "But let's get to Landon's unit first and hope the key is still there."

Mike and Caroline found a staircase that led to the upper floors of the condominium. There were random apartment items that they had to jump over on their way up such as books, chairs, irons, blenders, and several other kitchen items that had been dumped in the stairwell.

When they arrived on the third floor, they found that almost every door on the floor was either left open or had been torn down by looters.

"Apartment 313...314...aha! Here is 315," Caroline said.

They arrived at Landon's condo. The door had been kicked down and inside there was a complete mess.

"I'm not sure if this mess was first caused by that agent that came and searched this place on Kat Twain's order," Mike said, "or just the aftermath of random people searching for food or other survival items."

"Perhaps both," Caroline said jumping over an overturned sofa. "There's the bookshelf."

"That's where he kept the Communicator. There's a faux book on it that is actually a case," Mike said. "The spare key is there! We are one step closer to opening that underground door at that laboratory in Roswell!"

Mike's heart began to race as he looked through every single book to see if they actually opened up as real books.

"I think this is it!" Caroline exclaimed and Mike abandoned the search on the shelf below the one Caroline was sifting through.

Caroline opened the cover of the book to reveal that it was in fact hallowed and was a case to conceal items. The case was empty.

"No!" Mike yelled.

There was nothing in the case except for a small piece of crumpled paper. Caroline pulled out the paper and unraveled it. There was a message written in pencil that read, "THE FUTURE IS HERE."

"Are you kidding me?" Caroline said exhaustingly. "We came all this way for a message? What does it even mean?"

"That Agent Miller guy must have taken it. But that's a weird message, 'The future is here'," Mike said. "Agent Miller would have been the only one to know since he intercepted the letter that Landon sent us."

"Ok, well where is he then?" Caroline said.

"If he's still alive," Mike said and his heart dropped, "He could be anywhere."

"That key is lost forever," Caroline said defeated and her fatigue began to kick in.

"Hey do you feel that?" Mike said suddenly.

The condo's walls began to vibrate. There was a swaying motion as if the building they were in was moving back and forth. The vibration grew more violent and the bookcase where they found the message crashed to the floor along with several other items hanging on the walls.

"Is this an earthquake?" Caroline panicked.

"It feels like it. This is California after all," Mike said.

Mike grabbed Caroline's hands and urged her to follow him into a closet. They opened the door and took refuge in there, as there were no windows. Right before Mike shut the door closed, he saw the clouds through an opened window. They looked blacker than rain clouds. It was almost unnatural. He had a foreboding feeling.

"There's a light switch," Caroline said, and she attempted to turn on the light to the closet before realizing that there was no electricity any more.

"Wait!" Mike said. "I found a flashlight."

Mike clicked the switch of a heavy-duty flashlight he found in the closet and to his surprise, the batteries in them still had power.

"Light!" Mike exclaimed.

The room felt cold and then the flashlight went off. They could feel cold air seeping into the room that was coming from the opened window outside.

Mike and Caroline caressed each other in the dark as the earthquake finally began to settle. The ground was still and the building no longer felt as though it was swaying in an ocean.

"It stopped," Caroline said.

She hugged Mike tight and began to sob in his jacket. Mike loosened his grip on her.

"You alright?" She asked him.

"I am," He replied after a few seconds of silence, and he sounded happy. "We need to find that key. That needs to be our priority."

"What's the point?" Caroline said defeated. "That will be like finding a needle in a haystack."

"We need to find Agent Miller," Mike said. "He was wearing a key necklace. I remember...we were there eavesdropping on a conversation between him and Kat Twain at Shane's father's place. That is the key! He had it all this time! He was the one that rummaged through our mail and went to look for the Communicator in Landon's condo. He also took the key because he was *wearing* it!"

"It's the spare key Derek left for Shane," Caroline said matter-of-factly. "The last piece of his message."

Chapter Three:
Control Room

Shane was standing in a field of staggering black crystal rocks with Alice on his side. They were holding hands and looking back at the giant dome they were enclosed in that Shane knew was called Territory 3. They had broken through the enclosure's outer surface, which was a thick glass-like material. In the opposite direction of Territory 3's dome, was Territory 2, which just housed more fields of black crystals that had been harvesting light from nearby stars to use for the planet Threa's energy sources.

"And then there is Territory 1," Shane said after explaining to Alice how in the giant planet there were only three designated areas fit for living in giant domes. "Territory 1 is where I lived. That is where the government is as well. That is where Manuel leads. Nobody really ever ventures out here in these rocky fields unless it is your job to collect crystals and take them to Territory 2."

"Shane, this is so crazy," Alice said feeling her heart race. "I can't believe we've been held up on Threa for six months and had our minds wiped. Who would do such a thing?"

Shane had an idea that Manuel was behind all this since he first came across Territory 3's existence when his fellow Threa governmental colleague Ryker helped him escape to Earth. He recalled a message that the Eye Openers sent to a Communicator, which hoodwinked him to believe it was from Landon.

But why would Manuel wipe my mind and keep us at Territory 3, he thought. *Why would he bring Alice, who is one hundred percent human? Manuel did save us from the Empire State Building in New York City, right?*

"Our answers are in Territory 1," Shane said pointing at a much larger dome than the one behind them.

"These domes look like giant fish bowls," Alice said sarcastically. "They look like they are caging whatever is in them at least."

"It's not healthy to be out here in the crystal fields for a long time. Breathing here is only fine for a bit, but then it can become deadly for Humanoids. That's why our living areas are domed so that clean oxygen flows for our consumption," Shane explained.

"Oh my God!" Alice shrieked suddenly while making Shane jump in surprise.

Alice pointed at a skeleton of a deceased individual that was about four feet in height. Shane's first thought was that the skeleton belonged to a child, but when he looked closer at the skull and saw that there were large eye sockets, he came to the conclusion that the body was that of an…

"Elder," Shane gasped. "This is a dead Elder. It looks like it's been here for many years. It must have died before Genesis and her brothers evacuated Threa long, long ago."

"That is so freaky," Alice said hiding behind Shane as if she were afraid the skeleton would come to life.

"I wonder who it was," Shane said. "The Elders never stood a chance against the possession of the Dark Ones. And the Dark Ones could not find a host body in the Elders because they would die within minutes of trying to take them over."

"Let's keep on walking to Territory 1. I already feel lightheaded from breathing out here," Alice said.

They made their way through the rocky grounds of Threa. In the distance, they could see a mountainous canyon. It looked dark and foreboding. Territory 1 appeared nearer and nearer as the hours passed. Shane and Alice were beginning to feel thirsty and their breathing became more and more shallow. Alice's legs finally gave up and she collapsed onto the ground missing a sharp crystal stalagmite by inches.

"Alice!" Shane said with panic, "Are you ok?"

She moaned slightly but was unable to talk.

"You're dehydrated," Shane began to shake with fear.

"She can't handle this atmosphere," A voice from behind Shane whispered making him jump up in shock.

Shane looked at the owner of the voice and nearly did a double take.

"Ryker!" Shane gasped and he ran to him and gave him an embrace, as they were old friends. "It's so good to see you!"

"You too Shane! You're like a brother to me! Hey wait a minute, she's human," Ryker said. "We need to get her into the dome of Territory 1. I brought a Floater."

Ryker pointed at a silver, flat oval shaped looking disc that resembled a skateboard without wheels. Ryker lifted Alice's body and put her on the board. Ryker then jumped on it and gave his hand for Shane to join him. They all fit on it perfectly and an invisible gravitational force held them still on it as it began to speed over the crystal surface in the direction of Territory 1.

They flew through the clear dome that encompassed Territory 1 as if it were made of water. Ryker landed the Floater on the ground just a few feet away from the governmental building that Manuel ran. The building looked like a cross between a capitol government building and a castle. It had turrets on the sides, and a giant dome in the middle. It was easily the largest building in the community of Territory 1, which had several suburban looking homes as well as a few five-story buildings. None of the structures in the territory were taller than the government building.

Even though Shane was in a coma for six months, it felt as though he was only away from Threa for just a few weeks.

"You helped me escape to Earth," Shane said to Ryker who gave him a warm smile.

Ryker had bluish grey eyes, and shoulder length blonde hair that parted in the middle of his forehead. He had fair skin and was wearing a leather trench coat and high black leather boots.

"Why did you help me?" Shane asked. "Is Manuel furious? Why were we in Territory 3 with our minds wiped?"

"You have many questions, but I do not have enough time to answer them. Manuel will want to see you and the human now," Ryker said while giving a half glance to Alice who looked nervous.

They walked up the steps into the building and entered the main room. Shane and Alice both looked up at the dome ceiling which had painted planets and stars scattered all over it. It felt as if they were now in an observatory by the décor of that room.

Ryker escorted Shane and Alice into the same room that Shane was last in before taking an escape pod to Earth. Ryker knocked on the metal door and waited for a response.

"Come in," Manuel's voice sounded muffled through the door.

They entered the room that looked like it was a control center. There were several TV monitors up on the wall and Shane immediately recognized they were tuned onto live feeds of hidden cameras in Territory 3.

Manuel was sitting on a chair behind a desk in one corner of the room with a stern look on his face.

"Your venture to Earth has been disastrous," Manuel said not sounding too pleased. "You broke Threa law, by not only entering this room in which you did not have access too, but you also flew to Earth when I had made it clear that our contact with them had ceased indefinitely."

"But they were under a serious threat," Shane spat.

"They hoodwinked you into going so that the Dark Ones could use their minion of radical humans against Earth's government," Manuel said, his voice raising and echoing throughout the room they were in.

Shane looked at Ryker in the eyes. It was he that encouraged Shane to take an escape pod and he even left the door to the control room open. Ryker squinted his eyes and casually brushed a finger on his lip nonchalantly to signify that Shane was to keep Ryker's aid in his escape a secret.

"The Dark Ones deceived me," Shane said in a calm tone. "I made a mistake and fell for their tricks. I am sorry."

"Earth is a mess," Manuel said. "Over the last six months, most of the population was wiped out. They've lost power, food, and some humans were possessed by Dark Ones."

Alice clasped her hands to her mouth and looked as if she was about to cry.

"Why didn't you stop them?" Shane asked. "The Dark Ones, that is. You saved us from the Empire State Building, didn't you?"

"We brought you and Alice here. Your other party was saved too, however I'm not sure if they have survived on Earth in the last six months," Manuel said.

Shane felt like there was a large rock stuck in his throat. He was fighting back the urge to cry. He was about to open his mouth to say something when there was a knock at the door.

"Enter," Manuel called out.

A man that looked to be in his late fifties walked in. He had piercing blue eyes and shoulder length black hair that was currently in a ponytail. He had broad shoulders and looked to be very muscular and fit for his age.

Shane recognized the man whom he had met in a cabin in the woods and had helped him meet up with the Elders several years ago when he first discovered who he was on Earth.

"Dimitri," Shane gasped. "I haven't seen you in years."

Shane's mind raced to the night he left Earth for Threa for the first time. Dimitri and Manuel were by his side and filled him in on the planet they were headed to. Dimitri had put up a fight with the Dark Ones and was a big part of the reason they fled. Shane's crystal necklace helped significantly as well. Manuel had ordered Dimitri to set off into the far distances of space to finish them off, but they never heard from him again. It was assumed that he had died.

Manuel did not seem shocked by Dimitri's sudden presence, nor did Ryker.

"You're alive!" Shane said, and he ran up to hug Dimitri.

Dimitri returned the hug and after they let go of each other, he said, "The Dark Ones over powered me. I thought I was done for when I found their hiding place. I was saved by a higher power…a higher civilization."

"What do you mean?" Shane asked.

"There's so much to fill you in on," Manuel said. "Your venture to Earth caused such a rift in the universe that Dimitri was sent back to Threa a few months ago by another race."

Shane's mind raced back to a distant memory that was now coming back to him. He remembered a conversation with Landon:

"Shane," Landon said. "I was part of the Non-Human Relations agency. We dealt with Non-Human relationships. I…I never really spoke about this because Green just alluded to it, but I have reason to believe he was in contact with another race other than the Greys…which you know as your Elders."

"What?" Agent Holt said in shock. "I do not remember any records of such a thing in the Moonshadow files."

"It went undocumented," Landon said. "Green alone discovered something. Not sure what. But he was very pale in the face when he told me that there was a contact with another type of being. He was too shocked by it that he was afraid to tell even the rest of the NHR team. I was his second in command so he divulged just a little bit of information. He ordered me to never bring up our conversation. I nearly forgot about it as it has been so many years."

"Manuel," Shane began, "Landon told me that Agent Green learned about another race. He said he was too afraid to speak more about it."

Manuel nodded, "Yes, we speak of the same race here today."

31

"They are a very old and very advanced race, however they are not from this time period," Dimitri said.

Ryker looked at Dimitri and was studying him, but he seemed otherwise unperturbed by Dimitri's odd explanation of that civilization.

"What do you mean not from this time period?" Alice spoke up for the first time making everyone jump at the shock of her voice in the room.

Dimitri looked at Alice, then he set his gaze on Shane. "That civilization is among us. They could be here on Threa, or on Earth, or in other far reaches of the universe right now. They exist as their original form now—whatever it may be. However, in the future they exist as one cohesive race where all the males and all the females look exactly alike. I've seen them. Their features are the same. It's all very conformed. They are the perfected race evolved from trial and error and we are living during the trial—and mostly error—phase."

"I'm very confused," Shane said trying to rack his mind for some kind of understanding. "Do you mean to say that this race exists in the future?"

"Exactly," Dimitri smiled. "All the events that have been happening for the last years, decades, centuries, and millennium have been shaping up to this higher power civilization's conformed creation."

"Green met one of them?" Shane aksed.

"I was able to get information out of Green," Manuel said. "What it communicated with him did scare him."

"You knew?" Shane asked. "Did you tell Genesis?"

"I did. Genesis was already aware of these people from the future," Manuel said. "She left a message for me about them."

"I asked you about this message a few months ago!" Shane recalled a memory…

Earlier that day he heard Manuel talking to one of his colleagues about the Communicator going off with a scrambled signal that seemed to have been lost in translation. Manuel said it might have been a very old message from the Elders because he said he had received one a year previously. When Shane budded into the conversation and asked what that message was, Manuel looked slightly taken aback by his eavesdropping and told Shane not to worry. Shane did not really buy into that. Manuel looked like he had some sort of worry in the back of his mind.

"Was it from Genesis?" Shane asked Manuel.

Manuel stared at Shane and gave him a grave look. Manuel was wearing a suit just like any government official would wear in a government building on Earth.

"Your mother," Manuel began, "had prepared this message some time before she passed away. She sent it to Threa so that if we were to make it back we would be able to receive it. We did not have the Communicators functioning well for several years so when I finally got ours to work, the message came in garbled at first."

"What did she say then?" Shane insisted.

"It was very hard to understand. The code on the message said it came from a Communicator that was not the one the NHR was in possession of. We only had one pair of Communicators made, but if that code on the message—which is like a serial number on human manufactured goods—is real, then there was another Communicator in existence that I was not aware of."

"Where could it be?" Shane asked curiously.

"That," Manuel began, "I do not know. Genesis never told me anything."

"You told me there may have been another communicator," Shane said.

"You have a great memory," Manuel smiled. "There is a third Communicator, but the one I thought of is a one-way tool I left behind with the President of the United States so that I could occasionally check up on them. This one doesn't really count as a full Communicator because it does not work two-ways. I believe there was a third actual two-way Communicator. We have one here on Threa, and the other one was left in Landon's possession. That's the one that was used to bring you to Earth, Shane. That

Communicator has since been destroyed after the Dark Ones attack in New York City.

Anyways, a message from Genesis did come in. Would you like to here it?"

"I would," Shane answered and he squeezed Alice's hand.

Manuel punched a few buttons on the control panel at his desk. A holographic image appeared above his desk. It was Genesis and her image flickered on and off. She was speaking but it was difficult to make out most of her message.

"...the people were...uniformed....need to change the course...Shane...restart...over...fix...history...repeats...locked away...Earth...written in the cosmos."

"I did not understand anything," Shane said.

"The message was garbled," Manuel said. "There's no way to tell what her entire message was unless you find the original communicator she used to send it. Wherever it may be, I have no clue."

"But it makes some sense to me," Dimitri said. "I was there with *them*."

"Indeed," Manuel agreed. "Green told me that those visitors—these people—told him he was going to die at the hands of a Dark One. That freaked him out. They somehow showed him his fate."

"That's illegal," Dimitri said. "In their world order, they cannot show the past the future. It was malpractice."

"Someone was there that night at Sector 7," Manuel continued. "Someone from the future."

"What else did you learn when they took you to their world in the future?" Shane asked Dimitri. "And why were you brought back to the present?"

"The present is relative," Dimitri said. "I've been in the future so I don't really feel like this truly is the present. I feel like I'm reliving what those beings from the future have already lived. However, to answer your question, I learned more than was healthy. I was not brought back. I escaped back, but they didn't stop me."

"How do they travel time?" Shane asked sounding intrigued.

"Through a door. Once opened, time is bent and you are able to end up in a period of the past that you choose. Then you return through wherever their nearest door is set to the location of the universe you want to travel to. The door I came through here on Threa is located at the basement of this building. However, you cannot open it unless you have a special key. They also have this machine that's hooked up to people—"

"Manuel, did you know about this door in the basement?" Shane interrupted. "I don't remember ever seeing one."

"The door was hidden in the basement and obstructed by storage items. We believe one of those from the future is or was here on Threa and created it within the last decade and made sure we'd never see it. It was in a very obscure location in the basement. We cannot open it of course."

Shane had a dawning sense of realization and a look of excitement swept his face.

"I think I know where there is a door on Earth! And there is a key to open it. Where it all began..." He said.

"What do you mean?" Manuel asked with sparked interest.

"Sector 1. The laboratory used after the Roswell crash. Down in the basement through a secret trap door is a silver door that is locked. Derek apparently gave a message to my Earth father that he had the key to open it. Landon told me he had that key in his condo in Los Angeles. I need to get that key and open that door. That's what Derek wanted me to do."

"I was not aware of that message for you," Manuel said with shock. "I never told him to give a message to your Earth father."

Ryker spoke up, "Maybe it was someone from the future?"

"Possibly," Dimitri said giving Ryker an inquisitive look.

"Regardless of whatever or whoever told him," Manuel said, "we cannot go back to Earth. It's dangerous and has been overrun."

"It's my home," Alice spoke up. "Why was I brought here anyway?"

"You mean a lot to Shane," Manuel said. "After we brought him to Threa for the first time, he had a difficult time adjusting after leaving you behind. I figured it would make a good transition back."

"Yet you wiped our minds and made us live in Territory 3 which is a complete façade of a utopia of some sort," Shane interjected.

"I just thought that after the damages and events that happened back on Earth, we could let you live in complete happiness," Manuel said.

"Manuel," Shane said pointing a finger at him, "That world is like an ant farm. You have other Humanoids living there just like the NHR had a ranch where they kept Humanoids in a gated community where they were unaware of the real world outside those gates. How is that remotely normal?"

"The control room here," Manuel said gesturing to the monitors behind him that were surveillance of Territory 3, "is a testing ground to recreate Threa as a complete near-copy of Earth. Earth has failed in its course of time. We tried to help out the humans as much as they helped our race survive, but in the end they were self destructive."

"The Dark Ones ruined the planet!" Shane snapped.

"This is what they wanted," Dimitri said. "They are controlling our present right now. They want us to help shape the perfect race—themselves."

"Huh?" Shane asked sounding extremely confused.

"Them—the future of us," Dimitri clarified. "Their goal has been to create trials of life with species over the millenniums so that they have a superior race. They've set the wheels in motion so that every action we are taking now is shaped to better their lives.

They were not perfect at first, but with every instance of the past they change, the better their lives become."

"So we've been influenced to do exactly what they want us to do?" Manuel said sounding horrified.

"It's obvious, yes," Dimitri said. "The Elders wiped out dinosaurs once because they were a species not fit to rule the planet. They helped in the creation of humans, although they did not think they did. Genesis knew the truth though. That's what the future people told me. There is a link between all the work the Elders and we Humanoids have done. Shane is an example of a perfected Humanoid. Shane is the beginning of a line of Humanoids that will help against the resistance of the Dark Ones. The Dark Ones do not exist in the future, but they have become aware of it and are in search for a door to infiltrate the future so that their race can continue on and beings won't evolve to resist their possessions."

"Our destiny is being controlled and written for us?" Shane asked sounding uncomfortable.

"More than you and I will ever understand," Dimitri answered.

Chapter Four:

Unexpected Visitors

Shane and Alice followed Dimitri out of the control room as Ryker and Manuel continued a discussion about what the next steps they were going to take on the current stance of Earth. Dimitri was walking in such a hurried pace, that Shane and Alice nearly had to run to keep up because he was tall and every stride he took was twice theirs.

"What else did you see in this world—this future world?" Shane asked Dimitri as he ran down the steps outside of the governmental building.

"Manuel and I have had a few conversations about much of what I've learned, but I cannot say too much about it because anything I say can affect the future negatively," Dimitri said.

"You said earlier that the Dark Ones may know about this future civilization," Shane said. "Do you think they honestly know?"

"I know for a fact they do," Dimitri said and he had a grave expression on his face.

"How so?" Alice asked.

"Remember I told you that Agent Green met one of the individuals from the future and this individual told him he would die that night? I told you how that was against their rules. Well, Green was possessed by Noom. When a Dark One possesses a human, or any kind of living host for that matter, it can learn about their past and present. It's the ultimate weapon for them to live as someone they are not for any type of stealth reasons they may have."

"Noom then found out about the future beings?" Shane said with worry.

"He did. The Dark Ones know," Dimitri said. "They hid for a few years after that night in Sector 7 and when we left Earth, they came back with a plan to make it fall apart. Noom was able to communicate to his daughter Sunev that Earth needed to fall apart because it was the only planet in our universe that held a variety of life that was able to sustain itself for many years. The experiment known as Earth crumbled before us when they possessed humans to influence their population in a negative way. Hence, the leak of the United States government's secrets."

"Sunev must know that there is some door on Earth she needs to find," Shane said.

"You cannot be possessed by her Shane," Dimitri said seriously. "The knowledge in your head is very valuable to her and the fact that you know there is a key in existence that opens that door in Sector 1, would be catastrophic for our future. I really cannot say more about the future or what this race calls themselves because I could harm the future and our chances."

"They must know you escaped and will come back for you," Alice said smartly.

"Yes, which is why Manuel and I are meeting tonight to figure out a way for me to go into hiding. I'm more valuable here in the present than I am in the future."

"Is there something you are trying to change?" Shane asked.

"I do not have the power to change anything from the past," Dimitri said. "However, I could also damage the present and future and Manuel feels it is best I lay low somewhere until we can sort things out."

"What needs to be sorted exactly?" Alice asked.

Dimitri looked into her eyes then straight into Shane's.

"Shane," He said. "The Dark Ones will have made a connection by now that because you are the first Humanoid that can withstand a possession without dying at the hands of the Dark Ones, you are the key between the present and the future civilization. Sunev will want to see your mind and then kill you. This is the real reason Manuel had you living a fake life in Territory 3. We could keep an eye on you and protect you."

"I'm the key to the future?" Shane asked.

"If you die," Dimitri said with a stern look upon his face, "the Dark Ones win. They'll infiltrate the future and give them a chance to survive and one day have their own physical bodies. Sunev knows they do not exist in the future. She learned that from her father who learned it from the person who introduced himself to Agent Green back at Sector 7. They are going to try and change the future. The downfall of Earth's government caused a huge rift and change in the future and they knew that their actions would weaken the holes that lead from the now, to the future."

"This all seems so complicated and confusing," Shane said scratching his head.

"It's a lot to take in, and Manuel probably would not have wanted me to tell you as much as I just did. Your mother Genesis knew your value. Noom knew you were the beginning of their downfall because with a race of beings that could not be taken over by them, they would eventually die off as black smoky depressing clouds of nothing."

Shane nodded his head in agreement.

Dimitri continued, "The future has happened in the world I was in, but these people can rewrite it. They have to be careful how they do it. Everything happens for a reason Shane. *They* are the reason. They are watching over the universe and right now they are focused on this part of the timeline of the universe."

Ryker coughed out loud making Alice and Shane jump. He was walking down the steps of the governmental building towards them.

"Shane and Alice," Ryker said. "Manuel asked me to escort you to your temporary living quarters until he can figure out what is next in the game plan."

"We need to get to Earth," Shane demanded. "You helped me once. Can you help me find a way back again?"

Ryker gave Shane a dark look as if to suggest to him not to reveal that moment in which Ryker told Shane how to find an escape pod to Earth in Manuel's control room during his first escape from Threa to Earth.

"Please," Shane continued as Ryker remained silent. "There's a door I need to open. That's where the answers are. I know it."

"This door you speak of," Dimitri broke in, "is most likely a portal to their world in the future."

"Derek wanted me to find this door," Shane said. "He left a key behind and I need to find this key back on Earth. This key opens this very door. Ryker, are you still convinced that someone from the future might have tried to intervene with Manuel's help to give me the message about my existence as a Humanoid? Manuel did not tell Derek to come to my Earth father's house with the key left for me and the details on what it also opened...and that there were two."

Ryker remained silent again as if struggling with what to say. They were all distracted when a horn echoing around the confines of Territory 1 began to emit a loud sound.

"What is that?" Alice tried to yell over the sound while covering her ears.

"A safety alarm," Ryker said. "There is some sort of emergency!"

Manuel was running outside of the building and down the steps to where they were standing. Two government men also wearing black suits similar to Manuel's flanked him.

"We've detected an unidentified flying object reaching the atmosphere of Threa!" Manuel said with panic.

"You mean to tell me UFOs pose a threat to Threa too?" Shane said half sarcastically, but changed his expression at Manuel's grave look.

41

"My team in the control room is trying to get a reading of the ship. We've detected that it is made of material from this very planet, yet it is not a craft we built."

Dimitri's eyes widened as if he knew something. Manuel noticed and asked him, "What is it Dimitri?"

Both Ryker and Dimitri spoke in unison, "We need to turn that craft around!"

Manuel gave them both a quizzical look.

"Excuse me?" He asked.

Dimitri looked over at Ryker who just shrugged and muttered the word "hunch."

"It's the ship holding the last remaining humans—unless some are still on Earth alive after six months since the Moonshadow files were exposed."

"The USSA?" Shane asked. "The Noah's Ark Project?"

"Correct," Dimitri said. "I was informed about this very event by the future civilization. We cannot let them land. The ship bears about fifty humans, and male and female species of almost every kind of animal and plant known to human. It's a remarkable feat for mankind, but they believe Threa is the safest place for them now that their planet has been overrun by Dark Ones."

"That makes sense," Shane said. "The Moonshadow files documented this last resort approach in case of a world disaster so that human life could be preserved."

"I would like to be hospitable," Manuel said. "After all they are the reason our Humanoid race thrives and lives on. I'm not sure how I feel about animals roaming our planet though."

"We can't let them land," Dimitri said. "They are armed with weapons created from our own materials here at Threa. There was a path in our destiny where this very ship lands and you accept them as our own, Manuel. Over time during their stay here things started to become hostile and circumstances led the humans to create war with the Humanoids thus wiping out most of the Humanoids."

"Why would they do that? What circumstances?" Shane asked.

"The rule that Manuel would set for allowing them to live here was that they have their minds wiped and we create a larger Territory 3. He is overhead by the President who is on board in that ship and he tells his government officials that came with him. Landon tries to reason with them..."

"Landon is on the ship?" Alice asked excitedly.

"Landon is, however he gets killed by one of the government agents that came with the USSA. The President decides that they have a chance to fight for the planet Threa as it is livable and they begin a war to take out all the Humanoids."

"We don't come in peace?" Alice asked in shock.

"At first yes," Dimitri said, "but with time, humans cannot fathom the way of life here as subordinates. That's always been the flaw of the human race. They turn to war when it comes to rule and take over a land. There was another incident too with the captain of the ship—I've just forgotten what it was."

"Just like when Columbus came to America?" Alice asked.

"They killed off the natives at first," Dimitri said.

"How do we turn the ship away?" Manuel asked.

"The humans and animals in the ship are in a deep sleep. Once they reach Threa's atmosphere, they'll wake up and the autopilot will signal for the captain of the ship to take control and land it here," Dimitri said.

"Never in my life would I have thought I'd see the day that humans would be visiting us," Manuel said.

"Times have changed. They keep changing," Dimitri added.

"Shane should get in an escape pod and go to the ship and see if he could convince them to turn around," Ryker suggested.

Shane looked at Ryker and smiled. It would be a chance for him to catch a ride back to Earth.

"I'll do it. Alice will come with me and we'll take them back to Earth," Shane said.

43

"It's not safe there," Manuel said.

"Dimitri told me about your concerns and how important I am to the future," Shane said. "I'm trusting my gut instinct. I have to go back. I need to understand why everything happens for a reason."

Dimitri winked at Shane. Ryker nodded his head with confidence.

Manuel stood there outnumbered by this decision for Shane to board the USSA.

"Manuel," Ryker said patting him on the back. "Let the boy go. He's survived every path he has taken thus far. He survived his journey to Sector 7 and his journey back to Earth in an attempt to stop that secret society that was being controlled by the Dark Ones. Had he not, we would have been unaware that the Dark Ones were there and using humans and Humanoids to create an army to attack us. This ship that is coming to us would have been a vessel that the society would have used to open fire as soon as they reached us."

"That's an interesting theory," Manuel said suspiciously.

Ryker took a deep breath. "By law, I cannot tell you what I would like to say."

Dimitri's attention was immediately on Ryker as if he comprehended something nobody else could.

"Just trust me Manuel," Ryker said. "I've been one of your right hand men for the past few years. Just trust me."

Shane understood something. "You are one of them, aren't you? From the future?"

"Shane, ask no more questions," Dimitri ordered. "Trust me, the future is very sensitive and apt to major changes during this current time right now."

Shane nodded in agreement.

"Dimitri," Manuel said, "I'd like you to take Shane and Alice on an escape pod to get them on that craft. I won't allow you to use an escape pod back to Earth, even if it is faster, because you've already had one destroyed Shane."

Shane's face grew red, but he understood Manuel's rules.

"That's fine," Shane said. "And when we arrive on the ship do we just tell them we need to turn around and sorry that you have been asleep for half a year?"

"They do not need to be awaken," Dimitri said. "The ship is designed for them to hibernate for another journey back to Earth on autopilot. I'll make sure you get back to Earth safely."

"So you are coming then?" Alice asked Shane.

"I have to," Shane said. "We need to find that key. We need to open that door in Roswell. Some kind of answer is there."

"Just make sure that the Dark Ones do not beat you to it," Dimitri said. "Let's go."

"Wait!" Shane said as Dimitri began walking up the steps in the governmental building. "I want to take Penny and Peter with me."

"They are safer here," Manuel insisted. "And that would require us to give them a memory refresher."

"That's fine," Shane insisted. "They are trained in combat. They can be an asset to aid me on this mission."

"Very well then," Manuel agreed. "Ryker, fly over to Territory 3 and fetch them. Fill them in on everything on your way back."

"Thank you Manuel," Shane said, and he extended his hand to shake Manuel's. Manuel returned the handshake with a smile on his face. "Your mother Genesis would have been proud."

An hour later Peter and Penny Mills walked into the control room looking wide-eyed and nervous. Once they saw Shane sitting on a chair near Manuel's desk, they jumped with excitement and ran to him. They each gave him an embrace.

"Shane I can't believe we are not on Earth," Penny said.

"This is beyond crazy," Peter replied. "Ryker just filled us in on everything. Last thing I remember was being on top of the Empire State Building."

"I know, we had our minds wiped too," Shane said. "We've been away from Earth for a many months. I'm not sure what we will end up finding when we return, but I do not think it will be good."

"That creature—the female one who took over that woman agent's body—she's bad news. If she's still on Earth, well God knows what shape it'll be in now," Peter said.

"We just have to have faith. I believe we can stop the Dark Ones," Shane said. "I like to make my own destiny."

"Your destiny has been chosen for you already," Dimitri said. "By them."

"Who?" Penny asked sounding puzzled.

Dimitri briefed Penny and Peter on his stint of accidently ending up in the future and about the civilization that was paving their current lives.

"And the Dark Ones cannot find that door that opens up a path into the future," Dimitri said. "If they do, it can be catastrophic for our present."

Peter and Penny mulled over the information they learned. It appeared as though they had too much to process within the last hour of being released from Territory 3.

"Well," Peter finally spoke up. "I'm on your side. We'll stick by you."

"Same," Penny said and she stared deeply into Shane's blue eyes while her cheeks turned slightly pink.

Alice gave Penny a searching look, and put her hand on Shane's shoulder, then said, "I'm by your side too."

Manuel walked over to Shane and put his hand on Shane's other shoulder. He then pulled out something from his pocket and opened his hands to reveal a golden chain with a black crystal attached to it.

"My necklace!" Shane said in excitement.

"When we saved you from the incident in New York City, I took this from you for safe keeping," Manuel explained. "Your father Philip gave this to you for a reason."

"It helped me fight off the Dark Ones a few times," Shane said.

"Indeed it did," Manuel said. "But there is much more to this necklace. There is a legend behind it."

"Do share," Shane said.

"In due time you will learn about it, but that is part of your quest now," Dimitri interjected.

"Do you both know it? Why won't you tell me?" Shane asked Manuel and Dimitri.

There was silence for a few seconds and Manuel and Dimitri exchanged a few facial expressions. Dimitri spoke up.

"Once again you need to learn this on your own time. It will alter the future if you know because if Sunev or any of the Dark Ones were to possess your mind, the knowledge of what the necklace is, would be catastrophic. But as long as you are clueless until the timing is right, then the necklace is safe."

"This is confusing," Shane said scratching his head. "And when will I know when the right time is."

"It'll just happen," Dimitri said. "Just trust that they are watching over you and making sure everything aligns correctly."

"Ok then," Shane said. "Manuel—we are ready."

"Be safe Shane. Dimitri will take you all on an escape pod and into the humans' ship.

Shane, Alice, Penny, and Peter followed Dimitri into the entrance of the escape pod. They entered through a circular door and slid down a long tunnel until they were in a large room with a silver floating orb that was the ship. Dimitri put the palm of his hand on the orb and it began to glow brilliantly white.

"This is what you crashed into your Malibu house in?" Alice asked.

"Well, yeah," Shane said.

"Is it also a similar ship to what we saw flying over the desert skies those several years ago in Nevada?" Alice asked.

"Sure is," Shane answered.

"Guess I'm being abducted now," Alice joked and she gave a small chuckle.

"Let's walk under the ship and it'll beam us in," Dimitri commanded and the group followed his orders.

Once they were directly under the orb, it grew a little brighter and moments later they were inside the ship. The entire room was white.

"Ok, we've begun to rise up into the atmosphere. We'll be heading to the USSA."

"Let's do this," Shane said.

The ship flew up into the Threa sky and within seconds they were able to see the giant black crystalized planet before them shine with a dim white glow around the outer surface. The ship itself was shining much brighter and looked like a moving star traveling through the darkness that was outer space. A few miles ahead was the giant square shaped craft known as the United States Square Aviator.

"Do we just knock on the door?" Penny asked from inside the ship, as the USSA loomed closer and closer.

"I think I can hack into the ship's system," Dimitri said. "It is running off black crystals so their power source is the same as our ship that we are in. My plan is to use the magnetic energy of our crystals to sync our ships together, therefore giving them the ability to be controlled as one. As that ship's entire crew is in a deep sleep, it will be a breeze."

"What if they have some kind intruder alert system?" Peter asked smartly.

"I did not think about that," Dimitri said worried.

"Well we know Landon," Shane jumped in. "It's not like he'll attack us if he sees it is me trying to enter."

"True," Dimitri agreed. "However, I do not want them to wake from their sleep because they will want to land on Threa. I do not think they will like being forced back to Earth. Especially after everything that may be going on over there right now. Their home is being overrun."

"Dimitri," Shane said. "Do you think you can use this ship's power to give the USSA a speedier boost to get us back to Earth. I don't think I want to sleep for another six months. Besides, I don't want to waste any time that Sunev can have to find the key to that door in Sector 1."

"I can give you a boost," Dimitri said. "Your journey back to Earth will just take a day or two. I'll use the power of the crystals to energize the ones in the USSA. The U.S. government never learnt how to super charge these power sources."

Shane pulled his black crystal necklace out from under his shirt and examined it.

"There is so much to learn about this crystal and the crystals from Threa," Shane said.

"Yes," Dimitri said. "But as I said earlier, in due time you will know more about why a black object such as your necklace, can wield the power of a very bright light. It's the cosmos' biggest irony. And in the end Shane you have to choose between living on Earth or Threa."

"I have to choose...one?" Shane asked.

"You have to," Dimitri said. "Don't let the cosmos choose your destiny for you. Find a way."

Chapter Five:

Blood and Crystal

When the escape pod was within ten feet of the USSA, Dimitri shot a beam of bright white light on it making it give off a white glowing aura. He was then able to control the ship and transport Shane, Alice, Penny, and Peter through that same beam of light.

"Shane, trust your gut. You'll know what to do," Dimitri said leaving Shane with a confused look just before he disappeared from the interior of the escape pod only to end up inside the familiar steel-cold gray interior of the USSA.

"We're back in this thing," Penny said while she brushed her hands on the door that led to the large room where the possessed Kat Twain held a meeting with the Moonshadow Ranch residents alongside of James Carter.

"It feels so eerie still," Alice said. "Should we go down to that lair where all the cages are? I assume the people are in a deep sleep down there with the animals?"

"Sure, I guess so," Shane said. "This way right?"

Shane gestured down the hall while trying to remember when he was last on the ship. It was the day he went into a coma and his memory was still fuzzy.

"Yes," Penny answered.

They walked down the hall and entered what appeared to be a small storage room. There where cabinets lined up against the wall all the way up to the ceiling inside the room. Strange smells were coming from each and the mixture of the different smells did not make it pleasant for anyone's noses.

"Everyone— -stand over this circle shape on the floor," Shane ordered to the group.

Shane got on his knees to examine the circular shape on the floor. He put his hands over it and pushed it down slightly once the others were standing over it. Slowly, they began to descend down what became a cylinder shaped platform that lowered them down to a much larger room.

The sight before them was nothing like any of them had ever seen. The walls were all lined up with cages of different sizes. At first glance the room looked like a prison, but it was in fact a modern day Noah's Ark. Every cage had a different specie of animal, each both a male and a female, to preserve the life that was threatened after the government's secrets were leaked for all of Earth to learn about. Each animal was sleeping. In the middle of the room were about fifty egg-shaped capsules that had a clear casing. A human was in a deep sleep in each one.

"It's Landon!" Shane said pointing over at the first capsule closest to where they stood once the platform had lowered beneath the ground and the circle they were on was flat.

"And President Williams!" Alice said pointing to Landon's neighboring capsule.

"They look so peaceful," Shane said. "We will wake them up when we get to Earth. Dimitri put us on a fast course across the galaxy to get there much faster."

"What do you think it will be like?" Penny asked. "It's been half a year since the Eye Openers exposed the secrets to the world."

"And those Dark Ones were running amuck too," Peter added.

"I'm not sure," Shane said. "But Landon will be of use. He will take us to his condo and show us where he hid the key—the spare key that Derek left behind for me. This very key opens that door we could not access at the Eyes' headquarters—Sector 1."

"I remember a strange bluish light coming from the cracks," Alice said thinking back to that day when her and Shane were in that secret underground tunnel inside Sector 1 in Roswell, New Mexico.

"Yeah, it was an odd feeling there," Shane said. "A door stood between myself and countless answers I need to learn."

Shane began walking through the rows of capsules to see if there were any other faces he might have known. There were lots of distinguished looking men and women in uniforms, which must have worked for the White House or some branch of the government. Shane was also quick to notice there was a varying diversity of ethnicities too. He deduced that much like preserving different species of animals, the Noah's Ark Project was probably also set to have different races of people on board. Shane saw a man who looked vaguely familiar in one capsule wearing a black suit. He felt like he met the man, but his mind was working too hard to remember who he was. Shane figured it would come to him later, and kept on looking through the different capsules in hopes that there was a chance that Mike or Caroline were chosen to board the USSA.

"They're not here," Alice whispered into Shane's ear as if reading his mind. "I would have thought Landon would have brought them on board."

"I was thinking the same thing," Shane said. "Something must have happened. Manuel didn't bring them to Threa with us. What if they were killed in New York?"

Tears began to form in the corners of Alice's eyes.

"Don't cry," Shane said. "We need to have faith."

Alice gave Shane a tight hug. She made eye contact with Penny who was staring at them embrace with no expression on her face. Alice turned away and looked at a capsule near her. She screamed so suddenly that Shane fell backwards in surprise. Her yell echoed eerily around the room, but all the creatures in a deep sleep remained unconscious.

"What?" Shane said.

"JESSE!" Alice cried.

Shane could not believe his eyes. Jesse was sleeping in the capsule nearest them wearing a red plaid shirt that looked torn up from a scuffle. His jeans had dirt and grass stains on them and his face looked sunburnt.

"H-h-how did he end up here?" Alice sobbed. Oh m-m-my God!"

"Who is that?" Penny asked.

"Technically it's her husband," Shane said.

Penny and Peter both raised their eyebrows in confusion.

"You're married?" Penny said with a slight sneer.

"He left me though," Alice said. "Shane you were there. He chose to leave me at Sector 1 and he ran off when Kat Twain gave him the choice."

"Yeah," Shane said awkwardly. "You are going to have to face him eventually when we get to Earth."

"I have made my choice as he has made his," Alice said. "I will leave him too. I want to be with…with *you*."

Penny rolled her eyes and Peter stared uncomfortably at Alice. Shane felt his face turn red.

"Thanks," He said. "However, you need to sort that out first—your marriage."

"Earth has fallen apart, Shane," Alice said. "Laws and rules are being broken. I don't think I need to officially divorce him. We had just married when we were brought to Sector 1, the Eyes' headquarters, and he fled, leaving me behind."

"This doesn't feel right," Shane said.

"Feel right?" Alice said and her sobbing was becoming hard breathing. "Feel right? You left for fifteen years! I waited. I nearly gave up hope of ever seeing you."

"I had no choice, obviously," Shane said. "There are bigger things in the universe that I do not understand and I have no idea why it revolves around me."

"I want us to be together," Alice said. "Remember when you and I were in college and you had a crush on me. Remember when you were so shy around me that you only thought I wanted to be a friend? Remember when I came over to your parents' Malibu house to talk about that photo shoot you were going to do for me?"

"That was a long time ago," Shane said. "We're not kids anymore—well we're not that young anymore anyways."

"Ok, let's just end this now. I'm going to wake him up," Alice said.

"Wait what?" Peter broke in.

Alice walked over to a console that was in the center of the room.

"Don't, you'll wake up everything!" Shane said.

Penny ran after Alice and held her back.

"Are you crazy?" Penny shouted.

"Get off me!" Alice said. "Fine!"

Alice brushed herself off and walked to a corner of the room and sat down and began to sob into her arms.

"She's confused, I suppose," Peter told Shane.

"I am too," Shane said, and he was looking at Penny who was fixing her hair into a ponytail.

"Maybe we should get some rest," Peter said. "Let's sleep this day off and wake up tomorrow. We'll probably end up at Earth near mid-morning."

"Well pick the softest piece of floor you can find then," Shane joked. "There aren't any beds around here."

"Well there is one empty capsule. Who wants to sleep in it?" Penny asked.

"An empty capsule?" Shane said examining the capsule Penny was talking about. "How odd. They could have brought one more person on board."

"Well I'm going to get some shut eye," Peter said, taking off his jacket and crumpling it up to use as a pillow as he fell to the floor to sleep.

Peter and Alice were the first to fall asleep. Shane decided to get up for a walk not realizing Penny was still awake.

"Shane," Penny whispered. "Where are you going?"

"For a walk on the upper level," Shane said. "Can't really fall asleep. I was asleep for six months anyways."

"Can I join you?" Penny asked.

"Sure," Shane replied. "Don't make too much noise. Peter and Alice look peaceful. Alice has been through a lot today, and I want her to rest. She must be very confused."

"I don't like her attitude though," Penny said.

Shane shrugged and gestured for Penny to step on the circular platform on the ground. Once they were on, Shane pushed down on the center of it and it began to raise itself silently to the upper floor. When they reached the storage room they were in earlier with the cabinets that extended to the ceiling, they stepped off the circular platform and walked out into the main hall of the ship.

"It's so spooky what with the ship so silent and dim," Penny said. "The dim lights are to conserve the energy. I remember Kat Twain talking about its functions when she brought us on board this the first time."

"Let's go to the control room to see how much power the crystals are harvesting," Shane said. "If they need a boost, I can help."

Shane pulled out his black crystal necklace and showed it to Penny. Penny reached for it and touched the very tip of it with her index finger.

"I truly wonder what the legend behind this necklace is," Penny pondered aloud.

"I know," Shane agreed. "My birth father gave it to me and he never told me much about it. He died just after he gave it to me."

"I'm sorry," Penny said and she put her hands on Shane's shoulder.

"It's so weird," Shane said suddenly. "And then my birth mother wasn't even remotely human nor do I look anything like her."

"That was your uncle in that encasement back at Sector 8 that Kat Twain showed to the world in New York City, right?" Penny asked.

"Yeah. My mother looked the same," Shane said realizing how strange it sounded. "Same grey skin and large black eyes. They were about four feet in height. Their kind was so much more technologically advanced than the people of Earth."

"None of them are left?" Penny went on.

"No," Shane answered. "Humanoids are the next evolution of their DNA. "We—us—have been created to live on and continue their civilization at Threa and their work. I'm the only Humanoid that can survive being possessed by a Dark One. It's so bizarre. Why me?"

"We will figure this all out," Penny said and she kissed Shane in the cheek, making his whole face flush red.

Shane stared at Penny as if really looking at her for the first time. She was nervously twirling her auburn hair and avoiding Shane's eyes. Her green eyes kept looking at the entrance to the control room.

"Thanks," Shane said automatically.

Penny finally made eye contact with Shane again and smiled.

"I'm sorry, I know you and Alice—" Penny started.

"It's nothing," Shane said. "I mean I don't know what the deal is with Alice right now. I mean she is technically married and her husband is on this ship."

Shane gestured for Penny to follow him into the control room. The familiar room had several buttons and levers. Buzzing and beeping sounds were coming from various parts of the room. In the middle, was a tall cylinder glass encasement that housed several black crystals from Threa on the base of it. The crystals were glowing white.

"They look like they still have enough power," Shane deduced. "No need for an extra boost."

"Hey Shane," Penny called over from near a screen that showed a satellite image of Earth.

"Oh wow," Shane gasped as he saw what he believed was a live image of the planet.

The only way they could tell it was Earth was because everyone once in a while there was a break in the huge mass of dark smoky clouds that were encompassing the entire atmosphere of the planet, and they could see the landmass that was North America below it.

"Are those the Dark Ones eclipsing the planet?" Penny asked.

"Yes," Shane said. "They must be getting stronger too. They've been blocking out the sunlight from the planet. Who knows what kind of effects that will have on the people or anything living on the planet?"

"Hey look at this!" Penny said while pointing at a coffee mug that was on a table near a panel of buttons.

Shane examined the mug and touched it. It was warm as if the coffee in it had been made recently. Steam was slowly billowing out of the cup.

"This was made recently," Shane said with suspicion. "Is someone awake?"

"There was an empty capsule below..." Penny pointed out.

"Oh my," Shane replied. "You're right!"

"Let's go back down to the room with the capsules. I have a foreboding feeling," Penny said.

"Right, let's go back down," Shane agreed and they ran out of the control room and back to the storage room where the entrance to the Noah's Ark Project inhabitants were kept.

"Oh!" Penny gasped when they walked into the storage room and saw that there was a circular hole on the ground.

"Someone used it to go down!" Shane said.

Shane peered into the opening on the ground and saw bloody footsteps heading into a part of the room he could not see.

"There's blood on the ground," Shane said with panic in his voice. "I'm going to jump down."

"It's like a hundred foot drop Shane!" Penny said.

"There's no other way down!" Shane argued.

The lights in the storage room flickered slightly.

"Are we losing power?" Penny asked.

"The control room's energy source looked healthy," Shane said. "I don't know what that was about."

"There's rope in here!" Penny said after she had frantically pulled open several drawers. "I'll tie it to the room's door handle. I remember Kat saying these doors can withstand a bomb. I'm pretty sure it can handle our weight if we slide down to the ground down there!"

"You are brilliant!" Shane said and he tied the rope to the handle and then through the other end down the opening on the ground.

Once Shane felt that the rope was secure enough on the handle to hold his weight, he slid down to the room below.

"Ok, I'm fine. Slide down Penny!" Shane called up, however he did not wait for Penny to land.

Shane followed the point to where the bloody footsteps began. What he saw nearly made him fall over backwards. He put his hands to mouth.

"AAAAAAHHHHHHH!" Penny cried as she took in the sight of her dead brother.

Peter was on the floor facing upright still in his sleeping position with his head over his jacket. A pool of blood was spilling from behind his back. There was a wound on his chest that looked as though he had been stabbed with a knife.

"Alice!" Shane called out instinctively but there was no answer to his call.

Penny fell to her knees and put her hands over her brother's hands. She began to sob frantically and her tears fell onto his blood-soaked shirt. Shane had tears form in his eyes too, and he put one hand over her shoulder.

"Stay with me," Shane told Penny. "Follow me. We need to find Alice."

Shane pulled out his crystal necklace, as it was the only defense he had. They crept slowly passed the capsules and followed the bloody footprints. The footprints led them to the spot where they last saw Alice asleep, but she was nowhere to be found.

"She's gone!" Shane said with panic.

"You don't think she did it," Penny cried hysterically.

"Shh," Shane said trying to calm her. "And no! She would never hurt a fly!"

Shane's head turned suddenly to another corner of a room at the distant sound of a roar. He noticed that one of the cage doors was open and charging at them at full speed were two large tigers.

"AAAARGGGHHH!" Penny screamed as loud as her lungs would allow her.

Shane touched the crystal attached to his necklace with his thumb and it began to shine brightly with white light. The light appeared to have blinded the tigers like a deer in headlights. They stared at it confusingly and kept on growling. Shane rubbed his crystal again and the beam hit the tigers square in the faces.

When the crystal's light shut off after hitting the tigers, nothing but dust remained of them.

"It w-w-worked like a Disintegrator!" Penny sobbed.

"It did," Shane said feeling guilty about obliterating the tigers, however the fact that they did not maul them, was a much better feeling.

"Who let them out?" Penny said while wiping her eyes dry with her shirt.

"Let's find out," Shane said with his fists clenched. "Alice! Where are you?"

Once again there was no response to Shane's call for Alice. His heart began to race and he was afraid of what he would find as they continued to follow the bloody footprints which began to get fainter and fainter.

They reached the cage where the tigers had once been kept in and found Alice bound and gagged inside. Her eyes looked wide with shock.

"Alice!" Shane yelled and he ran into the cage and quickly untied her.

"Shane!" Alice screamed and she pointed. "Behind you!"

Shane turned around and saw a man grab Penny, and put his hands over her mouth to silence her. His other hand held a knife and it was raised up to Penny's throat. Penny had a look of horror and tears began to pour out of her eyes again.

The man had a captain's hat on his head and a badge on his blue uniform that read "Capt Bradley Wells, USSA." There was an American flag pin on his lapel. He had white hair that fell to his chin and a white beard. He looked as though he had not groomed in months and as if he had not had much sleep because there were dark circles underneath his eyes. His pupils were dark and dilated as well.

As Shane stared into the man's murderous eyes, it dawned on him…

"You're a Dark One!" Shane said walking out of the cage with one hand clasped in Alice's who was cowering behind him in fear.

"Aren't you smart Humanoid?" The man taunted. "I can't say that I am happy for you ruining my plans to infiltrate Threa. I was going to leave the body of this captain and go into the body of that president."

Shane remembered Dimitri saying that if the USSA landed, that the inhabitants of it would have taken over Threa. Now it made sense as to why that would have happened since a Dark One that snuck in for the ride infiltrated the USSA.

"Who are you?" Shane asked, not recognizing its raspy voice as Sunev's.

"I go by Leviticus," The Dark One answered in a raspy tone through Captain Wells' body. "This filthy Humanoid will not be able to live if I posses her."

Shane's heart began to race at Leviticus' threat to posses Penny. She would die instantly as her body would be unable to host the Dark One's possession.

"Slitting her throat would be a joke," Leviticus said. "It'll be more fun this way."

Captain Wells' body suddenly fell to the ground and the knife hit the concrete floor with a loud clank that echoed in the room. Penny was left standing in her spot and she ran to Shane instantly.

A black smoky cloud escaped the mouth of Captain Wells' body and he woke up in shock with a very fearful, "Where am I?"

The smoky mass that was Leviticus' true form was staring at Shane who had Penny and Alice behind him. Shane could see two red eyes and two formed arms with claws. While they looked deadly, they were nothing but mere smoke and vapor and were harmless.

"She's mine," Leviticus hissed.

"No!" Shane said and suddenly his crystal began to glow white without having touched it. It looked as though his heart was glowing white because that was where the crystal was hanging over.

Leviticus shielded his eyes with his clawed hands and floated further back to the room to put distance between him and the light that was protecting Shane, Alice, and Penny.

"Scared now?" Shane taunted with confidence. "You won't win this war. None of your kind will!"

Captain Wells looked so scared; however, he was able to mutter a few words. "It's World War Total!"

"I am Sunev's right hand," Leviticus hissed. "You will be sacrificed Shane Baker! Your death is inevitable. We will continue on into the future. The Dark Ones will have a future!"

The lights in the room began to flicker and then all the light bulbs in the ceiling exploded and glass fell to the ground. The room went entirely dark except for the light that was emitting from Shane's necklace.

Shane looked down at his necklace and noticed that the crystal was no longer black. It was clear and transparent yet the light it was emitting was still as white as ever.

"Did you see that?" Penny whispered behind Shane's ear.

"What?" Shane asked.

"A black substance escaped your necklace. I think a Dark One was inside your necklace!"

"What?" Shane said in shock.

Shane looked ahead of him and saw that Leviticus' bright red eyes were open in what he thought was a look of shock. Another Dark One was standing in front of Shane, except this Dark One's form looked more human and it's eyes were white. It was the most bizarre thing Shane had ever seen, and he had seen many bizarre things since learning he was Humanoid. The shadowy figure before him had its arms outstretched as if signifying its protection over Shane.

Leviticus flew up into the ceiling and through the hole on the roof that led to the storage room. They heard more explosions above them and the USSA shook violently.

The human-shaped shadowy figured before him turned around and walked back towards Shane, Penny, and Alice. While its form was smoky like a Dark One, it looked more solid.

The figure spoke in a male voice, but it had no mouth. Shane deduced that it was talking to him in his mind.

"Leviticus has fled. You are safe for now. I'll be with you on your journey and return when I am needed. You are the Bright One. Fulfill your destiny."

The figure before Shane turned into a shapeless cloudy mass and flew straight back into the necklace. One second Shane's necklace was transparent and clear in color, and the next it was back to looking shiny and black.

The USSA's emergency lights went on and an alarm echoed from up above the ship's main corridor. Shane's crystal stopped shining and felt warm to the touch. All of a sudden every single capsule's clear lid swung open before them simultaneously. Shane turned around and looked at all the cages, but they remained shut, however the animals inside them were awake and began roaring, growling, and making all kinds of noises in the confusion of their hibernation.

The people in the capsules began to crawl out of their encasements. Landon was the first one out, and his jaw fell open in shock when he saw Shane staring at him.

Chapter Six:

World War Total

"Shane?!" Landon said as he brushed off his jacket and stretched his arms from his six-month slumber. "Are we on Threa now? And why are the alarms ringing?"

"Um," Shane said trying to think of a way to explain the fact that they were now on a course back to Earth.

President Williams walked up beside Landon and fixed his tie. He eyed Captain Wells, who was still on the floor and looked shaken, with a raised eyebrow.

"Oh my God! There's been a murder!" A woman in a navy blue business suit yelled from another capsule.

"Secretary Lockhart," President Williams said, "What do you mean?"

Before the woman, who was apparently the United States Secretary of State could answer, President Williams spotted Peter's dead body in a pool of fresh blood.

"My lord!" President Williams gasped, which was echoed by gasps from other inhabitants of the capsules.

"Shane, what happened? That's the Mills boy!" Landon said rubbing his unshaven face.

"Alison!" Jesse yelled from nearby the capsule he was in. "You're alive!"

Landon took notice of Jesse and was surprised by his sudden appearance. Alice gave Jesse a very dark look and was about to say something, but Shane cut in.

"Look—everyone," Shane addressed the entire room. "The USSA was about to enter Threa's atmosphere, but Manuel made an order that we redirect this craft back to Earth. Myself, Alice, Penny, and Peter hitched a ride on this to go back to Earth because we have unfinished business with the Dark Ones that are causing havoc on the planet. Captain Wells here was apparently possessed by one and—"

"I had no idea!" Captain Wells cut in while getting up from the floor and trying to stand up straight with dignity. "I do not remember how it found me, but it was pretending to be me when I boarded you onto the ship six months ago. I think it found me before I closed the door on the USSA."

"That was right before Russia sent a missile attack on us," President Williams recalled.

"It's horrible Shane," Landon said. "The world has gone mad! The forty-eight hours after Kat slash Sunev exposed our government's secrets for the entire world to know, it was pandemonium. I figured Manuel came for you and took you home."

"It's a long story, but I was in a kind of coma after they brought me back from picking us up off the Empire State Building. I too have been asleep for half a year!" Shane said.

"Why did you send us back to Earth?" President Williams said. "Our government aided the Elders in their time of need. Humanoids exist because of our help. You exist. Why have we been sent back to where the danger is?"

"Your presence would have been a threat to Threa," Shane argued. "Obviously Captain Wells was possessed and that Dark One would have infiltrated our planet."

"One Dark One though?" Landon pointed out.

"A powerful one," Shane said. "It went by the name Leviticus and he is the right hand to Sunev, the queen of the Dark Ones."

"We cannot go back to Earth! We instated the Noah's Ark Project so that we would be saved!" President Williams said with panic.

65

"The alarms are blaring on the upper level," Secretary Lockhart chimed in. "The ship must be damaged."

"I'll go look into it!" Captain Wells said.

"I'm coming with you," President Williams said.

Landon also followed the president and captain to the circular platform. Shane decided to join and was accompanied by Alice and a still teary-eyed Penny. Jesse followed them up the platform as well and tried to reach for Alice's hand, but she folded her arms around her chest.

"I'll come as well," Secretary Lockhart said sternly giving Shane a very cold look.

The platform began to rise and they were transported back up to the higher level leaving the other capsule inhabitants behind.

"This doesn't look good," Captain Wells said when they arrived in the ship's main hall. There was smoke billowing throughout the corridor and pieces of broken bulbs on the ground.

They walked into the control room and saw that the control panels had been damaged. The ship was no longer on autopilot, yet it was heading for Earth.

"There's no control," Captain Wells said. "We're going to…crash into Earth!"

"What?" Landon and President Williams said in unison.

"We are very close too. We will enter Earth's atmosphere in T-minus twenty minutes!"

"Look at that!" Alice gasped pointing at the live satellite image of Earth, as there were no windows in the control room.

The dark clouds that they saw earlier eclipsing the entire Earth, looked even more menacing as it swirled over the planet as if it were a hurricane.

"We are going to crash into that?" Secretary Lockhart said. "We need to steer clear of the planet. In half a years time, it appears as if those creatures have taken it over."

"It was foolish of you to disrupt the plans of this government vessel," President Williams spat. "That is a federal offence!"

"Are you kidding me?" Alice spoke up, and then she turned red realizing she had just addressed the president rudely.

"There is no more government," Shane said matter-of-factly. "And as I explained earlier, your presence on Threa would have been detrimental to its survival. There was a stowaway Dark One possessing Captain Wells!"

President Williams opened his mouth as if to argue, but then closed it shut and remained silent.

"Captain Wells," Landon spoke up, "Is there some kind of safety procedure to land this vessel into a body of water or something? Do we have an escape pod of some sort?"

"There's no escape pod," Captain Wells said, "Once we enter Earth's atmosphere we'll be speeding down to the ground or ocean without any way to steer or control it. The controls were damaged by that thing that was inside my body!"

"What about the black crystals. Can we give them a reboot with Shane's necklace?" Penny asked.

"Um…" Captain Wells was at a loss for words.

"It's quite possible," Shane said, and he pulled out his necklace again, which still felt warm to the touch after the odd experience of it turning white and learning that some kind of black shadowy figure was living inside it.

"We'll be entering Earth's atmosphere in just a few minutes!" Captain Wells announced.

"What about the people and animals down below?" President Williams said. "We need to ge—"

A huge explosion knocked everyone in the control room to the ground. A fire erupted inside of cylinder where the black crystals were housed. Moments later, the cylinder encasement shattered into thousands of pieces and fell to the floor letting out the heat of the fire that was swelling inside.

Shane shielded his eyes as some of the glass flew in his direction. When all of the glass had fallen to the ground and was no longer flying through the air, Shane took his hands off his eyes and saw that there was dark smoke *flying* through the air.

"The Dark Ones!" Alice shrieked.

"We've flown through the Dark Ones' cloud barrier in the atmosphere and we are now falling fast straight down onto Earth!" Captain Wells exclaimed.

Shane could hear the hissing voices of the Dark Ones floating high above them in the control room. He could not make out what they were saying because of the extremely loud sound of the wind catching underneath the USSA as they plummeted to their doom.

I can't let them possess Penny, Shane thought. *They'll kill her.*

"We're going to die!" President Williams cried.

Shane's mind raced back to several years ago when he had first learned about the story of the Elders in their ship. There was a moment where the ship ran out of power and they were about to crash into the Nevada desert near Sector 7. He recalled that on that very night, his necklace turned bright white and saved them from the ship crashing onto Earth. It had just turned bright white and saved them earlier, even though there was a strange entity that came with the experience.

Shane remembered seeing his alien mother's look of horror when they all thought their fate would be their death when the ship's outer exterior would hit the cold desert sand below them. He remembered Dimitri being by his side as well that night.

The necklace's light made a connection with the moon and it saved the Elders' ship from crashing, Shane thought. *How did it happen? Can it happen again?*

Shane was not sure if he imagined it or not, but he thought he heard his mother Genesis' voice. Then he realized he was recalling what she told him about the crystal necklace.

"You use your mind to control the crystal technology," Genesis' words from Shane's memory rang in his head. *"I'm having it guide us to the landing site…"*

It was as if a light switch had turned on in Shane's brain. He had always subconsciously controlled the necklace, but it was still a mysterious object he did not fully understand. Shane imagined the moon outside of the USSA just beyond the dark clouds that were the Dark Ones eclipsing Earth.

"Light…" Shane said to his crystal necklace as he held it before his face. "Let's stop this ship from falling."

Shane imagined an energy that would cause the ship to slow down. Simultaneously the crystal in his hands began to glow white and the wind outside of the ship was roaring less and less.

I'm controlling the fall, Shane thought. *I'm doing it with the crystal. I'm going to have it guide us to Landon's condo in downtown Los Angeles. It will get us closer to the key!*

"What is happening?" Captain Williams said in shock. "We aren't falling!"

"Did the ship somehow regain control of itself?" Landon asked.

"It's my crystal!" Shane said and everyone else took at the bright light that was emitting from Shane's necklace.

It was then that Shane realized a beam of light had shot straight up into the ceiling creating a large hole. The Dark Ones that had entered the ship must have either fled or been destroyed by the light. The light was heading up into space and Shane knew that it had connected with the light from the moon.

"The GPS is showing that we are about a mile or two from the Santa Monica beach. We'll be flying over L.A. shortly!" Captain Wells announced. "Whatever you are doing Shane, just make sure you find a large space to land this. Might be wise to just land onto the beach near the Santa Monica Pier."

"Alright, I will try," Shane said and he imagined the USSA landing softly over the sandy beach.

There was a loud hiss from far away and sounds of gushing wind. Seconds after the sound rang in their ears, the USSA began to vibrate and there was a sudden falling sensation. The USSA was just a few hundred feet above the ocean and about a mile away from the coast of California when it plummeted and made a giant splash.

"We've hit the water!" Landon said. "Shane, what happened?"

"I don't know!" Shane said. "I think the Dark Ones used the weather to knock us into the water.

"The vessel is not meant to float. We'll sink!" Captain Wells said in horror. "And the people and animals below are trapped!"

As soon as Captain Wells had said that, water starting to spill into the vessel from the hole that the crystals' light beam created on the roof of the USSA. The entire ship was completely submerged underwater within minutes of impact into the Pacific Ocean.

"Arggh," Shane spat out salt water that fell into his mouth as he watched the water pour in from the ceiling above.

Jesse reached for Alice as if shielding her from a bullet, but they both slipped onto the floor as the strength of the gushing water hit them.

"Oh my God!" Penny cried. "Shane! Do something!"

Shane grasped his necklace and it grew bright white again. The water that had spilled into the ship began to evaporate and everything in the vicinity dried so quickly, it was almost as if the water had never even entered.

"Wow!" Landon cheered. "Good job Shane!"

Shane used his mind to image the giant craft floating back out of the water and then glide a few feet above the surface straight onto the sandy beach.

There was a soft thud as the USSA fell to onto the beach.

"We're on land now," Shane said. "Safe."

Captain Wells was able to manually open the emergency exit door that allowed for all the people in the room on the lower deck to evacuate.

"We're going to slowly let some of the animals into the wild and give them a chance to survive," Captain Wells said. "There's no point to let them stay caged up in here. They'll starve."

"The Noah's Ark Project was meant to have us all survive elsewhere. We're in danger on Earth," President Williams said as Captain Wells opened the cages of various types of birds that flew out of the emergency exit door without a backwards glance.

Shane walked onto the beach and saw the Ferris wheel of the Santa Monica Pier on its side hanging off the pier. The entire park looked as if it had been vandalized then knocked over. The skies were grey and dark clouds stretched over it for miles. It was evident that it was daytime because some sunlight would shine through a break in the clouds every once in a while, however those breaks were rare. It was very cold as well for summer in southern California. It looked like many of the trees and plants that Shane could spot in the distance were dead. None of the trees had leaves. The grass was brown as if there had been a drought.

"This place looks post-apocalyptic," Alice said, tears forming at the corner of her eyes. "I don't even see a living soul in sight. The cars are abandoned on the road. There are open doors as if they fled from the traffic jam they were in."

"Alice…" Jesse tried to talk to her but he stopped talking when she brushed him off with a hand gesture.

"I noticed that there are hundreds of footprints in the sand all leading into the ocean," Penny added pointing at where the sand ended and the water began. "And…oh my!"

Shane, Alice, and Jesse followed her finger and saw there were a few dead bodies of people drifting onto the shore.

"Do you have the Moonshadow Files?" Landon asked Shane from behind him, making him jump in shock.

"What?" Shane said. "Ah, no. I don't. I woke up in a coma in this part of Threa that Manuel created to imitate Earth. He must have it since he rescued me."

"Well, I wanted to read a paragraph from it," Landon said. "The section that talks about the aftermath of the population control."

"This wasn't done by civilization collapsing upon itself. This was the work of the Dark Ones!" Shane said.

"The Dark Ones started and aided in this event," Landon agreed, "however, humans greatly outnumbered Dark Ones. They would have to rely upon the human population to self-destruct. I'm pretty sure much of that has happened here. I want to refresh my memory about the teachings of the Elders. They foresaw this happening."

"We called this event World War Total," President Williams said. "The aftermath of the world war on itself. *Total* destruction."

"World War Total?" Shane repeated.

"You told me this, Parker," President Williams said to Landon.

"It's in the Moonshadow files," Landon replied. "The Elders' teachings on the aftermath of what would happen if the government's secret truths were revealed."

"We've lost the war then?" Alice said, taking in some of the nearby high rise hotels and condos, most of which had every single window broken.

"Earth will never be the same," Landon said. "We should have never kept our communication with extra-terrestrial life a secret, Will."

President Williams sat down on the sand with his legs Indian-style. He put his hands over his face making him look as though he was sobbing into them.

Secretary Lockhart and a few other government officials that were on the USSA walked over to him. President Williams gestured to them that he was fine. He got up from the ground and dusted sand off his suit pants.

"Ahem," President Williams cleared his throat. "Parker, you and I worked at Sector 7 long ago. You know that by keeping everything a secret bought us more time for a civilized and orderly country. We did all we could to prepare for the aftermath of World War Total. We should never have returned."

"Watch out!" Captain Wells called from the USSA just as an elephant and two leopards ran out of the ship and onto the beach looking very confused and scared.

"For goodness sake Wells," Landon said. "Can you maybe release them when we put a good distance between us and the ship?"

"Right then," Captain Wells answered. "You should head up into the city so I can release the rest of the wildlife. I'll catch up."

There were over fifty people in the party of USSA survivors. They all walked up to the streets and out of the beach. Many of them parted with words exchanged such as "good luck" and "survival of the fittest." They all knew that it was every man for themself. Most of the people in the party had a military background and understood the scenario.

"Landon, you will come with us, won't you?" Shane said as it was now just him, Alice, Penny, Jesse, President Williams, and Secretary Lockhart that remained behind and still within view of Captain Wells' releasing of the animal inhabitants.

"Of course," Landon replied. "We need to get that key from my place."

"Do you think we can use one of these abandoned cars?" Alice asked pointing at a van that could comfortably fit them all.

"We can try to start it," Shane said as he walked over to the van to look inside it. "This one still has the keys."

Shane turned on the ignition and the van successfully turned on after a few tries.

"Great!" Landon cheered.

"Ocean Boulevard is kind of packed with cars," Alice said. "I think we will have to drive on the sidewalks to get onto a highway and even those might look like a giant parking lot."

"We need bikes," Penny suggested. "Or a motorcycle?"

"Santa Monica has plenty of bike and motor bike shops," Alice said. "That would be easiest."

"Is that fine for you Mr. President?" Landon teased. "We won't have secret service in tow."

"Yes, that is fine," President Williams responded not sounding too thrilled.

"I am going to stay behind here and oversee Captain Wells' release of the animals," Secretary Lockhart said.

"Maybe I should too?" President Williams added.

"You go on Will," Secretary Lockhart said. "I think as a leader you will be beneficial in learning what the boy has to find. May you find luck and safety. I will stay around here and search for shelter and food."

"May you be safe too," President Williams said and he gave her a hug.

"I'm coming with you Alice," Jesse said.

"You abandoned me," Alice finally spoke to Jesse. "You left me at the Eye Openers' secret headquarters! You ran straight for freedom."

"How did you end up on the USSA?" Landon asked. "I had no idea you were even on the ship."

"After I ran out of that place in Roswell, the government people dressed in suits picked me up," Jesse said. "They said that I was a key witness in a federal crime and that they would need me to come with them to D.C. for some briefing. I had no choice, Alice. I was taken against my will to D.C."

"You had a choice to stay behind with me in captivity!" Alice snarled. "Kat Twain gave you a choice!"

"I was scared!" Jesse said, his voice rising in anger. "You and I married and were on our way to our honeymoon, then our flight was canceled and we were apprehended and taken to New Mexico from our layover in Texas. You tell me, how you would have reacted. Then, I learn that Shane's a freaking alien!"

"Humanoid, to be exact," Shane corrected Jesse sarcastically.

"Whatever," Jesse said glaring at Shane. "You left her man. You disappeared. I know you always missed Shane and you were trying to find a way to contact him, Alice. Your sister Kendra once let it slip. She read it in a letter. You knew he was alive and not missing like his family thought."

"Kendra read my letter from Landon?" Alice said.

"Now it all makes sense and that Kat woman explained what he was—*is*," Jesse said. "The government brought me on the ship by default because I had been briefed on the existence of these Humanoids. They felt I would have an easier transition if brought on that USSA ship."

"So you were given a chance to survive that most people on Earth were not," Shane spat. "There's no need to be rude or fight with Alice about this right now. You are alive because of her, technically. Otherwise you would have been at the Virgin Islands and maybe even stranded there during the beginning of this World War Total."

Jesse looked like he was trying to find an argument to rebuttal with, but he was at loss for words.

"Do you think we can search for my family?" Alice asked Shane. "My parents or Kendra?"

"This city is a ghost town," Landon said to Alice somberly. "My dear, I'm afraid that the odds of them still being alive are very slim."

"And what about Caroline and Mike, Landon?" Shane asked. "I noticed they were not brought on board the USSA."

"We could not find them," Landon said tearfully. "We searched for you, Alice, Mike, and Caroline. We somehow all got split up after the events at the Empire State Building."

"They might not be alive either," Shane admitted more to himself than anyone else. "This is tragic."

"You all should begin your journey," Secretary Lockhart chimed in. "It's getting late."

They parted ways with Secretary Lockhart and walked in the direction of the nearest highway while keeping their eyes open for a bike shop.

"It's almost nighttime," Alice said noticing the swirling dark clouds above were becoming harder to see as the sun was setting. "However, you can't even see the sunset."

"We should find a place to rest for the night," Shane said. "And some food."

"I brought some of the freeze dried food that was on the USSA," Landon said opening the backpack he was wearing. "It might just last us a few days so we should only eat sparingly and find maybe an abandoned grocery store or a gas station in the morning."

"Good thinking," Shane said. "Let's take cover inside that restaurant over there."

They walked into an abandoned Italian restaurant and at first glance saw every table turned over and broken dishware littered the ground.

"I guess the booths on the walls are the best bet for a bed," President Williams said. "Everyone pick a booth and let's get some sleep. I'm not sure I'll be able to sleep since I've been asleep for six months."

"Same here," Landon admitted.

Jesse pulled Alice away out of earshot from the rest of the group.

"Can we talk outside?" Jesse said, trying to smile.

"Fine," Alice said while rolling her eyes for him to see.

Alice and Jesse walked outside. There was no wind. The air was still and it was eerily quiet. There were no crickets or the sounds of birds chirping into the night. Everything was dead.

"I'm sorry," Jesse said. "You have to put yourself in my shoes. I was afraid I married someone I did not know! You did not tell me about any of your run-ins with the government and Shane's kind. How was I supposed to feel?"

"I…" Alice said trying to think of a good answer. "I guess if I were in your shoes I would have freaked out too. I just wish you had not abandoned me. What happened until death do us part?"

"I understand," Jesse replied. "It's just that at that moment, I did not think death would come too quickly into our marriage! I love you Alice. I really do and no matter what happened I want to put it behind us."

"It's not that easy, Jesse," Alice said. "I'm still in shock. I guess about everything. We've lost everything. I mean what is the point to live now? There's nothing here in this world. I kind of wished I never woke up from that coma in Territory 3."

"Territory what?" Jesse asked.

"Nevermind," Alice said.

"Look," Jesse said. "The government may have collapsed but I still believe in the sanctity of our marriage. Even if I did run out, I was under such duress and confusion from being kidnapped against my will."

"Excuse me!" A voice from behind Jesse said, which startled him and made him jump.

"Holy crap you scared me," Jesse said angrily at a man that was standing before him. He was an older man and was wearing disheveled clothing. He looked as though he had lost a lot of weight because the clothes he was wearing did not fit him well. They were too big on him.

"What's your name?" Alice asked nervously.

"What's your name?" The man asked back.

"I'm Alice, and you?" She asked.

"I'm Alice, and you?" The man repeated.

"Are you mocking me sir?" Alice said now beginning to sound irritated by the stranger.

"Are you mocking me sir?" The man said.

"Dude, what the hell?" Jesse spoke up.

"Dude, what the hell?" The man repeated.

"Are you off your rocker?" Jesse asked.

"Are you off your rocker?" The man mimicked him.

"This is not funny," Alice said.

"This is not funny," The man repeated.

Alice was about to say something, but Jesse covered her mouth and put his hands on her lips to stop her from saying anything. Jesse stared the man down for a minute. The man was smiling menacingly and his brown eyes began to turn dark and then they were a shade of red before going back to brown.

"Did you see his eyes?" Jesse whispered.

"Did you see *my* eyes?" The man said and then his eyes turned red again and his fingernails turned into claws and the fingers connected to those nails turned black. The man's pale skin turned into a charcoal black color and hair began to grow out of every pore on his body. The man was transforming before their eyes into some kind of creature. The clothes it was wearing were shred to pieces, as the creature grew two feet taller than it was when it was human. Its feet had five claws that were longer than its finger nails. He had a long pointed tail that was full of fine black hair just like his arms, legs, and face. The creature's face had a small noes and a thin mouth with sharp teeth. Its eyes were bright red and glowing slightly with cat-like pupils. It had a set of black sharp menacing horns growing out of where its ears were. Protruding out of its back was a set of wings that spanned about ten feet that had exposed skin on them. It gave its span structure that was held together by exposed bones the same color as its body. The creature was about seven feet in height and very slender with fine hair that looked very well tamed and shiny.

Alice screamed and both Shane and Penny came running out of the restaurant. They stopped dead in their tracks at the sight of the monster before them.

"Oh my God!" Shane said in surprise. "They've taken a true form!"

Chapter Seven:
The True Form

Shane stared at the familiar red eyes before him and remembered when he first saw the Dark One's nearly true form for the first time, however back then it was not solid like the one before him...

It was early in the morning past three A.M., when he was in mid-dream. His recollection of the dream was fuzzy. All of sudden he was conscious. He opened his eyes and everything was blurry since his contact lenses were off, and his vision was poor without them. However, at his window, he saw, or at least thought he saw someone peeking through the edge. It was a dark figure.

He ran to the window and squinted. There was nothing. He could no longer see the moon either, which was most likely due to the rotation of the planet, he thought.

Shane went to put his contacts back on, then walked back to the window and looked around outside. He was two stories high. There was no way anyone could be on the roof. With that in mind, he comforted himself by putting together in his mind, that he had just had a strange lucid dream. The only thing that bothered him was he remembered a similar scenario as a child where he woke up from a dream to see a dark figure framed at his window back at his parents' house. He shrugged and then made himself comfortable in his bed.

He fell back into bed and fell asleep almost instantly. He only had one more dream that night. He was in a dark room, and was bounded by an invisible force. He could not move. He heard strange whispers. Shane could not recognize the language the whispers were uttering. All of a sudden there was a flash of light in his dream, and he saw a black shadowy figure with red eyes staring at him before flying away into darkness.

Landon and President Williams ran out of the restaurant to see what was happening. Landon stopped dead in his tracks and instinctively reached for his gun. He fired three shots at the creature and it screamed a very loud high-pitched moan. The creature keeled over backwards and fell to the ground.

"I'm not sure bullets will kill it," Shane said staring into the red eyes of the creature.

Shane pulled out his necklace and held it into the air. Nothing happened. He assumed that it could trigger some light power from the moon, but nothing happened.

"I think I drained it," Shane said anxiously. "And the Dark Ones have clouded the atmosphere. Light cannot penetrate to recharge it!"

"I think it's dying though," Penny said as the creature began to moan and black blood poured out of its mouth as if it were a car leaking oil.

"I guess it is not invincible," Shane said. "It used a human body to transform into its real, true form. They have always wanted to have their own bodies, but Humanoids would die after possession. The Dark Ones have become strong enough to eventually use a host human's body to become the monsters that they once were. In the past they were not able to take over people's bodies to this extent, and humans were thought to have been possessed by a demonic entity."

"So basically because they are human," President Williams said, "they can die just like us?"

"That's the flaw in their plan!" Shane said with a look of hopefulness. "The only thing is they have their own powers and are physically stronger. I think the more powerful Dark Ones will be immune to human firepower though."

"The Elders never told us much about these alien life forms," Landon said. "Did you learn anything in the fifteen years you were living on Threa? I'm referring mainly to their past and how they came to be."

Shane walked over the dead Dark One and kicked it. It did not move and splatters of black blood landed on his shoe. Once Shane was sure it was dead, he answered Landon's question.

"They are the oldest specie in the universe. My mother Genesis told me about them very briefly, but not much detail about their past except that they lived in shadows and feasted on the bodies of solid, living beings. They were the reason my ancestors came to Earth so that they could birth Humanoids that would be able to withstand their possessions. They knew one day a Humanoid would be born that could survive a possession. I'm the only known Humanoid who can survive them and fight them off out of my body. I've done it before. A Dark One was inside me once and it died trying to take my body as a host. Penny here, for example, would not able to survive if she gets possessed. And now, any human is in danger because the Dark Ones can possess them in a way that they will transform their bodies into becoming an actual, solid being and not the smoky shadows that they are now."

"I remember when Noom possessed me," Landon said. "It was the most scariest thing I've ever encountered. He nearly forced me to kill you Shane."

"I remember that night so well," Shane said. "That night at Sector 7. You survived his possession."

"I think we should all stay inside," President Williams said. "There are some people walking around in the distance."

Shane saw silhouettes of some people walking around aimlessly in the distance. After the situation that had just taken place, Shane was convinced not to trust anyone still alive.

"They might be possessed by Dark Ones," Penny said.

"Yeah," Shane agreed. "Let's all go inside."

Everyone walked into the restaurant to find a booth to sleep on until it was daytime. It was very dark outside with no electricity or the light of the moon and stars visible for them to see much, so they had no other choice, but to remain hidden inside the restaurant.

The next morning, Shane woke up to find Jesse walking out of the restaurant. Everyone else was still asleep.

"Where are you going?" Shane asked him.

"Just seeing if the coast is clear," Jesse said. "I don't see anybody out. The sky is still grey, but at least you can tell it's daytime."

"Let's wake everyone," Shane said.

"Before we do," Jesse added, "can you and I both have a conversation...about Alice?"

"Um, sure," Shane answered awkwardly. "What do you want to talk about exactly?"

"I'm sorry about my fight with her," Jesse said.

"It's none of my business, nor do I want to be a part of it," Shane said automatically.

"I know she is special to you," Jesse said. "I think things have changed, um, around here in this world. I want to apologize about freaking out about you not being human as well. It was very naïve of me."

Shane felt that Jesse was being genuinely apologetic, yet he could not help but wish he was never aboard the USSA.

"It's a complicated time," Shane said. "I get that, but Alice is an adult as are you. I think that you both need to make an adult decision about how you will move forward, especially if you are going to stay in our group. It's not safe out there. You saw that *thing* last night. We're just lucky it had a weakness."

"I want to keep my wife safe," Jesse said. "Can you help me keep her safe?"

"Um, yes," Shane said scratching his head.

Once everyone had woken up and had a few bites of food that Landon had procured from the ship, they were on their way in the direction of the highway.

"I see a bike shop!" Alice said.

Everyone followed Alice, who took the lead, to the abandoned bike shop on their path. The windows to the store were all broken in and there were just a few children's bikes left.

"Damn it!" President Williams cursed. "Looters."

"It will probably be like this everywhere we go," Landon said. "Stores have been broken into. Things have been stolen. It might be just as difficult to find food. I can't imagine that grocery stores around here were not wiped clean of nonperishable foods."

Shane sat on the street curb outside the bike shop and sighed. He looked at the street that was filled with hundreds of parked and abandoned cars. He looked over to the highway that was just a mile away and noticed there were eighteen-wheelers.

"Hey!" Shane said. "What if we get in one of the eighteen-wheelers and just smash through the traffic?"

"Well I don't have a better idea," Landon said. "Will, do you oppose?"

"Let's do it," President Williams replied.

"I can't believe the President of the United States is hanging with us!" Jesse whispered to Alice, who gave him a half smile.

When they finally reached the highway and entered it through an on-ramp, Shane opened the door of the first truck he could find.

"Keys are in here!" He exclaimed. "I can fit two up here. The rest will have to go inside the trailer."

Jesse opened up the back door of the trailer and yelled, "Gold!"

Shane walked over to see what the contents of the trailer were. It was full of canned food items that had not been discovered by looters.

"Perfect! Stock up!" Shane said.

Shane took up the position as driver, with Penny in the middle and Landon on the passenger side of the truck's one row of seating. Alice, Jesse, and President Williams were in the trailer of the truck eating cans of beans.

"This truck is pushing all these cars as if they were paper being swept off the floor!" Penny said as Shane was pushing on the gas pedal.

"And we still have half a tank of gas!" Shane said. "That's plenty of fuel to get us to downtown L.A."

"Do you think we are making too much noise?" Landon asked. "I don't want to be discovered by the Dark Ones."

"I haven't seen anybody since daylight started," Shane pointed out. "I think they only come out at night when it's much darker. They are weaker in the light, hence why they created the dark clouds that have been blocking out the sun."

"I can't believe how cold it is right now for L.A. though," Landon said.

"We'll put an end to this," Shane said. "We'll find Sunev or she will find us."

"Once we get the key from my condo," Landon said, "we'll head straight to New Mexico. However, we'll need a vehicle that will be easier to maneuver. I can't imagine the highways outside of L.A. being as congested as these parking lot highways."

"Hey, be careful!" Penny shouted. "There's a woman on the street!"

Shane stepped on the breaks at the sight of an elderly woman wearing a nun's veil.

"She looks like she's very fragile," Penny whispered.

Shane jumped out of the truck and so did Jesse from the back trailer.

"Everything alright?" Jesse asked.

"Wait there!" Shane ordered as he got out of the truck and looked at the woman who was shaking nervously at the sight of Shane.

"P-p-please don't h-h-hurt me," The woman sobbed.

"I'm not going to," Shane said convinced she was not possessed. "What's your name?"

"Dulce," The woman said and she was covering her face slightly with her hands as if she feared Shane.

She looked as if she had not eaten in days. She was fragile looking and her green dress was torn up and severely stained. She had piercing green eyes, which were surrounded by dark circles around them as if she had not slept in weeks. Her hands covered the rest of her face and her hair was tucked behind the veil.

"Would you like to come with us? We have food," Shane asked.

The woman nodded her head. Shane turned to head to the back of the truck to grab some of the canned food, when Penny screamed. Shane quickly turned around and saw the woman's eyes turn red.

"It's a Dark One!" Alice shrieked!

The woman was attempting to transform into a similar creature as the one they encountered outside the restaurant they took refuge in the night before. It looked like she was not strong enough.

"RUN!" Jesse yelled out loud while grabbing Alice's hand and ushering her forward up the highway while jumping over parked cars.

Shane and the Dark One stared at each other. Shane looked into its dark red pupils and black irises. He pulled out his necklace and saw the Dark One's eyes widen in shock. Her thin mouth formed into a smile and sharp teeth were revealed behind its lips.

"You're *him*...," It said. "Sunev will be happy to know that I've found you."

"You won't get that far," Shane teased, but he was beginning to panic because his crystal was not turning white to his touch.

I need to recharge it with a light source, Shane thought to himself in distress. *The sun is covered by the clouds that the Dark Ones created!*

Landon and President Williams were standing shell-shocked by the truck with Penny inching closer to Shane.

"Give me the necklace," The Dark One ordered. "Give it to me or else I will possess the other Humanoid. She won't be able to survive."

"If you do that, then you won't have your true form!" Shane said realizing he did not know if that was true or not. He had not figured out the process of the Dark Ones' ability to transform their host body into their true, solid form.

"We are powerful now," The Dark One answered back with menace. "I will master the art of our transformation and turn that beautiful ginger girl into this."

The Dark One brushed her hands through her veil on her head in a mocking manner.

"Penny stay back," Shane warned her as he caught glimpse of her trying to sneak up by his side.

The Dark One suddenly turned into black smoke leaving behind the body of the woman he was possessing. Her body convulsed as if in shock, and then she stopped moving. It appeared as though in her old fragile state, she had a stroke and died.

The swirling black smoky cloud was hovering inches from Shane's face. He could see its red eyes contemplating trying to possess him instead of Penny. Shane knew it was coming before he could attempt to pocket his crystal necklace. He dropped it on the ground as the Dark One forced its way into Shane's mouth.

"SHANE!" Penny screamed.

Shane turned to look at her. He could still feel that his mind was his own. He remembered having experienced this sensation before at the farmhouse where he met Dimitri for the first time along with another Humanoid by the name of Agatha. He remembered waking up from what he believed was a lucid dream, however that was the first time a Dark One tried to possess him, however it failed and died.

Shane's head began to throb. He was no longer able to see. It was as if a black smoke had clouded his sight. He heard a whisper in his ear in a language he did not understand. It was a very eerie hissing sound and even though he could not see or feel the rest of his body, he imagined there were chills running up and down his spine from the Dark One's voice in his head.

You won't win, Shane said in his head knowing that the Dark One could hear.

You are special indeed, the Dark One's voice said in English. *I cannot take over your soul. You really are a powerful body vessel. No wonder Sunev is adamant about stopping you.*

You won't be able to escape alive," Shane said remembering that the last time he was possessed by a Dark One, it had turned into nothing and vanished.

And you are right, but the rest of our race will stop you, The Dark One replied to Shane's inner thoughts. *I am, however, sad that I cannot report to Sunev about this information in your head regarding a future civilization. It seems that they are helping you and…wait a minute…if we stop them then we can rule the universe at last?!*

Shane's head began to throb with pain again and he felt that the Dark One was getting angry. He could also sense its thoughts and knew that as long as it stayed inside Shane, it could buy itself more time to live, but once it escaped, it would die. Shane was imaging his body trying to push out the Dark One, but nothing happened.

I could stay inside you for all eternity, the Dark One said. I could leave you in this coma until your body dies of hunger and thirst.

You'll only be torturing yourself as well. I know it pains you to be inside me. You aren't much stronger than the last Dark One that was inside me, Shane replied.

Yes, it does hurt to be inside your soul, the Dark One agreed. *I cannot believe the fountain of information your soul has. I could put our race far ahead in this war of the universe…*

Shane could not feel any of his limbs and he wished he could pull his hair out because the Dark One was causing him agony while also causing itself tremendous pain.

STOP! Shane yelled to himself in his head.

In the distance, Shane could hear muffled voices becoming clearer and clearer. The dark shadows clouding his vision were vanishing slightly and he thought he saw a bright white light, but then he realized it was just his eyes adjusting to reality.

Shane was lying on his back and looking up at Landon, Alice, Jesse, Penny, and President Williams. He got up to his feet so fast, that a head rush made him dizzy and he fell back onto the street landing sitting down.

Shane noticed that Landon was looking off at another direction. Shane followed his gaze and saw that he was looking at a high-rise building just off the highway. There was a person standing on the roof. The person was wearing a brown cloak. The person must have felt Shane looking at their direction, because it lifted up the cloak's hood to cover up their face. The person was too far to technically make out its gender, but he could tell that the figure's skin was very tan and it was bald. Shane assumed it was male.

"Shane!" Alice said reaching for his hand to help him get off the ground.

Shane stood up and massaged his neck and looked back at the building where the person was standing a few seconds prior.

"It's gone," Shane said to Landon who was apparently the only one that saw the figure.

"Yes, it is gone!" President Williams said. "As soon as you came around, the black shadows escaped your mouth and it disintegrated into thin air! You killed it! But how?"

Shane looked at President Williams with confusion before realizing he was talking about the Dark One's destruction from his body.

"Yes," Shane said. "It cannot posses me. I'm special I guess."

"You truly are," Penny said with admiration and she gave him a hug.

Alice gave Penny a subdued look of shock and Jesse instinctively reached for her hand.

"Sorry we were running away out of fear earlier," Jesse said. "I'm human. I can't fight off that thing."

"I'm a Humanoid and I cannot either," Penny piped in.

Jesse just gave her a blank stare and then avoided her gaze and looked away.

"Do you know who that was?" Shane asked Landon.

Everyone but Landon looked at Shane as if he was not feeling well from the attack.

"There was someone on the roof," Landon said to the group. "I guess Shane and I were the only ones who saw it."

"I think I've seen that person before," Shane said racking his already tired mind. "In New York City, the night of the press conference and the Dark Ones' and Moonshadow Ranch residents' attack. Someone is watching over me. Maybe they are even helping me?"

"But who?" Penny said. "There's nobody from Threa left on Earth and we haven't seen any non-possessed humans since we landed."

"Was it Dimitri?" Alice asked. "Maybe he followed us? Or Manuel?"

"No – it was someone bald and with dark skin. It looked like it had a tan, but there can't be anyone left on this planet with a tan. The sun has been shielded from this planet for six months," Shane added smartly.

"Very good point," Landon said. He then turned to President Williams, "The cone! It's in the USSA isn't it?"

"I forgot about it," President Williams said.

"Cone? You mean a Communicator?" Shane asked in surprise.

President Williams explained to Shane how every president had been entrusted to keep the one that was left behind when all the Humanoids left Earth with Manuel at Sector 7. It was a one-way communicator only used in case Threa needed to send them a message.

"I had no idea about it," Shane said. "But if it is only one-way, then there is no real point to it."

"Unless Threa needs to give us a message," Landon said.

"Well Threa believes Earth is doomed, so there will be no reason they would send us a message," Shane said matter-of-factly.

"I suppose that's true," Landon agreed. "It was the first idea that came to my mind."

"How about we go get that key from your condo?" Alice suggested.

"Right," Landon said, "we should."

"Sunev knows about the future," Shane said. "Manuel told me that Agent Green met a person from the future back at Sector 7."

President Williams and Landon gave Shane confused looks.

"Listen up," Shane said. "I'll give you the details about what I learned recently since my return to Threa. I don't know all the details, just small bits. But there is a civilization out there that is watching over us..."

Shane stopped and thought for a second.

"Maybe that's who that person was!" Shane said. "It was someone from the future! But who?"

"Can you explain some more?" Landon said while trying to wrap the information around his head.

Shane explained what Dimitri and Manuel had told him back on Threa to the group, as not all of them knew the story.

Landon was the first to speak when Shane finished.

"I do recall this. And we have talked about this before Shane. Agent Green said he learned something that night, and he could not tell me," Landon said. "That was it, huh? He met someone from the future. All I knew was that it had something to do with our existence."

"Yeah," Shane answered. "Noom then possessed Green and learned about this person from the future and that was the key to their survival to win over Earth and Threa... even the universe.

As long as I get to the door and open it before Sunev, then we are safe. And I do hope she doesn't sniff us out before I am able to get to that door in New Mexico."

"Do you know what's behind the door?" President Williams asked Shane.

"I'm not positive but—" Shane began but was cut off by a scream from Alice.

"Oh my God!" Alice said while standing over the body of the nun that was possessed and left for dead.

Alice had removed the nun's veil and turned the body over. The lifeless green eyes staring back at them were…

"Is that Candy Adams?" Jesse said in surprise.

Chapter Eight:

Landon's Condo

Alice's face contorted into uncontrollable tears. Jesse kneeled down next to her and put his arm around her to comfort her. She returned the embrace by giving him a hug and sobbing into Jesse's shoulders.

"Mariette..." Shane whispered more so to himself than to anyone else in the group. "We thought she died years ago in a house fire..."

Landon shifted uncomfortably because it was his involvement with the Non-Human Relations agency that was ordered to burn down Mariette's house, bequeathed to her by her late lover and Shane's mentor, Derek Conrad, to silence her because she knew the truth about the beings living among Earth.

"She lived longer than she was destined for," Shane said aloud but to himself. "She survived the odds and spent her elderly days at Moonshadow Ranch. She survived the attack at the Empire State Building even after Sunev had possessed her momentarily. And here she lies in Los Angeles after years of a struggle and fight with her destiny."

"I remember when you were given the order to go to her house," President Williams whispered to Landon, but Shane and Penny could hear. "You did not want to set fire to it."

"And you offed Derek too," Shane said without thinking.

"I thought we were passed this," Landon replied. "I'm leading you to my condo to get the key that Derek left for you so that I can once and for all put this all to rest. This has been a heavy burden on my soul for many years."

Landon also fell to his knees and touched Mariette's cold, wrinkly hands. He began to sob uncontrollably and loud.

"Shh," Penny said. "There might be more Dark Ones around. We don't want to draw attention."

Landon wiped his eyes on his jacket and looked at Shane.

"I almost thought about jumping off of my high rise condo's balcony," Landon said. "The government put so much pressure on me during my young agent NHR days. It destroyed me. Will—don't you agree?"

President Williams looked at Landon uncomfortably then he nodded in agreement.

"The knowledge of all those secrets was such a heavy cross to bare," Landon went on.

"It still haunts me," President Williams added.

"You talked about a civilization from the future that seems to know what our destiny is, right?" Landon asked Shane.

Shane nodded.

"Well," Landon continued, "I believe I can choose my own destiny and I chose life so that I could do some good because Derek's innocence was taken from him when...when I pushed his car off that hill."

"Then let's go to your condo," Shane said. "If we go on foot we can be downtown before nightfall."

"Agreed," Penny said. "Those creatures will be out more when it is nightfall."

Out of respect, Landon covered Mariette's body with a jacket that was lying on the street.

"Let's go," He said after a few minutes of silence.

Shane and Penny took the lead in the group with President Williams and Landon behind them. Alice and Jesse took the rear and were holding each other's hands. Shane kept avoiding Alice's gaze because the situation was too awkward for him.

"You have your necklace back on?" Penny asked Shane.

"I do," Shane replied and he tucked it under his shirt.

The journey forward was like a maze. They had to jump and maneuver over the abandoned cars left on the highway. Jesse found an abandoned ice chest and was using it to store some of the canned foods he could fit in it from the truck they had to leave behind. The only break they took was so that they could have a quick lunch.

"I'm so thirsty," Alice said as she sat on the hood of a car. "There were not that many water bottles in that truck. How long will these rations last?"

"A few days at most," Landon answered. "We have to be smart and just eat for nourishment, not to become full."

"We'll just check every abandoned grocery store and market along the way," Shane said. "We'll leave no gas stations unturned and trucks unsearched."

"It's hard to tell what time it is as we cannot see the sun," Penny said, "but I'm guessing we have maybe two hours left of daylight. I say the word daylight sparingly because, well, there really isn't much light to begin with."

"It just gets way darker when it actually is nighttime, and without electricity, the streetlights don't work," Jesse added. "We'll need shelter."

"We can stay at my condo," Landon said. "Let's pick up the pace and get there before it's too dark."

The group made it to the downtown area of what was left of Los Angeles with twenty minutes to spare before it was completely dark. The skyscrapers downtown were still standing, however many of their glass windows remained broken.

There was a smell of death in the air. Alice and Penny screamed a few times as they jumped over the bodies of dead people. Some of the bodies were flattened on the ground as if they had jumped off from the top floors of the high risers.

"Gross," Shane said as he jumped over a decayed body of a man. "The smell is horrible here."

"I'm just up the street," Landon said referring to his condominium's building. I'm on the third floor. We can take the stairs three flights up."

"I can see some of those creatures flying around high up in the sky!" President Williams whispered pointing at the sky just beyond the roofs of the skyline.

"They are on some kind of aerial watch," Shane deduced. "Let's walk briskly. I don't want to run into any possessed people on the way over. Luckily...or I guess I should say unluckily for them at least...all these people on the ground are dead."

When they reached the door of Landon's building, they noticed that it was torn down.

"What a mess," Landon sighed.

They walked through the entrance and found the lobby in shambles. A glass chandelier that once hung on the magnificent ceiling was on the ground before them shattered into hundreds of pieces. They treaded careful over the glass and passed the concierge's desk where they found a dead concierge.

"This world is very post-apocalyptic. I doubt there is anyone alive anymore," President Williams said, tears forming at the corner of his eyes.

Shane absentmindedly put his hand on Penny's back ushering her in the direction of the stairs. His other hand was clenching the necklace around his neck.

They crept up three flights of stairs until they reached Landon's floor.

"My room is number 315," Landon said. "Take a left Shane."

Shane, who was in the lead, followed Landon's orders. They arrived at his door, which was left ajar.

95

"Someone's been here," Shane said.

Shane took a deep breath and pushed the door open. Landon's room looked as though it had been searched.

"This damage could have been from when Agent Miller did a search of this place for the Communicator he stole at the orders of Kat Twain," Landon said while looking at Shane's nervous expression.

"So where is the key then?" Shane asked.

"Should be in a case disguised as a book on my bookshelf," Landon said as he made his way to the bookshelf.

"It's not there," A voice coming from a broom closet in the condo said.

Everyone jumped, but when the door opened, Alice and Shane both yelled for joy.

"Mike!" Alice and Shane said with excitement.

Mike walked carefully out of the closet to take in the company that was with Shane and Alice. He appeared timid. Then he turned around and pulled the hand of another person that was hiding in the closet.

"Caroline!" Shane said.

"Oh my God!" Caroline cried and she flung her arms and ran to Alice. They shared a ten second embrace before Caroline's eyes moved from Shane to...

"Jesse?" Caroline said in shock. "But you..."

"I'm sorry," Jesse said bashfully. "I fled out of fear after those Eye Openers apprehended us and let me free. It's a long story, but I ended up on the USSA."

"And you aren't on the USSA?" Mike asked Landon. "We thought you left six months ago!"

"We did," Landon replied. "However when we got to Threa..."

"We brought them back to Earth," Shane said. "If they landed on Threa, there would have been trouble. There was a Dark One hiding inside the USSA preparing to attack Threa."

"So the Dark One failed?" Mike said sounding confused.

"It sure did," Penny jumped in.

"Killed?" Mike asked.

"It fled," Shane said. "It goes by the name Leviticus and it is Sunev's right hand partner."

"I see," Mike said. "Well I'm glad you are safe, but why would you come back to this hell hole? We've been hiding here for a few days. We were tired from our journey across the country. It wasn't easy. There's a few survivors we met a long the way, but as time passed, we found less and less living people. We came here to find the key! The spare key that Derek wanted you to have, Shane. It's gone! Someone took it."

"Dammit!" Shane cursed.

"But I think I know who has it," Mike said with triumph in his eye, "Agent Miller."

"How do you know?" Shane said.

"Do you not remember?" Mike said. "He was the one that ransacked this place on Kat Twain's orders. He must have found the key and kept it. If I remember correctly I saw him wearing a key necklace around his neck when we saw him and Kat Twain talking in the backyard of your dad's house in Beverly Hills."

"That's right!" Shane said, now remembering having seen the necklace that he thought was just a charm at the time.

"The only issue now," Alice started, "is how will we find Agent Miller? Landon?"

"There will be no way to track him down now," Landon said. "There's no power left. No way to communicate across the globe."

"Miller was discharged," President Williams said. "Was he not?"

"He was," Landon said. "But I have no idea where he would have gone for early retirement. We don't know if he's alive or not, and by the looks of how our world looks now, I doubt he's alive."

Caroline turned on a flashlight to give more light into the room as it was now nightfall outside and pitch black.

"We should stay here over night," Caroline said. "We've been here a few days and have not run into any trouble. Well, unless you count that earthquake that happened the day we arrived at this condo. It wasn't a strong one, but it sure did scare me."

"Well, then it is settled," Landon said. "We'll camp out here over night."

"What was that?" Penny said in shock.

In the distance, they could hear roars and screams from what could have been people or Dark Ones.

"It's a scary world out there," President Williams said. "It's like this is not even our home anymore."

"And you're not the leader of the free world, huh?" Jesse said sarcastically.

"Jesse!" Alice shouted at him and gave him a hard nudge.

"It's ok Alice," President Williams said. "It's true. I have no more power than any of you do, well, not including you Shane."

Shane felt himself go red. He smiled politely, but did not say anything in return.

Everyone had fallen asleep except for Shane, Alice, Mike, and Caroline. Shane was filling in Mike and Caroline on all that had happened from the moment he woke up in Territory 3 in Threa. Mike and Caroline in return explained how Earth fell apart in the last six months since the Dark Ones had their attack on New York City. The Dark Ones' coercion of the Eye Openers' leaks of the government's secrets, caused a rift in civilization.

"It was horrible," Caroline said while fighting back tears. "All of our families are dead. There's no doubt about that."

"Mine are for sure," Shane said silently.

"I wish I was able to say goodbye to my parents or my sister Kendra," Alice said putting her hands over her face.

"What's the deal with you and Jesse?" Mike asked bluntly.

"That's rude!" Caroline said nudging Mike in the ribs.

"It's ok," Alice said while avoiding Shane's eyes. "We're still married technically. He explained why he had to run. I guess it was not fair of me for keeping such a big secret."

"It's not like he would have believed you," Shane said bitterly.

"You left!" Alice snapped, and then she lowered her voice so as not to wake anyone else.

"It doesn't matter," Shane said. "You've chosen your path. Your destiny. Your fate. Whatever."

"No need to be harsh, man," Mike said. "This is a difficult time for all of us. We need to get that key as soon as possible, though."

"Penny seems to have a thing for you," Alice said through gritted teeth. "Go for her. She's a bit younger than you, but she's a pretty girl. And she's of *your* kind."

"My kind?" Shane said. "You say that as if it's an insult!"

"For crying out loud," Caroline cut in. "Stop yelling, both of you! There was a time when there was bitterness between us Alice. Remember I went on a date with Shane?"

"Awkward," Mike said sarcastically.

"Sorry," Caroline said. "I'm just proving a point that we can all get past this. We are a team. The four of us have been through this since Shane first learned he was Humanoid. We've been through so much in the last two decades. We cannot abandon each other now."

"I'm surprised we're still alive," Alice added. "The government was out for our necks, then the Eye Openers, and the Dark Ones. I just want to live a normal life."

"Normal?" Shane said. "Even though it's dark out there? Look around us tomorrow when it is light out. There is nothing! Nothing! Zip, zero, nada! Earth will never be the same again. I'm here to find a hope for the little survivors here and *my kind* back at Threa. It's my destiny apparently."

"Do you know what this means?" Mike cut in pulling out a piece of paper from his pocket. "I didn't want to show it to the whole room earlier when everyone was awake. I wanted you to see it first. This message was left inside the faux book. I'm pretty sure Agent Miller did not leave it. I don't recognize the handwriting either."

Shane grabbed the crumpled piece of paper from Mike and read it out loud: "The future is here."

"What does that mean?" Alice wondered.

"Future is the key word," Shane said. "This must have something to do with the future people. Mind if I keep this?"

"Sure. What else do you know about those people and what does that door open?" Mike asked sounding very intrigued.

"It could open to anything, but we'll have to wait and see," Shane said while he put the piece of paper in his pocket. "As for the people, I'm not sure, but I may have seen one of them earlier today."

"Really?" Caroline asked.

"Just a glimpse," Shane said. "I have seen this person before. I saw a glimpse of a dark-skinned bald man watching over me when we were attacked in New York City. And earlier today we had a run in with a Dark One that—oh I forgot to tell you..."

Shane explained to Mike and Caroline how Mariette was possessed by a Dark One and was left dead after the Dark One escaped her body to attempt to take over Shane.

"That's horrible," Caroline cried.

"So she's dead for real this time?" Mike said and he sounded almost sarcastic and not sympathetic.

"Uh, yeah," Shane replied. "Anyway, the person was wearing a brown cloak. He vanished before I could get a better look. I think it is someone from the future, but we're not allowed to see or talk to them as it could affect our present and eventually their future."

"That's confusing," Mike said, but he was hanging on every word.

"So how are we going to find this Miller guy?" Alice asked.

"It'll be like finding a needle in a haystack," Shane said. "I'm thinking maybe Landon can help us track him since he was a former NHR agent."

"How though?" Caroline said. "There's no power. It's not like we can track him via a GPS or something like that these days."

Shane knew that it would be nearly impossible to find the key now. It was perhaps lost forever.

"Let's get some rest and we'll figure out our next steps in the morning," Shane said.

It took an hour for Shane to finally fall asleep. He had been tossing and turning on one of Landon's couches trying to think of ways to obtain the missing key. When his mind had stopped racing with ideas, he was able to slip into a deep sleep.

"Wake up," Penny whispered to Shane in the morning.

"Hey," Shane yawned. "What time is it?"

"Seven, I think," Penny answered. "I opened up some cans of spinach. It's breakfast time."

"Oh, good," Shane replied. "I'm starving. How are you holding up?"

Penny looked like she was fighting back tears. Shane realized he probably should not have asked her that question.

"I miss Peter," Penny said. "I want to stop the Dark Ones once and for all. For you. For me. For Peter. For Threa. We need to kill them all."

"I know," Shane said. "They've become really powerful. All I know is that door is our key to ending this. There's something beyond it."

"Once you open that door, there's no going back," Penny said. "I'm afraid of what we'll find. Aren't you?"

"It can't be anything dangerous," Shane assured her. "We are going back to Threa if we can't stop the Dark Ones. We'll be safe there."

"They will eventually want to take over Threa again though," Penny said.

"We will prepare for that there and have a fighting chance," Shane said. "They won't take it over like they did when they took over the Elders."

"Good morning," Landon said walking into the living room where Penny and Shane were conversing.

"What's in the box?" Shane asked noticing that Landon was carrying a sealed cardboard box.

"Just some of my old NHR files," Landon said. "Nothing exciting. There's a few photos of people we kept tabs on. Some of the stuff in here were records of when I was tracking Derek and you when you went on his clue scavenger hunt that he left behind for you."

"Can I take a look?" Shane asked.

"Yeah," Landon said. "It's not so top secret anymore."

Shane sat on the floor and looked through the box. There were several surveillance photos of Derek being tracked. He found some of him and Mariette hanging out. Then Shane looked through a file that had photos of the clues that Landon and his NHR team stole from Shane's Jeep.

"Wow," Shane said. "Look at these Mike."

Mike had just walked into the room and he sat next to Shane and examined the photos that he was showing him.

"Wow these are the things Derek left behind for you!" Mike said excitedly. "Look it's the old camera, a picture of the original key, and look...this photo has the CD that Derek recorded that song 'I want Candy' on."

Shane grabbed the photo from Mike's hand and examined the photo of the CD.

"The handwriting!" Shane said excitedly. "Look at the handwriting!"

"It's Derek's handwriting," Mike replied. "What's so exciting about it?"

Shane pulled out the note that Mike and Caroline found in the empty faux book that read, "The future is here."

"What's that?" Penny and Landon asked.

"Mike and Caroline found this in the box where the key should have been," Shane explained.

"Really?" Landon gave an inquisitive look.

"Look at the H's," Shane said. The H in my name and the H on the note are very similar. There's a little curve on the letters. It's similar."

"How peculiar," Mike said. "The writing is in fact similar."

"But this note was written within the last six months," Landon said.

"Do you think that this piece of paper was another clue he created when he was alive?" Mike asked.

"That's what I'm thinking," Shane said. "But who put it in the case and how did they get it?"

"What's going on?" Alice said, walking into the living room with Caroline.

Shane explained his theory on the note that was found in Landon's condo.

"What if he's not dead?" Caroline said mysteriously.

"That would be impossible," Landon said uncomfortably.

"That's right," Mike said. "You killed him."

"Mike!" Caroline hissed. "That was rude."

"It's ok," Landon replied. "It's the truth. I was also with the police when his body was recovered out of the car. It still haunts me. He was cut up terribly from the fall off the cliff. I couldn't even recognize him."

"Don't think about that night any more," President Williams said as he joined the rest of the group in the room with a can of spinach in one had and a fork in the other.

103

"I had a lot of therapy after that night," Landon admitted.

"I have some information that could be useful," President Williams cut in while trying to change the subject. "I think I know where we can find Agent Miller."

"Where?" Penny and Shane asked in unison.

"Even though he was discharged from the NHR shortly before the leak of the agency's top secret information was spilled out for the world to know," President Williams continued, "all former NHR and active members that were not stationed at Sector 8 were asked to hide in a bunker at Sector 7 out of fear that their lives would be in danger if the Eye Openers leaked out names of its members."

"I guess I would not have been aware of that order as I was being held in custody at the time shortly before the New York City incident," Landon said.

"Correct," President Williams continued. "I think Nevada is in our plans now. The bunker was designed to keep people safe and alive for several months in case of an emergency. Even though Sector 7 was shut down, the underground bunker still existed. It would be smart for any agent or government official that knew of Sector 7's existence, to go there and hide after World War Total began."

"Then that is where we will head now. We should get a car," Shane said.

"Before we go," Landon said, "could I interest anyone in a glass of scotch?"

"I won't say no to that!" President Williams said. "We've been through quite an ordeal since we arrived back on Earth."

"Isn't scotch your favorite?" Alice asked Caroline. "You should have some."

"I can't have any," Caroline said.

"You always would have a small glass when you would do your writing," Mike said. "It can't hurt to kick back a few sips."

"Actually," Caroline said while taking a deep breath. "It can."

"Are you ok?" Alice asked. "You look worried about something."

"Remember when we went into that gas station a few days ago," Caroline said to Mike, yet she was also speaking to the entire room."

"I do," Mike said looking like he was trying to recall a memory.

"I went to the bathroom to deal with—" Caroline said and she used her fingers to signal quotations. "—girl issues."

"And?" Mike said sounding confused.

"And…" Caroline said. "I'm pregnant. *We're* pregnant."

Chapter Nine:

A Recording of the Past

"We are?" Mike said sounding flabbergasted.

"Yeah," Caroline replied. "I think I'm just a month in."

Mike took a seat on Landon's couch and put his hands to his face as if contemplating something. After a few minutes of silence he finally spoke up.

"We cannot bring a child into this world," Mike said. "Look out there. There's no telling how long even we will survive. We'll eventually run out of food."

"I know that," Caroline began to cry. "I kept it quiet for a while because of the circumstances out there."

"Let's talk outside," Mike suggested and Caroline followed him outside onto the balcony of Landon's condo.

Shane walked into Landon's kitchen and Penny followed him.

"So, do you think that Sector 7 will be where we will find Agent Miller?" Penny asked.

"It's a lead," Shane replied. "That's the only lead we have. It will be a good four-hour drive, but who knows what the roads look like. We have until nightfall to really travel, before the Dark Ones start flying around the skies again."

"I might have an idea," Landon said walking into the kitchen. "There's a news helicopter on top of a building a few blocks down the street. The news station must have abandoned it. It's a long shot that it works, but it can be worth a try. Will and I were trained to fly helicopters back in our NHR days."

"That would be great!" Shane said. "There's no telling how easy it would be to drive to Nevada."

"My thoughts exactly," Landon said.

An hour later, Shane, Penny, Alice, Jesse, Mike, Caroline, Landon, and President Williams were walking briskly down the abandoned streets of downtown Los Angeles to the building tower that housed one of the local news stations. When they arrived at the building they found that, much like most of the establishments in the area, the doors to the entrance were broken down.

They all walked single-file up about fifty flights of stairs until they reached the top floor which opened up onto the roof.

"Dammit," Shane cursed. "It's locked with chains."

"Let's go down to the news room, which is one more flight down, and see if we can find bolt cutters," Landon suggested.

They all walked down one flight and entered the newsroom. There were several upturned tables and chairs and smashed in TV screens. The room looked as if it had been vandalized. There was a pungent smell in the air that hit everyone's nostrils at once and instinctively everyone pinched their noses.

"Oh my God!" Caroline said in shock at the sight of a dead woman in a suit on the floor before a green screen.

"I recognize that woman," Alice said. "Her name is Sally King. She was a news reporter."

"I remember her," Shane said. "I saw the news report about Derek's house catching on fire—the one where we believed Mariette was first killed in. She was the woman doing the reporting."

"Yeah I remember that," Caroline said. "I was on the phone with you when you saw her report that news live on TV. Can't believe she still works here."

"She was a well known reporter," Jesse added.

President Williams and Landon walked over to where Sally's dead body was. She was lying face up and it looked like she had taken a blow to the head because there was blood spilled from underneath her head.

Landon made a gagging sound and ran to a nearby trashcan and threw up.

"She has a tape recorder," President Williams said, and he pulled out a small tape recorder from her suit blazer pocket. "I'll play it."

The tape recorder began to play and Sally King's voice echoed eerily in the vacated newsroom giving everyone chills up and down their spines.

"My name is Sally King, news reporter from KZLA Channel Nine. If you are listening to this recording, it is because I am not alive to tell my tale. Over the last few weeks, chaos has ensued across the world. The night that the President unveiled that giant craft known as the United States Square Aviator, all hell broke loose. The government was hoodwinked by a secret society known as the Eye Openers that revealed to the entire world watching the live broadcast, the dirty truth about what our government was hiding.

It is true that the crash in Roswell, New Mexico was actually from an extra-terrestrial spacecraft. We are really not alone. For decades we were visited by beings from another planet and all while this had been happening, there were beings walking among us that looked human. It also appears as though the dark shadows in the skies and the dark shadows that are possessing ordinary people are also another type of extra-terrestrial life form. Our universe holds life forms that are beyond our comprehension.

I've been doing my research since the attack on New York City, but those dark shadows now pose a threat. There have been many deaths. The numbers of fatalities keeps rising. People have gone mad. For example, some of the Channel Nine employees have stopped coming to work. People have quit and have attempted to evacuate and hide in forests or canyons from the cities where mass pandemonium has occurred. I've locked myself up here in the station and have a stash of food but it can only keep me alive for so long. I've even locked up the entrance onto the helipad in fear that ordinary people would overtake it and destroy or try to steal it.

It's hard to really understand the aftermath of the leak of files—from what I have learned—were called the Moonshadow files. I've done some digging around and even interviewed former agents that were part of this agency called the Non-Human Relations. It's baffling to know that we lived in a country where we were being lied straight to our faces. Our very own president, Will Williams, was part of this agency back when he worked for the military is his younger days. The face of our free world has been sitting in the oval office with knowledge about this advanced technology that the extra-terrestrial beings shared with them. One agent I interviewed told me that the beings were 'in the know' that the future of mankind would be jeopardized by over population. Our planet would run out of resources because our numbers would become too large. The government created that ship as a back up for something they labeled as population control. That very ship, the USSA, took off from a battleship in the Atlantic Ocean housing several animals and about fifty governmental and important individuals into outer space. This procedure, as I have recently learned, was call the Noah's Ark Project..."

The tape recorder went silent for a few seconds before it began to play again. It sounded like the next recording was done days later.

"It's been a difficult week for me. I've been hiding out in the station still. The screams and fires and explosions have lessened as the days have gone by. There's the smell of death in the air. I believe people are killing each other. They've all gone made. Electricity is down. I've been using our earthquake kit to help me survive. I have battery-powered flashlights and I was able to gather canned foods from a supermarket down the street one evening. I saw one of those dark shadows too. It took over the body of a young girl and it became this horrifying black furry monster with red eyes. Whatever those alien beings are, they are becoming much more violent and powerful. I haven't even seen the sun in ages. During the day, it's overcast and gloomy. I think this is the apocalypse. The end of the world..."

109

The tape ended for a few seconds before another recording began to play.

"Someone just tried to break into the newsroom. They gave up because I had my doors shut tight and held closed by furniture. I'm so scared. I wasn't even sure there were people still alive out there. I've been attempting to work the radio system the station has, but all I hear is empty static. I did, however, come across a voicemail that was left on my boss's phone from a colleague of ours that was reporting in D.C. the night that the president fled to the location of where the USSA would evacuate him out of Earth. The voicemail was from a reporter that said the entire White House was burned down by a riot that broke through the fence. The secret service was out numbered and nearby military helicopters began to shoot into the rampaging crowd, which started a lawn fire that spread onto the White House itself. The reporter said, and I quote 'It was symbolic of the fall of mankind. The fall of the free world.' What has become of the rest of the country? I wish I could know what is going on out there, but I fear the dark shadows at night fall and al—"

Sally's voice was cut off abruptly by the sound of banging on the door. She began to cry and sounded as if she was scrambling to hide. There was also the sound of metal hitting the floor and the tape recorder sounded garbled for a second. Sally had dropped the recorder on the ground, and then it sounded like she picked it up and at that point, then put it inside her jacket pocket because the noise it was recording sounded as though something was making everything slightly muffled.

"What do you want?" Sally's voice cried.

Shane and Caroline looked at each other worried. Their attention was completely on the recording.

"Let me onto the helipad," A man's voice was heard. "Open the chains, you bitch!"

"I will," Sally cried. "Don't hurt me!"

"Cut the damn chains or I will bash your head in with this hammer!" The man's voice snarled.

There was the sound of a struggle and a gunshot.

"How dare you try to shoot me?" The voice yelled and Shane began to listen more intently because it sounded familiar.

"P-p-please," Sally sobbed and there was a dull sound of metal hitting flesh with a sickening thud.

The tape recorder stopped.

There was an eerie silence for a few minutes before Landon spoke.

"Whoever killed Miss King picked up the tape recorder and rewound it and left it in her blazer pocket."

"Good catch," Shane said sounding very impressed. "That would make sense as to why when we pressed play it was rewound to the beginning.

"That voice..." Caroline said. "It's strange to say, but it sounded so familiar, yet it was so angry..."

"Hey Caroline," Shane said suddenly, "Can you come help me look through some of these news tapes. You used to work in a reporting type of role—even if yours was fashion—but you might be of some use helping us figure out if there are more stories recorded regarding the aftermath of the New York City attack."

"Ok..." Caroline said sounding confused.

"Everyone else keep looking for an ax or key to open up that chained door to the rooftop," Shane ordered.

Shane took Caroline into an empty office.

"That voice," He said. "I know you recognized it. I did too."

"It can't be," Caroline said. "He's been with me the whole time. That was not Mike on that recording."

"It sounded so much like him," Shane said. "It was slightly muffled so I don't think anyone else picked up on it."

"He didn't even look surprised by hearing it," Caroline said. "It could have been anyone with a similar voice. It was some looter or some deranged survivor."

"You sure he didn't leave your side one night to come over here?" Shane asked. "Maybe he left one night to find some resources for you guys while you were taking refuge in Landon's apartment?"

"That's crazy Shane!" Caroline said. "The father of my child would never!"

"You're right," Shane admitted. "It sounded so much like him. Whoever it was, however, did rewind the tape. I guess the person just wanted to listen to it? Maybe it was out of habit?"

"Shane! Come here!" Landon shouted.

"What is it?" Shane asked walking back into the newsroom.

"I've been looking over Sally King's body," Landon said. "She's not fully cold and the blood coming out of her head is fresh. She must have died shortly before we arrived here!"

"You think so?" Jesse asked.

"What?" Shane said walking over to the body.

"The killer might still be here!" Caroline panicked, and then she whispered in Shane's ear, "And Mike has been with us all morning…"

"Right," Shane whispered back.

"We need to find that key to the rooftop," Mike insisted.

"Here's the murder weapon!" President Williams said. "I found this bloody hammer behind one of the news cameras."

"What about the gun?" Alice asked. "In the tape, a gunshot was fired. It must have been Sally's gun."

"Where is that gun then?" Jesse said.

President Williams walked over to the back of the newsroom and was shifting through knocked over cameras, and tables searching for any clues.

"This is bizarre," Shane said to Landon.

"The killer might still be here," Landon said.

"What the—" President Williams yelled.

Everyone turned to look at where he was standing. He was outside of an office. There was a gunshot and President Williams fell backwards onto the ground. Before them was a figure in a brown cloak with its hand outstretched before it holding what must have been Sally King's gun. In the other hand, it was holding a set of keys.

The figure's face was hidden well behind the cloak so they could not make out its face, however everyone deduced it was Sally's male killer.

"Were you the one who saved us from the Dark Ones out there on that highway?" Shane asked the cloaked figured.

"That was not me," It said and the voice was much more clear than on the tape.

Shane and Caroline exchanged confused glances. Then Caroline looked over at Mike who was showing no emotion towards the scary situation.

"Step aside," The figure said with the gun outstretched and pointing at them as it walked sideways out of the room and onto the flight of stairs.

"We can't let him get away!" Mike said angrily. "He has the keys! We need that helicopter."

"Let me!" Shane said and he pulled out his necklace and touched it.

Shane ran up the flight of stairs and found the previously chained entrance open. The chains were left abandoned on the ground. Shane ran outside onto the roof and saw the cloaked figure getting into the helicopter.

"STOP!" Shane shouted.

Penny had run out onto the rooftop behind Shane and her eyes widened in horror as the cloaked figure aimed the gun at Shane. Shane hopelessly rubbed his necklace, but nothing was happening.

A gust of wind swept through the rooftop of the skyscraper causing the helicopter to shake and Penny's red hair to fly up.

"What the hell?" Shane said.

He was not sure if he was seeing things, but there was a strange point in the air just by the helicopter where a bright orange light was growing larger and larger. The bright light became the shape of a rectangle and then an arm appeared through it and grabbed the gunned brown-cloaked figure by the neck.

Shane turned around for a second and saw that Mike was running up the staircase and towards the rooftop. Just as he was about to run through the door onto the roof, there was another gust of wind and the door slammed on his face causing him to fall over backwards on the other side.

Shane turned back and saw that the mysterious arm that appeared out of nowhere and coming out of a white door-shaped light over thin air had successfully grabbed the cloaked figure. It happened quickly, but the figured dropped the gun onto the helipad and just as it disappeared along with the light and the other arm into thin air, Shane noticed that the cloaked figure's arm was black-skinned, and not olive like the figure he saw on the rooftop in New York City and the roof on the building off the highway where Mariette's possessor attacked.

"What was that and how did they disappear into thin air?" Penny asked in shock.

"I don't know for sure, but I think we'll find out in the future," Shane said.

Chapter Ten:

The Return to Sector 7

Landon pushed opened the door onto the rooftop with Alice and Jesse by his side. Caroline was kneeling over Mike to make sure he was fine.

"Where did that gunman go?" Landon asked.

"He just disappeared into thin air," Penny replied. "It was bizarre."

"Is Mike ok?" Shane asked.

"He's coming around," Caroline said worriedly. "He might have a bruise on his face."

"Will is dead," Landon said, tears forming in his eyes. "Shot right in the heart. That makes myself and Manuel the only people left that were part of the night we took Derek to Sector 7. Green died years ago. Carter was possessed by a Dark One and died at the press conference in New York City. It just feels so strange that we are about to go back to the place where I feel much of this whole mess began."

"I do hope Manuel comes to give us aid," Shane said. "We don't have a Communicator and the one aboard the USSA won't help us as it's only a one-way Communicator."

"Ugh," Mike said finally coming around. "What happened?"

"You were knocked out by the door," Shane said. "Some heavy winds blew it closed on your face."

"The helicopter is still here, I see," He said. "Where did that cloaked man go?"

"He vanished into thin air," Shane said. "I don't know what I just witnessed."

"Let's pack up and fly out of here," Landon said while wiping his eyes on his blazer. "Sally's recording mentioned she was stocking up on food. Perhaps we can find out where she kept the canned goods."

An hour later, Landon, Alice, Jesse, Mike, Caroline, Penny, and Shane boarded the helicopter with backpacks full of canned goods and bottled water that they found in a storage closet in the newsroom. Landon covered Will's body earlier with an American flag he found in one of the news station's closets out of respect.

Landon sat in the cockpit and ordered everyone to buckle up.

"It's been a while since I've flown one of these, but at least there is a full tank of fuel!" He said.

"Let's just make sure we get there before it gets dark," Shane said.

Landon was able to successfully get the helicopter into the air. He pushed it on forward in the direction of Nevada.

"The electronics and GPS do not work," Landon said. "Obviously, however, I'm a trained government agent. I can get us to Sector 7 before nightfall."

"Thanks again for flying us," Alice told Landon in a loud voice as the propellers drowned out her regular talking voice. "I'm sorry we couldn't do a proper burial for the president."

Landon smiled and nodded.

Shane sat in his chair daydreaming about the events that had occurred since they landed back on Earth. It seemed that there was no way he could save Earth or salvage any part of what it used to be. His concern now was to stop the Dark Ones and return to Threa. He always knew in the back of his mind that he would have to choose between Earth and Threa. It seemed like the choice was obvious as Earth was no longer fit for life.

As they flew over a mountainous forest, Shane took in the eerie sights. The trees were dead. There were no green leaves and it was summertime. The clouds above them were dark and menacing but it looked as though they were unable to produce rain.

Shane focused his thoughts on the hooded figure he saw on the helipad. He wished he knew what the man was up to and why his voice sounded so much like Mike's.

"Are you ok?" Penny asked Shane bringing his train of though back into reality.

"I...I don't really know," Shane answered truthfully. "I wish I knew what to do. I wish I knew my purpose. I wish I knew why this is all centered around me and why I was given this necklace."

Penny put her hand on Shane's and he accepted it and his fingers clasped over hers. Alice looked away when she noticed their intimate touch, and then put her head on Jesse's shoulder.

"What if the key isn't even at Sector 7?" Penny asked.

"The chances are slim," Shane said. "I don't know what to do except maybe find a way back to Threa. That door is impenetrable without a key."

"And can it really be a doorway to the future?" Penny questioned him.

"That or maybe more," Shane replied. "There's something about it, but I won't know until I open it."

"Can I go through the door with you?" Penny asked.

"Um..." Shane thought about it. "I don't know how dangerous it will be."

"Shane, I..." Penny was about to say something when Mike spoke up and distracted her.

"We're almost there!" He said.

"We sure are," Landon replied and he began to lower the helicopter in a descent to the ground.

"That crater..." Shane gasped. "That's the landing site!"

"It is," Landon said.

"What was the landing site?" Penny asked.

"The area where the Elders would land and communicate with the NHR. And this is where my first battle with the Dark Ones over fifteen years ago took place. That's where I defeated Noom with my necklace. Near that crater."

"My mother died at Sector 7," Penny said. "It will be so weird to walk those halls of the base."

Landon landed the helicopter just outside the torn down gates of what used to be Sector 7. The compound looked as if it had been burned down intentionally to hide that it once belonged to the military. It was nothing but old charred bricks and wood and much of the desert sand had buried its remains. There were no buildings left standing.

Everyone jumped out of the helicopter and onto the Nevada desert sand. It appeared as though the sky was becoming darker, which meant nighttime was approaching.

"I am so glad we didn't run into any Dark Ones in the air," Alice sighed with relief.

"I was very worried about that," Landon said.

"There's not much left of Sector 7," Shane said taking in the ruins of the once extremely secure and secretive government base. "Where is this bunker that former agents might be taking refuge in?"

"Follow me," Landon said. "I believe I can find the entrance."

"Interesting feeling...being here," Alice said as she walked side-by-side with Shane.

"Yeah," Shane admitted.

"I remember that night you left to Threa," Alice said. "I never thought I'd see you again…or be back at this place."

Shane shrugged his shoulders uncomfortably.

Jesse was eavesdropping and jumped in, "So now that you are back, what will you do after you find this key and complete your mission? Do you plan to go back to your *world?*"

"I do have a choice to make, and I will make that choice when the time to make it arrives," Shane said trying to brush off Jesse's prying question.

"You do have to make a choice, don't you?" Mike asked Shane.

"Well, eventually," Shane said hoping they would get off the subject.

"Stay here," Mike said. "Don't go back to Threa. You are my *best* friend."

"It's complicated," Shane answered beginning to sound irritated. "Can we get off the subject and just keep moving along to this bunker?"

"Don't be annoying," Caroline whispered to Mike.

Shane picked up his pace and caught up with Landon and Penny who were up ahead. Penny was asking Landon a few questions about his NHR days.

"…now some of the bodies that were recovered from this base," Penny was saying, "were buried at Moonshadow Ranch. My mother was one of them."

"The government found it to be a perfect burial place for the fallen personnel of Sector 7," Landon answered. "At least that's what I learned while I was being held up at Sector 8."

Landon brought the group to the torn down building that was once the main command center of Sector 7. They had to walk over rubble, which included bricks, twisted metals, and wires, to get over to what were once the walls of the building.

119

"The foundation is still here," Landon said. "And the door should be…"

Landon pointed to a corner of the ground that looked as though sand had been swept away from. There was a broom left on the ground. Upon a closer look at the corner of the ground where Landon was pointing, Shane saw that there was a small handle and a square shaped outline on the foundation.

"That's the entrance to the bunker," Landon said.

"Cross your fingers the key is here!" Penny said excitedly.

Shane's heart began to race with excitement. He had a feeling the key was near and that at long last he would have the final clue that Derek left for him and the next step upon retrieval of the missing spare key would be to go *where it all began…*

Landon reached for the handle and opened the door. There was a ladder that led to the bottom of the bunker, which looked like one large dark pit.

"There's no light down there," Caroline said.

"There should be battery powered flashlights available on the ground or at least some gas lamps," Landon said. "Either way there will be some sort of emergency supplies."

"I'll go first," Shane volunteered.

He stepped onto the ladder and began his decent down to the bottom of the bunker. When he finally hit the ground, he got on his knees and felt around. The ground was stone and felt very dusty. His hand brushed against several metal objects. He felt a specific object that was cylinder in shape. He found a button on it and pressed it. A light went on instantly and he sent a beam up to the top.

"Found a flashlight! Come on down!" Shane called up.

"Ok!" Landon called, and he was the next one to climb down the ladder.

Jesse was the last person to enter the bunker. Once they were all together, Shane shot the beam of light from the flashlight in the only direction that the tunnel they were in led to.

"Did anyone hide down here during the Dark Ones attack the night of the Nevada Lights?" Alice asked Landon.

"Yes, I'm pretty sure," Landon replied.

The tunnel they were walking in was sloping down deeper into the ground. It felt as if they had been walking for miles.

"How long does this go?" Caroline asked. "EWW!"

"What?" Alice shouted in panic.

"Mice!" Caroline screeched and she began jumping up and down to avoid a group of several mice running in the direction that they came from.

"Disgusting," Mike hissed. "I should kill that vermin."

"They won't hurt us Mike," Shane said. "How much further Landon?"

"Should be arriving at a door soon," Landon responded. "Normally the door would require a code, but as there is no longer any electricity here, I would assume we can just push it open."

Shane kept the lead in the group and they descended further down the tunnel. At long last, his flashlight beam ended on what looked to be a dead end, but was actually the door Landon mentioned.

"Here," Landon said and he walked up ahead of Shane and turned a handle that was on a door.

"It opened," Shane gasped.

They all walked through the door in a single file with Jesse bringing up the rear. They were inside a small chamber made of silver metal walls.

"A bomb could not penetrate these walls," Landon said. "This chamber is very safe."

A few gas lamps dimly lit the room.

"Someone's been living here," Landon said noticing empty food cans on the ground.

"There's also several articles of clothing on the ground," Caroline pointed out.

121

"Is Agent Miller here?" Penny questioned.

"The room looks empty," Landon said. "Perhaps nobody is home at the moment."

"Should we wait for them to come back?" Shane suggested.

"Either way, this is a great place to take refuge as night is about to fall," Landon answered. "And if there is anyone alive who has been hiding out here, I'm sure they know not to go out during nightfall."

"Anyone hungry?" Alice said while opening her backpack and offering cans of tuna to the group.

"Starving," Mike said reaching for Alice's offering.

After their meal, everyone began to yawn and feel heavy-eyed.

"I'm thinking we should sleep," Landon suggested.

"I'll stay up and keep watch," Shane said. "If someone randomly showed up at my home while I was away, it might scare me and I don't want them to attack us."

"Ok," Landon agreed.

Shane sat by the entrance of the bunker's chamber with his flashlight. He clicked it on and off absentmindedly and tiredly stared at the door waiting for the sounds of any movement on the other side.

"Hey," Alice whispered making Shane jump.

"You scared me," Shane whispered. "What's up?"

"I'm sorry that I've been so distant and cold lately," Alice said.

"It's fine," Shane said. "We have a lot on our plates."

"It's still no excuse to treat you this way," Alice said kindly. "I was just thinking about the night you left for Threa from this very base several years ago. It was such a difficult moment for me. It was almost as if you had died. I never thought in a million years that you would be crashing back on Earth *and* on my wedding day."

"Neither did I," Shane answered.

"Will you leave again?" Alice said. "Threa was livable and like Earth. There's nothing left for us here. Our planet is unlivable. I want to go back. We can stay in Territory 3."

"You want to bring Jesse too, I imagine?" Shane asked.

"Shane," Alice began but she seemed lost for words.

"I have to make a choice about picking Earth or picking Threa," Shane said. "That's obvious."

"And you have a choice to make about me," Alice lowered her voice.

"You?" Shane raised his eyebrow.

"Yes," Alice said. "Shane, I've decided I don't want to be with Jesse. No matter how hard I try, I just can't forgive him for running away from me when Kat Twain was holding us hostage."

"He's your husband, Alice," Shane said. "Till death do you part."

Mike opened his eyes at the sound of the hushed conversation between Alice and Shane. He listened intently.

"There's a chance that many of us will die," Alice said. "However, I want you to know that it has always been you on my mind. When I said 'I do' a few months ago at my wedding, I was thinking of you. It seems almost like a fairy tale that you crash landed from the sky moments after."

"This…this is no fairy tale," Shane told Alice. "I care about you Alice. You know that. We've known each other since we were children. Circumstances have changed unfortunately."

Alice began to cry silently into her arms. Mike was continuing on eavesdropping and he nudged Jesse who was sleeping a few feet away.

"What?" Jesse whispered, but Mike did not answer except for the sound of him snoring.

"I love you," Alice said through silent stifled tears.

Jesse's head shot up at the sound of Alice's words and caught a glimpse of her sitting next to Shane with her hands on his.

"Alice..." Shane said, but he felt as though he had a large rock stuck on his throat. "There are things out there in the universe that I don't understand. I do know that the stars did not align for us. The opportunity came and went. When we were in college you were on and off with Jesse..."

"...and when I broke up with him and went on that adventure with you....one that I risked my life for, mind you...I came to your side," Alice continued to cry. "He left me when my life was endanger. Jesse left me and ran away like a coward. *You* would never have done that to me. You only left because you had to learn about who—what you are."

"Alice," Shane said, and he took a deep breath, "I'm not the one you are destined to be with. And maybe Jesse isn't either. This might be difficult for you to realize, but I do think I'm developing feelings for Penny. There's just something about her that fits. She's a Humanoid, for one, and I just have to follow my heart. You come with complications and that ship has sailed."

"It only sailed because you got in that ship and flew away," Alice said feeling extremely hurt.

Shane shifted uncomfortably.

"Ahem," Came Jesse's voice from behind them.

Alice and Shane turned around quickly in shock.

"Jesse..." Shane mumbled awkwardly.

"Save it," Jesse whispered angrily.

"I..."Alice said nervously feeling her face turn red.

"Let me finish your sentence," Jesse said angrily. "Did you mean to say 'I love Shane,' because I already heard you say that?"

"Jesse—you left me. You weren't there for me when we were kidnapped," Alice sobbed.

"And you never told me about your run-ins with the government!" Jesse snapped. "This world may not be in order anymore, and there will be no need to sign papers or hire lawyers. I will say this with finality right here and now, but I am verbally giving you a divorce."

Alice began to sob into her arms. Jesse had a hurtful look in his eye and tears began to run down them.

"Jesse, I'm sorry about all this," Shane said.

"I'm off on my own starting in the morning when there is daylight," Jesse said. "I will take a backpack with food and fend for myself. I do not need to be on your pathetic adventure to find some damned key. That guy you were looking for is not even here!"

"You can do as you please," Shane spat. "Nobody will force you."

"Great," Jesse said. "I'm going to get some more sleep. Good riddance."

Jesse walked by over to the area near where Mike and Caroline were sleeping. He crouched into a comfortable position and wiped tears off his face. He was silent for the rest of the night.

"Shane..." Alice reached for Shane's hand but he moved it away.

"This is your mess," Shane said. "I do not want to be involved."

Alice cried herself to sleep and left Shane alone to keep watch.

Landon woke up the group the next morning. Shane had fallen asleep during his watch, but woke suddenly at Landon's touch.

"You kept quite the guard," Landon said sarcastically.

"I'm so sorry," Shane said rubbing his eyes and hoping last night's conversation with Alice was a dream.

"Jesse is gone..." Landon said realizing that he was unaccounted for.

"What?" Caroline said in shock. "Alice, where is he?"

Alice sniffled and spoke in a quiet voice, "He verbally divorced me last night and said he wanted to be off on his own."

"Oh my God!" Caroline said rushing to Alice's side to console her, and she cried vigorously into her arms.

Shane decided he would keep the situation that occurred last night between himself and Alice and made no mention of the argument that happened in the wee hours of the morning.

"I cannot believe he left you...again!" Caroline said angrily and Alice sobbed even harder.

Mike awkwardly patted her on the back and said, "I can't believe he took off without telling us."

"Jerk," Landon said.

"Hey everyone," Shane said suddenly. "Quiet down."

"What is it?" Landon asked.

"I hear an echo on the other side of the door," Shane whispered. "Someone is coming...or perhaps returning to this bunker!"

"Everybody just stay back," Landon ordered Caroline, Mike, Alice, and Penny.

Shane and Landon stood at the door waiting with bated breath and anticipation for it to open. They had no weapons and felt slightly awkward standing there defenseless.

Shane reached for his necklace as a precaution.

"I feel nervous about this," Shane whispered to Landon.

"It's probably someone who worked for the NHR," Landon assured Shane. "Who else would know about the existence of this place?"

"Be careful Shane," Penny called to him.

"I'm sure it will be fine," Shane assured Penny and looked her in the eye.

He then turned his face back in the direction of the bunker's chamber door.

The handle began to rattle and turn. Someone was on the other side and was about to open it.

The door opened and framed in the middle of it was an older woman.

"It can't be..." Shane gasped

"What?" Shane heard Alice whisper from behind him.

The woman stepped into the chamber with a look of relief on her face and tears began to pour down her face. She smiled at Shane and he returned the smile with a stream of fresh tears.

"I've been waiting for you to arrive," The woman said while making eye contact with only Shane. "He told me you would be arriving here around now and I've been expecting you."

Shane ran to the woman and gave her a tight embrace.

"Aunt Pam..." Shane cried onto her shoulder.

Chapter Eleven:

The Spare Key

"I cannot believe you are still alive!' Shane said happily to his Aunt Pam.

"It's a miracle," She said. "I was hoping I would see you again."

"Who told you that I would be arriving here?" Shane asked sounding confused.

"This man," Aunt Pam said. "I don't know who he is, but he saved me."

"The last time I saw you was in that underground tunnel on our journey to Sector 8," Shane said.

"I took that exit in that tunnel and ran off on my own in that Texas desert," Aunt Pam said. "I made it to the mountains and decided to hide and take refuge on a cliff. From my vantage point I could see that military base, but they could not see me. I saw it all, Shane. I saw the fights, the gunshots, and the military people running like crazy. Then I saw you enter that giant space ship and you flew off in it far, far away."

"How did you survive?" Shane asked feeling thankful that there was one last member of his Earth family still alive before him.

"A strange man in a brown cloak appeared before me and said I could live safely in Sector 8 for a while," Aunt Pam said. "I could not see his face, but he appeared friendly. And then he vanished into thin air. It was bizarre. I made my way down to Sector 8 because it was left abandoned. I was able to live off the food supplies they had.

I was there for maybe a day or two when strange things began to happen in the skies. One minute the sun was shining, and the next, it was hidden behind those dark clouds in the sky. I haven't seen sunshine since. That man in the cloak eventually returned to Sector 8 and told me that I needed to wait things out before he could make sure I was reunited with you. He said that you finding me would give you hope. He said that you finding me would be useful because he gave me the important task of helping you find something that's been lost. Something that belonged to Derek."

"A spare key?" Shane asked.

"Indeed," Aunt Pam smiled. "This man kept me safe here. I don't know if he is psychic or something, but he knows things. He knows things before they happen. I don't even know if this is real life. I feel like the loneliness might have driven me mad."

"You never saw his face?" Shane asked.

"Not clearly," Aunt Pam replied. "From a distance I did and he was bald and older looking."

"He wore a brown cloak...did he have olive skin?" Shane asked.

"I did see his hands and they were olive and very tanned looking."

"I think this same man has been watching over me too," Shane said. "So you know where the key is?"

"Yeah, where is the key ma'am?" Penny chimed in.

"The agent that was wearing the key as a necklace was living here for a while before I arrived. He was buried just outside in an area. I'm not sure how he died. When I arrived there were no more survivors or they had simply just fled this bunker. However, at one point there were living souls that buried the dead. There is a makeshift graveyard just outside. A simple rock marks each tomb, and their names had been engraved on the rocks."

"We need to exhume the body?" Landon asked.

"Yes," Aunt Pam said. "I never unburied it because the man told me as long as I was the only one that knew, then none of

129

those dark creatures could pry the information out of me. Luckily, living here has been safe for me. None of them have been seen in this area."

"Yeah I was surprised when I flew in that I did not see a single Dark One," Landon said.

"It's out of respect for the fallen king," Mike said randomly. "I mean, this is where Noom died, right?"

"Well, yeah," Caroline said.

"Maybe they would rather like to avoid this area because it reminds them of that terrible night," Mike said.

"Maybe," Shane said. "Well if the key is buried and you know where Agent Miller's grave is, then let's go dig it up!"

Aunt Pam took the lead up the tunnel and out of the underground bunker. When they climbed the ladder and were outside, they looked up to see another day of overcast and gloomy clouds.

"This way," Aunt Pam ushered for the group to follow her.

"Look!" Alice said pointing at the ground. "There are footsteps heading in that direction. They must be Jesse's. Did you see a man leave before you arrived, Pam?"

"I did not," Aunt Pam responded. "I'm sorry."

Alice grabbed onto Caroline's hand and held it tight.

"I'm sorry baby," Caroline whispered in Alice's ear. "Try to be strong."

Aunt Pam directed them to flat sandy area a few feet from one of the fallen Sector 7 enclosure walls. There were several rocks on the ground. Shane walked over to examine each one.

"Hey Mike," Shane called to Mike, "Keep your eyes peeled for one that says Arthur Miller on it."

"Will do," Mike said.

"I'll help," Landon jumped in.

"It's over here!" Aunt Pam called out.

Everyone walked over to the rock that had "Miller" engraved on it in barely readable handwriting.

"So who wants to dig up the body?" Mike said sarcastically. "Caroline?"

"I'm pregnant," Caroline said. "I should probably not do strenuous work.

"You're pregnant?" Aunt Pam asked. "Congratulations..."

"It's a complicated situation," Mike said to Aunt Pam. "We have eight months to find a functioning hospital."

"Ah," Aunt Pam said. "That may not be possible m'dear."

Shane got to his knees and began to scoop out the sand with his bare hands. Mike and Landon joined him.

"I'll help too," Penny offered and she got to her knees and joined the team as they dug into Agent Miller's grave.

The grave was not very deep. After about three feet, they felt something hard.

"Ew," Penny said and she backed away from the grave.

"His body..." Shane said while holding his breath because the odor that came from the body was not pleasant.

"Disgusting!" Landon yelled and he too backed away from the body when he saw the eyes of Agent Miller staring back at him.

The body had decayed, but oddly enough not as much as a body would normally have decayed being buried bare.

"There are no gross bugs or anything," Alice said.

"Humans aren't the only ones going extinct," Aunt Pam said. "I haven't seen a bird fly in ages, and have yet to even run into a snake or a scorpion in the desert here. I don't think any kind of organism can exist as there has been no rain or sunshine to keep life moving."

"There were mice inside the chamber," Alice said.

"I kept those around as pets. It has been very lonely here," Aunt Pam replied.

"There it is!" Shane shouted with glee suddenly.

He reached for the necklace that was around Agent Miller's neck. He unclasped the hook on it and threw the chain aside. He held the key up to the sky in triumph.

"At last!" Shane said. "I have the key, Derek!"

"I can't believe we found it!" Landon said. "Miller took it from my condo and he ended up here at Sector 7. That's some kind of poetic justice."

"Miller wasn't such a bad guy though," Mike said. "Kat was ordering him to get the Communicator from your condo and then he came across this key. I remember seeing him wear it in your dad's backyard, Shane."

"True," Shane said.

"Can I hold the key?" Mike asked excitedly.

"I would rather hold it myself," Shane said, and he put the key in his pocket. "It opens up a door that leads to many answers I need. I will not part with it. It will remain with me at all times."

"That's how it should be," Aunt Pam said. "I'm so glad I could be of help to you on your journey."

"Now what?" Alice asked. "Do we all go with you back to Roswell…back to that laboratory known as Sector 1?"

"If you want," Shane said. "Landon, I will need you to at least fly me there in the helicopter."

"Of course," Landon said and nodded his head.

"But first," Shane said. "I want to visit the crater…the landing site. The place where that first battle with the Dark Ones took place."

"Do you want to go alone?" Landon said.

"Yes," Shane said. "I'll meet everyone at the helicopter. Pack it up and bring our backpacks of food. Aunt Pam—bring any extra supplies you have been keeping here."

"I will," Aunt Pam replied.

Shane walked through the Sector 7 ruins alone. He zipped up his jacket to keep warm because it was cold out due to lack of sunshine.

He reached the crater and walked down to the center of it. He looked over to a canyon in the distance and closed his eyes.

That's where Derek, Manuel, Landon, Green, Williams, and Carter were when they asked Derek to take the photographs of the Elder's ritual, Shane thought. *I was part of that ritual. I don't have any recollection of it but I can imagine myself standing still on this spot and swaying as an Unknowing Humanoid. I was eighteen years old. That was twenty years ago. My mother Genesis walked over to me and touched my forehead. I'm not sure why I know that, but I feel that is what happened. She died here years later in this very spot during the fight we had with the Dark Ones. They killed her. Noom tried to kill me. He tried to stop the Humanoids but he could not possess me. He was destroyed in an attempt to take over my soul and body. He became nothing. My necklace saved me for the first time that night. It pulled the light from the moon and shined bright for miles. But the moon is covered and so is the sun, now. Maybe my necklace won't work anymore as it has had no time to recharge with the power from natural light.*

Shane sat down on the ground and put his hands behind him and looked over at the canyon ahead where Derek had once taken photos of him. Then he remembered that on the day of his battle with the Dark Ones, he saw another flash of light. He thought it was Derek, but later he learned it was his Uncle Robert who had been trying to uncover the secrets of the NHR and was taking photographs as well.

Shane could not help but try to piece together an event that he was present for but not conscious. The Elder ritual and the night Derek was brought to Sector 7 was where he truly felt it all began.

And also ended, when I left here to go to Threa leaving Alice behind, he thought.

"How long are you going to take?" Penny called from above the crater.

"Penny," Shane said. "You took me by surprise."

Penny carefully slid down the sloping ground into the crater and sat next to Shane. She put her hands on his.

"Are you thinking about home?" Penny asked.

"What is home?" Shane said. "I guess I lived on Threa for fifteen years, but you were brainwashed at Moonshadow Ranch for nearly the same amount of time and then brainwashed in Territory 3 at Threa. You must be confused about what home is."

"I am," Penny said. "But I believe that we'll find our destiny and that it is clearly written for us and waiting for us to discover it. I know home isn't going to be this wasteland of a planet now. Home will be something new. It may not even exist yet."

"You're talking nonsense," Shane said.

"Am I?" Penny said. "Home is where the heart is and I would like to create that home. I'm with you one hundred percent of the way."

"I want you to be," Shane smiled.

Penny closed her eyes and moved her face closer to his. Shane closed his eyes and their lips touched. Her lips felt so soft and warm on Shane's chapped and cold ones. He opened his eyes and looked into hers. He ran his hands through her wavy red hair.

"I'm sorry about your brother," were the first words that Shane could say after they kissed.

"I'm sorry about your Earth dad," Penny replied. "Lots of lives have been lost since this whole mess began in New York City. You need to stop it. I know you are the one."

"You saw those things—the Dark Ones in their true form," Shane said. "I don't stand a fighting chance against their sharp claws."

"They can't enter your body," Penny pointed out. "I am more in danger."

"I know that," Shane said, "but they can still kill me!"

"We'll stop them," Penny said. "One way or the other. And you have your necklace. Now let's get on that helicopter and find out what that door opens."

"Yes," Shane said excitedly. "Let's do that!"

Shane and Penny walked up out of the crater and stopped dead in their tracks. Jesse was standing before them with dark eyes staring daggers at them and a mischievous grin.

"Jesse?" Penny said.

"Stand back," Shane said to Penny and he moved in front of her with his necklace out.

"Give me the key," Jesse hissed in a voice that was not his own.

"Who are you?" Shane demanded.

"We've met before," Jesse hissed.

"What is your name, Dark One?" Shane asked.

"Leviticus," He replied.

"That's the Dark One that attacked us on the USSA!" Penny said in shock and she grabbed onto one of Shane's arms.

"Exit Jesse's body!" Shane demanded. "Or else..."

"Ha ha ha," Leviticus laughed. "His body is mine."

Shane rubbed on his necklace. It gave of a much weaker bright shine than before. It was losing its power because it had not had any natural light to store energy from. Shane took a deep breath and aimed the necklace at Leviticus and a small beam of light shot straight at Jesse's heart.

"AARGGHHHHH!" Leviticus's voice screamed in agony through Jesse's body.

A dark cloud escaped from Jesse's mouth and Jesse fell to the sand face down. Leviticus floated a few feet above Shane and Penny and flew straight up into the sky.

"Did he flee?" Penny asked.

"He's probably scared," Shane said, and he walked over to Jesse's body. "Jesse, are you ok?"

"He's breathing!" Penny said noticing his chest was moving up and down.

"He's been knocked out," Shane said. "I'll grab one arm, and you grab the other, we'll drag him to the helicopter.

Shane and Penny dragged Jesse's unconscious body to the Sector 7 ruins. As soon as they were within view of the others, Landon ran over to give Shane and Penny a hand. Alice's jaw dropped in shock to see Jesse's body.

"Is he dead?" Alice said worriedly as she ran up to meet Shane and Penny.

"What happened?" Landon asked running behind Alice.

"Um...," Penny replied. "He was temporarily possessed by that Dark One named Leviticus. He found us some how."

"That's the one that was on board the USSA possessing Captain Wells right?" Alice asked.

"Yeah," Shane replied. "My necklace is running low on light power. It just barely saved us and Jesse."

"Do you think he ran off last night because he was possessed?" Alice asked hopefully.

"I doubt it," Shane said. "He could have attempted to steal my necklace in my sleep, but he didn't. I think Leviticus found him while he was running away from here."

"Is that Jesse?" Caroline asked joining the group along with Mike.

"Is he dead?" Mike asked curiously.

"No," Shane answered. "Leviticus was possessing him. That's the name of the Dark One that was on board the USSA on our journey back to Earth."

"I see," Mike replied. "Is Leviticus dead?"

"He flew up into the sky," Penny answered before Shane could open his mouth.

"We should get him in the helicopter," Landon suggested. "Mike, give Shane and me a hand."

Jesse was still unconscious, but was still breathing. Landon rested him on the back seat.

"I'm sure he will be fine," Caroline comforted Alice as they boarded the helicopter. "Just be thankful that he did not transform into the true form of a Dark One."

"That would have killed him for sure," Mike said unsympathetically. "He did try to leave you though."

"That doesn't mean he deserved this to happen to him," Alice snapped.

"Hey," Shane cut in. "Let's keep tensions low. We have a mission to complete. Landon, take us up and away to Roswell."

"Everyone buckle in," Landon ordered. "Let's take off. We should have enough fuel to get us to Roswell."

"Use caution," Aunt Pam said. "Those winged creatures could attack us in the air."

The propellers began to rotate, and they lifted off the Nevada desert sand. Shane put his hands on Penny and rested his head on her shoulder and closed his eyes. He fell asleep almost instantly.

Alice looked over at Shane and turned away quickly when Penny made eye contact with her.

The flight was very quiet and peaceful. Nobody was talking as almost everyone had fallen asleep. Mike was sitting at the cockpit and was the only one awake aside from Landon.

"How much further, Landon?" Mike asked.

"I think we will arrive just before sunset," Landon said.

"Good," Mike said. "Do you think after Shane opens the door, you will finally feel at peace?"

"Excuse me?" Landon asked taken aback.

"I can tell that Derek's death still haunts you," Mike said. "I've had time to catch up with Shane and I'm just putting a few things together."

"Mike, I would rather not talk about this," Landon said sternly.

"Your head is filled with many secrets and experiences you learned during your time with the NHR," Mike said. "Doesn't all that make your conscience guilty?"

"Can you stop prying?" Landon asked. "You are making me uncomfortable and I'm trying to focus on getting us to New Mexico."

"You killed a man," Mike said sounding very rude.

"There are things I am not proud of," Landon said. "I've had to hide my career and my personal life for so long. I have gone to therapy. I have tried to clean my conscience in any way possible. Helping Shane is the only thing I can think of. Derek left behind a message in code to let him know he was Humanoid and to protect him from having the government abduct him. It was not easy."

"Do you think that whatever Shane finds," Mike said, "it will put your mind at ease to know that his death was not in vain?"

"Mike," Landon replied. "I really don't want to get into this very much."

"I'm sorry," Mike said. "I was curious. My apologies for prying."

"That's fine," Landon said. "So, you are going to be a father?"

"Yeah," Mike said. "It's strange isn't it? Me…a father?"

"I always wondered when you two were going to have kids and stop working so much," Landon said. "I guess now you'll have all the time in the world to raise a kid."

"I'm not sure how I feel about bringing a child into this world," Mike said. "There's nothing left of it and eventually we'll run out of food. It's a survival of the fittest type of world out there now."

"Don't say that Mike," Landon said. "We will all prosper. And I believe Manuel and Threa will give our planet some aid as we gave the Humanoid civilization a chance to thrive."

"What's that odd noise?" Mike asked.

"Static from the radio!" Landon said. "That's so weird because there's no electricity."

Landon tapped on his headphones and microphone on his helmet. He listened intently as the static became clearer. Then the static stopped and he heard a voice come through.

"Can anyone hear me?" The voice said.

"The radio is working? How?" Landon said stunned.

Mike remained silent.

"Yes, I can hear you," Landon said. "My name is Landon Parker and I am flying a news helicopter from Los Angeles. Who is this?"

"I cannot believe it!" The voice sounded excited. "My name is…"

The static became worse and they could not make out who the voice belonged to.

"Don't let him…the door…" The voice came in again and went during a few words.

"I'm sorry, I do not understand what you are saying," Landon yelled into the radio waking up Shane and Penny.

"What's going on?" Shane asked sounding groggy.

"That voice," Aunt Pam said. "It sounds familiar."

"Who is it?" Penny asked.

The static gradually became worse until finally it was clear again.

"Hello," The male voice yelled into the radio. "Can you hear me?"

"We can," Landon replied. "Name yourself."

"Whatever you do, do not let it through the door!" The voice said.

"Who is this?" Shane asked.

"Is that Shane?" The voice mumbled.

"It is," Shane replied.

"I have a message just for you," The voice said hurriedly. "Is there anyway we can have privacy?"

"Unless I ask everyone to cover their ears," Shane replied.

"Everyone, put on these earplugs," Landon said passing out several pink colored earplugs he found in a compartment.

"This might be important," Shane said to everyone as they obliged and put on the earplugs. "You too Mike."

"Fine," Mike snapped and he unhappily put on his earplugs as if it was the silliest thing the world.

"Ok," Shane said to the radio. "You only have my ears now."

"Shane," The voice rejoiced happily. "I will see you on the other side, just don't let…."

The static became worse and Shane was no longer able to hear anything and eventually there was just silence.

"I lost them," Shane said.

"What?" Landon yelled, then he pulled out his earplugs. "I mean what did you say?"

"The radio died," Shane said.

"I'm not sure how it even worked in the first place," Landon replied. "There's no wireless communication in this world anymore."

"Who do you think it was?" Penny asked Aunt Pam.

"It sounded like the cloaked man that helped me after your adventure in Sector 8," Aunt Pam replied. "When I parted ways with you in that Texan desert. The same man that told me to wait for you here at Sector 7."

"This guy is like a guardian angel," Caroline said. "Who is he?"

"AHHHHHHH!" Jesse woke up from unconscious state making everyone in the helicopter jump.

"Jesse!" Alice exclaimed. "You are alive!"

"Alice…" Jesse said looking very confused and taking in his surroundings. "Where am I?"

"You ungrateful fool," Mike said to Jesse. "You tried to abandon your wife."

"Mike..." Shane said kicking Mike on the knees because Mike was looking like he wanted to tell off Jesse for abandoning Alice.

"You!" Jesse said pointing at Mike and he looked scared.

Mike raised his eyebrows at Jesse.

"Shane, can we talk in private?" Jesse asked Shane.

Taken by surprise at the request, Shane agreed and walked over to the backseat where Jesse was sitting.

"I see we are about to land!" Mike yelled excitedly as Landon began their descent to the ghost town that was once Roswell.

Chapter Twelve:

Through the Door

"Where it all began..." Shane gasped. "We're back."

"I'm going to land us over the remains of the laboratory that the Eye Openers once used," Landon said.

"This is where..." Alice began looking over at Jesse.

"Uh," Jesse said taking his eyes off Shane.

"And you tried to leave me again last night," Alice began to cry.

"I can't deal with any of this," Jesse said frantically and loudly. "I was possessed by a devil-like creature! It controlled me and tried to force my body to attack Shane. I'm sick of this. I shared my mind with the creature that was inside me. He could see my thoughts and knew my whole life and I could see some of its thoughts too and..."

"Can we deal with this later?" Mike snapped. "You caused quite a scandal and I don't think we owe you the time or day for whatever crap you have to say. Shane, you've waited so long for this. You have the lost spare key. Now let's go open the door!"

"We'll talk later," Shane said to Jesse.

"Wait!" Jesse said, but Shane decided he wanted to be as far away as possible from the awkward drama that was Alice and Jesse's strained marriage.

Landon, Aunt Pam, Penny, Caroline, and Mike followed Shane out of the helicopter. Alice and Jesse stayed inside the helicopter and could be heard exchanging a heated argument.

"You would never abandon me, would you?" Caroline asked Mike with her hand over her stomach. "Or the baby?"

"Never," Mike said sternly.

Shane was digging through rubble looking for the underground trapdoor that led to the mysterious door him and Alice encountered before their venture into Moonshadow Ranch.

"Over here!" Penny said. "There's a huge hole on the foundation here."

"Perfect!" Shane said excitedly. "I can jump down into that pit. It's the hallway that leads to the doorway."

Shane pulled out both his crystal necklace and the key and held them tightly in his fists. He turned around and addressed the group.

"Hey everyone," Shane said. "I'm not sure exactly what lies beyond the door. All I know is that Derek wanted me to find this. I have the key now and hopefully there will be more answers on the other side."

"Are you going alone?" Caroline asked Shane.

Shane looked over at Penny who was gazing at him intently.

"I think I am supposed to," Shane said. "I think this door has something to do with my destiny and even...the future."

"Can I come with you?" Penny whispered into Shane's ear.

Shane took a deep breath and shrugged his shoulders. "I don't feel safe taking you. I've already put you and everyone else here at jeopardy."

"Oh my God!" Aunt Pam shrieked and pointed up at the sky.

There were about ten Dark Ones flying in a circle over the laboratory several feet up in the air staring at them all with their menacing bright red eyes and taunting them with their clawed fingers.

"What are they doing?" Landon said in a worried tone.

143

The Dark Ones continued to fly around in circles as if they were vultures scoping out dead prey. Shane reached for his crystal necklace but it merely glowed. It had lost most of its power. He was defenseless.

Alice came running out of the helicopter with tears streaming down her face. Jesse was running behind her trying to reach for her arm to stop her. Alice bent over and picked up a metal bar that was part of the Sector 1 ruins. She had a dark look in her eyes and was running at full speed towards Mike.

"Alice?" Shane said in shock.

"What the hell?" Caroline yelled when she saw that Alice was positioning the metal bar as if it were a bat.

The distance between Alice and Mike became less and less and Mike remained still and calm with no expression on his face.

"THAT'S NOT MIKE!" Alice yelled and before anyone could think, about what she said, she threw the metal bar square into Mike's face with a sickening thud.

Mike fell backwards onto the ground as blood gushed out of his forehead. He was yelling in agony.

"AAHHHHHH!" Caroline let out a blood-curdling scream as she fell on her knees to her husband's side. "What have you done Alison!"

Alice had fallen to her knees and began to cry. Landon reached for her to restrain her as if afraid she would attack again.

"He's a Dark One," Jesse said. "The Dark One inside me...Leviticus...is working for the Dark One that possessed Mike."

"You're crazy!" Caroline cried. "The Dark Ones are flying above us! Mike! Mikc! Can you hear me? Can you hear me?"

"It's Venus!" Jesse said. "Venus is inside of Mike."

Shane looked at Jesse and Alice as if they both had gone mentally ill. His first assumption was that they were possessed by Dark Ones themselves."

"In my head..." Jesse continued. "In my head I saw...I saw a memory of Leviticus writing the name of his queen although through his eyes everything looked backwards. It was as if I was looking in a mirror."

Shane looked at Jesse and then quickly turned his direction on a crying Caroline over Mike.

"Caroline!" Shane said rushing over to her. "Step away from him."

"What?" Caroline snapped. "Alice nearly killed him!"

"Caroline," Shane began to cry. "I think Jesse and Alice are telling the truth."

Caroline stopped crying and her face contorted into anger.

"Are you crazy too?" Caroline snapped.

"Jesse said he saw a memory of Leviticus writing the name 'Venus' in his head while he was possessed. "What is 'Venus' backwards?"

"Sunev..." Landon and Penny gasped simultaneously.

"No..." Caroline said looking at the unconscious body of her husband. "He was with me the whole time. There's no way that evil creature would have possessed him."

Shane felt for Mike's pulse. It was nonexistent.

"He's dead," Shane said trying to hold back tears and a swelling stuck in his throat.

Caroline collapsed onto Mike's body and began to sob profusely and hysterically.

"I killed him..." Alice said in shock.

"I told you the truth," Jesse said. "Sunev is dead now."

"That doesn't explain why the Dark Ones are still circling above," Landon said looking up at the sky as the Dark Ones lazily flew in circles and staring at the group below.

"Can you prove he was being possessed?" Aunt Pam asked Shane.

"Normally, the Dark One would have escaped the mouth of its host's body," Shane said. "If Sunev was inside him, then why didn't she transform his body to have a true form? And she would have had so many opportunities to kill me."

"Go to the door now," Landon urged Shane. "You might not have another chance. The Dark Ones seems to be circling lower and lower to the ground. They might be planning an attack. Go!"

"Alright," Shane said.

"I'm coming," Penny said and she grabbed Shane's hand.

Shane wanted to talk to Caroline and console her. He wanted to spend more time to absorb the shock of his best friend's death. He wanted find out what happened to Alice and why she snapped and attacked Mike.

Everything felt like slow motion as Shane ran towards the hole on the ground that led to the mysterious door. Before he jumped down with Penny, he glanced back at the company that came with him. Landon was gesturing for Shane to jump in. Aunt Pam was standing by Landon with gentle tears pouring down her face. Caroline had gotten up from her dead husband's side with bloodstains down her shirt. She picked up the metal bar that Alice used to give the fatal blow to Mike and ran with rage towards Alice. Jesse blocked Alice from Caroline's deadly swipe and smacked him right in the head, knocking him out. Jesse fell face-first onto the floor and was still. There were so many yells and cries. Caroline dropped the metal bar in shock before she could even think about attacking Alice out of rage. She fell to the ground and cried as if she were in physical agony.

Shane looked up at the sky and saw that the Dark Ones were now only staring at her. Caroline's cries were so powerful, but when Shane made his last eye contact with her, he could have sworn that they were empty.

Shane and Penny landed on the ground below in the hidden room that was once part of the Sector 1 laboratory. The small light from his necklace helped light their way down the dark hall. They stepped over skeletons of dead mice as they made their way closer to the door. Penny did not even flinch at the sight of the dead mice or the few spiders that had created webs in the ceilings of the underground tunnel they were in.

"Are you scared?" Penny asked Shane.

"I don't think I am," Shane said. "If I'm meant to do this, and if our destiny's are already paved for us according to what Ryker told me, then I should not be afraid."

"Shane," Penny said holding onto Shane's hand.

She remained silent and kissed him vigorously.

"I just want to make sure I gave you a kiss in case I cannot come with you," Penny said.

"You are not leaving my sight," Shane insisted.

"What happened up there?" Penny said. "Alice went crazy. Jesse went Crazy. Caroline snapped."

"This has all happened because I brought all of you along this dangerous journey. It's all my fault."

They heard a gunshot echo from above the ground where the rest of the group was. Aunt Pam screamed at the top of her lungs.

"Oh my God," Penny exclaimed. "What's happening?"

"I don't know," Shane began to cry. "I think the Dark Ones are getting to them."

Shane pulled out the key and knew that it was now or never.

"Here goes…" He said.

Shane used the fading light of his crystal necklace to find the keyhole over the metal door with a wooden sign over it that read "956."

"It's time," Penny assured Shane. "Unlock it."

Shane inserted the spare key into the door and turned it right. There was a clicking sound and instantly a bluish light peered from the cracks of the door as Shane slowly pushed it.

"It's heavier than I expected," Shane said as he pushed the door with all his strength.

"Let me help you," Penny added and she joined him.

147

Together they were able to successfully push the door open into a room with a bluish light coming from a silver object on the ground of a very small room the size of a closet.

"What is that?" Penny asked pointing at the silver object.

"I think it's a Communicator!" Shane said. "Strange. Look at that on the wall!"

Shane pointed at the wall directly opposite across from the door. It was metal, but there was an engraving on it of a strange creature Shane had never seen before. It had the shape and body of a human, but the fingers were webbed and clawed and its face looked like a reptile.

"Is that lizard or a dinosaur?" Penny asked in confusion.

"It's eyes are large like the grey aliens—the Elders, yet it looks like it has scaly skin drawn on it," Shane said. "Bizarre."

"This room is extremely small," Penny said. "All that trouble to find a way to open it and there is just a Communicator?"

"There must be a very special message," Shane said. "And it does not look like a normal communicator either. Sure it is the same shape as the ones I've used, but they don't glow with a blue light. This contraption is something more, I think."

They walked into the small room and the door swung shut behind them. They turned around and saw that Mike had walked in with a huge smile and large bloody gash on his face.

"Mike!?" Shane gasped in shock. "I thought you were dead."

"Mike is dead," A horse, raspy voice escaped from Mike's mouth.

"Sunev…" Shane said.

"We meet again Shane," Sunev said and Mike's face contorted into a menacing stare.

"Jesse was telling the truth then," Shane said matter-of-factly.

"And that darling Alison tried to stop me and save you by killing one her best friends...mind you, Mike's body is mine now and he has been dead since the moment I took him over."

"When did you take host in his body?" Shane asked.

"When his wife and him were searching for the very key you used to open this door, in the house of Landon Parker," Sunev's chilling voice escaped from Mike's mouth. "I possessed him in the darkness of a closet when Caroline and him thought an earthquake was happening. As soon as I jumped into his body and his mind was mine, I realized where the spare key was and as I posed as him for the last few days around you, I learned how important it is that I go through this door and not you. The Dark Ones do not exist in the future, but I will change that. It is our destiny to live on, especially now that we have the ability to turn human host bodies into our true form."

Shane looked around the cramped, small room. He looked at the Communicator that was sitting on the ground glowing ominously as if it were holding back more secrets.

"This room was meant for me," Shane told Sunev.

"She's here too," Sunev said sarcastically and pointed at Penny.

"That's not the point," Shane snapped. "I am meant for this room and if I choose to bring someone with me, that is because it is my destiny. You killed one of my best friends. You're kind is the reason for the death of mother."

"*You* killed *my* father!" Sunev spat.

Sunev pushed Shane and Penny against the closed door of the room with an invisible force. Penny got up quickly and tried to open the door, only to realize there was no doorknob from the inside.

"This door is only meant for entering and not exiting!" Penny said in panic.

"Your journey ends soon," Sunev said.

Sunev reached for the Communicator and handed it to Shane who accepted it. The Communicator felt warm to the touch and instantly as his fingers made contact with the warm metal, a bluish light hologram erupted from the tip of the cone-shaped Communicator. He recognized the image before him as an old recorded message Manuel had shown him back at Threa. The hologram was of his mother Genesis and Shane knew that this message would be full and not garbled like the one Manuel found. This was the lost message from his mother.

Genesis stood before him in a 3D hologram that looked almost life-like. She was a little over four feet tall and was thin and frail looking. She had two slits for nostrils and a thin mouth with no lips. She had two large black and glossy almond shaped eyes that slanted up on her face. Genesis' thin mouth began to move as she spoke.

"Dear Shane, this is your mother. I have so much knowledge I need you to learn, but I do not have enough time to record this message. I most likely have died by now, but I know how the future works and when we meet, I only tell you some of the story and not the full story about you, who you are, and why you are going through the journey you are going through. There is a group of individuals. They call themselves of the Cosmos of Destiny. They came to me one day and were all uniformed. They told me we need to change the course of your path, Shane. We need to restart the world all over again. We need to rewrite and fix history before it repeats itself. You have found this door locked away where it all began. Where our contact with a human government first began on Earth. From that day forward, it was written in the cosmos that our contact would taint and doom the planet through a series of unfortunate events. By the time you have reached this message those events would have already happened. It is written that my race...the Greys...would become extinct, however we used humans to create Humanoids so that our DNA could live on. Greys cannot reproduce. You, like myself, were created as a clone. The Cosmos of Destiny will welcome you with open arms and you will learn the truth about life in this universe and the chain of effects it has for any kind of life forced to struggle with the one thing all species' have in common: survival. Shane, you are the center of the future. You are the past, the present, and the future...you must find the white in the black."

The hologram vanished as the message ended, and as it did, the Communicator melted into a silver pool of liquid on the ground. The liquid turned bright blue and became wider and wider until it encompassed the entire room after spreading into every direction possible.

Shane felt his body leave the ground he was standing in. He could not see anything as everything suddenly went pitch black. He felt as though he was flying or moving extremely fast. He was reminded of a roller coaster ride. He could feel his cheeks being pushed back by a strong force as if wind was hitting him at several hundred miles per hour and pushing him into oblivion. He felt as though he was falling, yet it also felt as if he was falling up as if wherever his body was, gravitational laws did not exist.

He could feel the pit of his stomach drop and felt as if he was about to plummet fatally into a surface, but his body never forcefully came into contact with anything solid. The last thing he remembered of the strange sensation that began when the room he was in disappeared, was an orange glow that was peaking through his eyelids making the darkness disappear.

Chapter Thirteen:
Where it all Began

Shane felt blind. It was as if his eyes were closed, yet all he could see was an orange glow in every direction he would turn his head. He could feel his hands, his arms, his legs, yet he could not see them or feel what he was lying on. He felt as though his entire body was constricted. He could not move or talk. He could hear whispers. There was a group of people speaking so fast that he could not understand what they were saying.

Shane strained with all his might to try and make out what the voices were saying. He felt a pair of cold hands on his face, yet all he could see was just white light.

"Will you take him to 1947?" Someone with a very slow and calm voice said from the proximity of wherever Shane was. "Take him and let him see the beginning of the contact. It's key."

"What about the other boy and the other girl?" Another voice asked.

"They are subdued as well. I think we all know that the boy is not what he appears to be. There is a Dark One living in him. A Dark One in these times and this very place is very treacherous. Keep as many eyes on it as possible and let us make sure that we find a way to dispose of its soul."

"Yes sir," Shane heard someone answer.

"Ryker," The calm and slow voice spoke again, "Keep him safe. He's important to me...and his *brother.*"

Shane felt the surface beneath his back disappear. The orange light, which was all he had been seeing for a few minutes, was replaced with a black sky filled with thousands of bright stars. Shane got up off his back and realized he was lying on the ground just outside of a farmhouse that appeared to be located in the middle of nowhere in an arid area.

"Where am I?" Shane said out loud. "Hello? Is anybody here?"

Shane took a few steps forward and felt rocks, sand, and dry grass beneath his shoes. In the distance, he saw that the farmhouse had a few flickering lights and even though it was nighttime, he could tell that the chimney of the house was billowing smoke.

Where am I? Shane thought. *I feel like this could be Moonshadow Ranch, except there are no high fences and only one farmhouse can be seen in the vicinity.*

Shane walked carefully through brush and avoided rubbing against cacti. He finally reached the wooden fence surrounding the ranch and jumped over it. It was only four feet high. He saw two horses sleeping in one corner of the fenced area next to a feeder. Shane tiptoed over the sandy grounds, which were cleared of any brush inside the enclosure, so as not to wake the horses. However, his foot got stuck in an exposed root from a nearby tree and he fell face first into the damp Earth and cursed loudly.

"Dammit!" Shane's voice echoed into the night.

He looked over at the horses, but they remained asleep. He saw their chests moving up and down lazily. Shane walked closer to them to examine them. They continued to sleep.

Once Shane was within two feet of the horses, he extended his hand out to pet the horse's head. He put his hands through one of the horses' hair and it continued to sleep lazily without moving a muscle.

Strange, Shane thought.

"Horsey!" Shane whispered, but the horse remained asleep.

It can't hear me, Shane thought. *It can't feel me either. Am I even in a real world?*

Shane kicked the dirt in confusion and put his hands in his pocket. He could not even feel the wind or the temperature. The trees were swaying in a light breeze and as he was in the middle of a desert, he expected it to be cold, yet he could feel nothing. He thought back to his fall onto the ground and realized that he could not even smell the ground. He expected the farm grounds to smell like animals or manure, but it was as if his senses stopped working.

He walked over another fence and was within a few steps to the front porch of the farmhouse. He could hear the wind sweeping through the trees and the crickets chirping. He looked over into the distance and saw stalks of cornfields also swaying slightly to a very light breeze.

There were two gas lanterns that gave light on the porch. He walked up the wooden steps of the porch and knocked on the door. There was no answer.

"Hello?" Shane called out. "Is anyone home?"

He waited another minute before trying to turn the doorknob, but the door was locked. He decided to walk around to the back of the house and jumped at the sound of an owl hooting. He shook off the surprise and made his way around the house walking over a damp lawn. He saw a very old-looking pick-up truck parked in a driveway. Shane figured the truck was easily over sixty years old, yet it looked to be in good condition.

Shane found a door in the back of the house and he could see that someone was definitely home. There were lights on inside. Shane peered through a window and saw a man, a woman, and two male children having dinner.

Shane knocked on the window.

"Hello, can you help me?" Shane said, but the family inside paid no attention to Shane's call.

They can't hear me either, Shane panicked in his mind.

He walked to the door and turned the knob. The door creaked open. Shane walked in, but the family continued to eat their dinner without noticing Shane.

Shane walked up to the man, who appeared to be a rancher judging by his western-looking clothing and cowboy hat. Shane

154

moved his hand in front of the rancher's face. The rancher did not blink and instead continued to eat his food while conversing with his family.

"This steak is very well cooked," The rancher said to the woman.

"Thank you darling," The woman responded. She appeared to be his wife.

"Can we stay up to listen to the radio show?" One of the boys asked.

"We have to wake up early to go into town to run a few errands," The woman responded. "You can listen to the radio show tomorrow."

Shane took notice of the furniture around the kitchen. He felt as if he was in another century. Everything was old-fashioned. It looked like a much more old-fashioned Moonshadow Ranch. There was a Benjamin Franklin stove, a fireplace with a large pot in it, and all the lights were from candles or gas lamps.

"Martha," The man said to his wife, "I'll let them hear the radio programming for a bit while I help you with the dishes."

"Timothy, that is very kind of you," The woman said with a slight blush and smile.

The rancher got out of his seat and pulled a vintage-looking radio.

"It has fresh batteries," The rancher said. "Ok let me find that station. You boys like to listen to the ghost story station, correct?"

"Yes, papa!" One of the sons said. "We love a good haunted story."

"Here we go!" The rancher said as the radio dial fell onto the station the children wanted to listen to.

Shane followed the wife to the sink of the kitchen as she began to wash the dishes from their meal. She looked very content and warm, yet she took no notice of Shane.

Am I a ghost? Shane thought tuning into the radio program the children were listening to about ghosts.

155

"…and there were handprints on the dusty bookshelves, but no one had touched them in ages," The radio program host was saying through the radio. "One by one the books began to fall off the bookshelves and…"

Static cut into the program and the voice of the host was inaudible.

"Papa, I thought it had fresh batteries," One of the sons asked.

"The signal must be weak out here tonight," The rancher told his sons.

The static grew louder and stranger. There was eerie sounds emitting from the radio's speakers, but they had nothing to do with the programming. Something was interfering.

Without warning, a huge explosion was heard outside. It sounded like a sonic boom. The sound cracked through the air and the horses in their stables were now awake and neighing loudly.

"Stay put!" The rancher told his children and wife as he ran towards the door.

There was a shotgun propped right by the same door Shane came in that he had not noticed before. The rancher picked up the gun and grabbed a flashlight out of a drawer.

"I'll be right back," The rancher said with a worried look on his face.

"Timothy please be careful," The wife said.

Shane followed the rancher out of the house. Shane was running out of breath to keep up with the man who was about ten years older than him.

"What the hell?" The rancher yelled staring up at the sky.

Shane nearly tripped over a bush in shock. A white light was streaking across the sky. It looked like a meteor was about to hit. It was gaining momentum and falling closer and closer to the house. The noise was becoming louder and louder and then the streak of light flew over the house causing some of the windows of the home to shatter from the vibration. Shane did not feel any vibration, but he knew it must have caused one because even the truck began to vibrate in its parked position.

The light made impact with the ground about a mile away from the house causing fire and smoke to erupt from where it crashed. It appeared as though some of the dry bush in the vicinity had caught fire as well.

"Lord have mercy!" The rancher gasped and he ran back past Shane and got into his truck. "I'll be right back! Something crashed! It might have been an airplane!"

Shane jumped onto the back bed of the truck just as the rancher put it on drive and sped off in the direction of the crash.

There was a crate of old, empty milk bottles in the truck's bed that Shane took refuge in. He pulled out one of the bottles and read a label that read "Enjoy before 06-30-47."

"47?" Shane said aloud. "That can't be right...I'm either in the future or the past. I'm pretty sure this is not the future."

A donning sense of realization hit Shane like a whip. He was in the past and he was not sure how he had arrived there. He realized that the crash that occurred was a crash he was familiar with.

"The Elders' ship!" Shane gasped. "Jax and Steg..."

Within a few minutes, they were within proximity of the crash site. There was a large fire and smoke rising into the night sky. Another truck had arrived on the scene before the rancher, Timothy.

Timothy turned off the engine and quickly jumped out of the truck with his shotgun pointed in front of him. There was another man standing before a large silver metal disc shaped object that Shane recognized as one of the escape pod ships from Threa.

"What's your name?" Timothy asked the other man who was holding a small pistol in front him and looking startled.

"John," The man said, and by the looks of his attire, he was a rancher as well. "I own the neighboring ranch. I'm sorry I drove onto your property, but I was afraid this might have been a plane crash."

"What the hell is it?" Timothy asked.

"This here is no plane," John responded. "It's some kind of metal shaped disc. I think it might be something from the government."

"It looks very odd," Timothy said. "I've never seen anything like it. I don't have a phone on my property, but we can put this thing on the back of my truck and I can drive into town to the sheriff's office. Or maybe we can store it in my shed? I have space."

"I brought some buckets of water," John said. "Mind giving me a hand and we can turn out this fire."

The two men worked together to put out the brush fire caused by the crash. After half an hour of intense labor, they were finally able to extinguish the fire.

"This flying object has a door," Timothy said as he took a closer look at the metallic ship.

Shane inched closely behind him and watched in awe as Timothy opened the door and immediately jumped back in horror and yelled into the night.

"What the hell is that?" John exclaimed putting one hand on his chest and the other tightly over his pistol.

A four foot Grey alien was clawing its way out of the door that Timothy had successful propped open. Its black glossy eyes shined as Timothy was pointing his flashlight at it. The alien squinted its eyes as if trying to block the light. Shane could hear it gasping and breathing heavily. He saw that the frail creature had wounds all over its body.

"Steg…" Shane whispered to himself remembering the story his Elder mother Genesis told him about the crash of his alien uncle.

Shane's mind reflected upon the night Genesis told him her tale…

"Sadly, on a trip to visit Earth, Jax and Steg's ship ran out of light and crashed in what is called Roswell, New Mexico. The mini ship was just a smaller ship that was an emergency pod for our current vessel, which you are in now.

Both of them were killed, although Jax lived a week after."

"Where's Jax then?" Shane said to himself noticing that there was only one occupant in the ship. "He supposedly lived a week after the crash…"

"Never in my life have I seen such a thing!" Timothy gasped. "Is this some kind of experiment? Is it the Germans or the Russians?"

"Is that a mutilated child?" John said.

Steg extended his arm out to the ranchers as if asking for help, but then his arm fell limply to the ground. Steg's body was silent and still.

"I think it's dead," Timothy said prodding the body with his shotgun.

"That's not a human child though, is it?" John asked.

"I'm not sure," Timothy replied. "I have some blankets inside my truck. I'll grab it and we can wrap the body. Perhaps you can give me a hand to put this craft in the back of my truck? I will go into town in the morning and talk to the sheriff."

"That sounds good to me," John said. "I don't want that…that thing on my property."

Shane watched as the two men worked together to carefully place Steg's body in a fleece blanket. Once the body was carefully placed in the passenger seat of Timothy's truck, they worked together to lift the damaged silver ship onto the truck's bed.

Timothy shook John's hand and bid him farewell as he got back into his truck with both the dead body and the craft. Shane ran onto the bed of the truck and was able to barely fit in small nook that was not taken up by the craft.

Shane had fallen asleep without realizing how tired he was. He woke up at the sound of the truck being turned on. He was still

159

on the bed of the truck, however it was now morning and the craft had been removed. He glanced at the farm's shed in the distance and saw that there was a large blanket covering what he believed was the craft. Shane looked around to see if the dead body was in the passenger's seat, but it was not. Instead, one of Timothy's sons was buckled in.

The drive into town was about twenty minutes. There was a small wooden sign that read "Welcome to Roswell" as they arrived in the city limits. Timothy drove the truck straight to the sheriff's station and told his son to wait in the truck. Shane jumped out of the truck's bed and followed Timothy into the station.

"Timothy!" The voice of a plump man with a handlebar mustache and a cowboy hat yelled as soon as Timothy was in the door. "What brings you here? Any more trespassers on your property?"

"Actually," Timothy replied. "Someone—something crashed on my land last night."

"Like an airplane?" The sheriff replied. "We actually received calls last night about some lights in the sky or people saying they thought a shooting star fell just outside of town."

"Well I can assure you it is not a shooting star," Timothy said. "Why don't you follow me back up to the ranch? I've never seen anything like it, Dylan."

"Right," Dylan, the sheriff replied. "Bob, come with me. We have something to investigate this morning."

Shane rode back on the truck as it sped up the highway with Dylan and his partner, Bob, following behind them in their patrol car. When they arrived back at the ranch and through the gate onto the property, Timothy picked up speed on the truck. The sheriff's car followed suit.

As soon as they parked outside of Timothy's farmhouse, his son ran out in the direction of the shed where the ship was covered.

"Over here sheriff!" The son called out.

Dylan and Bob walked over to the shed following Timothy's lead. Timothy pulled the covers and the sheriff and his partner gasped in shock.

"Well that's something I have never seen," Bob said.

"That looks like something from the government," Dylan said. "I'll have to contact the military when I get back into the station. Maybe they were testing some kind of new aircraft."

"That's not all," Timothy said and he walked into the shed and picked up a bundle of blankets.

Steg's frail arm fell out and both Dylan and Bob backed away in shock before Timothy could unveil the entire body. He set the body on the ground and pulled the covers to reveal the dead alien.

"Lord have mercy!" Dylan gasped.

"What the hell is that?" Bob asked.

"What the hell was it, is more like the question," Timothy said. "I think this creature came from outer space."

"Keep the body and this craft covered," Dylan ordered. "Do not tell anybody about this. I do not want word out to the media at all."

Dylan and Bob left in haste and jumped into their car. They sped off at full speed with the sirens blaring.

"Dad, is this some kind of monster?" The son asked.

"I'm not sure," Timothy responded.

Shane spent the rest of the afternoon exploring the ranch out of boredom. He was not sure how he was going to end up back in the present and at Sector 1 where the door was. He came up with a theory that he needed to end up at the Sector 1 in the current time he was in and he would perhaps find an answer and way out of the time warp he was trapped in.

Or maybe this is one bad dream, he thought.

Around noon, a caravan of military vehicles sped onto Timothy's ranch. Shane watched in fascination as a bunch of military men in uniforms marched straight towards the shed without even knocking on the farmhouse's door. Timothy ran out and was ordered to stay on his porch by someone in the military.

Shane watched as the military men unveiled the ship and Steg's body. Many of them backed away in shock. Shane was surprised to see a familiar and very young face in the group. It was a younger version of Agent Green who would eventually grow to become the leader of the Non-Human Relations agency, which was created because of this exact event Shane was reliving.

"Where it all began," Shane said aloud to himself. "This really is where it all began."

"It really is," A voice from behind Shane said making him jump.

"Ryker!" Shane said in shock recognizing the voice, however not the face of the man that was behind him.

The Ryker Shane knew form Threa was young and around his age. The Ryker standing before him was about the same height but his face looked older. It had many wrinkles and his skin tone was a dark tan color as if he had been in the sun for an extended amount of time. He was completely bald and had no trace of hair on his skin. His eyes were a darkish brown in color. Ryker did not look much like Ryker at all. He looked like an older man of a different race wearing a brown cloak. He had a hood that was folded behind him as he was not wearing it over his head.

"It was you!" Shane said. "You were the one watching over me in New York City. You were there in L.A. when that Dark One that possessed my friend Mariette, attacked us! And my Aunt Pam said a man in a brown cloak told her to wait for me at the ruins of Sector 7. It was you!"

"Ah," Ryker said calmly as the military men were scurrying about in a hurry and lifting the spacecraft onto one of their trucks and putting a tarp over it. "That was someone else. You'll become reacquainted soon enough with him. I can see how you would mistake me for the ally that has been watching over you, but we all look very similar. I'll explain in time. I promise."

"Where are we?" Shane said. "I mean I know we are in Roswell, but how can I be in 1947? Did I travel back in time?"

"Yes," Ryker replied. "In essence you have, but there is more to the process and I wanted you to experience this very important part of human history firsthand."

"Why can't I hear anything the military is saying now?" Shane said rubbing his ears as if he had gone deaf because he had realized he could no longer hear any sounds in the location he was in.

"I've tuned out the sounds to speak with you," Ryker said. "Grab my hand."

Shane reached out for Ryker's hand and everything went bright orange. Moments later they were standing in another part of the ranch surrounded by military men and trucks.

"They are about to discover Jax's body," Ryker said. "Jax tried to eject himself from the ship before the crash, but he hurt his legs upon his fall onto the ground. The military discovered that he was still alive. Jax will live on for a week and in that week the communication begins. Greys and humans—well the human government at least—begin to learn about each other."

"I know those men!" Shane said in shock.

He pointed at two men dressed in slacks and wearing lab coats. One was a younger Dr. Felix Morgan, the scientist who once tried to erase Derek's mind and later in the future would save Shane from a near run-in with the NHR at Derek's old storage facility the day Shane learned he was a Humanoid. The other man was the motel manger of the place where Shane stayed when he visited Roswell for the first time before his first encounter with the Moonshadow Ranch. His name was Eddie and he had told Shane that he was once a scientist who worked at the Sector 1 laboratory. Shane explained this to Ryker as he tried to wrap his mind around being in the past.

"Sector 1 will be established tomorrow," Ryker said. "Well, tomorrow in this time period. That's where they take Jax's body and run tests. Then they begin communication. Your maker, Genesis, will begin visiting and talking to the government and the Non-Human Relations agency thus begins."

"My maker?" Shane asked confusingly. "Don't you mean my mother?"

"Genesis used the term mother because it was a human term you could understand," Ryker said. "But Shane, she would be appropriately labeled as your maker because she created you."

"Created me?" Shane was baffled.

"Would you like to relive your creation?" Ryker asked.

Shane gave him a blank stare.

"Derek's final message was to get you to come to where it all began...but also to where *you* began. And how..."

Chapter Fourteen:
Mother, Father, and Sons

A blinding orange light engulfed the scenery he was in. The ranch disappeared as well as all the military vehicles, Dr. Morgan, and Eddie. Shane closed his eyes and felt as if his body was being thrown around by an invisible force. He could no longer feel the ground beneath his feet.

Shane opened his eyes when he felt a surface beneath his feet. He was in a room, and judging by the electronics in the room, he was no longer in the 40s. He deduced that he was still not in the present day because the electronics looked vintage to him. He was in a child's room. It was nighttime, and the only source of light was a dim table lamp that gave off a faint orange glow. There was a crib up against the wall, and a window with its blinds drawn right near it.

Ryker was standing next to Shane and he gestured for Shane to walk to the crib. Shane obeyed and looked into the crib. He saw a baby boy in blue fleece pajamas sleeping soundly and peacefully. Shane recognized the face of the baby from a picture that once sat on the fireplace mantel of his foster parents' house. The dirty blonde hair and rosy cheeks were what gave the identity of the baby away.

"That's me…" Shane gasped. "As an infant."

"Not necessarily," Ryker said awkwardly. "It's your *other*."

"My other?" Shane said with raised eyebrows.

"I rather you witness this time period than for me to explain," Ryker replied. "It will make much more sense."

The lamp sitting on the table adjacent to the crib began to flicker on and off. Shortly after that, it went out completely. There was a white light shining through the blinds that was so bright, Shane had to shield his eyes.

The light finally began to dim and three figures appeared before him. They were Greys, and they were all surrounding the crib. They were inching closer to the crib and examining the infant. One of them outstretched its arms into the crib and picked up the baby. It woke up and looked into the Grey's almond shaped black glossy eyes. Shane's heart was racing. He did not understand why he feared for the baby—the baby he believed to be him.

The door behind Shane and Ryker swung open suddenly. Framed in the doorway and looking right through Ryker and Shane was Philip, Shane's birth father.

"My real dad!" Shane said in surprise.

There was a crying baby, but it was not coming from the baby that was in the arms of one of the Greys. There was another crying baby in Philip's arms.

"Please, take me," Philip cried. "Do not take any of my sons!"

The Greys looked at each other as if contemplating what Philip was saying. It was then that Shane realized the Grey holding his baby self was Genesis and the other two were her brothers Renner and Starro. They were the last surviving beings of the Grey race.

"Please..." Philip begged. "Not my son."

Ryker turned to Shane and whispered into his ear as if the other bodies in the room could hear them, even though they could not, "Philip had been visited by the Greys for some time. They marked him. They had abducted him as a child. They followed him throughout his adult life. They knew he would have children that would be born stronger and much more different than other regular humans. But even though they were born different, they still needed to be...*made*."

"I'm confused..." Shane began, but then two other people ran into the room behind Philip.

An older boy who looked to be in his twenties was standing in a tank and shorts with a pistol raised in front of him. The look of shock in the boy's face meant he was not expecting the intruders to be extra terrestrial. The boy had a familiar face to Shane as if he had seen him before somewhere, yet he could not figure out where.

"Dad what are they?" The boy said in shock.

"Stand back!" Philip ordered and the baby in his arms cried even louder.

The other person was a woman with blonde hair and blue eyes. Her facial features looked so familiar. It was as if Shane was looking into himself.

"You're real birth mother," Ryker said as if he could read Shane's mind. "As I said before, Genesis was your maker."

"Who was she?" Shane said in awe as he looked at the woman who gave him half of his DNA and was the wife of his birth father Philip.

"Vivian," Philip said to his wife. "Take the boys. Run!"

Philip passed the baby that was in his arms to his wife. The baby was younger than the infant Shane. He looked like a newborn.

"That boy and that baby that Philip just passed to my mother. They are my brothers..." Shane said with disbelief. He had always believed he was an only child.

"Yes," Ryker said.

Renner and Starro blocked the doorway out of the room. It was either Renner or Starro who took the newborn from the woman's arms. The other Elder put his hand on the oldest son's arm. With a flash of white light, the newborn and the older son disappeared along with Starro and Renner. The mother screamed bloody murder and then fainted and collapsed onto the bedroom floor.

Shane had his hands over his mouth in shock. Philip's two sons were abducted and he knew the infant version of himself was next.

Philip was on his knees and sobbing as he looked into the black eyes of Genesis. Genesis was caressing the baby before she too vanished with a flash of white light. The room was left in darkness for a few seconds before the lamp turned back on.

"The Elders…" Shane tried to put a few words together. "They kidnapped me…and my brothers."

"Philip's family was marked," Ryker said. "The Greys were allowed to take a few human subjects to help them continue on their race and legacy. The NHR granted them permission in exchange for advances in technology. The government was experiencing sharp changes and technological advances thanks to the Elders. And the Elders then created a sub-race of themselves they deemed as Humanoids."

"I guess that makes sense," Shane thought out loud. "I mean I remember the Moonshadow files mentioned the exchange in technology and much more about the communication between the races. Not much was documented about allowing the Elders to abduct human subjects, but I guess the landing site ritual I was once a part of makes sense. Obviously I was returned to my family though."

"Once again, you need to see what happens. It will make more sense than if I explain," Ryker said. "Let's go."

There was another flash of orange light and then Shane found himself standing in a large white room. He recognized it as the inside of one of the Elders' ships.

"There they are!" Shane said pointing at three silver tables. One of them had the oldest son strapped onto the table. The other two had the two babies sitting upright on them staring around the room with curiosity, and they looked peaceful.

Genesis, Starro, and Renner were prodding each of their subjects with metal objects. It was as if they were extracting blood, yet they were not using a syringe or anything of human familiarity.

There were also three large glass cylinder tubes that began from the ground and stretched up to the ceiling. Each of the elders placed the blood specimen of their human subjects into each tube and then extracted some of their own blood into the tube as well after injecting themselves with the same tube. The oldest boy was the only one asleep. The babies were awake, and they did not even cry from being poked and prodded.

"What are they doing?" Shane asked.

"Giving life…to you and your brothers," Ryker explained.

A man walked into the room taking Shane by surprise. It was Philip.

"Will my original self's mind be wiped?" Philip asked Genesis.

"Yes and so will the spouse," Genesis replied to Philip. "He will be fine. It will be as if they never had any children."

"What about the human originals?" Philip asked. "Will I care for them?"

"For now," Genesis replied. "Their others will be sent to live back on Earth. They will be perfect clones much like yourself. They will live on as Unknowings until the time is right. The human originals should stay in your care until we can figure out another experiment to use them with."

"The oldest is almost twenty five in human years," Philip said. "Would it be best to keep him as an Unknowing?"

"Yes," Genesis said. "Only because one of these three Humanoid clones we are creating today will be very special. One of them will be the perfected body to fight off the Dark Ones and hopefully he will be able to pass on his DNA and mate and his offspring will thrive and the Dark Ones will hinder."

"Your race was a clone race too, was it not?" Philip asked Genesis.

Genesis nodded.

"We were created by another race long, long ago," Genesis said softly. "They gave us life, but no way for us to reproduce. We have decided to clone using the human race because of their complex bodies. We had to resort to the same method of how we Elders came to be."

"Do you know which of the three clones will be able to survive a Humanoid?" Philip asked.

"Not yet," Genesis said. "You are not strong enough to withstand one yourself. You were one of the first Humanoid creations."

"He's Humanoid?" Shane asked.

"The Philip you see before you is a clone of the Philip that you saw fight to try to keep his children," Ryker said. "And in those tubes are the creations of your Humanoid self along with your brothers. Genesis is your maker, and therefore, technically your mother."

The tubes before them began to glow with a dim white light. There was water inside the tube and it began to form streams of bubbles. Shane saw three bodies form from the bubbles within the tube. They were suspended in the water in the three tubes with each of their eyes closed shut. They were nude and looked exactly like their human originals that were on the silver tables before them. The three bodies floated lazily in the water.

"Each of these three Humanoids," Genesis said pointing to her newly created clones, "will go back to Earth but end up with different families that will hopefully foster them. We can see them grow in a human world. As for the oldest, we just need to get him some kind of mentor figure to guide him. I think Manuel will be very helpful in making sure he grows into his middle aged years, however Manuel cannot be too informed on our project because of his close work with the human government. I do not want his cover to be blown. He is our liaison with them."

"So Philip ends up taking me to my foster parents," Shane asked Ryker.

"He does," Ryker said. "But you already know that story. Your foster father told you the story of Philip's mysterious appearance in the Nevada desert."

"He did," Shane said. "But what about the other two. My brothers?"

"The originals stayed with Philip on the ship with the Elders. The two children died not long after. They had side affects from the cloning extraction of their blood. They were too young to handle such a procedure. The oldest lived for several years with the Elders and his mind was wiped to make him believe he was a part of their world. Then one day he would be of great importance to the Elders because his Humanoid self was in danger back on Earth."

Shane was about to question Ryker's statement, but then he had a lump in his throat.

"Wait a minute," Shane said after he cleared his throat. "I'm dead then?"

"Your human self never grew up, Shane," Ryker said. "However, the way you look today is how he would have looked. You're his clone. A Humanoid. An exact human replica and copy. I think by now you put together that you were the one meant to fight off the Dark Ones."

"Did my two Humanoid brothers die?" Shane asked. "If I'm the one destined to fend off Dark Ones, then what became of them and what makes *me* special?"

"Even I don't know why it is you and not—" Ryker began but then the fell silent and looked as though he was in deep thought. "We are all learning together."

"So Humanoids are all clones of an actual Human that lived?" Shane said. "I guess I never really knew what the birthing process of a Humanoid was for certain. Manuel never explained to me."

"It's true," Ryker said. "You are a clone. As am I. Sometimes a Humanoid runs into its human original and they believe they are long lost twins or become extremely confused. That's rare though, and it only happened once in a situation. But yes, we Humanoids from Threa all derived from another human that looked just like us—because it was part us."

"My head hurts trying to understand," Shane said rubbing his temples. "And why do you look so different in your old age? And what year are you from?"

"That story is for later," Ryker said. "In the cosmos, we work with time because we have so much of it."

"Ryker," Shane said. "What happened to my Humanoid brothers? If they are still alive then they may have been living on Threa when Manuel took all the Humanoids from Earth after my first battle with the Dark Ones and Noom."

"One of your brothers died," Ryker said. "The other lived on."

"One of them is still alive?" Shane said. "Assuming you are from the future, you must be talking in present tense as if we were in your time period. Is he alive in your time period then?"

"He sure is," Ryker said with a smile. "I guess I could say…I sure am."

Shane looked at Ryker with disbelief.

"You are…" Shane began and tears began to stream out of his eyes. "My brother?"

"That was me…" Ryker said pointing to the tube that had the sleeping newborn clone baby. "And that was my human original."

Ryker pointed to the newborn baby sitting on the silver table.

"And you never told me?" Shane said. "When I last saw you on Threa before making my journey back to Earth with Alice, you hinted you might have known something about the future."

"My current self," Ryker said taking a bow, "asked my past self to help you, but I never revealed who I was to him because that could alter my future and become a disaster. I had my past self help you escape to Earth for the first time since you left it fifteen years before because of the threat of the Eye Openers that formed due to the Dark Ones. Ryker—me—has been your ally."

"Wow," Shane said still in disbelief and shock. "What about our other brother? You said he died?"

"He did die…in a car accident on Earth," Ryker replied. "He was an Unknowing."

Chapter Fifteen:

The Cosmos of Destiny

"Derek…" Shane gasped.

Ryker nodded.

Shane took a step back in shock. Over the past couple of years he had learned so much about himself, his past, and where he came from, but he never had any idea that he had a brother, let alone two. He always believed he was an only child, especially having been fostered as an infant.

Shane looked over at the table where the twenty-something year old Derek was asleep and strapped in. He really did look like the older Derek he once knew. It had been nearly two decades since Derek died at the hands of Landon and the NHR. Looking at Derek's original finally made sense as to why he looked familiar when he was experiencing the time period of their abduction.

"How?" Shane said while not able to figure out what to ask even though several questions were piling on top of each other.

"Genesis," Ryker said. "Our maker…never told any Humanoids about our connection as clone brothers. Manuel never knew either. He did not know that his task to help Derek assist you was because Derek was your family. There is a lot more to this than I have time to explain at the moment, but as we journey on to the future you will learn so much. Your entire journey has led up to the point upon when you would finally open the door to the Cosmos of Destiny."

"The Cosmos of Destiny?" Shane whispered, not entirely sure why he had done so as the Elders in the time period he was experiencing could not see or hear him.

"I would like to take you to the Cosmos of Destiny. It is both a people and a place," Ryker said with a warm smile that made his face look even more wrinkled.

"And I'm a clone?" Shane asked.

"You are a Humanoid," Ryker said, "but technically you are a clone. A clone of the human child Shane that unfortunately never lived to grow into the individual you have become. My original died as well."

"What about Derek's original?" Shane asked.

"He served an important purpose, however he lived for a while among the Elders," Ryker responded. "Our Visionary, as we call him, knows what the purpose was. But he is the only one. The Visionary is the leader of our people. I—and my people—well, we call ourselves the Cosmos of Destiny and we are located in an area also called the Cosmos of Destiny."

"Who is the Visionary?" Shane asked.

Ryker took a deep breath, "He keeps himself hooded. He is the one who actually has been keeping an eye on you. The individual you thought was me was actually the Visionary."

"Do you even know who he is?" Shane asked in shock.

"No," Ryker said. "But I have my beliefs about who he once was before he became and created the Cosmos of Destiny."

Shane thought hard about the things he had experienced recently. His thoughts fell to Dimitri.

"You said that you could not reveal to your past self who you were or it would alter your future—um, current self?" Shane asked.

"Yes, I did," Ryker replied.

"But Dimitri went to the future," Shane said. "He found a door that led him to the Cosmos of Destiny. He came back to the present—"

"Stop right there," Ryker interrupted Shane. "Dimitri does not exist in the Cosmos of Destiny and that is why we allowed for him to return without a struggle. He plays a role in the past—your present—that will be pivotal for our current state of existence."

Shane slapped his hand to his forehead.

"Aha!" Shane said suddenly. "The Visionary never revealed himself to me nor showed his face. Could it be that the Visionary is—me?"

Ryker smiled.

"Between you and I, I think that is the truth," He said. "Shane, I've always had my suspicions that you were the Visionary—that he is the future you. Being the one that is destined to stop the Dark Ones and the one with the black crystal necklace, it has always been an unspoken knowledge that the Visionary is Shane Baker. However, we do not question it. The Visionary has his reasons for his secrecy."

"It must be me," Shane said. "Will I get to meet him?"

"That is for him to decide," Ryker said.

"Ryker," Shane said abruptly, "If you are in the future, what becomes of my friends Alice, Caroline and Landon? I know Penny and Mike—who was possessed by Sunev—went through the door with me."

"I can take you back to the time period you left," Ryker said. "But as you have already entered the Cosmos, I'm afraid that the past has already happened. We can alter it, but there are a few things we are careful about altering and in that situation at the location of Sector 1, a few events occurred after you disappeared through the door. As for Penny and Mike...Penny is at the Cosmos and you will be reunited with her. Mike is currently being quarantined because a Dark One lives within him, and not just any ordinary Dark One, but the queen of that race!"

"Will I learn what becomes of my friends then?" Shane said with uncertainty and worry in his tone.

"If you would like to," Ryker replied. "I think I should introduce you to the Cosmos first. Let's leave this time period."

Ryker reached for Shane's hand and led the way towards a door that Shane had not seen before. The door looked very similar to the one that he entered in Sector 1. Ryker turned the doorknob with his free hand and everything around them turned bright orange again. Shane closed his eyes and could feel the ground before him disappear. The similar feeling of being on some kind of rollercoaster hit the pit of his stomach and then everything stopped.

Shane opened his eyes. He was still holding onto Ryker's hand. In front of him were about twenty figures all wearing brown cloaks. He was in a very large chamber. There were high windows around the room and through the windows all he could see was bright orange light. Shane deduced that the windows were not windows at all, but a light source for the grey-stone chamber he was standing in.

Shane looked up and noticed there was another level to the chamber. There was a balcony, and he saw another figure standing alone on it. He was holding a thin silver stick that looked as if it could have been a walking stick. On top of the silver stick was a black crystal that was giving off a faint white glow. It looked much larger than the one on Shane's necklace.

Shane stared at the hooded figure on the balcony for a minute before it turned its back to him and walked away into another room without a backwards glance.

"Welcome Shane," Ryker said. "To the Cosmos of Destiny."

The figures in front of Shane all lowered their hoods to reveal that each and everyone one of them looked identical and just like Ryker. They were all hairless with dark-brown skin that looked as though they had been tanning endlessly. Their eyes were dark brown. The only difference in their appearances was that the older individuals had wrinkles on their skin. They all wore the exact same garb, which consisted of a brown wrapped cloak and a hood. Their feet were exposed below the cloak and all the individuals wore brown sandals. Shane could not tell the gender of the individuals but he was almost sure that he was standing before men and women.

"Is everyone here a clone?" Shane whispered to Ryker as it was the only thing he could conjure up in his mind to explain the sameness in everyone's features and dress.

"Some of them were at one point, technically, because they were Humanoid decades ago," Ryker explained. "Here in the Cosmos we all look the same because the one flaw about several past species' of the universe has been diversity. There was never a normal, and whatever civilizations deemed was *normal*, meant that individuals that were not seen as normal were chastised or treated unfairly. Humans had most of those flaws. In the Cosmos there are no races, true gender, sexuality, ethnicities, birth defects, hair or different eye colors. We all are of the same skin tone and height, and the only real difference is we eventually age. We cannot avoid the natural disease we call aging. Our civilization has overcome the process to prolong life and slow down the aging process, but eventually our bodies become too weak to function and at that point we follow a specific procedure to terminate our life span."

Shane looked at the other individuals in the room. Each one of them was staring at Shane with their dark brown eyes, yet they did not show any change in emotion.

"The Elders wanted to create the perfected life form," Ryker continued. "We are a very long and evolved version of some of their work. In the time period you lived in, Shane, our people did not exist. However, we have since been able to use the power of light and technology we've created to travel back to time periods we choose."

"Choose?" Shane could only muster one word from his already racing mind.

"Have you ever experienced déjà vu?" Ryker asked.

"Yeah, I guess I have," Shane answered although he could not pinpoint an exact memory of an incident that he experienced where he felt he had experienced it before.

"Time travel," Ryker said, "Is not what your time period's definition would have called it. It's not some sort of science fiction film or story of using a machine to go back in time. Time is parallel. The universe is parallel. The Cosmos are in a parallel universe to what Earth and Threa are in."

"But we were just back in time in Roswell and during the procedure of my making," Shane said.

"You were back in time, yes," Ryker explained. "You were reliving an event that took place...and keeps taking place like a video on repeat. Follow me."

Shane followed Ryker out of the chamber they were in. He could feel the eyes of the other Cosmos following him out of the room. They walked down a very long corridor that was also lit up by the strange orange glow. Shane looked at the light source and realized it was in fact a window overlooking a very bright orange substance.

"What's outside of those windows?" Shane asked.

"That is our protection. The ultimate light source of the solar system," Ryker said. "Shane, we are inside a star. The sun, to be specific."

"What?" Shane said with shock. "How come we are not burning up? Did you not just say the Cosmos are in a parallel universe?"

"The crystals from Threa have given us a barrier to protect us from the intense heat," Ryker explained. "The sun protects us and guards us. No other life force can ever enter the sun without dying. We found safety in the core of it and created the Cosmos. The sun gives infinite light and power to those crystals. I'll explain more about how the parallel universes work shortly."

"Are there threats out there?" Shane asked.

"Not any more," Ryker said. "It's our past that haunts us. As you very well can see a Dark One found its way to the Cosmos via your friend Mike. That door was a hole to this universe. Eventually they need to be sealed, but only once we have corrected the past to benefit this future and our upcoming futures."

"Are you taking me to Mike and Penny?" Shane asked.

"Mike, as I said before, is quarantined," Ryker said. "I'll take you to Penny, but first I want to teach you about our time traveling methods."

Shane followed Ryker to a door at the end of the corridor. The door was ten feet high with two large metal doorknobs. Ryker knocked on the door twice, and it opened on its own accord. Shane took a step back in awe of the enormous room that the doors led to.

"Whoa," Shane gasped.

The room expanded for what looked like miles. There were several capsules similar to the ones that were on board the USSA that Landon and crew had used to hibernate on their journey from Earth to Threa. Shane noticed that theses capsules were completely made of blue glass and were rectangular in shape and stacked high upon each other. Each capsule had a person in it.

"Are they asleep?" Shane asked.

"They are what we like to call Age-Dead," Ryker explained. "We conquered death in our learnings and evolution in the Cosmos, and the price for that is immortality. One might find that to be wonderful, but if Humans, for example, were immortal, Earth would have overcrowded, which was why the Earth government always had their plan for Population Control inspired by the Greys."

"Interesting," Shane said.

"But age is a disease to us," Ryker said. "Because it is the only negative thing nowadays that impacts our bodies. We do not get sick or catch the diseases that plagued humans. We just grow too old and too weak to even move. We enter a vegetable state, yet we are still alive and we can think and some of the really old Cosmos can talk. We created this system called Age-Dead because it puts us into a deep slumber as our bodies never die naturally. We can be killed by force or accidents, but naturally we can live forever."

"So all of these bodies, are people who are technically still alive, but they are extremely old?" Shane asked.

"Yes," Ryker replied. "Most individuals in here average five hundred years old. You, Shane, were the first person to have been created to naturally live longer than what was normal for any kind of race. You helped birth the Cosmos of Destiny half a millennium ago."

"So the Visionary must be me," Shane said.

"Obviously, that is everyone's thought," Ryker said. "The Visionary keeps to himself. He's very old as well, but not yet ready to be Age-Dead. He does however appear to be a few years shy of being able to walk. He relies on a cane."

"That was him on the balcony then," Shane said thinking about the mysterious hooded figure he saw when he first arrived at the Cosmos of Destiny.

"Yes," Ryker said. "He resides on that second floor. Alone."

"You said earlier that you were going to explain about time travel," Shane said. "Can you?"

"Yes. Each of the people in these Resting Cases have memories of the past that spans back in time for centuries. We created a technology—these glass cases before us—that allow us to study the memories of each of these individuals. We can look into our memories and pinpoint a time and place we want to travel in the parallel universe they came from. All of us Cosmos once started off in the parallel universe to this one."

"We did not go into their memories did we?" Shane asked.

"No," Ryker replied. "Their memories told us where to go and what to keep an eye out for so we could study exactly what happened at that time and be prepared so that we don't alter the future negatively The unique thing about studying someone's memory is that you can roam that world freely, therefore being able to experience other parts of that world that happened simultaneously that the subject did not experience. The world is recreated in their heads and we are free to explore it to study the past. We create a sort of mind map."

"Bizarre," Shane said feeling his body with his hands.

"Memories are a real thing," Ryker said. "But they are not tangible and you can alter someone's memory—even make them forget events like the Elders did with their Mind Scramblers—but you need to go into the real past to make actual changes."

"You brought Dimitri here before, and you even showed your hooded self to Ryker in Threa," Shane said, "but if we are from a universe that those times have already taken place, then you can't technically alter your future without damaging the past."

"You are correct," Ryker smiled. "We went back and revealed ourselves to an Age-Dead person's past. We altered their future by accident. We do not intend for our Age-Dead subjects to die because everyone's memory and past is very important to us in our studies. The end result was they just vanished into thin air. They don't exist now."

"Can you explore your own memory?" Shane asked.

"That would be impossible Shane," Ryker said. "I have to be in an Age-Dead sleep for anyone to enter my mind and nobody can enter their own memories. It is impossible."

"You entered Threa through that door at the governmental building I assume? That is how Dimitri returned," Shane asked.

"Yes," Ryker said and he gestured over at the nearest Resting Case and noticed a wire was hooked up to a nearby chair.

Shane walked over to the blue glass case and saw a person in the case who looked just like the other Cosmos and the Ryker from the future.

"Who is that?" Shane asked.

"Manuel," Ryker said. "He evolved with the rest of the Humanoids and a few of the human survivors from Earth and joined the Cosmos of Destiny. Manuel's memory was useful for helping understand where we could create a hole to have us land on Threa."

"Hey!" Shane said suddenly. He had so many questions, but he had an idea. "If we are in the sun, can we visit Earth?"

Ryker gave Shane a very uncomfortable look.

"Earth doesn't exist any more," He said.

"What?" Shane clenched his black crystal necklace.

"Threa now orbits where Earth once was," Ryker explained. "It is a recreation of Earth before the Eye Openers revealed the United States' government secrets. Threa was a project. Territory 3 on Threa was created as a testing ground to create a world that was an almost exact replica of Earth. Threa was eventually transferred over to the solar system Earth resided in."

"Can we visit it then?" Shane asked.

"We can see it," Ryker said, "but it is only an image because it is in an alternate universe…the one that runs parallel to ours."

"This is beyond confusing," Shane said scratching his head. "I don't understand any of—"

"You won't," Ryker interrupted. "Not easily. Much of the future is beyond your comprehension. Do you want to see what becomes of your friends?"

"Um, yes," Shane said.

"Follow me," Ryker instructed. "All these glass cases are intertwined so we get the full story of the past. Whatever happens to one person in the past can be linked to someone with a similar or conjoining history. We have hundreds of Age-Dead subjects. It's a very complicated experiment but with purpose," Ryker explained.

Shane's head was beginning to throb as he tried to make sense of everything he was experiencing.

"How am I here?" Shane asked. "If I was just in my present, how can I be allowed into a future I apparently helped build without causing detrimental affects?"

"That's what we will learn together," Ryker said. "The Visionary might have answers for us as well. He wanted you to come here on your journey."

"And Mike and Penny came through too," Shane added.

"That was not expected," Ryker said. "However you were given clues to find that key that opened that door and brought you here. At least you made it through."

"Derek left those clues for me before he died," Shane said.

"I've been studying your journey of self discovery through his clues," Ryker said. "But our brother may have had more help than just Manuel."

"What do you mean?" Shane said.

"I believe that he had a second ally," Ryker said. "That's what I need to discover. I need to find out who that ally was because this ally was also trying to help you as well. My guess is that ally was the Visionary."

"Why doesn't anything make sense here at the Cosmos?" Shane asked.

"Can I confide in you something interesting, brother," Ryker said.

Shane took in the word "brother" and looked at Ryker as if seeing him for the first time. While his future self in the Cosmos looked nothing like his former self from Shane's time period, he could sense the truth about his relation to him.

"Sure you can," Shane said. "Brother…"

"I've always had a feeling that there was someone even more higher than the Visionary," Ryker said. "It is odd to say that aloud to someone for the first time. There are so many questions that both you and I have that need answers and together we will learn them. I trust it."

"I want to know why I'm the one who is destined for…" Shane began. "Come to think of it I don't know what I am truly destined for. I mean I'm the one who can stop the Dark Ones. I have this necklace too…"

"Your destiny is already written. It has already happened. I just don't know what it is. Only the Visionary does and if you have not noticed you do not exist in the Cosmos of Destiny," Ryker said. "And if you do exist, then you must be the Visionary because you helped pave a way to create the Cosmos in your future and my past."

"That makes sense," Shane said. "Can I meet the Visionary?"

"When he's ready he will come to you," Ryker said. "But don't you want to go back to where you left off with your friends?"

"Will I be able to interact with them?" Shane asked already knowing the answer to his question.

"No," Ryker replied. "It will be just like the last time periods I took you to. They won't be able to see or hear you. Are you ready?"

"I guess so," Shane said with a feeling that Ryker was not completely honest about Shane being able to interact with his friends.

"Follow me," Ryker told Shane.

Shane obliged and the walked over to a metal door in a corner of the large room they were in.

"Don't worry," Ryker said taking in Shane's look anxiousness. "We won't be in the past long. I'll be right by you as we travel. Put on these sunglasses. You can see how the time travel process works if you aren't blinded by the sun's light."

Shane accepted the pair of sunglasses from Ryker. The lenses were so large; they covered nearly his whole face. The entire pair was a metallic silver color. The lenses were as well and they did not look transparent. When he put them on, he was able to see through them regardless.

Ryker reached for the doorknob and opened the door. They walked into the closet-sized room then closed it shut.

"When one door closes..." Ryker began and instantly they both felt their bodies tighten up as if they were falling faster than the speed of light.

Shane could see what was happening as the light was no longer blinding him. Even though their bodies felt to be free falling really fast, everything he was looking at appeared in slow motion. He saw the bright orange gas that was the sun and was expecting to feel heat, but there were no sensations except for the feeling of fast winds brushing against his skin.

It was as if their bodies passed through the sun and they were falling into space. Shane thought they were flying towards another star, but it remained bright white. It turned out to be a hole.

A white hole, Shane thought.

Shane and Ryker fell into it and he thought he saw lightning strike on all sides of him. Then he saw what he thought was Earth rotating backwards faster and faster as if on rewind. He deduced that time was passing and by the look of the dark clouds swirling over the once bright blue planet, he knew it was the era of the Dark Ones and he was about to experience the present he left.

In a flash of white and orange light they no longer had the sensation of falling. When Shane felt solid ground beneath his feet again he opened his eyes to see that he was standing over rubble of a torn down building surrounded by a desert. It was Sector 1.

"I'm back!" Shane said, and he caught the last few seconds of himself running down to the chamber where the sliver door that led him to the Cosmos was. "That's so bizarre...seeing myself!"

"It is, isn't it?" Ryker said, but he was looking up at the sky at the Dark Ones that were circling high above in the sky preparing to attack the group below.

Shane followed his gaze up, but then heard a gunshot that distracted him, and he saw where the source of the sound came from.

Chapter Sixteen:

The Dark Guardian

It happened in slow motion. Shane heard Aunt Pam let out a high-pitched scream that echoed and reverberated off the ruins of Sector 1. Caroline, who looked as though she could not produce any more tears, fainted. Alice and Jesse's jaws dropped and finally Alice was the next to scream.

Landon fell to the ground with a gun in his hands that slipped out of his fingers. His head hit the cement foundation with a soundless thud due to the screams from both Alice and Aunt Pam overpowering any other sounds.

"He shot himself," Shane cried. "Why?"

Ryker put his hand on Shane's shoulder and took a deep breath, "His job was done. He wanted to make sure you got through the door. He was living with guilt from Derek's death, his work with the NHR, and could not see any escape from the current state of the planet. He took his own life because he did not see his destiny."

"Did he have a destiny? Can we change this from happening?" Shane asked wiping off tears off his cheeks.

"We can't be seen," Ryker said.

"How come we were invisible to the rancher and my birth parents when you took me back in time to those two periods?" Shane asked realizing that he was able to see the Visionary in a few instances when he traveled to Shane's present.

"The only way we are seen is if we do something to alter the past," Ryker informed him. "The Visionary helped save you back in New York City and when Mariette's possessor tried to kill you. He gave you light and that made him visible to anyone there."

"I want them to see me," Shane said. "They saw me go into the door so it's not like I will be seeing myself."

"I don't advise it, but you are destined for something great, therefore I should not stop you," Ryker replied.

The Dark Ones began to close in on Caroline, Jesse, Alice, and Aunt Pam. Shane stepped out from behind the rubble of Sector 1 and pulled out his necklace, which seemed to have recharged from his journey through the sun. A bright light emitted from his necklace and shot at the first Dark One that made a swipe for the unconscious Caroline.

Jesse, Alice, and Aunt Pam quickly looked at the direction of the light and nearly fell over backwards in shock to see Shane. Ryker was still invisible to them judging by how only their eyes were on him.

"Shane!" Alice yelled in shock. "I thought you—but you just—we saw you go down to that door a few minutes ago."

The light from Shane's necklace still wasn't strong enough to hold the Dark Ones. There were so many of them.

"What do I do Ryker?" Shane said. "Can you help me?"

"I don't have any special powers," Ryker said. "Or a necklace for that matter. The Dark Ones can see you now. We need to get out of here. I do have the ability to connect us back to the future...my present."

"Shane, help us!" Alice cried.

"I'm going to save them," Shane said. "Had I not returned they probably would have all died!"

"Yes," Ryker said. "I wasn't going to tell you that coming here, but I wanted you to know. We shouldn't risk altering the future. Let's go Shane. You aren't strong enough yet."

Shane ignored Ryker and ran towards his friends.

Caroline came to her senses from fainting and her eyes met Shane's with a confused expression, "You're back already? Mike is dead! Sunev has possessed him, Shane. Landon just committed suicide!"

Caroline sounded unhinged. Her eyes were not focused, and it appeared as though she was about to collapse again.

"Why did you come back?" Jesse asked Shane once he joined them.

"I went into the future," Shane said while still holding his crystal necklace up towards the Dark Ones who kept dodging the light beams. "I'm here to pave the path of your destiny. You won't be fated to end at the hands of these terrible shadows."

"Thank you for coming back Shane," Alice sobbed.

"You're my nephew still. Blood or not," Aunt Pam said with pride and she hugged Shane from his side.

"Thanks," Shane said beaming proudly.

"The necklace is not strong enough!" Ryker called from where they first landed unnoticed by Shane's friends. "Come back over! We need to get out of here!"

Shane kept staring up as the Dark Ones closed in on him. He was outnumbered and the necklace's light was waning.

"This is my present," Shane said to Ryker. "I'm not going back to the future right now."

Assuming Shane was talking to them, Alice responded, "You're so brave..."

"Where's Mike—Sunev I mean?" Caroline cried.

"Where's Penny?" Jesse chimed in.

The light in Shane's necklace had depleted. It was nothing but a black, empty rock now dangling on a chain.

The Dark Ones' menacing red eyes locked on Shane and they outstretched their shadowy, clawed fingers and flew at him. As they neared Shane's face, a strange sound like thunder cracked above in the clouds, echoing across the canyon. It distracted the Dark Ones and they focused their attention to the sky.

Shane's necklace started to feel warm in his hands. He looked down at it only to realize the crystal was no longer black, but clear in color just like it was when they were in the USSA right before...

"It's happening again!" Shane shouted happily knowing that the strange black figure that acted as a guardian to him once when they came face-to-face with Leviticus for the first time, was probably about to reveal itself again.

"Why does that one look different?" Aunt Pam yelled pointing behind Shane.

There it was. It stood about eight feet tall. It had a slender build and even though it was shadowy and not solid, the black figure before them looked muscular. It had a pair of bright, white eyes that glowed brilliantly. The eyes gave the figure a look of peace, where as the Dark Ones had dark red eyes, claw-like fingers, and wings.

The Dark Ones flew up to the sky in fear. The black figure did not have to do anything. They disappeared into the swirling gray mass of clouds above them and were out of sight.

The black figure looked at Shane. He was speaking to him, but through his mind.

"This planet is doomed my dear boy," It said. "Altering its fate is not wise. You need to focus on destroying the Dark Ones. You are the Bright One. You have a destiny to fulfill."

"Who are you?" Shane said aloud even though the figure was talking to him telepathically.

"I'm the past, present, and future," It answered.

"I've carried you around for years," Shane said reaching for his currently white and normal-looking crystal necklace. "And you can't even give me an answer that makes sense?"

"Answers are given to the deserving," The dark figure replied. "And a point shall come where you will be deserving."

Shane took his eyes of the figure and looked at Alice and Jesse who were huddled together and shaking with fear. Aunt Pam was hugging Caroline who had finally stood back on her feet. Ryker was looking at the dark figure in awe, but his expression showed that even he did not know who or what the dark figure before him was.

"I've helped you and protected you as your guardian for a long time," The dark figure said. But for now I must leave you so that your true strengths can be learned and tested. I bid you farewell for a limited while…"

The dark figure raised both arms into the sky and majestically floated up towards the sky. With every second, he was floating fast and faster, and once he reached the clouds they swirled away from him as if in fear of him. The sun's rays came shining down on Sector 1 from where they parted to let the figure through. Shane instinctively raised his necklace to the sun, but it did not glow.

"It's a regular crystal now," Shane sighed.

"Shane, let's go back to the Cosmos," Ryker insisted still invisible to everyone but Shane.

"This is my future," Shane told Ryker. "This is where I left off, therefore I'm not doing harm in altering anything."

"I suppose you are right," Ryker said with a pensive look.

"Who are you talking to?" Alice asked Shane with a slight worry to her tone.

"Long story," Shane said. "No time to explain. We need to get you all to safety."

"Where is Mike's body?" Caroline asked.

"His body is still being kept hostage by Sunev," Shane replied. "She's being restrained so we stand a fighting chance. She's not in this time period anymore."

"Does that mean it's over?" Aunt Pam asked.

"The Dark Ones are still flying in the skies up there," Shane said. "This isn't over yet."

Shane found a tarp in the rubble of Sector 1 and placed it over Landon's body out of respect. A tear formed in his eye. He knew that Landon's life had been plagued with challenges and secrets that came from his agency years with the government, but it was not until that moment that he truly understood how broken Landon really was to take his own life.

"What is the plan now?" Alice asked Shane.

Shane looked into her eyes. They felt emptier than he remembered them to be. The newly changed world had left them expressionless devoid of the warmth he once knew. Caroline who was now holding onto Alice's hand was still sobbing and mourning the death of her husband in the confusion of learning that he had been possessed by the queen of the Dark Ones for several days.

"It's only a matter of time before we are all gone," Caroline whimpered. "Mariette is gone. Mike. Landon. President Williams. Peter. One by one our group is dying off much like the human race. They won, haven't they?"

"No. There are still people around the world fighting and hiding," Shane said. "We need to ban together to stop them."

"But how?" Jesse asked while eyeing Shane's clear crystal necklace. "Your jewelry doesn't seem to have any powers left."

"I have a guardian," Shane said. "You saw him. I'm sure he'll be watching over us. We need to get you all to safety."

Shane turned back and looked at Ryker. He was silent as if contemplating what to do as Shane planned his next steps. After a few seconds of eye contact, Ryker finally spoke up.

"Help is coming to you shortly," Ryker said. "You can live out your present further, but the door below this foundation is open and ready for your return. I'm needed back at the Cosmos of Destiny. Having a Dark One in our midst is very unsettling."

Shane nodded in agreement.

"I will see you soon, I hope," Ryker said, and he walked down to the underground basement where the door labeled 956 was so that he could head back to the future.

"What are you looking at?" Alice asked while following Shane's gaze to where Ryker was once standing.

"I'm, um, thinking," Shane said.

"What's that?" Aunt Pam said pointing at the dark, gray skies.

There were rays of white light peering through the clouds. The clouds seemed to be buzzing in frenzy to the abnormal source of light that could not have been from the sun.

"I think help is on the way!" Shane said with delight and his heart skipped a beat when he saw that a bright light orb was floating down to Earth from several miles away.

"Is that...them?" Alice asked.

"Threa has come!" Shane said. "I wonder how they knew where to come?"

The orb was slowing down the closer it came to where the group was standing. It was a beautiful site in the very grim atmosphere of the planet Earth. The light it was emitting spread for miles around the canyon.

"It's beautiful," Jesse said.

"It's a ship from Threa," Shane said as it grew closer to them and finally stopped a few feet above them.

"Are they taking us?" Caroline said while wiping her eyes dry.

"I hope," Shane responded.

A beam of light shot from the ship to the ground and moments later Manuel and Dimitri were standing before them.

"You came!" Shane said and he walked up to Manuel.

Jesse flinched at the sudden appearance of Manuel and Dimitri and inched back out of fear.

"The most bizarre thing happened," Manuel said. "We were monitoring Earth and saw a disturbance in the clouds. A hole appeared for a short while and something strange and dark flew out of Earth and towards the sun."

"It was whatever has been residing in my crystal necklace," Shane said.

"The Dark Guardian has revealed himself?" Manuel asked.

"It looked like a Dark One, but it had white eyes and did not appear or sound threatening. It saved me twice already," Shane answered.

"I told you there was a legend to your necklace back at Threa," Dimitri said. "It contains history and much, much more. I learned a bit about it from my journey into the future."

"I was just there!" Shane cut in. "The Cosmos of Destiny."

"You were?" Dimitri said in shock. "You made it then? But why are you here? What happened?"

"I chose to come back to my present to help my friends," Shane said gesturing to his party behind him.

"The door is open then?" Dimitri asked.

"Yes," Shane said.

"Manuel, do you fancy a trip to the beyond?" Dimitri asked.

"Would that be safe?" Manuel asked.

"I only was allowed back because I don't exist in the Cosmos," Dimitri clarified. "But you are a part of the Cosmos so I don't think by their law you can walk into your future."

"I apparently was part of the movement of the Cosmos," Shane said. "And I time traveled."

"You're an exception perhaps," Dimitri said.

"Who is under that cover?" Manuel asked noticing the covered body that was Landon.

"That's..." Shane began and he felt like a rock was stuck in his throat. "It's Landon."

Manuel put his hands to his mouth in shock.

"No..." He said in almost an inaudible whisper.

"I'm sorry," Shane said. "I know at one point you both worked closely together during your Sector 7 days. He killed himself because of the circumstances that Earth is now in. I think he was bottling guilt because it was he that helped fake Derek's death as an accident."

"He was a very smart human," Manuel said. "The government put so much pressure on him. This world does not stand a chance at thriving anymore. Look at this place. There's gloom and doom."

"I need you to help," Shane asked. "Manuel, you can be of great assistance. The USSA is lying on a beach in the Santa Monica area in California. Can you give it a power boost and help find any survivors and take them to Territory 3. We need the human race to live on. If they die, how will we be able to replicate the Humanoid race if we are created as clones?"

"You know about the creation process?" Manuel said.

"You left out those details," Shane said nonchalantly. "But someone from the future filled me in."

"You are right Shane," Dimitri chimed in. "Just as much as the Dark Ones need host bodies to live—and humans seem to be a good fit for consumption for them to become stronger—we need humans to replicate our race. Humanoids, like the Greys, are unable to conceive naturally. Every one of us came from a human that looked and talked just like us. We are mere clones."

"It's true," Manuel added. "The NHR were not entirely let in on the truth of the Grey's experimentations with abducting people. They had no idea they were cloning humans with their DNA. It's not even written in the Moonshadow files."

"Do you have the Moonshadow files?" Shane asked. "Landon said he wanted to read about the aftermath of what would happen when World War Total began."

"I do," Manuel said and he pulled out the documents that were encased in a book, from his inside jacket pocket. "You could read it, but it's just a hypothesis that the Greys came up with."

"Is that hypothesis happening?" Shane said grabbing the files from Manuel and flipping it to the last pages.

"It's more than a hypothesis," Dimitri said. "Genesis was very much in contact with these people. They communicated with her so they could help shape our current present."

"So did they fail?" Alice said suddenly. "The Eye Openers exposed those secrets. The Dark Ones coerced them like puppets. This world is practically a wasteland. If the Elders had help from the future, why wasn't any of this prevented?"

"It was written in the cosmos," Dimitri said. "Earth was bound for doom. The Greys warned the humans to give them a fighting chance even though Genesis was advised not to communicate that information because if the Dark Ones got wind of the future, they would be able to find a way to use that knowledge against the future people."

"But they know now," Shane said. "Sunev followed me into their world. She's still there now!"

"You need to go back Shane," Dimitri said with a very serious look on his face. "You're the only one that can go from this group without causing disaster with the future people. You need to bring her back here. She cannot be let loose in that world. If the Cosmos are destroyed, our future and the future of races from around the universe are in danger."

"Do you mean to say there are other races out there besides your people from Threa and the Dark Ones?" Caroline said all of a sudden.

"We've not met them all," Manuel said. "But we know that there are other civilizations out there. Explain Dimitri."

"The Cosmos is made of many civilizations that spanned all over the universe," Dimitri said. "I learned that in my time there and you will learn more from them, Shane. The Dark Ones will want to rule the entire universe. The Cosmos governs under one rule as one people. In that time only one civilization exists. By conforming as one type of specie, they eliminated many intergalactic wars. Peace is one."

"This is all very confusing," Jesse said scratching his head. "What becomes of Earth?"

"It…" Shane began and he took a deep breath avoiding the gaze of his friends. "It doesn't exist."

"We become extinct?" Alice said in shock. "The planet is destroyed?"

"I'm not sure what happens exactly," Shane said truthfully. "However, Threa replaces Earth in this solar system as a replica of what Earth once was."

"So then we can live on Threa!" Alice said while looking at Manuel and Dimitri.

195

"You owe it to them," Shane said. "They have helped me as much as their race has helped all Humanoids."

"There's no denying that they have earned the right," Manuel said. "And we need them if we want civilization to continue to grow. We can't replace the millions of humans who have perished here in the last six months, but we can replace the world they created. We've begun a project called Territory 3. You know about it Alice as you lived there for six months. Anyways, here is the deal. If we stop the Dark Ones once and for all, then you will join Shane and the rest of the population on Threa."

"And we will take any Earth survivors too, right?" Shane asked.

"Yes," Manuel agreed. "There's another group we need to meet with that is living on Earth."

"Manuel, what are you talking about?" Dimitri asked puzzled.

"I must confess to another secret that was between myself and the Elders," Manuel said apologetically. "There is something special about this star system that Earth is a part of. It holds thousands upon thousands of species of life in one planet. Dimitri mentioned earlier that there are other civilizations in the cosmos far, far away in different star systems. Earth is a rarity because it holds more than one specie of life. There are animals, bugs, and sea life on this planet. It's special and unique. Our people of Threa have always wanted to see what made this world so unique for life to flourish and live simultaneously with one another. Earth has been visited by more than the Greys. The ancestors of the Greys began visiting during the time of the dinosaurs and early human civilizations such as the Egyptians. The ancestors of the Greys created the Greys as clones to be used for slavery purposes. The Greys became intelligent and eventually overthrew the reign of their ancestors."

"Who were their ancestors? Did they look like the Greys?" Shane asked baffled by the new information he had just learned.

"They were called the Reptilians by the NHR," Dimitri said. "They created the Greys and they spawned the life of the dinosaurs."

"I remembered something Genesis once told me," Shane said. "She said her ancestors found Earth inhabited by the dinosaurs. That contradicts what you just said about those ancestors creating the dinosaurs."

"Genesis wasn't fully disclosing the truth because our lives and destiny have been unfolded for us by a more advanced and intelligent civilizations that created us." Dimitri said. "That's just something I learned while at the Cosmos of Destiny. Genesis knew the truth, but chose to hide it from the other Elders and Humanoids much like the government hid our existence for decades for Earth's population. If other Greys knew the truth, our own social order would have crumbled much like what has happened here on Earth."

"Is that so?" Manuel said sounding fascinated.

"Every civilization has one thing in common. They all question 'where did we come from?'" Dimitri continued. "An answer that no civilization has never been able to answer, technically. We know the dinosaurs were created on Earth, but the planet was already inhabited by organisms. The Reptilians also mastered the art of cloning and created the Greys, a sub species. The Greys created Humanoids from Human DNA. The question I've been wondering since I left the Cosmos of Destiny was who created the Reptilians? That race is extinct because they could not survive without the help of the Greys once the Greys took matters into their own hands and fled to the star system where Threa is."

"What about humans?" Aunt Pam spoke up. "Who created us?"

"It wasn't the Reptilians," Dimitri responded.

Manuel was very quiet. He was thinking hard and it was apparent that Dimitri was speaking of this information for the first time with him.

"I don't know how humans came to be on Earth," Dimitri said. "The answer, I believe, is linked to you Shane. Somehow you will discover that answer and we will go back in time and trace the existence of all life. I do know one thing, however. The Dark Ones are one of the first species known to universe kind, which

197

ever existed. They are the oldest race still living. They are the key to questions we may never have even thought of asking."

"Why are you just telling me this?" Manuel asked.

"I couldn't risk confusing Shane on his journey," Dimitri said.

"There's a person known as the Visionary," Shane said. "He hasn't spoken with me yet. Apparently he will when the time is right. Have you overstepped boundaries by telling me this?"

"I might have..." Dimitri began.

All of a sudden it looked as though Dimitri was turning into a ghost. His body was becoming transparent almost as if he were a hologram that was slowly disappearing into nothing. He closed his eyes and the last words he said were, "I broke the code of Destiny..."

Dimitri had vanished into thin air. Even the sand below where his feet once stood left no imprint. It was as if he had not existed at all.

"He did break the code," A voice from behind Shane made him jump.

"Ryker!" Shane said suddenly making the whole group turn to him in confusion.

Shane was the only one who could see Ryker.

"The Visionary will explain to you about the secrets of life. Dimitri was briefed slightly on it, but it was not his duty to tell you. By doing so he destroyed his own existence."

"That's why he doesn't exist in the future..." Shane said more to himself than anyone else.

"Who are you talking to?" Manuel asked. "And what happened to Dimitri?"

"Can I talk to the Visionary now?" Shane asked ignoring Manuel's question. "I'll walk through the door now."

"We need to eliminate the Dark Ones," Ryker said. "Our future at the Cosmos is unstable because Sunev is there currently being restrained. And your necklace has changed..."

"Seriously who are you talking to?" Alice asked.

"Has he gone mad?" Jesse whispered.

"That necklace was the key to stopping the Dark Ones," Ryker said with worry. "Now I'm not so sure what is going to happen. By choosing to stay in your present you altered your path"

"I'm going through the door and back to the Cosmos," Shane said. "I'll see you on the other side."

Shane ran towards the entrance of the underground lair of Sector 1 where the door to the Cosmos lay hidden. He put the Moonshadow files in his jacket pocket for safekeeping.

"Shane, where are you going?" Manuel called for him. "And who were you talking to?"

"I'm going to appear back here in a few seconds," Shane said. "I'll make sure to come back to the present. I just need to bring Sunev back."

"Ok," Manuel said. "When you return we will travel to a very cold region of Earth. There is another race living among Earth, and I know where they are hiding."

Shane stopped dead in his tracks.

"Another alien race?" Shane asked. "Here?"

"Yes," Manuel replied. "The NHR worked with this other race almost at the same time they were working with the Greys. They ended up on Earth because they followed the Greys here out of curiosity. This race is very advanced as well, but they have been keeping to themselves for a few decades, especially once the Dark Ones made their presence known here. They are not an enemy to Greys or Humanoids. In fact they are almost Humanoid themselves as they look almost like a human, however they do have strikingly different features. They are living in the Nordics somewhere."

"Why are you telling me this now?" Shane said. "I lived on Threa for fifteen years and so much history is now just becoming available to me?"

"I wanted to keep this race out of Threa history because we could not fully trust them," Manuel said. "I did not want anyone to go looking for them, but now desperate times call for desperate measures, and they can help us because I have something that can help them."

"I'm tired of all these secrets!" Shane said out of frustration. "I'm going to find out the answers to all this and why I'm so important to our destiny."

"Then go to the beyond," Manuel said. "Upon your return we will travel in our ship to the Nordics to meet the race the NHR called the Whites."

"The Whites…" Shane whispered to himself and he remembered a verse from Genesis' hologram message: *"You are the past, the present, and the future…you must find the white in the black."*

"Go on!" Manuel said, and he looked up at the dark skies, but there was no sign of a Dark One anywhere.

Shane walked down the basement of Sector 1 and ran up to the door, which was already opened. The cone was glowing inside the room just as it had when he first opened the door. Shane took notice of the wall in front of him and saw that strange engraving he saw the first time he went through with Penny. The reptile-like creature with webbed feet and claws stared back at him looking as though it was moving because the glow of the cone was causing shadows on the reptile's face.

Shane deduced that the engraving was of the now extinct species known as the Reptilians.

Chapter Seventeen:

The Queen Rises

Shane closed his eyes as the familiar sensation of being flown into another dimension grasped his entire body, and he could not feel anything except the rush of wind. His eyelids were too heavy to lift this time as he saw the orange glowing light he knew was the sun trying to peak beneath the cracks of them.

Shane felt his back come in contact with a cold, stone floor. He was finally able to open his eyes. He was in the chamber he had ended up in previously. Ryker was the only one there waiting for him.

"Glad you came back," Ryker said. "Sunev is being restrained in a holding cell, but we don't know if the power of light can keep her at bay. She's very aggressive. Follow me."

Shane followed Ryker as they walked briskly down a long corridor and down a spiraling stairwell that appeared to be leading them to some underground dungeon-like room.

"Where are we?" Shane asked.

"The prison area," Ryker said. "However our civilization is in perfect harmony with one another that this area has just become an old ancient reminder of our past and when evil intentions existed."

A group of hooded men and women were standing outside of a large bronze, metal door. They each took off their hoods when Ryker arrived.

"The medications we injected her with are no longer working," One of the men said.

"Is she still in human form?" Ryker asked.

"Yes," Said another member of the Cosmos, and while they all looked alike, her voice sounded feminine, leading Shane to believe she was female.

"So she is still in Mike's body?" Shane said more to himself than to the room.

Shane felt a presence behind him and he turned around. Another hooded figure walked into the room. He appeared to be slightly taller than the rest of the people in the room. He was holding a thin silver stick that he used as a walking stick. He walked very slowly, yet with a powerful energy about him. Shane could not help but think that he was most likely looking at his future self. The man walking towards him was the Visionary, yet his face was concealed by the dark shadows that his hood cast on where his face would be.

"Sir…" Ryker began, but the Visionary waved his hands as if to gesture for Ryker to remain silent.

Ryker closed his mouth and watched as the Visionary walked to the bronze door without even glancing at Shane or acknowledging his presence. He opened the door and shrieks were coming out from Mike's mouth. The bronze door closed shut, but the rest of the group of Cosmos walked over to a window in which they could see into the holding cell.

Shane found a free space to squeeze into and saw the Visionary stand in front of Sunev. She was screaming obscenities to him.

"I will kill you," Sunev spat.

The Visionary just stood before her, unperturbed by her spitting insults.

"I will leave this body and take yours!" Sunev shrieked.

"I need to do something," Shane said to Ryker who was standing beside him.

"She's already fully invested into Mike's body," Ryker explained. "She's ready to become her full form. She's bluffing. Even if she could escape the body she is bound to, we are all a strong, evolved race. We cannot be penetrated by the Dark Ones, just like you cannot."

The lights in the room began to flicker and then they exploded. The windows of the cell shattered as Sunev let out a high pitched scream that had everyone falling to the ground with their hands over their ears. The Visionary flew back onto a wall and keeled over.

Sunev ran out of the room and down the corridor.

"Chase her!" Ryker ordered the group of Cosmos, and they stood up and chased her.

Shane looked back and saw the Visionary back on his feet and running as if he de-aged several years and was young again.

"Where's he going?" Shane asked Ryker.

"To deliver a message to your past," Ryker said. "Emergency protocol. He's going to call the helicopter that Landon is flying to Sector 1."

"But he's dead!" Shane said.

"He's sending the message to right before he dies," Ryker said.

"That's right!" Shane said. "There was a strange voice coming through the static of the radio in the helicopter. The messenger asked me to not let Sunev through the door, but that did not work out."

"We need to fix the past so that she does not come through the door!" Ryker insisted.

A member of the Cosmos came running back into the prison area.

"She found a way into the past—*your* past," The Cosmos man said.

"What part?" Shane asked.

"To the time period of when you were in the news station. She killed a reporter and almost sabotaged that helicopter you were going to use to get to Sector 1," He replied.

"Oh no!" Shane said remembering how Caroline and him thought the person in the hood they saw disappear into thin air sounded like Mike.

"That was her then?" Shane said. "I thought it was Mike on that rooftop even though he was right by us. Of course it was her. She came from the future and is still in his body."

"Sunev is back at the Cosmos," The man said. "We pulled her out."

"Thank you Zeb," Ryker told the man.

Zeb walked out of the room and Ryker gestured for Shane to follow them out into the corridor.

There was chaos in the corridor. Many of the Cosmos were running around and tripping over their brown robes, which made it clear that they were not accustomed to running in their garb.

"Where is the Visionary?" Ryker called out.

"He's been secured in his chamber," Zeb responded. "Sunev is heading to the chamber of the Age-Dead."

Ryker picked up his pace, and Shane followed in pursuit clutching onto his now clear and empty-looking crystal necklace.

When they entered the large chamber they saw Mike's body hunched on the ground breathing with a deep, raspy breath. Mike's eyes locked onto Shane's and his brows furrowed in anger.

"I have waited a long time to find my true form," Sunev's voice escaped Mike's mouth. "I kept a low profile to secretly live among you and your friends because I knew you could lead me here to the future. My people will have a chance to exist here when I am done with this place. I've never felt stronger in my life. Long gone will be the days where I will be mere shadow and smoke. Long gone are the days where I will have to possess a host body to feel solid. It's time for my one, true form as the heir to the thrown of the Dark Ones and the rightful daughter of Noom. I will avenge his death, Shane Baker!"

"I won't let you taint the past, the present, or the future," Shane said through gritted teeth.

"AAAAAARGGGHHH!" Sunev let out a high pitch scream and fell to the ground.

Shane stared in horror as his best friend's body slowly began to morph into the monstrous creature that Sunev had yearned to be. Mike's arms began to grow thick, black fur. His fingers turned to long, thin claws with razor sharp nails. Wings sprouted out of his back and claws protruded out of his feet.

Mike's body was no longer recognizable. A ten-foot tall creature was hunched on its knees and hands. It shifted its head up to reveal two large horns, a dark face with sharp teeth. The two red eyes locked with Shane's and he knew that they no longer belonged to Mike.

Sunev's true form looked much bigger than the other Dark Ones Shane had encountered. She did not have any feminine features. Instead she was quite muscular and had broad shoulders.

Several of the Cosmos walked into the room holding silver rods, which Shane assumed were weapons. They aimed at Sunev and beams of white light hit her in the face. She keeled over onto a few Resting Cases causing them to shatter and break. The inhabitants inside them were still alive, but weak. They opened their eyes in horror, yet they were in a vegetative state and could not move.

"You fools!" Sunev screamed. "Stand away!"

She spread her wings open and knocked over more Resting Cases and she began to flap them and flew a few feet off the ground and then sped towards a group of Cosmos instantly killing two with her clawed hands.

"Stop!" Ryker said to his people. "Take refuge. We are not equipped for a war or fights in this time period. We must take her out of here and back to your present, Shane."

"Try to get me," Sunev teased and she flew straight through the wall of the chamber causing the bricks to crumble through as she made her way into the corridor.

Sunev was clawing at every inch of the walls she could get her hands on and causing damage and pieces of the roof to fall to the ground.

"You can destroy our fortress," Ryker yelled at Sunev, "But your people do not exist here. You can destroy us today, but you will have nothing left and no way to get back to your filthy past."

Sunev stopped causing damage and contemplated what Ryker had just told her. It seemed to have made sense to her. She reached for Ryker and grabbed him.

"I will not harm your people...right now...if you send Shane and me back to our present." Sunev said.

"I'll go back," Shane said bravely.

"There's no point," Ryker said.

"Your future will not exist if I don't," Shane said. "I'm supposed to be the one that begins the Cosmos of Destiny."

Ryker turned away from Sunev's red eyes and looked at Shane. "You are choosing your own destiny."

"I am," Shane said. "That's what makes me different. My destiny is not written out for me. It's obvious that anything can happen right now to change the course of this future."

Sunev threw Ryker into a wall and he slid down to the ground in pain.

"Are you ok?" Shane asked him as he ran to his side.

"Fine," Ryker coughed.

"I can destroy the balance of light," Sunev said and she flew straight up and through the roof of the fortress. Orange light and heat entered the room.

"The sun is the ultimate source of your rocks," Sunev said. "Without it, you have darkness. My favorite feeling."

Sunev stretched out her arms wide. From the palms of her claws, dark shadowy orbs appeared. She brought her claws and both orbs together to create an even larger orb.

The black shadows wrapped around Sunev's body like growing vines.

"What's happening?" Shane asked.

"She's protecting herself from the light and the intense heat of the sun. She's really strong," Ryker replied.

"I could easily dive into the gases of this star," Sunev said. "I could unbalance it and cause it to die from the core. I could create a supernova. Something my father once did to a star in another galaxy where he killed off two entire civilizations with one cosmic blast of a dying star. This entire solar system will be destroyed. However, if I cause a supernova in my present, then the Cosmos of Destiny will not exist. I will obliterate everything."

"Is she bluffing?" Shane asked.

Zeb walked into the corridor shielding his eyes from the bright light of the sun.

"She knows that without light we are all weak," Zeb said. "And she and her people will be strong. There will always be darkness in the far reaches of space, but as long as stars exist, so does life. Her race was one of the very first to come into existence. We can stop her here in the Cosmos and hope that the Humanoids and humans of our past are able to stop the remaining Dark Ones. We cannot let her go back to her time period."

Shane took his necklace off and held it at the palm of his hand and walked directly under the hole left on the ceiling. He shielded his eyes slightly because the brightness of the sun was too strong. He held the crystal high above him expecting it to foster the sun's light, but nothing happened.

"Your crystal won't work right now," Ryker said. "Whatever that thing was that was living inside, it was what was giving it the ability to have power."

Sunev flew back into the chamber and used her wing to push Shane to the ground. Shane grasped his necklace and quickly put it in his pocket.

"You're coming with me," Sunev said and she grabbed Shane by the shoulders and lifted him with ease as she flapped her wings menacingly at the rest of the Cosmos who were each holding up their weapons at her.

"Drop him Sunev," Ryker said.

"I need to kill him in your past," Sunev spat.

"Let me go!" Shane yelled trying to slip out of her grasp, but she kept squeezing him hard and her nails began to scratch the surface of his skin after tearing through his clothes.

"I'm going to give Manuel a head's up," Zeb whispered to Ryker. "I'm sending a message to that time period because that is where Sunev will take Shane."

"Go!" Ryker said.

Zeb ran out of the room just as another hooded person came running into the room.

The hooded figure was not the Visionary, which was Shane's first thought as he followed the figure sneaking behind Sunev with one of their weapons tucked in its robe's pocket.

Ryker eyed the person curiously, but remained silent.

"I will find my way to the door," Sunev spat at Ryker. "No need to show me."

The person who was hiding behind Sunev raised its weapon and a beam of light hit one of Sunev's wings making her scream with pain and causing windows of the chamber to shatter.

Sunev let go of Shane as she winced in pain. Shane fell to the ground and landed on his already scratched shoulder. He yelled in agony, and while he could not hear anything else but the sounds of Sunev's pain, he imagined the sound of his shoulder dislocating as it impacted with the ground.

"Their wings!" Ryker exclaimed. "It's their weakness because they have exposed bones!"

"That was a lucky hunch," The figure said.

It was a woman and she took off the hood of her robe. It was Penny. Shane locked eyes with her and smiled even though the pain on his shoulder was excruciating.

"Penny," Shane tried to call to her.

"Shane, I was being taken care of by these people," Penny assured Shane as she ran to his side.

Sunev was flailing on the ground and crying. She tried to flap her left wing, but it was not enough to help her fly.

"You've damaged my right wing you bitch!" Sunev shrieked. "I cannot fly!"

"You are as weak as a washed up bee," Penny hissed.

"I'm going to tear you apart from the inside out," Sunev threated with her claws and she crawled to reach her.

Penny shot the weapon straight at one of Sunev's eyes and once again left her screeching so loud it shook the entire fortress.

"MY EYE!" Sunev screamed. "I CANNOT SEE OUT OF IT!"

"You are well trained in weaponry," Ryker told Penny. "You hit her in her weakest spots."

"I learned this in training at the Moonshadow Ranch," Penny admitted.

"Good job," Shane said. "I dislocated my shoulder."

"We need to get you back to your time period," Ryker said. "She will chase after you, therefore leaving this current time period."

"We can fight her off in the past...our present," Penny said. "May I take this weapon?"

"Yes," Ryker said. "It's called a Light Rod. You can take one too, Shane. I don't think taking a future weapon to the past will cause much trouble with the future."

Ryker handed Shane one of the weapons. Shane grabbed it with his unharmed hand.

"Go!" Ryker said pointing at a door down the corridor.

Shane put his good arm on his dislocated shoulder to add pressure to the pain as they took off at a run to the room of the Resting Cases. Once they were in, Shane directed Penny to the door that would lead them to their present.

"Put these on," Shane said handing over a pair of sunglasses to Penny.

Once Penny had the large glasses on her face, Shane turned the doorknob and swung the door open. They walked in and the door shut behind them. Shane heard the door open again and looked into a pair of red eyes. One was bloody and glazed over. The other eye looked angry.

Shane, Penny, and Sunev were instantly warped through the parallel universe into the present day Earth. Shane felt his body hit dirt. He opened his eyes and tossed aside the glasses. He grabbed Penny with his good hand and they saw Manuel, Alice, Jesse, and Aunt Pam looking at where the entrance to the door to the Cosmos of Destiny was.

Manuel turned to look at the sudden appearance of Shane, Penny, and a screaming Sunev.

"Oh my God!" Alice yelled in surprise.

"You're back in seconds of when you left, just as you promised," Manuel said. "Run!"

Sunev was on her feet. She extended her unhurt wing and began to flap it in hopes that it would lift her off the ground. Nothing happened.

Shane pointed the Lighting Rod at her good wing and shot a beam of light at it. Sunev screamed in agony and kicked Shane ten feet into the air, and he landed once again on his hurt shoulder. Shane screamed in pain, but the sound was overlapped by Sunev's call for help.

"LEVITICUS!" She roared.

From above the clouds, three Dark Ones came flying to her aid. They were two feet shorter than she, but the three of them grabbed her by the arms and lifted her into the sky.

"You will pay for this," Leviticus hissed at Shane.

The Dark Ones flew up into the sky, and as soon as they disappeared into the clouds, there was a crack of thunder and it began to rain.

Shane noticed that the drops were staining his skin and clothes red.

"It's blood!" Manuel said feeling the red drops that fell onto his hands.

"Gross!" Jesse exclaimed, and he tried to cover Alice's face.

"It's starting to fall harder," Aunt Pam cried. "We need to take cover."

Shane closed his mouth in fear of getting the taste of blood in his mouth. He got up and winced with every step he took towards Manuel.

"Let's get into the ship," Manuel said. "We will heal your arm. Everyone, follow me quickly."

The group followed Manuel onto the ship. Caroline was the last one to board. Once she was in, the door closed behind her. The entire room had white walls, floors, and ceilings. There was nothing else. The floor was now stained red as everyone dripped onto the ground. Everyone was drenched head-to-toe in dark, red blood.

Manuel touched one of the walls and a white beam fell from the ceiling and covered everyone. Within seconds, the entire party and floor was wiped clean of the blood.

"Wow," Jesse said. "With that kind of technology you could kill someone and hide the evidence."

"Shut up," Alice snapped looking at Caroline who was on the verge of tears. "Don't say that."

"Sorry," Jesse said.

"Is your shoulder better?" Manuel asked Shane.

"Actually, yes," Shane said realizing that the light had also healed his dislocated shoulder.

"Why was it raining blood?" Penny asked.

"That was the Dark Ones' warning to us," Manuel said. "It's their foreshadow of Earth's fate. They want to bathe it in the blood of their victims. Their victims are every living thing on Earth. The seas and land will be completely red upon their victory. That's the mark they leave when they take over a civilization according to the history Genesis taught me about them."

"It's morbid," Alice said.

"Very," Aunt Pam agreed.

211

"We made Sunev weak," Shane stated. "She's can't fly and she's blind from one eye."

"For now," Manuel said. "Just as our technology was able to clean and heal you, the Dark Ones have powers of healing too. She'll be restored eventually. It did buy us time."

"I had to bring her back to the past," Shane said. "I couldn't allow her to destroy the Cosmos of Destiny. She has a plan to cause a supernova...to the sun."

"She can't be that strong, can she?" Manuel asked more to himself than to anyone else on the ship.

"She seemed sure of it," Shane replied.

"What's the plan now?" Penny asked. "We have these weapons from the future, but there are more Dark Ones than us."

"Those weapons are great," Manuel said, "but it won't be enough. You are right. They will hunt down any surviving people on this planet. The population has dwindled to near extinction point. We need to find that race of beings that have been living among Earth as well. The Whites."

"Genesis definitely wanted me to find them," Shane said. "It was in her hologram message...find the *white* in the black."

"Makes sense," Manuel agreed.

"You mentioned they live in the Nordics, right?" Shane asked.

"I did," Manuel said. "We can fly there on the ship. Last I heard they were living in a snow-capped mountain. It will be cold and dangerous. They are difficult to deal with and gaining their trust will be like pulling teeth, but they have technology that can help us. We need to join together...all life forms that live and are a part of this wide universe. Humans have always thought they could be alone is this wide expansive universe, but that is not true. We share the stars with other cultures and civilizations. Some, as we know, don't exist yet. Some live now in the farthest reaches of space, but we have not met or discovered them. We have to preserve what is left. The Dark Ones want to be supreme masters of this universe because they feel entitled to as one of the earliest species ever. Alice, Jesse, Caroline, and Pam. You are humans. We are slightly different, but we look the same. Today we are all equal. Today we are the same. Today you are family. We should have come to Earth's aid long ago. Shane came alone and tried to stop the Dark Ones' powerful coercion to leak out the secrets that the American government was hiding. Maybe we can go back in time, but changing the past is probably not going to happen. We need to think about our future and the future people who have been trying to help us."

Manuel stopped talking and he pressed an area on the wall.

"We are on our way to Northern Europe," Manuel said.

"We are all in this together," Shane said, and he grabbed Penny's hand, then reached for Caroline's hand.

Caroline grabbed Alice's hand, and Alice grabbed Jesse's. Jesse reached for Aunt Pam's hand who in turn reached for Manuel's hand, and at that moment, they were joined together as one.

Chapter Eighteen:
Nordic

They all let go of each other's hands and remained silent for a bit. After a few minutes, Manuel broke the silence.

"You all may sit on the ground," He said. "The ship will get us to our destination in a few minutes time. I did not want to risk flying through space to get to Europe because of the clouds of Dark Ones."

"It's weird how it does not feel like we are moving," Jesse whispered to Alice. "It's amazing."

Shane walked over to Manuel who was looking extremely nervous and was fidgeting with his jacket buttons.

"Something is bothering you, isn't it?" Shane asked.

Manuel put his arm around Shane's shoulder and gestured him to put some distance between the group and them.

"I'm nervous about encountering this civilization," Manuel said. "The Greys and Whites did not get along. They weren't allowed to be near the Whites, but they lived harmoniously on Earth just as long as they did not run into each other. The planet is big enough for that, but at one point the government had them only two bases apart in the same Nevada desert."

"But they are friendly, right?" Shane asked.

"Friendly is not the right word," Manuel said. "I would say they are cordial if they feel safe and that they can trust you."

"How do they look?" Shane said curiously.

"They look almost human actually," Manuel said, "however they are abnormally tall. Most get to be about eight feet tall. They live to be between six hundred and eight hundred years old. However, they die naturally around then because as they age, they get taller and eventually their bodies cannot support their organs. They die of organ failure. We call them Whites because their skin is pasty and pale. They have eyes that are slightly larger than ours, and the younger Whites have really bright blue eyes. The older ones tend to have pinkish eyes. Both the males and females have shoulder length, platinum blonde hair. They are extremely thin. No body fat at all. They look frail, and they are, but they are fast and smart. If they feel you are threatening them, they won't hesitate to kill you. They are afraid of humans as much as the humans are afraid of them—well the handful of them that were privileged enough to meet them in top secret bases. Sector 6 was just a few miles away from Sector 7. Sector 6 is where another group of NHR personnel housed them and communicated with them. Unlike the Greys and Humanoids, the several Whites actually chose to live on Earth to learn about our world and in return they would sometimes teach us about theirs. I never interacted with the Whites. I am glad too, because they would have known I was part Grey. That would have been dangerous for my cover while I was working as an insider for the NHR to help Derek help you."

"Why didn't Genesis or you ever talk about them?" Shane asked.

"The easiest answer would be pride," Manuel admitted. "Genesis was not a fan of their race and how they could instantly kill someone if they felt threatened without warning. She trained us to not speak of them as if they were some kind of curse word."

"Why now then?" Shane asked.

"Look at the condition that Earth is in," Manuel said. "The Whites have been visiting Earth for years. It was longer than our ancestors, in fact. Our ancestors helped pave a path for life and humans, but the Whites had more of a role with shaping how humans led their life. I don't really know what that means, but I think we need to learn that bit of information. Genesis, as always, was selective about what she told me and even you."

"Do you think they can help us?" Shane asked.

"I'm out of ideas," Manuel said. "I just have a hunch that we have to."

"Remember what I mentioned earlier?" Shane said. "When I opened the door at Sector 1 that led me to the Cosmos of Destiny, Genesis' full message that you received scrambled and played for me, was emitted in full in a hologram right before I went into the future. The last words I can remember clearly: *You are the past, the present, and the future…you must find the white in the black.*"

"Right!" Manuel said. "The white in the black…"

"Was that her way of telling us we needed to reach out to the Whites without properly mentioning them?" Shane questioned.

"Yes," Manuel said. "Genesis was very clever. And the message came to me as well, so maybe she hoped I'd help you decipher it. Ah, we have arrived!"

Manuel addressed the rest of the group.

"It's going to be extremely cold out there. We are at the top of a mountain in the Nordic region of Europe miles away from any cities. I don't think the Dark Ones will be looking for us here. We are looking for a very unique type of people. We will approach them with caution and you must always compliment them and, dare I say it, suck up to them. You must make them feel that they are better than you. If you see one of them with a child, you must say that their kind loves their children more than we do. They hold their children to high regards and protect them above anything else. If you make one false move on your part that might make them anxious or frightened by you, they will kill you instantly."

"That sounds horrible," Caroline said.

"We have weapons too," Penny said showing Manuel her Lighting Rod. "Would they be threatened by them?"

"Yes, leave them here on the ship," Manuel ordered.

"I don't feel comfortable not having protection," Shane said. "I want to take them just in case. We can ditch them before we confront the Whites."

"We need to trust our communication skills for this," Manuel said. "That will be our greatest ally as we embark down into the mountain. I believe they live inside it. This was the last known location where they moved to after the NHR disbanded during the attack of the Dark Ones. The one thing that will bring us together is both our disdain for the Dark Ones. The Whites hate and fear them. The Dark Ones can possess their bodies, but as the Whites are very thin, they die easily just like the Greys do if they become possessed."

"Ok, but let us take the weapons for safety," Shane urged.

"Fine," Manuel said curtly.

"What if they aren't here? What if they left?" Penny asked.

"I strongly believe a few of them would have stayed behind because Earth provides resources to them that their home planet does not," Manuel replied. "Now, we will need to keep warm, so I want everyone to wear these suits. Just put them over your current clothes."

Suddenly, a pile of metallic jumpsuits appeared on the white floor at the group's feet. They each reached for one and put them on.

"They look like onesies," Jesses said.

"These are the uniforms the Elders wore," Manuel said. "It helped them keep their skin safe from the various environments of their travels on Earth."

Once everyone had put on their jumpsuits, a hole appeared in the middle of the floor. Manuel gestured for everyone to follow him and jump down into the opening.

Shane followed Manuel and jumped into the hole and in seconds, he was standing on the top of the snowy mountain. His entire body was warm, but he could feel the cold on the exposed skin of his face. Alice landed softly next to him and her cheeks turned pink instantly.

Penny was the last one to come through. The ship continued to hover above them with a soft white glow.

217

"How exactly are we going to get into the cave?" Caroline asked Manuel.

"We need to search around here for something that does not look normal or natural," Manuel said. "It could be camouflaged for all I know. It would be some kind of entrance that will lead us into the cavernous mountain. It won't be simple to get to where the Whites reside either. They are very intelligent creatures and they believe that any other specie that deserves the privilege to speak with them should be intelligent too. That being said, there could be obstacles along the way that will test our minds. The Whites are sneaky and their technology is impeccable."

"Why don't we all split up?" Alice suggested.

"Good idea," Manuel said.

Alice, Caroline, and Jesse became one team, while Aunt Pam and Manuel joined together. Shane and Penny paired up and took off to part of the mountaintop that the other groups were not covering.

"It's so cold, yet I can only feel it in my face," Penny said, "These bodysuits are great."

Shane smiled and reached for Penny's hand. They walked hand in hand to the edge of the mountain. They could see nothing but snow and trees for miles. There were no cities or signs of any kind of life in the vicinity.

"It's so beautiful out here," Shane said. "No destruction here and the clouds above us don't look as abnormal."

"It's so quiet and peaceful looking," Penny added. "What happens when all this is over? I mean, if we stop the Dark Ones?"

"I guess I have a choice of either staying on Earth or going to Threa," Shane said.

"But you said Earth does not exist in the future," Penny said.

"I feel I can change that," Shane said. "As much as this planet has been damaged with the near extinction of humans, I still feel that I could change the course of the future. I want to be responsible for my own destiny."

Penny smiled, squeezed Shane's hands tight, and kissed him on the lips. They shared the kiss for about a minute before breaking away.

"I needed that," Shane said.

"Me too," Penny replied. "I'll be here by your side. You know that."

"I do," Shane told her. "And I know things are awkward with the whole Alice situation, but I know that the stars did not align for her and me. I want you to know that I have feelings for you, and just you."

"I feel the same way," Penny said. "I don't know what I would do without you. I would feel so alone, especially after Peter's death."

"Your brother's memory will never be forgotten," Shane said while putting his arm around Penny. "He was a fighter and a good man."

"I'm sorry about Mike," Penny said. "And Landon."

Shane was quiet for a while. He took a deep breath and fog escaped his mouth into the cold air.

"Mike was my best friend," Shane finally spoke up. "It seems like another lifetime ago, he and I were in college and I was getting off work at this camera shop I worked at to meet him up at a bar. It seems like it was in another world I was a young adult in college where the biggest worry in my life was a job after I graduated Pepperdine. I guess that life will be unknown to me as I left for Threa before I ever had a chance to graduate or learn what I would become if I stayed on Earth. Part of me wishes I could use the Cosmos of Destiny to take me back in time and never learn about being a Humanoid. Maybe if Derek's clues were never given to me, I could be living a normal life."

"We don't know that," Penny said. "It's a probable future, but the Dark Ones were still lurking among Earth."

"It still baffles me," Shane said. "I'm almost forty years old in human years, and nearly two decades ago I was just a kid trying to make a living on this planet with two parents who adopted me, yet treated me as if we shared the same blood. And then I think back to my childhood when my Uncle Robert and Aunt Pam would visit us. Uncle Robert introduced me to Derek Conrad and Derek introduced me to my love of photography. I remember Derek would like to play games with me. He'd give me challenges to figure out, and if I was successful in deciphering his clues, I would be rewarded with an opportunity to shadow him at his job. I remember he took me on the set of Marriette's show *Candy's World*, back when she was a young actress by the name of Candy Adams. He gave me these photographs to look at and I figured out where he wanted to take me. It was the studio where the show was filmed. He was always guiding me. A part of me wants to go back in time to the moment where he took those pictures of the alien activity at the landing site of Sector 7. That night, his whole life changed."

"You weren't as close to him as an adult, were you?" Penny asked.

"When I started college I was really busy with my school and work load," Shane said. "He became an A-list photographer about town and was very busy himself. I had not seen him in years. I remember the day he died so well."

Shane's mind raced to a memory of a younger version of himself seated at the dinner table with his father Todd and his mother Emily in their Beverly Hills home.

"How are classes, Shane?" Mrs. Baker asked.

"Intense," Shane said through a mouthful of pot roast he had just inserted into his mouth. "Mmm, this is delicious mom."

"Is it too late to steer you into the medical field?" Mr. Baker asked hopefully. "You can be a doctor like your mother and me."

"Weren't you the one who said you would let me be creative?" Shane asked after he swallowed his food.

"Well, yes," Mr. Baker replied in a defeated manner. "We did say you could do what you wanted and to follow your heart. However, photography might be difficult. I want you to be able to make money and make a nice living."

"My goal is to be a big-time photographer just like Derek Conrad is," Shane said. "Maybe I can reach out to him in two years because I will need an internship for my senior year of college."

"Maybe you should reach out to him sooner," Mrs. Baker chimed in. "It does not hurt to start looking around early. The more experience you have, the better your chances of finding a job when you graduate."

"I've actually tried, but he's so difficult to get a hold of," Shane said while cutting into his pot roast with a knife. "He doesn't have an assistant. I was thinking of maybe potentially pitching him the idea of letting me be his assistant. I wish he would return my calls or e-mails."

"Pam told me that Robert has not been able to get in communication with him either," Mrs. Baker said. "She mentioned it to me briefly the other day on the phone."

"I haven't seen much of his work around either in magazines or anything in a while come to think of it," Shane added. "I hope he's doing fine though."

A few days after that conversation the Bakers had at dinner, Mr. and Mrs. Baker received a phone call from Mrs. Baker's sister Pam with the news about Derek Conrad's accidental death. They called Shane, who was at his off-campus apartment at the time to share the tragic news.

When Shane got off the phone with his parents, he went online to search for the local news story of his late mentor's death. He found several news articles that had just been posted. Later that night it was all over the news and the next day it was splashed all over the entertainment trades' front pages.

"Shane?" Penny spoke and brought Shane back to reality. "Sorry," Shane said. "I was daydreaming just now."

"We should probably begin our search for this entrance," Penny said. "I feel like whatever these people are, they are probably watching us right now. I have this eerie feeling."

"Yeah, I have that same feeling," Shane said. "Part of me feels like we should not barge in on their territory."

Shane began to kick around snow and rocks as they searched for a sign of an entrance into the mountain. They eventually ran into Alice, Jesse, and Caroline as they made their way over to the other side of the mountaintop.

"Th-this is useless," Jesse said through chattering teeth. "It's so c-c-cold."

"Find anything?" Alice asked Shane while noticing that Penny had her hands clasped in his hands.

"Nothing," Shane replied. "I'm not sure what we are looking for really. I was thinking we would find a cave or something."

"I'm so tired," Caroline said. "I should not be doing a lot of physical activity because I'm pregnant."

"I agree," Shane said. "I can ask Manuel to take you up to the ship."

"I don't want to be alone either," Caroline said. "I'm afraid. Look what happened to Mike, and I was with him the entire time."

Jesse sat down on a boulder near the edge of the mountain. As soon as he put his entire weight on it to rest, the boulder began to roll over. Jesse jumped up quickly as the boulder rolled down the side of the mountain causing lots of snow to tumble down the peak.

"Oh no!" Alice yelled. "Are you ok? That was close!"

"I'm fine," Jesse panted.

The falling snow began to build up, and an avalanche formed and tumbled down into the forest below causing a loud echoing sound as it crashed into the several trees below.

"So much for subtly," Caroline said. "What if those people hear us? They may not take kindly to us."

"What happened?" Manuel's booming voice came from behind them.

"It was an accident," Jesse explained. "I sat on this rock and it was loose and tumbled off the mountain."

"The Whites may not be happy about this," Manuel said worriedly. "They may think we are trying to destroy the mountain. This could be a deadly disadvantage."

"Deadly?" Aunt Pam gulped from behind Manuel.

"I told you earlier that they are very difficult to earn trust from," Manuel said. "They may believe we are hostile. They won't come out and attack us here, but if we go in, they could be ready to off us all."

"Then maybe we should scratch this plan," Shane said while examining his clear crystal necklace that felt powerless in his hands.

"We need them," Manuel said. "They should understand that we have a common enemy. If I can convince them how much we hate the Dark Ones, which really won't take much acting at all, then that would be the beginning of an open conversation we can have. Humans had an advantage with communicating with them because humans, in their eyes, are a weaker, less intelligent race. They sometimes treated NHR agents as pets."

"They really don't sound like a pleasant bunch at all," Aunt Pam said matter-of-factly. "But after the craziness that those Dark Ones caused and how they coerced my husband to leak out that top secret government information, I feel it is our duty to fight back for what they have done. Earth is my home. They have tainted our world."

"You're right," Shane agreed. "If you and Genesis believed that the Whites could help us, then let's find a way in."

"I think I may have actually found that way in!" Jesse said excitedly. "Look at this! There is a flat metal foundation under where the rock that I accidently knocked over, was sitting."

Everyone gathered around Jesse to see what he was talking about. Manuel got on his knees and wiped away excess snow that was covering the metal surface. There were strange symbols that looked like Egyptian hieroglyphics.

"Can you read that?" Shane asked Manuel.

"No," Manuel said. "But these symbols are from the Whites. They are here."

"Is this some kind of entrance?" Shane asked.

"Yes, but to open it we need to decipher the language," Manuel said.

There were three symbols etched cleanly on the metal surface, which was a bronze color. The first symbol was a square with what looked like a person trapped inside a box. The figure inside the square had a head, legs, and arms. The second symbol had a weapon that looked like a sword inside a circle. The third and final symbol was a triangle with a circle inside it and short lines around it.

"The third symbol—is that the sun?" Shane asked.

"It is," Manuel said. "And the one in the middle, the second one, is a weapon."

"The first one is a person who looks to be enclosed in a box," Caroline said.

"It symbolizes a prison," Manuel said. "I think the message is actually quite clear. The figure in the box represents an enemy. The weapon is how they kill that enemy. The sun, however, can represent light, a God, or warmth. I'm not entirely sure."

"This is going to sound weird," Shane said while unclasping his necklace from around his neck, "but it appears as though those symbols represent my necklace."

"Interesting," Manuel said mysteriously.

"There was a dark figure trapped inside it," Shane explained. "We saw him escape into the sky when he saved us back at Sector 1 from the Dark Ones. The necklace is also a weapon. It's my weapon and it is what killed Noom, the king of the Dark Ones. And it gets its power from the sun or any kind of light."

"You really are the Bright One," A voice said from behind Shane that made him jump.

Apparently he was the only one that heard the voice. Shane turned around and saw Ryker standing before him.

"Don't give me away, and don't say a word," Ryker said. "I came to this time period in your life to talk to you about what you are about to do. If you go about this right, the Whites will be an asset to you, but if you are not careful, it could be detrimental. The symbols signify a way to enter. The middle symbol shows a weapon. A weapon that is used to kill their mortal enemy is the key to enter their cavern. The Whites have their own weapons that they use to fight the Dark Ones and that is how they access their own cave. You, Shane, have that necklace which has knowingly killed Noom. The metal surface will register your weapons memory. It will read it like a story and it will grant you access to the depths and the lair below. That will be the first sign that the Whites will be able to begin to give you their trust. The necklace will prove to them your worth but you must be careful because they are quick and smart. The Whites know there is a legend behind your necklace and they will want to know what it is. You must tell them that you have not earned the right to that secret, but when you do you will gladly share it with them. The way to learn this secret is to stop the Dark Ones once and for all. Every single one of them. Good luck. I must head back to the Cosmos."

Ryker disappeared into thin air.

"Earth to Shane," Jesse said waving his hands in front of Shane.

"Sorry," Shane said. "I just had a moment of realization. I think my necklace can get us in. I have a hunch that because it is a weapon that has been used to kill their mortal enemy, it will give us way into their lair. It will also help them trust us. It's brilliant too if you think about it because the Dark Ones would never be able to enter their layer because they are the enemy."

"Did you come up with that on your own?" Manuel asked sounding impressed.

"A hunch helped me," Shane said more to himself than to the others.

Shane walked over to the bronze metal plate and placed his necklace on top of it.

"Nothing happened," Alice said after a few tense seconds.

"Maybe that's not what the symbols mean," Penny said.

Shane did not respond. He kept quiet and concentrated hard on his necklace. He reached for it and picked it up off the metal plate. He took a deep breath and sighed.

"It was a good theory," Manuel said.

Shane put the necklace back on over his head. It rested on the middle of his chest. He paced back and forth and kicked some snow out of frustration. He could not understand why Ryker was wrong.

"Are you ok?" Caroline asked. "No need to beat yourself up over the first attempt and idea to open this entrance."

"My necklace's power has been drained," Shane said. "The being that was living inside it has gone making this crystal ordinary."

Shane realized that because his necklace was out of commission, so were its memories, which he believed the dark guardian that protected them took with him when he flew up into the sky.

"Penny!" Shane said so suddenly that it made everyone jump. "Pass me the Lighting Rod that Ryker gave you."

"Here," Penny said, handing him over the thin, silver rod.

Shane held it up to the sky and then slowly placed it on top of the bronze plate.

"You used this weapon to harm Sunev," Shane said. "This has to work."

Once again, nothing out of the ordinary happened. The weapon rested on top of the metal plate unperturbed.

"Another good guess," Manuel admitted.

"I'm pretty sure my necklace would have worked if it was still black and had the power of the light still," Shane said.

He walked back over to the plate and examined it with his gloved finger. Shane decided to take off his silver gloves, which were part of the body suit, by unbuttoning the buttons on his sleeves that connected the gloves to the rest of the suit.

Shane's hand felt as though he had dipped it into an ice, cold bucket of water. Shane put his hand on the bronze metal plate and instantly something happened.

"Whoah!" Manuel said as the bronze plate began to melt away into the snow leaving behind a dark hole into the ground.

"You opened it!" Penny said and she hugged Shane. "But how?"

"I'm the weapon," Shane deduced. "I stopped Noom. I possess the necklace. I'm the Bright One."

"The Dark Ones cannot possess you. That makes you special and an asset. They Whites will have no choice but to trust you," Manuel said. "You are the weapon of hope."

"So do we just jump into that hole?" Aunt Pam asked.

"Shane, you lead the way," Manuel said.

Shane looked into the hole. It looked as though the entrance was a pipe and it sloped down as if it were some kind of slide.

"I'll go first," Shane said, and he jumped into the hole.

In an instant, wind was blowing through his hair and he enjoyed an exhilarating sliding sensation down the tube.

Chapter Nineteen:

Obstacles

The ride down the tube ended suddenly, and Shane flew off the end of it into a cavernous room that was dimly lit by a strange blue light. The light appeared to be coming off the rock itself. There were several stalactites and stalagmites made of ice. For a second, he was reminded of the terrain at Threa. Shane picked himself off the ground. The room was very cold, but because he was wearing the bodysuit that Manuel had given him, he could only feel the cold on his face. Shane rubbed his cheeks in an attempt to keep warm. He saw his breath fog before him with every inhalation and exhalation he took.

Manuel was the next person to arrive in the room. Penny followed shortly after. Once Aunt Pam, Caroline, Alice, and Jesse had tumbled onto the ground, they began walking to the opposite end of the cavern to what looked like the beginning of another cave.

"This place is very spooky," Caroline said.

"Ouch!" Jesse yelled.

Jesse had tripped over a large rock.

"It's very dim in here," Alice said. "I wish your necklace still worked, Shane."

"Yeah," Shane agreed. "Manuel, do you have any kind of light source from the ship to guide us?"

"I brought a crystal power source," Manuel said, and he pulled out a piece of black crystal from his jacket pocket that was glowing brightly. "It will do."

Manuel handed the crystal to Shane who had taken the lead of the group. Shane was about to enter the entrance to the cave, when his face smacked hard onto an invisible surface.

"Ugh!" Shane howled. "There's an invisible wall."

Manuel walked up to Shane and put his hand on the invisible surface.

"It feels like glass, but we cannot see it," Manuel said. "This material is invisible to Humanoid and human eyes. The Whites can see it though. There is probably some kind of way to open it, however, I'm unsure how."

Shane wiped the entire surface as if cleaning it for smudges while he tried to feel for anything that could give him an idea as to how to penetrate through.

"What if I throw a rock at it?" Jesse asked.

Shane ignored Jesse and pulled out his Light Rod that the Cosmos had given him.

"Stand back," He ordered to the group.

Everyone shifted a few steps back and Shane aimed the Light Rod at the surface. He produced a beam of light but as soon as it hit the surface, it disappeared through it.

Shane walked over to the entrance and felt the invisible wall. It was still intact and otherwise undamaged from the use of his weapon.

"What else can you tell us about the Whites?" Penny asked Manuel. "Are you familiar with their technology?"

"Some of it," Manuel said, "however as I mentioned earlier, they will have left obstacles and traps to protect them from unworthy beings. They feel that anyone that tries to get to them would only be worth their time if we could safely get through their obstacles."

"This must be one then," Penny said smartly. "If only a White can see this, then we are screwed. But there must be a way for us to get through. We just need to use our minds. They admire intelligence right?"

"That they do," Manuel said. "These beings are extremely smart and dare I say it, much wiser and more advanced than the Greys or we Humanoids are."

"So," Shane began, "if we could see this invisible wall, what would we see. It's flat, so there is no doorknob. The first entrance outside of this mountain allowed us in because I was worthy of opening it. Nothing happened when I touched this wall so there has to be another way. What if there is writing on it?"

"Not a bad guess," Penny said giving Shane a warm smile.

"How can you read what you cannot see, though?" Caroline added.

"How do the blind read?" Aunt Pam said while rubbing her arms out of apparent coldness.

"Braille," Alice said.

"The wall is flat," Shane said. "I tried to feel for even the smallest change in the surface."

"Fair enough, but the blind use their other senses," Aunt Pam said.

"Interesting," Manuel said as if looking at Aunt Pam for the first time. "The Whites have different senses than we do. They have amazing sight. They can hear very well. In fact, they can probably hear us right now. They can touch and taste. They don't smell. That sense is not needed for their survival. They also have telepathy. That is how they communicate to beings that do not speak their language."

Shane walked over to the entrance of the cave and instinctively said to himself in his mind, *I would like to pass. Would you give me access?*

Nothing happened, or so it seemed, yet when Shane put his hand on where the invisible surface was, his hand kept going through. With a rush of excitement, Shane walked straight into the cave.

"I did it!" Shane said. "I used my mind to get what I wanted. I said I would like to pass and asked for access. I was granted it."

"Great!" Penny said and she ran to Shane but smacked straight into the wall just as Shane had done earlier. "Ouch!"

"Use your mind to ask," Shane told Penny who began to rub her forehead.

Penny had done as Shane asked and was also able to walk through the surface.

"Come on!" Shane said excitedly to the rest of the group. "Ask for permission to pass."

Every single one of them was able to enter the cave. Their discovery of how to enter had worked like a charm. Shane led the group into the hole of the cave. The cave was very tight so they had to walk in a single file.

"Everyone grab hands with the person behind you," Shane ordered. "I'll lead with the light."

They walked through the cramped dark cave for what felt like ages.

"Is it a bad time to admit I have claustrophobia?" Caroline said.

"I think so," Jesse added.

"I'm a bit scared to come face-to-face with these creatures," Alice said.

"I would highly advise you not think of them as creatures," Manuel urged. "Think of them as something greater than your existence. It's about stroking their ego to get them to even give us the time of day and also making them feel safe."

"I'm still afraid of them," Alice said.

"I think we are almost out of this tiny tunnel!" Shane said excitedly. "Yes the end is—"

Shane's words were cut off as he fell off a ledge to a six foot drop below. The crystal he was holding tumbled a few feet away from his hand, but it lit the entire room he had entered.

"Are you ok?" Penny yelled worriedly, and her voice echoed in the room.

"Ugh," Shane moaned. "I'm fine. That hurt though. Good thing I let go of your hand before falling."

"Charming," Penny said trying to make light of Shane's good fortune of only falling a few feet.

The rest of the party carefully jumped down to meet Shane in the room. Aunt Pam struggled a bit, but Manuel was able to help her slide down as gracefully as possible.

"Is it me or did the temperature get colder?" Alice shivered.

"It is significantly colder in here than in that tunnel," Caroline added.

"AHHHH!" Aunt Pam yelled.

Her echo bounced all around the walls.

"Shh!" Manuel snapped. "What happened?"

"Bones!" Aunt Pam cried pointing at the skeleton of a tall creature.

The bones were not human. The skull of the deceased creature had a long snout and large sockets where its eyes once were.

"What the hell is that?" Jesse said.

"You mean, what was that," Shane corrected him.

"That everyone," Manuel addressed the group, "was a Reptilian. The ancestors of the Greys. The beings that cloned and created the Greys, that is."

"Why was it tethered to the wall?" Shane asked after first noticing that its arms were in shackles that were connected to charcoal colored chains that were attached to the wall of the room.

"This place looks like a torture chamber," Shane said.

"The Reptilians are extinct," Manuel said. "The Greys thrived on thanks to them, but they also became their enemy. The Whites despised the Reptilians as well for interfering on Earth when they were trying to first explore it. However, they were also afraid of them too. I think the Whites were able to find a way to overpower the Reptilians. This one might have been a pet to them or they used it as an obstacle to attack anyone that came through this room."

"Well I'm so glad we do not have to deal with it," Shane said. "But how did it die?"

"By a knife," Manuel said. "I found this in its rib cage."

Manuel pulled out a small knife from the skeleton.

"It looks manmade," Manuel said. "A human must have been through here. But as the body has decayed, this Reptilian died long ago."

"A human was able to come through here?" Shane said. "How?"

"That is my first question too," Manuel said. "It must be someone who was worthy to the Whites some how."

"Should we keep on walking?" Penny said pointing to a door at the other end of the room.

"Yes," Shane said.

Shane picked up the crystal and led the way to the door, which was left ajar and unlocked. He opened it, and as soon as he did, the ceiling of the room began to dimly glow blue.

The room's walls were tiles stacked on the left and right side of the room from the ground to the ceiling. Each tile had a picture depicted on it with a symbol on the bottom of the picture. There were thousands of tiles with symbols all over the walls much like the one at the entrance into the mountain.

"Do we need to decipher all of these?" Shane said to Manuel.

"I am unsure," Manuel admitted.

"What are those?" Caroline asked pointing at three pyramids in the center of the room.

"Weird," Shane said, and he walked up to the three pyramids at the end of the room.

The pyramids were made of solid gold.

"They look like the famous pyramids from Giza in Egypt," Alice said.

233

"That's not a coincidence," Manuel said. "The Whites helped the Egyptians build those pyramids. I learned that during my talks with fellow NHR agents who were working and communicating with the Whites."

"That changes history!" Jesse said.

"Obviously a lot of history has been changed since the leak of the Moonshadow files," Shane said coming off much more rude than he meant to.

Alice gave Shane a dark look, but remained silent.

"Well, yes, that is true," Jesse said. "But how many other world wonders are really wonders from another world? What else in our history of mankind has been shaped by these—creatures?"

"Once again, do not think of them as creatures," Manuel said. "That is insulting. The Whites played a pivotal role in shaping mankind. I know bits and pieces, but I want to learn more about them. The Greys helped in the last century, but the Whites are older, wiser, and have been around Earth for centuries just like the Greys' ancestors, the Reptilians."

"I don't see any other way out of this room," Shane said.

"Dead end?" Caroline said.

"There has to be a way out," Shane replied. "We just need to figure it out."

Penny began pacing up and down the room. She was taking in the symbols and scratching her head as she thought. Shane examined the pyramid with Manuel.

"It's pretty much an exact replica of the pyramids," Shane said.

"Almost," Manuel said.

Shane knocked on the pyramid only to discover it was solid. Alice, Jesse, and Caroline sat on the floor to rest. Aunt Pam was also examining the symbols, but kept to herself.

"Hold on a minute!" Penny said suddenly.

"What is it?" Manuel asked.

"I think the symbols are a timeline of Earth," Penny said. "They appear to look ancient like hieroglyphics, but some of these symbols depict modern things such as cars and airplanes."

"Oh they do," Shane said. "And it ends here with…"

Shane placed his hand over a symbol of what looked like Dark Ones flying over Earth. It was the last symbol and there were empty spaces after it. The symbol before that one showed a square object over a city skyline.

"That was the incident in Times Square," Shane said. "This is some kind of historical map that shows big events that changed Earth. Look over there just a few squares down is a symbol of an airplane crashing into twin towers. September 11…"

"There's more historical symbols too," Penny said. "I see Roswell, Pearl Harbor, the first landing on the moon even!"

"It's like a timeline of Earth," Manuel said. "Look over here! There's one of a ship crashing near an ocean. If I have my time period correct, that must have been your crash onto Earth when you returned back, Shane."

"The day of our wedding," Alice said to herself, but loud enough for all to hear. "This wall is still being updated. Someone definitely lives here."

"What is the first one then? The beginning of Earth?" Jesse asked.

Shane turned around and ran to the other wall of the room on the complete opposite corner. He found the very first tile of the timeline. There was just a figure of a person on it and no symbol below it. The next symbol showed that same figure with a few other shorter figures around him.

"What does it mean?" Penny said as if reading Shane's mind.

"There was a leader and that leader had followers," Shane guessed.

"This map starts at a specific time on Earth though," Manuel said. "There are no mentions of the dinosaurs or even the

Egyptians, even though this very room we are in has a model of their pyramids made of gold."

"Wait a minute," Alice said taking a closer look at the first tile. "This map is only an A.D. time period and not B.C."

"Whoah," Shane said. "This could contradict the fallen religions. After all, many lost faith in religion when they learned that government had a huge cover up. Could that figure be Jesus?"

"Yes," Manuel said.

"I've never really talked religion with you," Shane said to Manuel. "Can you tell me what you know about it?"

"The Greys and Humanoids do not have anything to do with religion, unless you count that their existence to the civilian world population of Earth caused them to disbelieve anything they were taught. Mass chaos has broken out and the Dark Ones are running free now."

"The Whites know something," Shane deduced. "They must. There's some kind of connection between all these events. The Cosmos said they helped pave our destiny, but who created destiny before the Cosmos even formed since they are from the future? The past happened, at one point, unperturbed by the future."

"Excellent point," Manuel said sounding impressed. "From what Dimitri filled me in on, the Cosmos of Destiny want to fix the flaws from the mistakes of Earth's past, which has led it down the road it is on now."

"When I visited the Cosmos of Destiny, Earth no longer existed," Shane said. "Maybe I'm supposed to be the one to stop it from its extinction in the future."

"So we figured out what the hieroglyphics represent," Penny said. "Even if we cannot read the symbols below each one, the pictures are self-explanatory. But where is the way out of this room?"

"Hey everyone!" Jesse said suddenly. "Come over here to this tile. I swore it was glowing blue."

Everyone walked over to where Jesse was. There was a tile that he was pointing at that looked like a campfire. The image depicted flames over logs.

"Is this the discovery of fire?" Caroline said thoughtfully.

"It can't be," Penny said. "Fire was definitely around in the B.C. era."

"Very good point," Manuel said.

"This tile is out of place," Shane deduced. "It does not belong in this time period in which this room is dedicated to. It represents the last two millenniums and the present."

"You said it was glowing?" Manuel asked Jesse.

"I thought it did. Maybe it was a trick of the light from Shane's crystal," Jesse answered.

Shane put the crystal in his pocket, and the whole room fell dark except for the dimly lit blue light in the ceiling.

"There!" Aunt Pam said. "I just saw that tile glow blue!"

"Just as I suspected," Shane said. "You can see it better in the dark."

"It's only glowing every few minutes and only for a second," Manuel said. "It's to grab your attention. It is a clue."

Shane pulled the crystal back out and the light lit up the room again. He put his had on the tile and felt that it was loose and slightly raised out of the wall unlike the rest of the tiles. Shane put his fingers around the square tile and gently wiggled it. The tile became loose until it was freed from the wall.

"Wow," Caroline said.

"It's meant to be pulled off," Shane said. "Fire..."

"Is that a button?" Penny asked while pointing to a small raised circle that looked as if it was engraved on the wall where the fire tile was once resting.

"Maybe," Manuel said. "Should I push it?"

"Yes," Shane said.

Manuel touched the button gently with his index finger. A fire erupted from behind them all around the three pyramids. The temperature in the room rose exponentially causing everyone to shield their faces as the bodysuits were helping in protecting them from the heat.

"It's a trap!" Jesse yelled running to the opposite side of the room to put enough space between him and the fire.

Everyone else decided to run to where Jesse was standing to escape the fire, which kept burning strongly.

"It looks like it's controlled," Shane said. "The fire isn't spreading."

"It's not a normal fire," Manuel said. "It feels much hotter. Can you feel that?"

"We're going to bake in here. Feels like an oven," Aunt Pam cried.

The fire licked the pyramid as the flames rose higher until it looked like it was starting to melt.

"The gold is melting!" Alice said in shock.

The pyramids began to twist and warp into a puddle of gold liquid unnaturally fast. The fire stopped abruptly leaving the room's temperature to drop once more.

The gold liquid on the ground began to drain into the ground. Once it had fallen through what turned out to be a hole, the group gathered around it to investigate.

"It appears to be another tube," Shane said.

Shane pocketed the tile for safekeeping. He felt as though he needed to take it with him as they continued on their journey.

"Want me to go first this time?" Penny asked.

"You're quite brave," Shane said admiringly. "If you insist. I'll follow behind you."

Penny jumped into the hole and slide down the tube. Shane jumped a few seconds right after her and wind gushed through his dirty blonde hair as it took several twists and turns. He started to feel queasy from the abrupt turns. He kept picking up speed and wind all at the same time. It felt as though it was never ending.

Shane could hear screaming from behind him. It sounded like Alice was not enjoying the slide down deeper into the mountain. At last the tube ended and Shane shot out of it into another room. He looked down, and his heart dropped. They were in a large well that dropped about five hundred feet further to what looked like a pool of water below. The water was glowing blue. Just as he thought he was about to drop to it, he realized that his fall was slowing and he saw Penny flying up towards him.

"This is amazing!" Penny shouted. "There is a gust of wind blowing from the water below. Not sure where it's coming from, but it appears as if it magically starts from thin air!"

"We're flying!" Shane shouted as well.

The rest of the group fell into the giant well and were immediately confused by the sudden appearance of their ability to fly in what reminded Shane of indoor skydiving.

"I'm going to be sick," Alice said, and she ended up throwing up to the side, which was fortunate enough because it flew up high above her as there was a gust of wind holding them up.

"Good thing this wind broke our fall," Jesse said. "Now what Shane?"

"Where did that gold liquid go?" Penny asked.

"I think it fell into the water," Shane said. "I can see something shining at the bottom, but we are too high up for me to tell what it is. I don't even know where this wind is coming from. The only way forward is through the water."

"The water is rising!" Manuel shouted. "We are going to drown!"

The water began to fill up the well. It was getting closer and closer to them, yet the wind was still blowing and keeping them afloat.

"Wind is air, air is oxygen…" Shane said thinking about what this room's challenge presented to them. "We need air to breath. What to do, what to do…"

"Look!" Caroline said pointing to a certain point on the wall of the well. "Is that a tile?"

Shane began to flap his arms as if he were swimming through the wind. Surprisingly his actions were helping him propel forward to the wall. Manuel mimicked his actions and propelled himself to the tile as well.

"There is a symbol and a picture on it. It's a cloud with lines moving in the same direction," Shane said.

"Wind," Manuel said.

"Yes," Shane replied. "I'm starting to think there is a pattern. There are four elements on this planet. Fire, Wind…"

Shane pointed below to the rising water.

"Water," He continued, "and Earth."

"Fascinating," Manuel said. "That would make sense. The Whites admired the elements of this planet because their planet lacked most of them."

Shane pulled the tile out of the wall and pocketed it in his jumpsuit where the fire one was resting. There was another small button beneath where the tile once hung. Shane quickly pressed it and suddenly the gust of wind picked up and pushed them all the way to the ceiling of the well.

"The only option is to go back up that tunnel!" Penny said. "We'll drown!"

"What the hell are those?" Jesse said pointing at what looked like golden rings.

"There are exactly six rings," Shane said. "Enough for all of us."

"Grab them!" Caroline said. "What other option do we have? The water is about to fill up this well."

Shane was the first to reach for one of the rings. It was the perfect size to put over his head. Instinctively, he put it around his neck and wore it. The sensation that happened next was unlike anything Shane had ever experienced. It was as if the gust of wind that was keeping them afloat was now coursing through his skin and into his lungs. It was the most bizarre sensation to him. It felt as though the ring had some kind of power to make him breathe without having to open his mouth. Immediately it was evident to him that the rings would help them to breathe under water.

"Put the rings on!" Shane ordered. "Around your neck! It will help you breath."

Everyone reached for a ring and wore them around their necks like some kind of awkward piece of costume jewelry. Penny fumbled with hers as her hair flew to her face by an unexpected extra rush of wind. She was able to grab the ring finally, but as soon as the ring touched the water, it slipped out of her hand and began to sink.

"Nooooo!" Penny panicked.

Shane immediately kicked his foot off the ceiling and fought the wind for about three feet until he was able to touch the water. The water pulled him under, and he immediately began to swim as fast as he could to the ring that was slowly sinking to the bottom.

He took one glance back and saw that everyone except for Penny had the rings over their necks. Manuel grabbed Penny's arm and gestured for her to hold her breath for as long as possible. He pulled her closer to where Shane was. Shane extended his fingers and made contact with the sinking golden ring. He grasped it hard and turned his torso in the water and kicked back so that he could meet Manuel halfway.

As soon as Shane reached Penny, he forced the ring over her head while Penny pulled her red hair up to allow for the ring to fall onto her neck. Penny's body exhaled and bubbles blew out of her mouth. The look on her eyes meant she had oxygen and could now breathe under water like the rest of the group.

Penny swam towards Shane and kissed him. When they broke apart, he gestured for the group to follow him. Shane once again took the lead and swam down into the depths of the well. He was fumbling for the crystal, which was in his pocket. When he pulled it out he dropped it and it sank down lighting the way down to the bottom.   Several hundred feet down the light stopped sinking.   It had hit the bottom of the well.   Luckily for the group, the water was mysteriously glowing blue so it gave off an eerie light.

The swim down felt like an eternity.   Shane was particularly good at swimming, but he looked back and saw that his Aunt was struggling.   Manuel was kind enough to let her put his arm around him so he could guide her down to the depths.

Shane took another look back and saw that Penny was now helping Caroline swim down.   He just realized that she was a few weeks pregnant and that type of strenuous activity was probably not the best for her.   Shane swam up to Caroline and put his arm around hers to help her along with Penny.

After what seemed like an hour, but in reality was probably about twenty minutes, they finally reached the bottom of the well. Shane reached for the crystal and put it back in his pocket.   The bottom of the well was made up of several pebble-sized rocks packed tightly together.   Shane patted the ground.   A few of the pebbles were looser than others.

What now? Is this a dead end? There has to be some kind of sign as to what we do next, Shane thought.

Shane was not expecting what happened next.   A soft-spoken voice answered him in his head.   It had a strange accent that sounded British, yet the dialect was slightly different.

Would you like me to help you? You've made it so far…

Who are you? Shane said in his mind.

In time, the voice responded. *You are him, aren't you? The Bright One?*

Yes, Shane said. *Are you one of the people that created this place in the mountain?*

In time. They told us you would come one day. They really know so much. They are part of the future. We've been expecting you. The only reason you were able to enter was because the door was designed for just you. Only your touch could bring you in. The rest of your party was allowed in out of courtesy. The voice explained.

What do I do now? Shane asked the voice in his head. He was beginning to think he was hallucinating.

To find the answer you need to dig a little deeper. You're just above the surface. If you are truly the one, we will meet.

Shane felt his mind become at ease. He realized that the voice inside his head had left and the communication was cut.

Shane looked around at the group who were all staring at him as if waiting for him to give them direction as to what to do.

Dig a little...deeper. Dig, Shane thought.

Shane began to shift the loose pebbles. The more he freed them from their confines, the easier it became to dig through them. The rest of the group followed Shane's lead, and they began to shift and move the rocks from the ground.

Penny pulled out her Light Rod and began to zap away some of the rocks, which instantly disintegrated into dust. Shane followed her lead and zapped away at the loose rocks. Their time was exponentially cut until at long last Shane gestured for Penny to stop once he saw something near the end of the small hole they created.

Shane shifted the rocks that were covering an object that caught his eye. It was a tile with waves.

Water, Shane said to himself. *Another element.*

With excitement, Shane lifted the tile and placed it in the opposite jacket pocket from where the fire and wind tiles were. Like the other tiles, a button was hidden behind where the water tile once rested. Shane pushed it. Instantly the entire well began to vibrate as if an earthquake was happening. Everyone had looks of fear on their faces. The water around them began to spin around as if it was being flushed out. Shane had realized then that the button he pressed caused the entire rocky floor to give way and crumble.

A large hole was left that looked as if it led into another tube. The water began to slowly drain down the hole all while pulling the six of the group with it.

Shane knew they could all breathe, but the pressure of the water on their bodies was intense. They began traveling fast down the tube. He was afraid of hitting the edges of it and getting hurt. Luckily, the current of the spinning water kept him from not hitting the edges.

They picked up speed, and then all of a sudden Shane fell face first into sand. The fall was soft, but then the five others landed on top of him. Jesse's leg smacked Shane's head and his face was pushed deeper into the sand.

The water that came from the well sank into the sand leaving them in a pool of mud. Shane took off his ring because he could no longer breathe with it on, as they were not under water. The rest of the group did the same. Shane rubbed his face from where he was kicked, then took in the room they were in. The ceiling was glowing blue and giving off a dim light.

"We're sinking!" Aunt Pam shrieked.

The sand had become quicksand after soaking in the large amount of water from the well. Shane was unable to feel his legs. Half of his body was already under the sand, and he was slowly sinking into the earth with the rest of his party.

Chapter Twenty:

The Four Elements

Shane looked over at Manuel and saw a look of horror on his face. His head sank below the sand and he was gone.

"NOOOO!" Shane yelled, and he attempted to swim in the sand to where Manuel was.

"The more you move, the deeper you sink," Penny advised Shane. "Stop moving."

"It's not helping," Alice retorted. "I have been still and I'm still sinking. However, I'm sinking much more slowly."

"What do we do?" Caroline cried. "Can you figure this one out Shane?"

Shane thought hard. He was not sure what his next step would be. The sand was coming up to his mouth and only his head remained above. Jesse and Aunt Pam had already gone under. Alice and Caroline began to cry hysterically and they too went under within seconds. Shane took a deep breath before the sand ate him up and he sank below the surface.

A minute later, Shane found himself falling onto dry dirt and landing on top of someone. He pulled out his crystal and the dark area he was in was lit. Everyone was there safe and sound.

"Shane!" Penny said. "You're kind of heavy."

"Sorry," Shane said, and he rolled off Penny. "What is this?"

They were in an underground crevasse of some sort. Shane looked up and saw the ceiling in which he fell through was the sand

245

they sank through, but it looked as though it was drying up and hardening. The ceiling began to glow dimly blue.

"We're buried alive!" Caroline cried. "And I'm starving. We are starving."

Caroline put her hand over her belly.

"What now?" Alice asked Shane.

"Well, it seems that the obstacles we have encountered have had something to do with the four elements on Earth," Shane said and he put up four fingers to count them off. "Fire, wind, water, and now…well…we are buried in earth."

"Is there a tile around here with a button we can press?" Jesse said while kicking around dirt as if something would be buried.

"This is our grave," Manuel said. "We must have failed and the Whites are burying us."

"I don't think so," Shane argued. "I think one of them was communicating with me telepathically. He helped me figure out that we needed to dig through those rocks in that well."

"Dig!" Penny said making Alice and Caroline jump. "Let's shoot our way out of here."

Penny pulled out the Light Rod.

"The only thing is," Shane said. "This place is designed to escape without the help of a weapon. Even though digging by hand would have taken ages, we could have easily escaped from the well without the Light Rods."

"Let's not endanger ourselves," Manuel said. "We could cause this place to cave in on us and really bury us."

"Do you think we need to dig our way out of this hole?" Aunt Pam asked.

"That's the only possible way I can think of," Shane answered.

"As soon as we start digging, that dirt will give in," Jesse said. "It looks like it is no longer mud anymore."

Shane noticed something in a corner of the underground area they were in. There was a piece of rolled up paper wrapped in string. Shane grabbed it and unwrapped the string.

"That wasn't there before," Manuel said. "It must have appeared out of thin air."

"Nothing is as it seems here," Caroline chimed in. "I would not be surprised."

Shane opened the paper and saw a message in English written on it. He read it aloud:

"What happens when you die? Do you fly above the sky? Why bury your body underground and forgotten? Will not the bugs and worms make you rotten? You cannot claw your way out. You are dead, no one can hear you shout. In your chest, there beats a heart. Where will your soul go to depart? Would you like to find out the answer? Death is but a cold-blooded dancer. Let death take you to that place. Where a God has a face…"

"What the hell does that mean?" Alice said. "That's very creepy. It sounds like whoever put this place together, wants us dead."

"Admittedly, the text is disturbing," Manuel said.

"Is that some kind of riddle?" Penny questioned. "It sounds like we need to figure out what the message is referring to."

"In human culture, people are buried when they die," Shane said. "Or cremated. But religious teachings have always said there was a beyond. However, learning who I was and where I came from, made me question human beliefs in religions. Is there really a God? The place this text refers to is heaven."

The cavern they were in began to shake. Everyone dropped to the ground and braced for the worst. Shane took a look up at the ceiling expecting it to collapse and fall, but it never happened.

The paper where the text was written on, transformed into a tile that had a symbol with a picture of what looked to be a mountain. It represented earth, the fourth element.

"We did it!" Shane punched the air. "We figured out the riddle. It was not that hard though."

"Where is the button?" Penny asked. "Before, the tiles were stuck on some kind of surface with the button concealed under it."

Shane turned the tile in his hand and saw that there was a small button behind it. Shane raised the tile up in the air to show the group. They all clapped with excitement, and Shane pushed the button.

The ground beneath them dissolved into nothing and they all immediately fell into a much larger tube, and were once again sliding around deeper into the mountain.

"I hate this!" Caroline yelled as they slid down through the dark tube.

It was over before they knew it. They all fell on top of each other once again into a large empty room that was lit by a blue ceiling. The room was magnificent compared to the other rooms they had encountered. The walls were made of stone. In front of them was a giant stone door with two columns. There was a column on the right and one on the left. The door was made of some kind of metal substance. There was a large square divided into four smaller squares inside it, engraved on the door.

Shane walked quickly up to the door then heard a strange growl. He looked up and saw a large cage dangling from a chain. It was being lowered slowly into the chamber they were in.

"Oh my goodness!" Penny shrieked.

"A Dark One!" Aunt Pam cried.

Inside the cage was an angry-looking Dark One in its true form flapping its wings madly. It had its claws wrapped around the bars of the cage.

"Is this place actually run by the Dark Ones?" Shane said to Manuel.

"It appears as if that Dark One is prisoner, don't you think?" Manuel said, although he did not sound so sure of himself.

The cage opened on its own accord and the Dark One flew out of it. It appeared as if it was more interested in finding a way to escape. It realized it could not fit through the tube that the group fell through, and then turned around and attempted to break down the door with the square on it.

"Let me out!" The Dark One hissed. "I will rip you to shreds for entrapping me like some common pet!"

The Dark One kept punching the door with its fists, but nothing happened to it. The door remained solid and stable.

It turned its angry red eyes and saw Shane.

"You!" It shrieked and it flew straight at Shane, but Shane was prepared and shot the Dark One right in the eyes with the Light Rod.

Shane dodged out of the way as the Dark One came crashing to the ground and hit its head on the wall. Penny pulled out her Light Rod and shot both of its wings with a beam of light. The Dark One screeched so loud, everyone had to cover their ears. Shane felt his head pound as if it were about to explode by the intensity of the screech.

"Kill it!" Manuel said.

"Ready?" Shane mouthed to Penny because he knew she could not hear him.

Penny nodded and both of them shot beams of light at the Dark One. It flailed around hopelessly in pain. Shane and Penny focused their light on the forehead of the Dark One because it seemed to be giving it the most agony. After what seemed like a minute, smoke began to billow out of the forehead as the light created a hole through it. The Dark One let out one final screech and keeled over without moving another muscle.

"Is it dead?" Penny said.

"I think so," Shane said as the body of the Dark One began to smoke and shrivel up into dust. "Well, I guess that answers your question."

"Why was there a Dark One in here?" Alice asked.

"The Whites must have trapped one," Manuel said. "I would not be surprised if they were studying it."

"It looked more like they were using it as a final obstacle," Shane said. "Anyways, check out that door. There's a square on it with four panels that look to be the size of the four tiles I collected. I had a hunch I should bring them with me."

Shane placed the four element tiles on the door. They fit perfectly and snug. Once they were all one, they all began to glow blue and as if they were magical. They blended into the door and were now a part of it. They were no longer tiles, but smooth images engraved on the door.

The door began to open slowly. Shane stepped back out of caution for the unknown beyond the door. He tightly gripped his Light Rod and gestured for the group to follow him.

The room they entered was much colder than the chamber they were in. There was a light breeze, which was unnatural because they were in an enclosed space.

"Where's the wind coming from?" Jesse said more to himself than anyone.

"This place is creepy," Caroline said.

The room was smaller than the chamber outside of the door, but it was still vast. They walked to the other end of it and saw an archway that led into another room. As soon as they all entered, flames shot up from the ground and engulfed them.

Aunt Pam, Alice, and Caroline all screamed in unison. Shane instinctively jumped around, then stopped when he realized that the flames were neither hot nor burning them.

"This is crazy!" Alice said after she realized that the fire was harmless. "We can walk through this."

"I'm guessing that other room over there is going to be something with water or earth," Shane said.

The group walked through the flames and into another room that had an archway entrance as well. This room had trees, sand, and rocks. It looked as if they were outdoors.

"Earth," Shane mumbled.

"Once again, nothing life threatening here," Alice said.

The group commenced to the next room and when they entered it began to rain lazily from the ceiling. The water was ghost-like, and it went right through everyone, without getting them wet.

"And we are staying dry here," Shane said.

Ahead of them was another archway. Shane walked over to it with a nervous feeling. He felt as though this final room was the end of the obstacles. It felt as if they had been traveling to the bottom of the interior of the mountain for months.

"Ready?" Shane whispered to Manuel while gripping his Light Rod.

"Let's hope we've proven ourselves," Manuel said.

"I'll go in first," Shane said.

Shane stepped forward and proceeded to walk under the archway. The next room confused Shane at first. It was as if he had walked into a forest and was no longer inside of the mountain. There were giant trees and a light breeze causing the branches to sway lazily. He looked up at the ceiling and could see stars, which were giving off light to the entire room.

"Are we outside?" Penny asked as her and the rest of the group walked in.

"There's no way that is possible," Shane said. "But then again, everything inside this mountain was not even humanly possible."

"It feels so peaceful," Aunt Pam muttered.

The ground had well kept green grass that reminded Shane of a golf course. The walls on all sides of the enclosure are what made this forest seem unnatural and proof that they were not outside. There was even a small pond inside the room that was filled with water, which was glowing blue.

Shane kept a slow pace as he walked through the trees to the other side of the room. It became slightly darker when they were under the cover of the trees. He could still feel the cold air against his cheeks. There were a few breaks in between the branches above them where light from the stars and even the moon would give way to the path they were on. A strange barking sound echoed through the trees, causing everyone to jump.

"Did you hear that?" Alice whispered.

"Was that a dog?" Caroline added.

"I'm not sure," Manuel chimed in. "Stay quiet. I do not like the feeling of this room."

"Guys—shh," Shane told the group while putting one index finger to his mouth. "There's someone over there."

In the distance, a tall figure was standing with its back facing them. It had long platinum blonde hair. Even at the distance they were from the figure, it was evident that it stood about eight feet tall. The figure turned around and looked at them.

"Ohhh," Caroline gasped and she covered her mouth quickly.

They had come face-to-face with one of the Whites. It was a female. She had a face that was something Shane had never seen before. In her own way, she was beautiful, yet mystical. She seemed almost unreal or like a dream. Her face was very white, almost pearl-like. The skin on her face looked tight and smooth. Her eyes were slightly larger than a human's, and they were a bright, crystal blue color. Her hair fell to her shoulders and was slicked back and perfect. There was not a loose strand or frizz on it. Her body was very slim and much like a human she had breasts. She wore a body suit, similar to the one that Manuel lent to the group. Her suit was silver in color and was form fitting all over her body like spandex.

She proceeded to slowly walk in their direction. It appeared as though she was using caution with every step she took. She had her eyes locked on only Shane. The closer she was, the higher Shane would have to look up because of her height to make eye contact.

At last she stopped about ten feet away from Shane and the rest of the group. She opened her mouth and let out a strange barking sound that seemed unnatural and even wild compared to her impeccable image. Shane could see that both Alice and Caroline were shaking in fear because the sounds she made seemed threatening. Jesse was backing away slightly. Both Aunt Pam and Manuel, however, were standing still with confidence. Shane could not tell what emotions Penny was feeling. She looked poised and ready, but the slight quiver of her eyebrow gave off a look of nervousness.

"My name is Shane Baker," Shane addressed the White.

The White opened its mouth and more barking sounds came out.

"I don't think she speaks English," Penny said.

Shane reached his hand out as if to shake the Whites hand. It was a mistake. The White quickly pulled out a pencil like object and pointed it at him threateningly. Shane did not flinch, even though it did scare him. He wanted to show the White that he was not afraid of her.

"Get on your knees," Manuel whispered to Shane. "Just show her some kind of respect. Actually, we all should."

Shane got on one knee, and the rest of the group followed. The White stared at them curiously and fidgeted with the object in her hands.

"We mean you no harm," Shane said softly and very slowly.

The White barked again with its strange voice. Shane could feel Penny begin to shiver out of fear. She was no longer able to hold her courageous poise.

Do you communicate telepathically? Shane thought in his head remembering the strange voice he spoke with at the well.

Yes, but we also have a means to translate our languages to understand each other, the White said in Shane's head.

The White pulled a silver ring out of thin air and placed it over her head as if it were a necklace. It reminded Shane of the rings that helped them breathe under water.

"You've made it through our challenges," The White said. "It appears as if you have proven your worth and intelligence."

"She speaks English now?" Jesse whispered behind Shane.

"That ring around her neck is translating her language for us to understand," Shane whispered back.

"You mean her barks and cackles?" Jesse said sarcastically.

"Shush," Alice snapped at Jesse.

"Can you tell me your name?" Shane asked the White.

"Venus," The White said. "I was named after a planet in your solar system by your government. Our people do not have names as we do not see the need to define anyone with difference."

"I understand," Shane said. "That is very wise. Venus, why are you hiding in this mountain?"

"We came here by choice," Venus said. "We arrived when the Non-Human Relations agency disbanded several Earth years ago. We created these caverns with obstacles to protect us from the evils outside. Only those who are truly worthy would be able to enter. The only reason you were able to enter was because of your significance to the Cosmos."

"You know about the Cosmos of Destiny?" Shane said sounding impressed, and he added for the sake of stroking Venus' ego, "Your knowledge must be vast and great."

"Greater than yours, Humanoid," Venus said in a mocking way that sounded slightly derogatory. "I see you come with two other Humanoids and four humans. That is an interesting party with which you have arrived. It is also surprising that the humans were smart enough to survive with you as their leader."

"We all worked together," Shane said. "Humans are the reason for my existence. Their DNA lies within me."

"No need to lecture me, I'm quite aware," Venus said roughly as if Shane had insulted her.

"Please, we mean no disrespect," Manuel chimed in. "My name is Manuel. I worked with the NHR. I was posing as human to make sure that they would operate efficiently and safely. I was not assigned to the sector your people lived in, but I'm aware of your communication with the United States government. I worked with the Greys. Naturally."

"The Greys are extinct now because they were an inferior and non-intelligent race," Venus said.

"Yes, they—we are not as smart as you," Manuel said and Shane could tell he was biting his tongue, yet he knew that appeasing Venus was a priority.

"Why have you come?" Venus asked only Shane. "You are the Bright One, are you not?"

"I am the Bright One," Shane answered. "And truthfully I'm not even sure what that really means. Manuel here said he had a hunch we needed to find you. You can help us with this war against the Dark Ones. They are filth. They are our mortal enemy."

Venus' expression did not change, but the tone of her voice did when she spoke, "The Dark Ones are a threat to the universe. My people are outnumbered greatly. Humans stood no chance. Their population has dropped significantly. Eventually the Dark Ones will enslave the remaining living humans. I estimate there might be only a million humans left in the world out there. It is a significant decrease from the billions that populated this planet. I do not believe we can be helpful in stopping the filth. I do know that in this mountain, we are safe and untouchable."

"Venus," Manuel spoke up. "If I may address you. With great respect for your people and your intelligence, let me, the governor of Threa, be the first to say that we would like to become allies."

Venus walked closer to them. Jesse backed away suddenly and surprised Venus. She pulled out her weapon and Jesse was stunned. He passed out.

"Oh my God!" Alice yelled.

Venus was taken aback by Alice's yell and then stunned her too.

"Please," Shane said, once again on his knees, "do not hurt them. They are my friends."

"I did not trust them," Venus said. "You should be fortunate that they have only just been immobilized temporarily. I could have easily killed them."

"While I could never be on your level," Shane said, "I want it to be known that we could end this war of darkness. Together."

"You are the only one in this room who has real significance," Venus said bluntly. "You are the Bright One. You are a legend written in the stars."

Venus gestured up at the stars.

"I only met Genesis once," Venus said. "She made you. She was wiser than the Reptilians. She was the only Grey I ever trusted."

"You met her?" Shane asked with a feeling of surprise.

"Oh yes," Venus answered. "She was the one that killed that Reptilian in the obstacle course through which you came. The Reptilians enslaved the Greys, but only because they were created as clones at their hands. Genesis was the leader of the Greys. Vizar, the dead Reptilian whose skeleton you passed, was the king of the Reptilians. I had the pleasure of catching him ages ago. The president of the United States was what other alien races considered the leader of Earth because of his power and influence across the planet."

"Ours was killed recently," Shane said. "Sunev killed him."

"That is unfortunate," Venus said but she did not sound like she cared. "Sunev is the queen of the Dark Ones. Every race has a leader. Manuel, your governor of the Humanoids, is not the leader of your race. *You* are."

"Me?" Shane said while pointing at his chest.

Shane took a side-glance at Manuel who felt uncomfortable by this piece of information.

"You did not know?" Venus asked.

"Not necessarily," Shane admitted truthfully.

"He's young," Manuel jumped in. "I thought after we abandoned Earth we would not have to deal with the Dark Ones any longer—"

"Silence," Venus yelled at Manuel. "I sense greed in you."

"Shane, I helped Derek help you learn about your existence," Manuel pleaded. "I just felt you were too young to lead a group of people you were not born knowing existed."

"I agree," Shane said. "It would have been a heavy burden. You are forgiven."

"Really?" Manuel said with a sigh of relief.

"You are quite generous," Venus said to Shane. "I would have killed him on the spot."

"That's not the Humanoid way," Shane told Venus. "Our people's tactics differ. However, we all have one common enemy, so as of today, we are all the same."

"You do have the voice of a leader," Venus said. "The Visionary would be proud."

"You know of the Visionary then?" Shane asked.

"I thought we discussed that I had knowledge of the Cosmos of Destiny," Venus said rudely.

"Apologies," Shane replied. "The Visionary is the leader of the Cosmos of Destiny, yet I know nothing about him."

"No one does," Venus said. "His identity remains a mystery to us all."

"Apparently I'm the reason for the Cosmos of Destiny," Shane said. "It could be possible that the Visionary is me...in the future."

"That is possible," Venus said. "He is also the only one who knows why you are the Bright One—the one destined to bring light to the universe and fade the darkness. If you are him, then somehow you will learn the truth. I do know the legend as to why there is a Bright One, but as to why it is you, that's a mystery to me and my people."

"What is the legend?" Shane asked excitedly.

"Show me your necklace," Venus asked, but it sounded more like an order.

Shane pulled out his crystal necklace, which was still empty and white.

"The Visionary knows the legend of this crystal, and so do my people," Venus said as Shane handed her his necklace. "It's not black..."

"I can explain that," Shane said.

"No need," Venus said while feeling the crystal with her long skinny fingers. "He has left the crystal. He will return."

"You know about the guardian that was inside my crystal?" Shane asked.

"Guardian?" Venus replied. "He is more than a guardian. He's responsible for so much, yet he's quite mysterious even to us."

"What happened?" Jesse said.

Jesse had come out of his trance and was rubbing his forehead as if he had a massive headache. Alice was shifting around too and her eyes were slowly opening.

Shane ignored Jesse's question and continued, "Who is he?"

"He will tell you who he is, when he is ready," Venus said.

"I'm tired of everyone telling me things like that and not being able to fully give me an answer!" Shane said angrily making Venus jump and point her weapon at him. "I'm sorry Venus, I made a mistake. I was a little worked up with the stress of the unknown."

"I also know the legend of the crystal necklace," Manuel spoke up.

Venus looked at Manuel and studied him with her eyes for a few seconds. She looked as though she had smelled something foul as she gazed at him.

"Then you know that the necklace is everything?" Venus asked.

"Um," Manuel said while scratching his head. "The legend is that the crystal, a piece of Threa, has powers from the past that will choose the person who will wear it. That person it chooses is the only one who can survive a Dark One possession. The crystal will make the chosen one live for a very long time. It has the power of a star. I really shouldn't be telling Shane this. He needs to earn the right to learn about it."

"You're wrong," Venus taunted. "Genesis did not know the full legend behind the crystal. She only knew of the watered down version. And the necklace does not have the power of the star. The necklace posses powers of four elements. Those very elements are the ones you encountered in the obstacle course to our habitat grounds. Fire, water, earth, air. These elements are what make the planet Earth unique because they all exist here. Threa also has all those elements only because they were created and modified onto the planet from the Greys' ancestors' earlier visits to Earth. The elements' energies are engrained in the crystals that make up the planet's surface. That's why the Dark Ones wanted to take it over ages ago. Then they discovered where the elements came from—Earth. Our home world only has fire and air. What made Earth interesting to other civilizations like ourselves, the Dark Ones, the Reptilians, and the Greys, was that the four elements present in one world means life. Our race survives in our planet because of the resources we borrow from Earth. Why else does Earth house so many creatures? Because it has all four elements. Why was it important for the government to create the Noah's Ark Project? To save the uniqueness of planet Earth and various animals. Earth is the pearl in the vast expanse reaches of outer space. The Dark Ones know that and now in their true form, they can manifest those elements for themselves to continue their race and prevent its own extinction."

"So that is why they want our planet? That is why aliens have visited us?" Alice spoke up.

"The human spoke to me," Venus said, sounding offended. "Her rank is not great enough for me to care to answer."

Alice scowled at Venus' rude response, but Shane gave her a look that suggested she ignore her comments and let it pass as if it had not offended her.

"So why was Genesis wrong about the necklace?" Shane asked. "My friend Dimitri told me that the Dark Ones fear this crystal, and the crystals on Threa, because of their innate power to harvest light from distant stars and moons. That light could be unleashed to destroy them."

"That much is true," Venus said. "It does harvest light as you were taught; however, a normal crystal from your planet does not turn white."

"She's right," Manuel said. "I was wondering about that ever since it turned crystal clear. This necklace was not made on Threa, was it?"

259

"It was not," Venus said mysteriously and softly. "To answer your question, Shane, I can tell you why Genesis was wrong about it. Because when I gave her the necklace myself when she came to visit us here decades ago, I fed her an untrue story because she was not worthy of knowing the actual truth about it. I made her think it was made of the crystal from her home planet. I did ask her to make sure the necklace fell into the hands of the Bright One, the one who would be able to outlive a possession of a Dark One. The first person who could actually help thwart the darkness of the universe. And she followed my request because you have it."

"My Humanoid father gave it to me before he died," Shane said more to himself than to anyone in the room.

"Genesis gave it to him to give to you then," Venus replied.

Shane's eyes were distracted by a sudden appearance several figures walking behind Venus in the distance. Some were much taller than the others. When they came into the light from the ceiling of stars above, everyone shivered with nerves. There were about twenty Whites standing behind Venus. About half were male and the other half was female. There were even children in the group, and they were at least seven feet tall.

Venus turned around to address her people.

"Should we share the legend of the black crystal necklace with the Bright One? Will the Visionary mind?"

Chapter Twenty-One:

The Legend of the Black Crystal Necklace

Shane could see that Alice, Caroline, and Aunt Pam were shivering with either fright or because the room's temperature kept dropping and the skin on their faces was exposed to the elements. Penny's face was alert and attentive and Manuel had a dazed look about it that signified he was having issues dealing with the scenario in which they had found themselves.

"The Visionary would show himself now if he wanted to stop you from telling the legend," A male White said in the distance. "As he is from the future, this would have already happened."

"I have not yet decided in my mind if I am going to tell him or not," Venus responded.

"He would have already showed up as he would know before you would decide. Remember our destinies are paved as well," The male White said.

"Then I suppose I will have the privilege of telling you this fascinating tale, young Bright One," Venus said airily.

Venus reached into a pocket in her bodysuit and pulled out a large blue crystal.

"This is a very valuable piece of technology," Venus explained. "It looks like a diamond, but diamonds don't have the ability to show memories."

Venus awkwardly kneeled down with her long legs onto the ground. She used both of her hands to carefully place the diamond on the ground. The diamond was about the size of a regular dinner plate. Once it was flat on the ground, she touched the very tip of the diamond with her finger and a blue light emitted out of the tip and created a holographic world around the forest. It reminded Shane of Genesis's Communicator cone message, however this holographic image was much more intriguing. Eventually the bluish light became vivid and colorful as if they were in a television set.

A world of nothing but stars unfolded above them and it began to play like a movie. The image zoomed into what appeared to be one of the stars, but as the holographic image zoomed into that one particular ball of light, it turned out to be a crystalized planet that reminded Shane of Threa. The main difference was that this planet was made up of white crystals. The closer the image presented the planet, the more detailed it became with every zoom into it. Soon, the holographic image around them made it appear as if they were walking on that very planet made up of millions of bright white crystals.

Shane waved his hands around the hologram as if he could actually touch it. Venus gave him a look of disbelief as if she thought Shane believed he could actually touch the crystals.

"What are you showing us?" Shane finally asked because there was no more movement in the image.

"We call this white rock planet *Ab Aeterno*...from the beginning of time," Venus said.

Manuel and Shane exchanged shocked looks. Shane felt goose bumps running up his arms. Caroline absentmindedly grabbed Penny's hand as if she was afraid that the image before them would explode.

"Whoa," Jesse said in a barely audible whisper.

"The creation of the universe?" Shane asked Venus.

"Yes...and no," Venus said.

"Is this the Big Bang?" Penny asked out loud.

"The Big Bang theory is a human joke," Venus said. "A theory that is not true...at all. This is the beginning of the journey..."

"And what journey would that be?" Manuel asked.

Venus ignored Manuel and looked at Shane without saying anything for a few seconds.

Shane added, "Yes, what journey would that be?"

"The journey of life," Venus responded. "Your journey has been about discovering who and what you are, and how you are the perfect vessel against the oldest living creatures of the universe. How did we get here? Where did we come from? We Whites share the same curiosities and face the same questions that humans do. As well as Humanoids..."

"Well we were created by the Greys," Manuel said smartly. "The Greys were created by the Reptilians."

"Who created the Reptilians?" Venus asked. "Who created my people? Who created the humans? The Reptilians and the Whites may have shaped the consciousness and rise of the human culture, but we did not create them. We all share a very similar bond...a bond that is not DNA nor blood. A bond of existence and being."

"God?" Alice asked.

"God..." Venus gave Alice a stern look, "is what all civilizations consider a higher power. Whether civilizations thought Gods or beings of invaluable strength and intelligence monitored them, it is neither here nor there. Gods have been fashioned to all civilizations across the universe in some way, shape, or form. For humans, we are responsible for the Earthling's beliefs in a higher power."

"What do you mean?" Manuel said nearly dropping his jaw in surprise.

"Millenniums ago there were ancient cultures on this planet that my ancestors would visit," Venus began. "They saw us as Gods. We looked almost human, except we are taller and we have such a strange pigmentation to our skin that seems very, *holy*. The truth is, humans were not civilized. They were destined to become Earth's dominant and most intelligent specie, but that would take hundreds and thousands of years. We fashioned Christ. We sent him to your world to teach and show humans the unordinary. We deliberately changed the consciousness of human life and gave them a belief in a higher power that would forever keep them stable and civil. They learned of the fear of hell to prevent them from falling off the path of good. While not all humans were good, the majority were able to coexist harmoniously after hundreds and hundreds of years."

"Jesus was not real then?" Caroline asked.

"If you believe in something strongly, then it is as real as you and I," Venus said. "Without us helping the human race, it would have never become civilized. However, as the latest millennium approached in the 2000s, we realized that once again Earth would have a very difficult problem of overpopulation. The Greys were aware of the same issue that would happen. Both our civilizations came to Earth to borrow resources and help humans on different accounts, although separately. The Devil has risen, but the devil is not what religions have taught human culture. The Devil is Sunev...it is all the Dark Ones. The beginning of pure evil."

"My head is hurting trying to make sense of this," Shane said. "How can this be possible?"

"It took years and years of traveling and studying to learn what the meaning of life is," Venus said. "And we are very close to learning. It somehow has to do with all of our different races, the fashioning of Gods in our races to keep us in order, and something to do with the image we will continue to show you in this hologram. The legend of the black crystal necklace stems back to the *Ab Aeterno*. And I will explain how I came to be into possession of it and how I learned of the Bright One...you."

Shane's heart began to race. Ever since he learned about his identity as a Humanoid, he kept on encountering more and more deep secrets of his past, present, and future. It was as if at that moment he felt that he could actually be the Visionary of the Cosmos of Destiny.

The holographic image began to play before them again. The image panned to the ground and two feet were visible. The feet were walking into a two-foot deep pool of water. Shane looked down at Venus's legs and realized that the holographic image they were watching...

"It's your memory," Shane said.

"I did say the diamond has the ability to show memories," Venus answered rudely.

"Yes, of course," Shane tried to say with politeness. "So then we are not about to see the beginning of time then."

"You try and find me a living being who can give me that earliest memory and you might just be the king of the universe," Venus said sarcastically. "Now pay attention to my memory that is playing."

The image through Venus's point of view and what she was seeing out of her own eyes was still showing the room a view of the ground. Once she was out of the water, she was walking on the crystals. Several of them broke with every step she took. The image panned back up forward, and it was apparent that Venus was now looking up. In the distance, there was another pool, but instead of water there was fire. Venus began to run because the image was zooming in faster. She ran through the fire. Everyone, minus the Whites, jumped as the holographic, yet seemingly real flames, swept through them.

Once Venus had left the fire, they saw another pool in front of them that looked empty. As soon as Venus stepped into it, she looked down and it was as if some invisible force was pushing her back. She was struggling with some kind of barrier to walk forward.

"Air," Venus murmured.

Once she had walked out of the pool, there was another one ahead, and Shane was wondering what kind of earth would be inside.

"That one always fascinated me," Venus said as her holographic perspective showed the room what was in the pool.

There was dirt and a grass growing. Venus got to her knees and outstretched in the hologram before them, were her hands as she began to dig through the dirt and lift it up to her face as if she could smell it.

"It was the first time I felt earth. It was beautiful," Venus said. "I took some of it that day to our home planet."

"So this planet," Shane began, "apparently has all four elements."

Before Venus could answer, a strange figure appeared in the hologram. The image was blurry. But it looked like it was a tall person. They could make out a silhouette of a person. Its arms were moving around and making gestures.

"Why can't we make out that individual?" Manuel asked.

"His image can only be seen in real life, not in memories," Venus said. "But you have seen him before…"

"I have?" Shane asked unsure about what she meant.

"Watch," Venus ordered.

The blurry figure in the hologram raised both its arms. Dirt and grass began to float from the pool into a ball that was floating in between his hands, which he brought down and extended in front of his chest. Then a stream of flames flew into the ball apparently from the pool that Venus had walked through. The blurry figure was holding a ball of fire.

"This is beautiful," Penny whispered to Shane after she had released Caroline's hand to exchange it with his.

A stream of water flew into the fireball and then a blob of water formulated into a sphere in front of the figure. It began to grow bigger.

"It looks almost like a planet of water…" Shane gasped.

Then suddenly Venus fell face first into the ground. She lifted herself up and watched as an apparent gust of wind hit the ball of water and it flew up high into the sky, as it grew bigger. However, it flew far away into outer space and out of sight giving off the appearance of it becoming smaller with the distance.

"Fire is the core. Water is the ocean. Wind is the oxygen. The dirt completes the land," Venus said.

"Was that the creation of Earth?" Shane asked.

"Yes," Venus said. "But at the time I did not know to which galaxy it was sent off."

"Who was—was that the person who created life?" Shane began, but Venus gestured for him to stay quiet.

266

The holographic image continued playing and the blurry figure broke off a small piece of the white crystal plant and fashioned a gold chain out of thin air so that the crystal became a necklace.

The figure began to speak in Venus' language, so Venus translated it for Shane and his group.

"You will find the light in that world. You must help shape it so that our destinies are positive. The Bright One will live and be birthed through that world. This crystal necklace I have created will be the last remaining piece of creationism. This planet on which you have discovered in the center of the universe will fade away on this day forever. The four elements you have seen that have created that world, are engrained in this crystal. Save it. Keep it. It will restore the balance. The Dark Ones must never possess this. It has powers that will give them control of this universe. You must guard it, because guarding it means you are guarding my very being. I will be inside the necklace. The Bright One will be able to stop the Dark Ones. It's written in the Cosmos. Give the necklace to the Bright One's creator, as I, *your* creator, have given it to you."

The blurry figure transformed into what looked like a smoky cloud and it disappeared into the crystal necklace that Venus was holding. The white crystal turned into the shiny black crystal Shane remembered so well.

A large fire began to spread and encompass the entire white crystal planet. Venus had set off at a run into the direction in which she came from. In the distance was a disc shaped craft. She was in the craft, the next second as if she had teleported into it. Venus looked out of the window as the craft flew away and they saw the crystal planet disappear into flames, which extinguished on its own accord into nothingness.

The hologram image ended and Venus lifted the diamond and put it in her pocket.

"I'm surprised none of you asked how this could be my memory when it occurred billions of Earth years ago," Venus said looking around the room.

"Right!" Manuel said. "You cannot live that long."

"True," Venus said. "Something we never shared before with anyone outside of our civilization is that our souls are reincarnated and we are born again as someone different. This diamond technology we created can pull out memories from our past lives that have been forever lost—until now."

"Your people are amazing," Penny said. "You all are a very old race. I mean that with gratitude, respect, and with the utmost privilege to be in your presence."

"Thank you Humanoid," Venus said to Penny and it sounded almost pleasant.

"I appreciate you sharing this story with me," Shane said honestly. "I had no idea how much history and story was behind the crystal and how it contains the four elements of life."

"The honor is mine, Shane," Venus said. "Now you understand what I meant by how you've seen the entity that I spoke with on *Ab Aeterno.*"

"I do," Shane said. "He was a black figure. At first glance I thought he was a Dark One, but he was not evil. He protected me. He protected my friends. It is still a shock that a living soul has been housed in this crystal the entire time."

Shane took the crystal necklace off and held it in his hands. He caressed the white crystal.

"That planet," Shane said. "This is only last piece of it. Was that first planet...ever?"

"Yes," Venus said. "However, I would not call it a living world."

"That individual lived there, did he not?" Shane asked.

"He lives everywhere he wants to," Venus said. "He lives inside all of us. He's the link between us all. He created my people. He created your people that created your people that created you. He created worlds for us to explore. He allowed for different types of peoples to live separately and unaware of each other. We now have the answers that we've always asked and wondered."

"Who is he?" Shane asked. "Because he flew out of my crystal and left Earth."

"He is…" Venus began.

Venus fell to her knees and put her hands on her forehead with her elbows bent out side to side. The rest of the Whites behind her followed her lead.

"Shane," Venus said with her eyes closed. "It is now or never. The Whites have studied the stars created by that entity that resided in your necklace. They have finally aligned. The Cosmos of Destiny came to me one day and said we would meet and we would help you on your journey to the brightness. The Visionary is the last person to help tell you the story of our worlds and the universe. But the stars are aligned right now in this time period and now is the only time to stop the Dark Ones once and for all. Extinction of them—is the only way. That entity is the Creator…the one who is the reason for all of us standing here in this room today. Legends…folklore…tales…religions…they all refer to him as God. But God, is just a fashioned human word."

Chapter Twenty-Two:

Banding Together

Shane had to sit on the floor for a few minutes to take in what he had just been told. Aunt Pam was breathing very hard and had tears forming in her eyes. Manuel looked as though he did not believe he was alive. He kept looking at his hands and feeling his face as if discovering them for the first time.

"Humans always knew a higher power created them, or at least they hypothesized it," Venus began. "Should this really be a shock?"

"God was in my necklace the whole time?" Shane said dumbfounded.

"He is the Creator," Venus corrected him. "Religions have taught Earth of a God, so to speak, but you must eliminate that history from your mind and look at the Creator as your reason for being. Now you must think about why he chose to be united with you before you were even born and what your significance in the cosmos is. That is something I have been wondering."

"And the Visionary," Shane began. "Could I be him...in the future?"

"It is possible," Venus said. "It is almost certainly possible the more I've thought about it. The Visionary is the leader of the Cosmos of Destiny—a world far advanced than all of us and not even in existence in this current time period. It is a utopia. A place where there is no hate or evil. Everyone looks the same and is taught the same. There is no wealth or poverty. There is no difference in facial features or skin color. They are all one in the same.   It could be the only civilization meant to survive harmoniously but the Dark Ones have learned of their existence and they will try to get back to the Cosmos through a door."

"Venus," Shane said while getting back onto his feet, "as the Bright One, I invite you and your people to join us in the fight. Would you accept?"

Venus turned her back on Shane to address the other Whites in the room.

"On this day, the day of the alignment of the stars and our planets, I declare a bond between humans—Earth's mankind. I would also like to declare a bond between the Humanoids, heirs of the Grey race. Earth is the focal point of the universe right now because it was created long ago to bring us together. I saw it created from the four powerful elements. My past lives searched for decades for it. My soul is old, but my mind is fresher today than it has been before."

Venus turned back to Shane and then addressed Manuel.

"Manuel, you will have to eventually come to terms with the fact that Shane is the rightful leader of the Humanoids. As you currently command post on Threa, we would like to offer you the use of our technology to send your people a message to come to Earth and help us. Do you accept?"

Manuel shifted uncomfortably then spoke, "I rightfully agree that Shane is the true leader. He has earned it and was meant for it. I was wrong for believing he was not ready, but he is not that young anymore. Please, with all respect, lend us your technology to send a message to Threa."

"Rightfully so," Venus said. "And I will send a message to the home planet of the Whites to call for their help to join us on Earth."

"Do you think our weapons can stop them?" Penny said holding the Light Rod.

"The necklace will be our weapon," Venus said. "It still has a bond with the Creator. He did not leave you forever, Shane."

"Then it is settled," Shane said. "We will work together and all races and civilizations will become one."

271

Shane felt a sense of pride swelling in his chest. Long gone were the days when he was a shy college student trying to get a date with Alice, or when he was running around with a camera working at his internship with Fashion Rack magazine. He was nearly forty years old now and for the first time, he felt like a real adult. He felt like he had a sense and a purpose. He spent fifteen years living on Threa, yet he never felt it was home or that he fit in. He always felt different. Even as a child when his mentor Derek would take him on photo shoots, he felt older than he really was. He felt beyond his years.

Maybe I am the Visionary, Shane thought. *Maybe I can change my destiny and make it my own.*

"Would your people like to join us on our ship?" Manuel asked Venus. "We can take you to the last place we encountered Sunev."

"Yes, the place where it all began...Roswell," Shane said.

"We will gladly accept the ride," Venus said. "Follow me onto the platform."

Venus walked to one end of the room onto a giant square tile that had the symbol and elements of the pieces that Shane and his group found in the obstacles inside the mountain.

Once all the Whites, Shane, and company were on the platform, it began to rise up what appeared to be a tube leading them up to the top of the mountain where they started.

Once they reached the end, the ceiling opened up to the bright clear day atop the mountain. Instantly, cold hit Shane's face and he rubbed his cheeks for comfort. The ship was still glowing silently where they had left it.

"Will they all fit in there?" Caroline whispered to Shane.

"Yeah. It may be a bit packed though," Shane replied.

"Ready?" Manuel addressed the group. "I'll beam us up."

Shane looked around at the odd group, which consisted mostly of the Whites. He had never been in the company of such a strange team.

A beam of white light beamed everyone into the ship and then they were inside the large empty room in the ship that was nothing but all white walls, floors, and a ceiling.

"Would you like to send your message to Threa?" Venus asked Manuel while pulling out her diamond.

"Yes," Manuel answered. "How do I use your technology?"

"Simply stand where you are and it will record your image," Venus explained. "When you finish your message I will beam a signal to Threa. It should arrive almost instantly. Alert them to meet us at the location of Sector 1."

"Ok," Manuel said. "Should I practice what I'm going to say?"

"Just wing it," Shane insisted. "We don't have a lot of time."

"Alright, I'm ready to record my message to Threa," Manuel told Venus.

Venus touched the tip of the diamond and pointed it at Manuel. Penny and Alice both flinched in fear that Venus would attack Manuel, but all that occurred was a beam of blue light scanned Manuel from head to toe.

"You may begin your message," Venus said.

Manuel fidgeted with his blazer jacket and absentmindedly brushed his hair with his hands. He took a deep breath.

"I'm ready," He said.

"Go on," Venus responded.

"Citizens of Threa, this is your governmental leader Manuel. I have a very important and serious message. Today I must announce that the continued war on the universe's oldest and most powerful civilization, the Dark Ones, must come to the end. However, for that to happen we must band together with other civilizations. Today, we unite with the Whites. Many of you might find that shocking, but they have also walked among Earth longer than us Humanoids, yet they never interrupted our observations and surveillance of the planet. The United States president has been killed at the hands of Sunev, and they are now without a leader. We have a few humans by our side right now, but we plan

273

to rally up the rest of Earth to join us to help take back their home. I am also announcing my resignation as your governmental leader. The power will now be upheld by Shane Baker who is the Bright One. He will lead us to end World War Total on Earth. With the darkness that has spread around the world and the universe, we will find the light. We only hope that our Creator—the one responsible for all of our lives—will come to our aid in the darkest hour. I now turn the table to Shane…"

Manuel stepped out of the light and waved for Shane to come over.

"Me?" Shane mouthed in shock.

Manuel nodded and kept on waving him to step into the light of the diamond.

Shane walked over slowly and found himself being scanned by the blue light. Surprisingly its brightness did not hurt his eyes.

"Threa…" Shane began with a gulp. "There are many things we have yet to learn. Many things even I am about to learn. About our worlds…about myself. There is a higher power out there that once said it would be me that would stop the Dark Ones. Let us make that happen. Join us on Earth. We need your help. I order anyone of you that is willing to fight, to fly out here via escape pods right now. We need you. We cannot let the Dark Ones win. Our future needs to be bright. It depends on it. I thank you for your time and respect. Well wishes Threa."

"Very well done," Manuel said, and he patted Shane on the back.

"Spoken like a true leader," Penny said and she kissed Shane on the mouth.

Alice turned away uncomfortably and Jesse put his arm around her instinctively.

"I will send the message to Threa, to my planet, and then to other galaxies," Venus began, "in case other civilizations exist and want to help us if they have the technology and means to do so."

"Wonderful," Shane said with pride. "Send that message away!"

"We are almost in New Mexico," Manuel announced. "Landing shortly. The ship moved pretty fast with no disturbance across the planet."

Without warning, the ship shook violently. It caused everyone to tumble onto the ground. Some of the Whites yelped with pain because their bodies were fragile. Shane noticed that some of their pale, white skin became instantly bruised because it had appeared as though some Whites had broken bones from the fall.

Venus looked unharmed, but she was crawling on the floor and trying to reach for the diamond so she could send the message.

"What happened?" Aunt Pam asked Manuel.

"We're being attacked by the Dark Ones," Manuel said and he pointed to a part of the wall that became a window.

"Oh...my...God..." Penny gasped.

There was a giant black tornado sweeping through Roswell. Several vehicles and houses were upturned. There were several people running for their lives that were survivors of the initial Dark Ones attack.

"What is that?" Jesse asked.

"The Dark Ones have joined forces," Shane said. "When Noom ruled them, he did the same thing. They have some kind of control of the weather."

"Look!" Caroline screamed. "Is that Sunev?"

There was a group of Dark Ones flying in front of the tornado and heading towards the ship. The one in the middle looked to be the tallest.

"It is her!" Shane said.

"I thought I damaged her eye and wing!" Penny said in shock.

"She's been healed," Venus said. "She's very powerful. We need the light to shine through and stop her for good."

Shane glanced at Venus as she put her finger on the tip of the diamond. The ship violently shook again and began to plummet down to the ground building up speed as it lost its battle with gravity.

"I've lost control!" Manuel panicked.

Shane felt as though everything was happening in slow motion. He saw the Whites and his friends slide to the side of the ship that was facing the ground as it plummeted below. The window showed the desert below them become closer. He saw the diamond was still out of Venus' reach. The messages had not been sent out into the universe.

This is the end, Shane thought. *This is what happens when I tried to change my destiny.*

He could see Penny crying on one end of the ship. Shane could not reach her, however he extended his hand out to her. She was hugging Caroline who was also crying and had one of her hands over her stomach.

Shane felt a sudden rush of wind inside the ship. There was a warm feeling on his chest. He looked down and saw that his necklace was black again.

"He's returned!" Shane shouted over the yells of the ship's passengers.

Shane raised his necklace up high over his head and used his mind to channel its strength. It was as if he could read its inhabitants mind. For some reason he knew why the Creator had left. He left Earth to channel the power of the stars because light kept him alive, just as it keeps life alive on Earth and other worlds. He also knew the Creator left for another reason, but that reason was being kept from Shane.

Light is what gives life…

Shane understood the Creator's message to him and suddenly his black crystal necklace began to glow bright white. Everyone in the room shielded their eyes. They felt the ship's fall onto Earth slow down.

"You did it Shane," Venus said and she smiled for the first time.

There was a soft thud as the ship landed onto the sand of the desert. It stopped glowing bright as it was damaged, but a door appeared on the wall.

"Let's exit," Shane ordered to the group.

Within seconds everyone was out of the ship and standing outside, just a few miles from Sector 1. The tornado was about to sweep over it.

"The door!" Shane screamed.

Venus reached for the diamond and held it in her hands for a few seconds before a gust of wind blew it out of her hands and it flew up into the sky towards the tornado.

"No!" Shane shouted.

Venus put her hands to her mouth in shock. She was showing real emotion, which she had not done once at all.

"The Dark Ones took away our chance to band together as a universe," Venus said.

"Are you sure you were not able to transmit a message?" Manuel asked.

"I attempted to in the ship, but then they attacked us," Venus said.

"Manuel, do you think you can get the ship to work?" Shane asked.

"Yes, if you give it some light," Manuel responded.

Shane aimed his necklace at the ship and instantly it began to float a few feet above the sand with a soft white glow.

"You are aware of where the government was keeping military personnel right?" Shane asked.

"Yes, from my NHR days," Manuel said. "Why?'

"Go find them and bring them," Shane said. "As well as any survivors. Help arm them all. This is World War Total. There are no civilians anymore. We are all an army of one."

"Ok," Manuel said. "Is this my first order under your leadership?"

"As my second in command, yes," Shane said, and he patted Manuel. "It feels so weird to say that."

"Thank you Shane," Manuel smiled and entered the ship.

Once he was inside, the orb took off at light speed and disappeared into the distance. The tornado was getting closer to the ruins of Sector 1.

"We can't let them destroy that door," Shane said while pulling out his Light Rod. "I'm heading over. You all stay here until I give you the clear."

"I'll go with you," Penny said.

"No, stay behind. Please," Shane said.

Penny nodded in agreement. Shane took off in the direction of the tornado and Sector 1 at full speed on foot.

"Going somewhere?" A voice from behind Shane spoke.

Shane turned around and saw a Dark One glaring at him, but the voice was male.

"Leviticus…" Shane gasped.

"Right you are," Leviticus said. "Come with me!"

Leviticus grabbed Shane roughly by the shoulders with his two hands and flew him the direction of the tornado. Once they were close by Shane spotted Sunev flapping her new wings around the ruins of Sector 1. When she saw Shane being brought to her, she landed on the foundation of Sector 1 and relaxed her wings.

Leviticus swung Shane over to the foundation and he landed hard on his stomach, but was otherwise unharmed. He dusted himself off and got to his feet.

"You think that weapon will truly stop me?" Sunev taunted Shane as he pointed to the Light Rod at her. "I was able to heal myself. I can see out of this eye again."

Sunev blinked and then snapped her teeth threateningly at him.

"Your stay here is no longer welcome," Shane said through gritted teeth. "You must go…or else."

"The Bright One is threatening me!" Sunev said sarcastically, and it was followed by a cackle of laughs from nearby Dark Ones that were flying around Sector 1.

Sunev extend her long claws and grabbed Shane by the throat.

"I have been waiting to get my revenge for destroying my father," Sunev hissed. "I will snap your back in half!"

"STOP!" A booming voice from behind Sunev called.

It was the future Ryker and several of his fellow Cosmos of Destiny people. They were walking out from where the door to their future was. Several cloaked and similar looking individuals walked onto the foundation of Sector 1 with Light Rods pointed at Sunev.

"We have come to your aid," Ryker told Shane.

"Th-thanks," Shane coughed and he rubbed his crystal necklace, which immediately emitted sparks of white light.

Sunev screamed in agony as the light had burned off one of her fingers.

Sunev reached for Shane again but he rolled out of her way on the ground. Ryker and the rest of the Cosmos sent light beams at Sunev and she flew off to dodge their hits.

Leviticus and several other Dark Ones closed in on the Cosmos as they fought. Shane ran to their aid.

"Shane, we need to seal off the door," Ryker said.

"Permanently?" Shane asked.

"Yes," Ryker said. "We've done more damage than good by interfering with the past. The Dark Ones' knowledge of us has given them an edge. We are not sure why, but the Visionary asked us to leave the Cosmos and come to your aid. He believes the future will be destroyed."

"How?" Shane asked.

"The Visionary did not tell me," Ryker said as he hit one of the Dark Ones in the face with the Light Rod causing it to fall from the air with a hard smack onto the foundation.

"You killed it!" One of the Cosmos cheered.

"How could the future be destroyed?" Shane said dumbfounded.

"The Cosmos of Destiny will be destroyed by the Dark Ones some how," Ryker said. "The Visionary foresaw it. If we shut the door closed, then the Dark Ones can do no harm."

"But that means you are stuck here in this time period," Shane said.

"That is a risk we are taking for our leader," Ryker said.

Sunev flew at one of the Cosmos and grabbed a female one judging by the sound of her screams. Shane had to look away as Sunev clenched her claws around her throat until she was decapitated. Shane felt the head hit his back with a sickening thud and a splash of warm blood. Shane took one look at the Cosmos' head and nearly threw up. He ran a few feet away from the head to put as much space between him and it.

"See how dispensable the future is," Sunev said. "This is the future you have to look forward to. The Cosmos of Destiny is not a perfect and unified civilization…they are blood and bones."

"We are all blood and bones," Shane spat back.

"Shane, take this," Ryker said, and he handed Shane a signed photograph of Candy Adams.

"What is this?" Shane said taken aback by the random photograph Ryker gave him.

"It's from the Visionary," Ryker said while dodging a swipe from Leviticus' claws. "He said you would know what to do with it."

"This is a photo of Mariette," Shane said while pocketing the picture in his jacket pocket. "A very old photo from twenty years ago."

Leviticus grabbed Ryker by the shoulders and flew up into the sky.

"Drop him!" Shane ordered to Leviticus and he shot a beam of light at him with the necklace, but missed Leviticus by inches.

Sunev was glaring at Shane with murderous red eyes. She was closing in on him, but then she turned to look up at the sky. Shane followed her gaze and saw three white orbs of light heading towards them.

"Threa!" Sunev spat. "How did you alert them? You don't have a Communicator."

"Venus' diamond object must have worked!" Shane cheered as he swelled with pride as the sight of his people.

The three ships landed and out walked hundreds of his fellow Humanoid citizens of Threa. Each of them had Disintegrators armed at the ready. Instantly a few Dark Ones were killed. The sudden appearance of the Humanoids distracted them.

"NOOOO!" Sunev shrieked and she flew up high in the air.

The present day Ryker was running to Sector 1 with his Disintegrator aimed in front of him. Ryker smiled at the sight of the future Ryker who did not look anything like the present day Ryker.

"This is quite a surreal feeling," Ryker said while still being restrained by Leviticus.

"We received yours and Manuel's message," Ryker said. "The Whites had it transmitted to our planet."

"I'm so happy!" Shane yelled.

Sunev turned to look at Shane and gave him a menacing smile. She turned back to look at Ryker and she opened her mouth and a ball of fire shot out of her mouth and hit the present day Ryker before he could register what Sunev had done.

"NOOOOOOO!" Shane cried and he fell to his knees.

Ryker's body fell to the ground in flames and continued to burn. Shane took one look at the future Ryker and saw a tear form under his eye before he vanished into thin air because he no longer existed.

"Fascinating," Sunev said when she saw what happened to the future Ryker.

"Amazing!" Leviticus jeered.

281

Shane locked eyes with Sunev. He felt a surge of rage because he had recently learned that Ryker was his brother. He always thought he was an only child, but his venture into the Cosmos of Destiny taught him otherwise and that both Ryker and Derek were his siblings.

"You're going to die like your father," Shane said.

"No," Sunev replied. "You're going to die like yours…"

"My father died in a helicopter incident," Shane spat.

"He died on Earth," Sunev teased. "You will too."

"That was my brother you just killed," Shane spat.

"Sunev!" Leviticus shouted. "Look!"

Sunev and Shane looked in the distance and saw that the Whites, Shane's friends, and a group of regular looking humans and military men and woman were walking towards the Sector 1 ruins led by Manuel. Two disc shaped ships flew appeared in the sky and landed near the ships from Threa. Several more Whites had arrived from their home planet and were running to join their brethren.

"Manuel did it!" Shane said to himself.

"What!" Sunev laughed. "Does he think an army of humans and those lanky and wretched Whites can stop us?"

"Every single civilization in this universe is against you, Sunev," Shane said calmly. "Can't you see this is *your* end? Not mine, not Earth's or anyone else's. You will pay for the harm you brought to this planet, for the death of my best friend Mike, and for all the lives lost innocently at your hands."

"I'm not afraid of you," Sunev said. "The Bright One means nothing to me."

"Seal the door!" Shane ordered to the Cosmos that were lingering a few feet away from them.

Sunev turned her neck fast and roared at the Cosmos as they made their way to the underground door. She extended her wings and slapped Shane with them. He fell onto the floor, but quickly grabbed onto Sunev's tail. He was dragged through the rubble and saw a couple of the Cosmos get thrown out of the way as Sunev made her way into the chamber where the door to the Cosmos of Destiny was.

She shot a fireball at two of the Cosmos who had arrived at the door. They caught fire and fell to the ground to their death.

Sunev opened the door and walked inside. It was then that she realized Shane was grabbing onto her tail. She swung her tail to the wall and Shane hit the part of it that had the Reptilian engraving. Shane tried to pick himself up, but Sunev had already closed the door. He could feel his feet lift off the ground. They were traveling to the Cosmos of Destiny.

Shane felt the cold stone floor of the familiar chamber he had landed in once before. Sunev extended her wings and roared at the sight of a brown-cloaked figure. Shane was expecting an army of the Cosmos to be waiting for them, but there was only one. This Cosmos had a familiar silver walking stick.

Chapter Twenty-Three:
The Visionary's Broken Destiny

Sunev extended her wings and flew at the Visionary. The Visionary lifted his cane and shot a beam of white light at Sunev's throat. She screeched so loud, that Shane had to cover his eyes and ears. The sounds reverberated around the room and glass shattered onto the ground. Apparently the same glass, which Sunev had destroyed earlier, had been replaced. The new glass fell onto the ground and pieces of it cut Shane's arms as he shielded his face.

Sunev was twitching on the ground. The sounds escaping from her throat ceased, and she was no longer stirring.

"Is she dead?" Shane said more to himself than to the Visionary.

"I believe so," The Visionary said in a barely audible whisper.

Smoke began to billow out of Sunev's dead mouth and float lazily up into the ceiling and it escaped from the broken windows. Shane thought the smoke was probably from her ability to breathe fire. It looked like Sunev had finally been extinguished.

The Visionary bent down to the ground on his knees and pulled a vintage-looking camera from inside his cloak.

"Examine this, then follow the music please," The Visionary said.

The Visionary turned on his heel and walked up a stairwell to a room on the second floor. When the Visionary was out of sight, Shane walked over to the camera.

"Wow," Shane murmured. "It's an exact replica of the one Derek gave me."

Shane's mind raced back to the Santa Monica Pier nearly two decades ago. He met Penny's mother Peggy, there and she handed him a similar camera that Derek had left behind for Shane as a clue. It was originally given to Mariette to give to Shane, but she had Peggy do it for her.

Shane grabbed the camera and walked up the stairs to the room where he saw the Visionary disappear into. As he climbed up, he remembered the photograph of Candy that Ryker had handed to him. Shane pulled it out with a puzzling look on his face. He continued to climb up and heard music playing in the distance. It was echoing eerily off the walls.

Shane entered the room on the second floor. It was a library. There were stacks of books on the left and right walls. At the end of the room was the Visionary sitting on a chair with a record playing before him. Shane recognized the song as "I want Candy."

Shane's heart began to race, the closer he was to the Visionary. His mind was racing with impossible thoughts, but something told him nothing was impossible in the Cosmos of Destiny.

"The camera...the photograph Ryker gave me...that song...those are clues," Shane said. "You purposefully placed them, like you always did when I was a kid. You always wanted me to end up at my own conclusions and figure out answers for myself."

Shane's heart was beating so fast, he thought that the Visionary could hear it.

"So you know who I am then," The Visionary said with his hood still on and covering his face in dark shadows.

"Yes," Shane said and he took a deep breath. "You are my brother..."

The Visionary stood up from his chair with the help of his walking stick. With his free hand, he lifted off his hood to reveal his face. Shane was expecting him to look like the other Cosmos,

285

but he didn't. He looked like a man who had been aging for centuries, yet his face was still recognizable as the man who had once taught him all he knew about cameras and who left behind a set of clues for him to decipher the truth of his own identity.

"Derek..." Shane gasped and he began to cry. "I thought you were dead. The NHR killed you!"

"My dear Shane," Derek replied. "It was my other who died that night. Remember Ryker informed you that we were cloned from a human? Well my original—who was human—died for me that day."

"How?" Shane asked in utter shock.

"Put on these glasses," Derek said. "It will show you that memory."

Shane put on a pair of silver glasses that Derek handed to him. His eyes were watching what appeared to be a movie, but were in fact a memory of Derek's.

Shane saw Landon pushing Derek's car through the rearview mirror. His vision looked blurry, but then Shane realized it was because Derek was intoxicated. He turned to the left and saw another Derek.

The Derek on the passenger side of the car said, "Genesis does not know I came here. A shadowy man that came out of this crystal necklace that has been in Genesis' possession, sent me here. He says you are the future and might be the Bright One. The Bright One will save the universe one day, but it is either you or your brothers Shane and Ryker."

"Shane?" Derek said drunkenly. "I don't have any brothers. I was adopted."

"The shadowy man will guide you, but your existence must be kept a secret in case you are the Bright One."

The human Derek touched the Humanoid Derek and Derek found himself in a white room. The Creator was standing before him.

"I'm sending you into hiding. I will explain to you more about why your life has been spared and why your original other will help fake your death," The Creator said.

The images stopped and Shane took off the glasses.

"Your death was orchestrated by the person who you were made a clone of..." Shane said in awe.

"Yes," Derek replied.

"I just—I can't understand," Shane said. "The Creator wanted you to live because he thought you might be the Bright One?"

"Or Ryker..." Derek said. "But it was evident it was you and Genesis learned you could survive a possession of a Dark One before Noom killed her."

"I have so many questions," Shane began. "I just don't know where to start."

"You were tested," Derek said. "You earned your right to learn about your Humanoid secret. You learned about life on Threa. You came back to Earth when you learned its secrets were threatened to be revealed, and even though you were unable to stop that, you continued your fight. You came back to Earth again even after Manuel took you to live in Territory 3. You came through yet another door labeled 956. Remember the one in that storage facility of mine that had my old photographs and that video of me that revealed to you your identity? Well, once again you came through another door by copy of the same key and this time it is not a video of me. It is me...in full flesh and blood."

"In a drunken stupor you told my Earth father Todd to go where it all began," Shane said. "You did not know you were going to be saved that night—how would you even know about this door."

"You're right, I did say that," Derek said clasping his hands together. "But only because Genesis said I had to. She was aware of the Cosmos of Destiny, but she did not elaborate that with me."

"Genesis was not aware that your original human self was going to sacrifice his life for you," Shane said. "I just saw him say that in your memory."

"And she did not," Derek said. "She was to believe I truly died trying to protect your secret and left behind clues so that you could one day learn your secret without her breaking her own code set before by the Elders because you were not of age to become a Knowing."

"Right…" Shane said. "I had no idea you were a Humanoid, let alone my brother."

"I was an Unknowing as well," Derek said. "The Creator filled me in. The Creator helped me pave this path of enlightenment and towards the creation of the Cosmos of Destiny."

"Why did Ryker and a few other Cosmos come to my present time period?" Shane asked. "He said something about the Cosmos of Destiny being destroyed, yet I don't understand how it could have been. You just killed Sunev. She cannot do any harm here."

"They call me the Visionary because not only can I help us look into the past, but I can see the future that has not happened," Derek said. "It was a gift granted to me in my journey to a longer-than-normal lifespan with the Creator as my mentor. I also helped create this world. I envisioned it with him."

"And I thought I was the Visionary because I did not exist in the Cosmos of Destiny," Shane said.

"That is because in your paved out destiny," Derek said, "you chose to not become a part of us. You chose a different path."

"Where are the other Cosmos?" Shane asked realizing that there was more of their population there when he visited the first time.

"They don't exist anymore," Derek said. "The ones who went back to your time period have another chance at life outside these chambers."

"How do they not exist anymore?" Shane questioned.

"Because of the choices you made in your time period that prevent the Cosmos of Destiny from ever existing," Derek replied.

"Then why are you still here?" Shane asked.

"The Creator came to see me after he escaped out of your necklace," Derek answered. "After doing so he made sure that my life path was unaffected so that you could meet me here. He knew it would be the only chance we could have to meet. You saw how I watched over you in New York City, and when I saw my dear Mariette be taken away by the Dark Ones. I even helped your Aunt Pam survive at Sector 8 and helped her to reunite with you at Sector 7. I stepped in when I could to get a glimpse of you. This is the only way you and I could ever reunite and meet."

"But if you are alive now—in the future," Shane said. "Then you exist in my present. Where were—are you in hiding?"

"That's not important," Derek said. "What is important is that you learn about your purpose, which is more than being the one destined to defeat the Dark Ones…"

"Tell me," Shane insisted.

"In your current time period as you became the leader of Threa, you brought together different civilizations. You helped them put aside their differences to work as one to fight the Dark Ones. That is what set in motion the creation of the Cosmos of Destiny. The idea of this place sounds wonderful in theory, but as we meddled with the past, we only brought upon ruin and destruction and we failed to successfully save Earth from its current status. In the Cosmos you visited previously, Threa replaced Earth, because Earth was destroyed. Things have changed, but that is for you to learn on your own. You do not need to know the future that you have not rightfully lived yet."

"I need to get back," Shane said. "I need to stop the Dark Ones and help my friends."

"You will," Derek said. "But our time here is very short. My destiny is broken. Your destiny is now being controlled by you and not by an advanced future civilization—us."

"Broken?" Shane said with a raised eyebrow. "How is your destiny broken?"

"The Cosmos of Destiny tampered with the past. There are consequences for that," Derek explained. "The Creator warned me, but I ignored him. The future has been altered. There no longer will be a future perfected civilization anymore. I don't know what your future holds, but I've grown here alone now. You will need to leave the Cosmos because the door will be destroyed and there will never be a connection to the future again. You will go back to Earth and fight with all your might. In the end, you have to choose between Threa and Earth. When the Creator saved my life to allow my original to play me and fake my death, he gave me the same choice. Obviously I chose Earth, but he asked me live far away from where I was known. I chose a different country and started a new life."

"I cannot believe you were alive all that time," Shane said still trying to process all the information.

"I was believed to be the Bright One, but when it was learned that it was you, the Creator said I would be destined to lead a group of survivors into the world I created here," Derek said.

"So this journey that I have been on...why am I on it and what makes me so special?" Shane asked as if he had been waiting an eternity for the answer.

"As the Bright One," Shane said, "you were born through an evolutionary method where the genetics and the stars aligned perfectly that you became the one born with the light. That is why you are called the bright one. *Light is what gives life.* The Creator gives light to the universe. Through his private teachings with me, I learned all I know today. He creates the stars, the planets, and our lives. He created worlds through fire, air, water, and earth. Subsequently, the Creator also created the Dark Ones not realizing that as a life form they would have their own free will and because they outnumbered the Creator, they wanted to take over his thrown. The Creator is powerful, but he needed help from other life forms and knew it would be millions of Earth years before he could have help in stopping the Dark Ones."

"If he's powerful enough to create life," Shane said, "why can't he just stop them?"

"The Creator is made of the same substance as the Dark Ones' original form," Derek said while touching Shane's necklace. "That is his weakness."

"Why is it a weakness?" Shane asked. "He's been helping me stop the Dark Ones for a long time while inside my necklace. He's inside it right now."

"Exactly," Derek said. "He's protected inside the crystal. Without its barrier, the Creator can be destroyed. He's outnumbered by the Dark Ones and needs the crystal and its elements to fight. The only one who can share its powers is the one born with light. You...the Bright One."

"So because of my destiny and my life's binding to the crystal's legend, I have to work together with the Creator to stop the Dark Ones for good with the power of light."

"The power of all light," Derek added. "I'm proud of you Shane, and the man you have grown up to be. You survived all the challenges I left behind for you, and the challenges left behind for you in my time of faked death. The Creator has been by your heart for so long. The Cosmos of Destiny is what you make of it. This is my Cosmos of Destiny, but your Cosmos of Destiny will be what life path you choose when you end the darkness. This destiny is broken."

Shane had tears forming down his eyes. He walked over to Derek and gave him a tight embrace that lasted for a minute. He felt Derek's cold tears falling down his shoulder. They broke away from their embrace and Derek stared Shane in the eye.

"You are giving people a chance to live," Derek said. "In many ways you are like me. You are a Visionary of your own accord. Let's get you back to your millennium."

The temperature in the room began to rise. Flames were engulfing the entire chamber.

"What's happening?" Shane asked in shock.

"Let's get you back to the door—RUN!" Derek ordered and he led the way down the stairs without his walking stick.

"Is something wrong with the Cosmos?" Shane yelled while dodging pieces of the ceiling that were falling to the ground.

"Supernova..." Derek cried.

"WHAT?!" Shane yelled.

"We are inside the sun. It is dying," Derek said.

"And you knew all along this would happen?" Shane asked. "Why would you build a civilization in the core of the sun?"

"Untouchable by anything," Derek said.

"But you ideally would not have any more threats in this future time frame," Shane said.

"Right," Derek replied, "but Sunev's more powerful than we know. Instead of dying when I killed her true form, she escaped back as her shadowy, smoky self. She's so powerful that the sunlight is not even fazing her. She's causing the sun to self-destruct. I foresaw this."

"How can you see the future?" Shane asked.

"An ability that the Creator gave me," Derek said.

Derek pushed Shane towards the door. He reached for the handle and opened it.

"Wear these glasses to protect you from the sun's light," Derek said. "I'm so glad I was able to give you a proper goodbye this time."

"You are coming with me," Shane said grabbing Derek's arm.

"Shane—don't!" Derek yelled trying to free himself from Shane's grip. "Trust me, I need to stay here."

The chamber caught on fire and black smoke began to fill the room. Shane and Derek began to cough. Derek collapsed to the ground and hit his head hard on the stone floor. Shane could have sworn he heard a hiss ringing near his ear.

Shane knelt down and lifted up Derek's unconscious fragile body and walked into the door. He took one last glance at the Cosmos' chamber knowing it would be the last time he would ever see it. Shane closed the door and bright orange light filled the room. He felt his feet leave the stone ground, and with his glasses on, he saw himself being pulled through the parallel universe, which was his current time period. For a few seconds it was as if he was floating away through space. He could see the sun in the distance. It exploded and flares and flames lit outer space as if some brilliant

292

fireworks show was taking place. The Cosmos of Destiny was gone.

Shane felt his body land in the room where the Reptilian engraving was. He began to feel the temperature rising quickly. Shane kicked open the door and dragged Derek's body out of it and up the stairs.

When he arrived at the top of the foundation of Sector 1, he walked into what looked like a full-on war. There were humans, Humanoids, Cosmos, and Whites, each using their own weapons to take down the Dark Ones. The tornado was still spinning furiously in the background, but it did not look like it was moving.

A huge jet of fire exploded high into the sky from where the door was behind them. Shane knew that at that moment, the bond between his time period and the future had been closed permanently.

"It's time to make my own destiny," Shane said. "No one else will shape it for me."

"Shane!" Penny yelled after dodging a claw swipe from a Dark One. "You're ok!"

"Yes," Shane said. "I'll fill you in later, but some crazy things just happened at the Cosmos."

"Who is that?" Penny asked while pointing at the unconscious body of Derek.

"It's the Visionary!" One of the Cosmos yelled with glee. "Is he alive? Did you save him Bright One?"

"He's just unconscious," Shane reassured them. "Penny, can you help me drag him to safety?"

"Yes," Penny replied.

They pulled Derek by the feet and moved him under some some rubble where he was hidden from the war that was occurring.

"I'm not sure leaving him near Landon's body is appropriate," Shane said realizing that Landon's covered body was a few feet away.

"Why?" Penny asked.

"This is Derek Conrad," Shane said.

"He's alive?" Penny said with shock.

"Yes...long story," Shane said with haste.

"Oh Shane!" Aunt Pam called with a gun in her hand. "You are safe!"

"Where did you get that gun?" Shane asked.

"From one of the military men," Aunt Pam replied turning red. "Although I don't think I can do much damage to those wretched creatures with it. Who is that man?"

"It's Derek," Shane said.

"Derek Conrad?" Aunt Pam said in disbelief. "But he's dead and this man looks like he's really, really old."

"Derek's death was fabricated by a higher power so that he could help me and help others," Shane said. "I'll explain to you all in detail what I learned about the Cosmos, but right now we have World War Total to fight."

Shane got up off his feet and saw Alice and Shane holding Disintegrators from Threa shooting at any Dark One that would come their way. Even the United States military men and woman had Disintegrators, which were probably from Sector 8.

"Where's Sunev?" Penny asked.

"She stayed in the Cosmos and caused a supernova," Shane said. "She's done for."

"The Cosmos is gone? For good?" Penny said in a sorrowful tone.

"Yeah," Shane said. "But for the better. We can choose our own paths and not have to worry about anyone from the future telling us what to do or controlling how things happen."

Penny hugged Shane and kissed him feverishly. They broke away and had a silent agreement to fight the Dark Ones.

"I have dibs on Leviticus," Shane ordered and he pulled out his Light Rod and ran in the direction of where he was flying.

As Shane approached Leviticus, he had to shield his eyes for a few seconds as Leviticus ripped the head off a White child. The scene was bloody and gruesome. Rage began to build inside Shane, and he tossed the Light Rod to the ground and pulled out his crystal necklace.

Leviticus looked shocked to see Shane's sudden appearance, but his expression quickly changed to menace. Leviticus flapped his wings hard making dirt fly up in different directions. Shane shielded his eyes once more to prevent dirt from falling into them. He thought hard with his mind to channel the light of the black crystal. He knew the Creator was bonded with him. The necklace began to glow really bright that the light had encompassed Shane fully. It looked as though Shane was a walking white light bulb.

Leviticus stalled from flying and began to back away as Shane drew closer to him. The military were aiming their guns at Leviticus but the bullets did minimal damage to him.

"You belong in Hell," Shane said, and he channeled the light towards Leviticus.

It was as if lightning had struck Leviticus through the heart. The bolt of light created a clean hole straight through his chest. Leviticus shrieked with pain and agony. Shane watched in shock at how powerful he felt and how easy it was to cause the creature before him great anguish.

The military that was aiming fire at Leviticus, stopped to cheer. Leviticus looked at Shane with his red glaring eyes, which turned to shock almost instantly.

Alice and Jesse had both used their Disintegrators to shoot off Leviticus wings into nothing but dust. Leviticus screamed and fell face first into the desert sand. Venus came running and she jumped into the air and stabbed Leviticus in the back with her pencil sharp weapon. Leviticus raised his head and looked at Shane in defeat.

"We've lived for millions and millions of years," Leviticus moaned. "We deserved Earth and we deserved the true form. We deserve to lead the universe. You are an accident—an experiment. We were the first civilization to thrive in the universe."

"You are the one that is defeated," Shane said. "You've had more than enough time to leech and prey on other souls. Now it is time for me to take yours."

Shane channeled the light at Leviticus' face and in seconds he was nothing but black ash lying on the desert sand. Leviticus had been defeated. Cheers from everyone fighting for Earth met his death. Several other Dark Ones that were flying in the sky began to retreat in the direction of the tornado. They disappeared into it and the tornado began to move towards them slowly.

"They're angry," Alice said to Shane. "Can you use that really cool light trick on that tornado?"

"I can and I will," Shane said.

"That tornado is going to destroy everything in its path," Caroline said. "Shane, you need to stop it quickly."

Shane rubbed the crystal necklace again and felt its power of light surge through him. He felt energized and wiser as it coursed through his body. He had a connection with the Creator and in that moment it was as if he was being taught many things. He knew that those teachings would be useful to him one day, but at that point in time, his greatest concern was to end the war.

"Everyone, stay here!" Shane ordered to his army.

Shane ran as fast as he could through the desert sand. He kept running even though the distance between him and the tornado was a few miles. He was not even breaking a sweat. It was as if he could run forever and never need a drink of water or a break for rest.

Images flashed in Shane's mind, but he did not have time to even concentrate on what they were. He felt as if there was truly someone with him. He knew it was the Creator.

Even though I know my purpose, I still wonder, why me? Shane thought.

Shane's mind raced to images of his Earth mother Emily and his Earth father Todd. He thought about his best friend Mike and his mentor Manuel. Shane swelled with emotions knowing that Landon took his own life prematurely. If only he knew that the Derek Shane loved was still alive. Shane began to pang for Mariette who was one of the most interesting individuals he had ever met. There was also Dimitri who helped him during the first discovery of who he was. Shane could never forget about Dr. Felix Morgan's brave attempt at helping Shane escape from the NHR. James Carter was at one point just someone who was doing his job for the government before he was coerced by evil much like his Uncle Robert. Shane thought about how lonely Aunt Pam was now that his Uncle Robert was deceased and wrongfully used as a ploy for the evil doings of the Eye Openers. Shane's mind then rested on Ryker whom he had just learned was his brother. He was happy that at least his other brother Derek was not really dead after all these years and had been watching over him as a big brother normally would.

Normal, Shane thought. *I've always been anything but normal. Here I am trying to save what is left of the world. So much has changed. Where do I go from here? I still have my friends Alice and Caroline. I still have my Aunt Pam. And I know my heart has fallen in love with Penny. But I have to choose Earth or Threa. I know I cannot do both.*

Shane was a couple hundred feet from the tornado before the strong winds lifted him off his feet. Shane was pull up into the air at high speed into the swarm of Dark Ones.

"I'm not afraid!" Shane yelled.

Shane closed his eyes as he neared the swirling black clouds. As soon as his body slipped through it, he felt as if he fell into a bucket of ice. Chills shot up and down his spine, as he was whirling around in the tornado at high speeds. He felt as if he was going to be sick. He opened his eyes and saw several Dark Ones in their true form looking at him with their hands outstretched.

"You killed our leader!" The Dark One said. "But in here there is only darkness.

The necklace Shane was wearing began to strangle him. It was as if an invisible force was pulling it away from his neck until finally it was freed and flew into the abyss of darkness.

"NOOOOO!" Shane screamed, but his voice could not be heard over the roaring of the winds.

Two Dark Ones flung themselves at Shane and grabbed him by the shoulders and flew down to the ground inside the center of the tornado to hold him down. Shane's feet were dangling up in the air as the wind was trying to pull him, but the Dark Ones had restrained him.

Shane's heart began to race. He did not think this was how things would end, but he knew that without his necklace he was powerless.

"Goodbye Shane Baker," The Dark One hissed into his ear and then opened its mouth wide to reveal sharp teeth.

Shane saw a blinking light spinning around the interior of the tornado above them. It was the necklace.

"Light is what gives life!" Shane shouted as loud as his lungs would allow him. "But that rule does not apply for your kind! The Creator created you. How could you disrespect that?"

"Die!" The Dark One yelled and as it was about to bite Shane the glowing necklace fell straight through its head leaving a gaping hole in it.

Shane tried to hold in the desire to throw up as the Dark One was pulled into the air of the tornado and disappeared. The other Dark One that was restraining Shane fled and flew away. Once it had taken its grip off Shane, Shane was flung into the air and was spinning again, however he had a tight grip on his necklace.

The necklace began to glow even brighter and a beam of light shot straight up into the sky. It broke through the black clouds and for the first time in a long time, Shane could see the clear blue skies of Earth's atmosphere. The sun was shining bright and its rays fell into the inside of the tornado.

Shane felt the crystal necklace become warmer and warmer, and suddenly it did something he had never seen it do before. A huge flame shot out of it and the flames began to lick every inch of the tornado until the black clouds twisting in fury were a fiery inferno.

Shane's body was sweating profusely in the heat, but the fire was not hurting him. The flames burned every inch of cloud and he even saw some true form Dark Ones fall from the sky and onto the ground. Once they hit the ground, the dirt began to swallow up their bodies as if it became quick sand. Then there was a gust of wind that began twisting the tornado in an opposite direction than what it was originally spinning. The Dark Ones lost control of the weather.

There was a huge lightning strike that went straight through the tornado and the fiery twister fell to the ground into a large field of flames. Shane landed in the middle of the fire with the necklace still in his hands. The fire did not harm him. Thunder echoed across the desert and then rain began to fall onto the earth. Shane was soaked, but the water was cool on his body. The rain put out the fire that was blazing around him.

Screams and shouts of Dark Ones could be heard as they fell from the sky since the clouds they created dissipated into nothing. The rain stopped and all that was left was black ash falling from the sky.

Shane punched the air in victory with his necklace at hand. As he did so, he saw the Creator escape from the tip of it and float high in the sky above Shane.

"You have chosen your own Destiny, Bright One," The Creator said. "You have a life ahead of you to live, but today you have done something I never would have imaged—you brought together different civilizations for one cause. You created unity and that, to me, is a perfect world. I've created worlds and watched them grow. I've watched those worlds experiment and create other worlds too. Whatever your beliefs are, even after today, keep them true to you. Beliefs are not something you learn from a book. Beliefs are seen and they are true. The Dark Ones wanted to rule all civilizations. You wanted to unite them. That is all I have ever wanted. You unlocked the powers of the necklace. Not me. I was just a guide and guardian. Use this necklace to help you with your future endeavors. You already know what your choice is going to be and you already know what you will do with the necklace. I'll be watching among the stars *above us*..."

The Creator flew up high into the clear skies in the direction of the sun. It was a surreal moment for Shane. He had never experienced anything unworldly as in that moment, and he was not even from that world he had just saved.

299

In the distance, Shane could see a large group of people running and cheering in his direction. The Whites were walking slowly but as they had long legs, they were able to keep up the pace. Manuel and several of the Threa Humanoids were running as fast as they could while clapping high into the air. The humans and their military were beyond happy that the dark days on Earth were at last over. It was a momentous day for everyone.

Shane began walking towards the hoard of survivors because the dirt he was standing in was muddy and he wanted to get to dry land.

"You did it!" Manuel cheered.

"I'm so proud of you!" Alice shouted.

"Well done nephew," Aunt Pam beamed.

"You're quite the hero sir," Jesse exclaimed.

"I'm proud to call you my friend," Caroline said. "Mike would have been really proud too."

"I love you!" Penny said and she jumped at Shane and put her arms around his back as they exchanged a long kiss.

There were many cheers and whistles coming from the crowd. The applause was so loud that Shane was sure one of the mountains would probably have a landslide from the noise.

"We all did it," Shane said when he and Penny had finished kissing.

"I can't believe that the Dark Ones are finally gone," Manuel said. "Genesis would be so proud. We are all just in awe at how well you did. Even Derek would be proud."

"We can ask him," Penny said nudging Manuel and pointing to Derek who was carried over by one of the surviving Cosmos.

"That's Derek?" Manuel said in shock. "Dear Creator!"

"Yeah," Shane said. "He was the Visionary of the Cosmos of Destiny. Sadly I have to report that the Cosmos are no more."

"You can put me down," Derek told the Cosmos man that was holding him.

Derek got on his feet and walked towards Shane. He was smiling with his eyes closed. It looked as though tears were forming beneath them.

"I'm sorry about your broken destiny," Shane said with honesty.

Derek was silent, but he walked towards Shane and grabbed his hand.

"Walk with me…alone," Derek said.

"Of course," Shane replied.

They walked for about a hundred feet before they stopped. Derek turned and faced Shane and opened his eyes. Derek's pupils were dilated and dark black.

Chapter Twenty-Four:
Where It All Ended

Derek's eyes flashed red for a second before Shane could register the truth. A Dark One possessed Derek, yet he believed he had just destroyed them all for good. A few tense seconds passed before Derek began to sway side to side.

"Sunev..." Shane whispered.

"Yes," Hissed the sound of Sunev's voice coming out of Derek's.

"He will die," Shane said. "He's Humanoid. His body cannot survive."

"I know," Sunev said. "But because of my new abilities I was able to keep him alive just enough to see you face-to-face."

"You could have come to the aid of your kind," Shane said. "You had a chance to fight me up in the clouds, but you chose to hide in Derek's body."

"A choice I regret," Sunev whispered.

"When did you possess Derek?" Shane asked.

"Right as you entered the doorway to return to this time period," Sunev said. "I'm stronger. When Derek killed my true form I was able to go back to my original self. I used my powers to destroy the sun and then came right back as Derek. It was his death sentence."

"You can't win," Shane said. "Because you've already lost."

"I am the last survivor of my race," Sunev began, "so it would be wise of me to surrender. You and I both know I would never do that."

"The Creator will find you if you try to flee," Shane warned.

"They all speak of you as the Bright One," Sunev said. "They all say you can not be possessed by us. Noom could not. Many of my kind were afraid to try. I will try. And when I leave Derek's body, he will finally die. He should have died years ago in that car crash. I remember reading reports about it when I was posing at Kat Twain. Her mind taught me so much, but now as I read his mind, I've learned even more about how he went on to be the Visionary and his work with the Creator. Now, Shane...now I have the upper hand. You see, this knowledge will help me find the Derek from this time period and it will lead me to the Creator and I will find a way to stop the Creator."

Smoke escaped from Derek's mouth and flew above his head. Derek's eyes went back to normal for a few seconds before his life escaped them and his body fell to the sand.

"Derek!" Manuel yelled.

"Shane, there's a Dark One!" Penny shrieked and she ran towards him.

"Stay back!" Shane ordered. "All of you!"

The army stopped at Shane's request, but it looked like each of them were fighting the decision to disobey it.

"No matter what happens..." Shane said.

Sunev flew into Shane's mouth and Shane could feel her thinking inside his head. She was reading his mind and learning his history, yet she was also in pain. She was screaming inside his head, but was not able to control Shane's mouth.

You cannot hurt me, Shane thought.

Shane felt his body go rigid. He fell backwards on to the sand. Immediately his friends ran to his aid and were hovering over him. Shane could see them as they looked into his eyes.

"His pupils are not dilated," Manuel said. "Sunev cannot posses him. She will die trying."

"Can we do something?" Caroline asked.

"He is the Bright One," Venus chimed in. "Let him be."

Shane was not hurting. He could feel Sunev reading his entire history and living the life he lived. Shane was aware that Sunev firmly believed she could escape Shane's body alive now that she was much more powerful.

"Should we kill him?" One of the Cosmos said. "If he dies, so does she. She may be able to stay inside him for as long as she wants."

"We are not going to kill him!" Penny snapped.

Sunev was becoming frustrated inside Shane's body. She was not sure she could survive if she escaped, but she knew the chances were high that she would not. She was unable to control any part of Shane's body. He was immune to her powers. She was aware that Shane was wearing his crystal necklace, but it remained white and empty, as the Creator had left. She was beginning to think the Creator would come back to his aid.

You are fighting a losing battle, Shane thought.

I am? Sunev responded in Shane's head. *I could always fly up to the sun and cause a supernova here in the present. That would destroy your world and solar system.*

You would die too, Shane responded.

There is no point to my life. As you said, I lost, Sunev teased. *But you killed someone I really loved. My father. And here in your head, the one person you love that is still alive is that girl Penny. Consider us even…*

Smoke escaped out of Shane's mouth and he felt his whole body become warm again. He could feel his fingers, toes, and his heart beating. Shane could make out Sunev's red eyes in the cloudy mass floating above him. She somehow survived after possessing him. Sunev turned her shadowy head in the direction of Penny.

Penny's eyes widened in horror. She took a few steps back as Sunev loomed closer. Manuel shot a beam of light with his Disintegrator at Sunev but nothing happened. The light went right through her.

"FAATTTHHHEERRRRR!" Sunev shrieked and she flew full speed at Penny's mouth.

Penny was hit hard and she fell over backwards onto the sand.

"Penny!" Shane cried and he got up off the sand and ran to her aid.

Everyone circled Penny's unconscious body on the ground. Shane put his arms around her and began to cry.

"No," He sobbed. "I love you."

"There, there," Alice said running her hands through Shane's hair. "She's going to be in a better place."

Shane smacked the dirt with his hands and rubbed his necklace hoping something would happen, but it remained still and cold.

"I could not penetrate her," A voice from above them said.

Shane looked up and saw Sunev's shadowy figure floating above them.

"What?" Shane said in surprise and then he looked down at Penny and saw her stir.

Penny opened her eyes and smiled at Shane.

"When she was inside you," Penny said, "you destroyed her powers. You really are the Bright One. She was strong enough to still live, but you've destroyed her power. She cannot possess *anyone.*"

Shane smiled and he could hear murmurs of excitement among the group. Sunev had a look of worry in her eyes.

"You lost, as I said before," Shane said sternly to Sunev. "Your kind is now about to become extinct."

Sunev was silent. She turned her head and flew away into the distance.

"We need to kill her!" Jesse said.

"She's powerless," Venus said. "I believe it is punishment enough to roam the world and universe alone without any significance. She's been defeated. Her whole kind has been. Well done Bright One."

"Hey look at that!" Alice said pointing at the distance.

There was a strange light in the sky entering Earth's atmosphere.

"UFO?" Jesse said.

It zipped over a distant mountain canyon and then landed a few miles away from where they were all standing.

"I'm going to go investigate," Shane said.

"It could be another civilization," Venus said. "I sent a message to different galaxies, even to ones where I'm not sure life exists."

"Excuse me sir," A man in a U.S. military uniform said, "You can use my ATV."

The man pointed at a dusty four-wheel ATV that he had apparently used during the war with the Dark Ones.

"Thank you," Shane said, and he hopped on the ATV and turned it on.

Shane took off at the highest speed possible. It took him ten minutes to arrive at the landing site of the unidentified flying object. Shane saw a man standing just outside of the square shaped object. The object was the USSA.

"Hello…" Shane said timidly.

The man's back was facing Shane and was looking up at the USSA, which appeared to have been repaired since the crash onto the Santa Monica beach.

"Captain Wells?" Shane called out.

The man turned around and Shane's jaw dropped. It was not Captain Wells. He was familiar with this face, as it was much more recognizable than the Visionary's face, because this face had only aged almost twenty years.

"Derek!" Shane said. "Of course you are alive and well in this time period. Where did you come from? Santa Monica?"

"No," Derek replied. "But I did pick this ship up there. It will be useful for me while on my quest for the future."

"The Creator is guiding you, isn't he?" Shane asked.

"That, he is," Derek replied. "I believe my future self has just died?"

"He did—I mean you did," Shane said confusingly.

"May I future rest in peace," Derek said happily.

"The Cosmos of Destiny was destroyed," Shane said. "Are you sure you want to continue your quest to create that?"

"No, the Cosmos of Destiny is the path you choose now," Derek said. "You are the rightful Visionary now. I pass on that responsibility to you."

"What does that mean?" Shane asked

Sunev suddenly appeared from behind the USSA and looked at Derek.

"When are you going to really die?" She taunted.

"One day," Derek said. "In the future. But you made sure that the future written for us changed and was destroyed. Therefore the future ahead of me now is uncertain. I'm not even sure I'll live for hundreds of years more. I might have a normal Humanoid lifespan for all I know. But you did us a favor."

"Enlighten me with what I did," Sunev said not sounding too thrilled.

"You shifted the course of the universe into a much more stable flow," Derek said. "We can now pave our own paths and not have the future decide for us how it should happen."

Derek then pointed at Shane's white crystal necklace.

"Can I borrow that?" He asked.

"Sure," Shane obliged.

Derek took the necklace and then pointed it at Sunev. With a last second look of horror, Sunev's shadow was sucked into the tip of the crystal and encased…

307

"Forever," Derek said. "This crystal will remain black with her forever. She will live on entrapped in it and there is no way she can escape unless the crystal is broken. Only then will she die because she will be weakened by the elements in which this crystal was created. I figured this would be a wonderful souvenir and a final inheritance to give to you. My gift to you brother."

"Impressive," Shane said.

"The Creator has taught me a few tricks," Derek replied. "I have a journey to continue on as his living apprentice. I want you to know that I will be ok. My future is undefined, and that makes me happy. Yours is too, but I think in your heart you have already made your choice of what path you would like to take."

"I think I do," Shane said.

"Good," Derek smiled. "Gosh, long gone are the days that I would bring you to work with me at the studio. I never knew that my calling would be otherworldly one day."

"Can you at least tell me where you are going or if I will ever see you again?" Shane asked.

"That I cannot," Derek said somberly. "I'm so sorry. I know you've only just found out about me still living, but it is for the best that we go on our own separate paths. Our brother Ryker would have had an amazing path, but his was served to help you along your journey—and me when he was part of the Cosmos."

"You know about the future then? I mean it sounds like you were just there," Shane asked.

"The Creator showed me my future memories," Derek said. "It was quite the gift. Speaking of gifts, I have another one for you."

Derek pulled out a thin cylinder, silver shaped object.

"That's a Mind Scrambler!" Shane asked. "Are you about to wipe my memory?"

"No," Derek said. "That would be unless you wanted me too, but your memory and the accounts of everything that you witnessed and just happened must be kept on record, but only for your eyes. You still have the Moonshadow files?"

"I do," Shane said pulling out the leather-bound book from his jacket pocket.

"Don't destroy it," Derek said. "It's a record of the truth. I want to you fill out the rest of it with information of the accounts you experienced during World War Total and the banding together of different alien species. I ask that this book does not get leaked, and it won't because I will have my eye on Earth from time to time. I think you understand why I'm giving you the Mind Scrambler, right?"

"You are asking me to write down real history," Shane began, "but something tells me you want the rest of the world to learn a different history?"

"You are wise at this age," Derek said. "You will always be able to have contact with the Whites and the Humanoids and the humans of Earth. However, the Whites and the Humanoids can live harmoniously as they are in their own planets. Humans will need to continue to thrive on Earth without any knowledge of these recent events. You know why?"

"Their flaw is their inability to accept the abnormal?" Shane thought out loud.

"They cannot live in order after the events that occurred," Derek said. "Some can, but not all. It could be your responsibility or someone else's to restore it."

"I see," Shane said deeply in thought.

"Shane, whatever choice you make," Derek said, "will be the right choice, because it is your choice. Think of it as a chance to start over. Things got out of hand and went awry, but you have a chance to start over. That's why I say your path is the Cosmos of Destiny, because in this journey you have been on to discover yourself, where you came from, and who you truly are, you have excelled with great maturity and growth. I'm proud of you. I'm proud to be your brother."

"Thanks brother," Shane smiled.

Derek handed Shane the Mind Scrambler and they embraced. When they let go of each other, Derek pulled out a cone from his pocket.

"Oh...another last gift...the Communicator left behind in the ship. It works two-way now. It can be left here on Earth and Threa has one that can communicate back with it."

"Thank you," Shane said gratefully.

Derek walked into the USSA and closed the door behind him.

The USSA lit up and took off high into the sky and out of sight. Shane stared up at the sky for minutes knowing that he would probably never see Derek again. He wondered what his future would be like. It was strange to see Derek leave for his path of fulfillment and destiny because now he truly understood how Alice felt when Shane had to say goodbye to her in the Nevada desert when he left for Threa for the first time to learn about his Humanoid self.

The drive back to where the rest of his peers were waiting for him felt like an eternity. Shane had so many ideas in his head that he was considering, but at last he knew that Derek was right. Shane knew exactly how the rest of his destiny should be written. Deep down inside, he always knew this would be his and solely his decision.

"Who was that?" Manuel asked Shane as soon as he shut off the ATV.

Everyone was looking at Shane with peaked interest.

"Someone from my past, present, and future," Shane said.

"Shane!" Penny said. "Your necklace is black again. Was that the Creator? And you have a Communicator cone and a Mind Scrambler?"

"No that was not the Creator," Shane said. "Sunev's soul is now trapped in my necklace for all eternity. The cone and Mind Scrambler were a gift."

"Wow," Penny said. "Glad to hear Sunev got what she deserved!"

"Rightfully so!" Aunt Pam said.

"That's great," Alice beamed while holding Jesse's hand.

"I can't believe this is over," Caroline said. "After all you put us through Shane."

Shane laughed and gave Caroline and Alice a hug.

"Thank you two for sticking with me from the beginning during my Pepperdine days," Shane told them. "Mike would have been so proud of us…and he would have been a great father."

A tear formed in Caroline's eyes, but she gave a very powerful smile. Alice reached out for Penny and gave her a hug, which surprised not only Penny, but Shane as well.

"You take care of Shane," Alice said. "Make sure he leads Threa well. He'll be a great leader and man. I'm also sorry about losing your brother. My condolences."

"That's very sweet of you Alice," Penny said honestly. "Thank you so much."

"It has been a privilege to trust and work with you Shane…with all of you," Venus addressed the crowd.

"Are you heading back to your planet?" Manuel asked Venus.

"We are," Venus said. "I think our time is done here."

"Where are you from?" Manuel asked. "What galaxy?"

"That is our secret," Venus said and she gave Manuel a friendly smile.

"So you are leaving us again, huh?" Caroline asked Shane. "Kind of feels familiar doesn't it. Like déjà vu all over again."

Shane smiled and looked at Manuel.

"You knew you would have to make a choice one day," Manuel said. "We can always visit Earth, but I think Earth is better off being alone for a while."

"This place needs a good leader," Shane began. "It needs to be rebuilt. The people of Earth need a faith and a hope. Much of this place has been left in ruins, but that does not mean it cannot be salvaged. Threa has lots more work to do with Territory 3, before expanding it to the rest of the planet to allow for a nearly similar world and lifestyle as one would find here on Earth. In one alternate future in the Cosmos of Destiny, Earth was destroyed and Threa replaced it as a near exact replica. I changed that. Earth has another chance to revolve around the sun."

Shane took a look up at the clear skies and took in the warmth from the sun.

"What are you trying to say?" Manuel asked.

"There is peace with all civilizations," Shane said. "And for those that we have yet to encounter or meet—if there are any others—well, we extend a friendly hand to them if ever the stars align for us to cross paths."

"Well said, like a true leader," Manuel said with pride. "Have you made your choice then?"

Penny held Shane's hand and whispered, "Whatever your choice is, I will be a part of those plans.

Shane nodded and smiled.

"I assume Threa," Manuel said. "You have a civilization to lead."

"Actually," Shane said. "You have experience with that. Threa thrives well with you. You should be its rightful leader. I have made my choice and it is..."

Penny smiled and squeezed Shane's hand tight. Alice and Caroline looked at each other and smiled. Venus showed no emotion, but Shane was sure that his answer would meet her approval.

Shane looked around at the group, then to the sun, then back to Penny. He gave her a short kiss on the lips and then turned to Manuel.

"Earth."

Epilogue

It was a clear sunny day in the city of Washington D.C. Caroline Lu was driving her vintage Jeep that had been gifted to her from an old friend. She was afraid she would be late to drop off her eight-year-old son at school because of heavy construction on the roads on buildings that were in her route. While she was used to heavy construction as the nation and the world was rebuilding itself, today was much busier than normal because of traffic due to the last day of the current President's term in office.

"You are going to have to tell your teacher that we got into a bit of a traffic jam, Mikey." Caroline said to her son.

"Ok mommy," Mikey replied from the backseat of the Jeep. "I have a question."

"What is it dear?" Caroline asked.

"Someone in my class asked me why I don't have a daddy," Mikey said. "I did not want to tell him the truth because it might make him sad."

"Don't feel like you cannot talk about your father Michael, who you are named after," Caroline said. "He died in the military fighting for our freedoms before you were born, but he expressed to me how much he really loved you. You should be proud of him."

"Ok, I won't feel bad about talking about it next time," Mikey said.

"Ok. We are almost there sweetie," Caroline said.

She pulled up to the curb of the elementary school, and she ran to the other side of the vehicle to get her son out. She tucked in his shirt in the parking lot, and then grabbed his arm and ran into the school with her heels clicking away on the concrete grounds.

"Ok baby," Caroline said. "Have a good day at school. You know how to get to your classroom right?"

"Yes mom," Mikey replied. "What time are you picking me up?"

"Three o' clock," Caroline answered. "We have a big dinner to go to tonight. Have a good day in class."

Caroline kissed Mikey on the forehead and he sped off towards his class with his oversized backpack in tow.

Mikey opened the door to his classroom and everyone looked at him. His teacher raised her eyebrow. She was an elderly lady with dark rimmed glasses in the shape of rectangles and her gray hair was in a tight bun. She was wearing an argyle cardigan.

"Michael Cambell Junior," She said. "Why are you late?"

"My mom ran into traffic Mrs. Richmond," Mikey said.

"Well then, take a seat please," Mrs. Richmond responded.

Mike sat down in his assigned desk seat and unpacked his pens and notebooks.

Mrs. Richmond wrote "World War Total" on the chalkboard.

"Today is a better day than any to teach you all the history behind World War Total," Mrs. Richmond said, "which happened only eight years ago and shaped our country and even the world. World Wart Total began with a radical group—a group of people that wanted to not follow the rules or laws of the United States— set out to make up lies about our country that people believed. They went around saying things such as our history books and religions were not real and they were made up. Of course, that was not true. Our history of the world is very accurate as is religion. This radical group called themselves the Eye Openers. They were led by an evil woman by the name of Kat Twain who was working for our government, but she was secretly passing along inside information to people that did not work for the government. They were terrorists. They created, I guess you could say, a lot of lies.

Well the world went into a panic and lots of people did bad things. There were many laws and crimes broken. People broke into banks, stores, and schools. Cars were racing up and down the streets and many, many, people were hurt and killed. The population of our world was just over seven billion. After World War Total ended, our population was less than a billion. It is known as the largest loss of life in human history.

World War Total ended because our current President Shane Baker, led the army that stopped them. He was a general in the military that banded together with regular people that were not in the army and together they helped restore order to the world. It was such an amazing feat that he inspired so many people. He was offered the position to become president because our former President Will Williams was killed during the war.

Today the White House stands tall again. It was rebuilt immediately, and the First family moved in shortly. President Baker helped shape the world to what it is now. Several countries across the world are still working on being rebuilt, just like ours, but it is all under President Baker's leadership. I wanted to talk about this history lesson with you today, because tonight there will be yet another major historical moment in your lives. Since the nation banded together again eight years ago, there has not been another president, and sadly President Baker's two-year term ends today. Our new president will start tomorrow. We hope that the new president will be able to effectively mange the rebuilding of our nation and our planet after it was left in such a mess. That is why there has been so much construction going on for nearly a decade now."

Mike raised his hand.

"Yes Mikey?" Mrs. Richmond asked.

"My dad died in that war," Mikey said. "My mom said it is ok for me to talk about it, and that I should be proud."

Mrs. Richmond smiled and had a tear in her eye.

"You should be very proud Mikey," She said. "Your father was part of a movement that would bring back balance to this country. My son was a victim of the riots that occurred after the outbreak. I'm happy to know that there was a group of people who stood up to the evil that the Eye Openers brought upon us."

"I have his uniform in my house," Mike spoke up. "It is hanging in my closet. When I'm old enough to join the army, I'm going to join and make sure that our country does not ever go into war again."

"You're such a good child dear," Mrs. Richmond said admiringly, "but the world learned so much after World War Total and since those days there have not been any crimes or wars. President Baker has made sure that our streets are safe. The only dangers in our streets are the ones left damaged from the war, but those can be fixed eventually."

A few of the students clapped and even patted Mikey on the back.

"Did everyone do their homework on the movie we saw the other day starring late actress Candy Adams? Hollywood is another part of history. We hope that one day we will have the ability to make movies for pleasure, but Los Angeles is still being rebuilt."

There was shuffling in the room and the students pulled out their essays from their backpacks or desk cupboards.

A tone sounded in the intercom of the school and the principal spoke.

"This is principal Schwarz, could you all please rise for the Pledge of Re-allegiance?"

Everyone in the class stood up and put their hands over their necklaces and grasped them. Everyone in the room had a small black crystal necklace attached to a gold chain.

"I pledge Re-allegiance to the crystal the Reunited States of America. And to the republic for which it stands tall again, one world under Creator invincible and strong, with life and freedom for all mankind."

"Alright class, it is now time for you to head to religious studies," Mrs. Richmond said. "I hear you will be learning about how our Lord Creator rose from the core of our world to help save us from the apocalypse and darkness that World War Total brought on to us by the devil. Happy prayers children."

Three o' clock rolled around and Mikey was picked up by Caroline.

"How was your day?" Caroline asked while walking Mikey to the Jeep.

"I learned so much today," Mikey said proudly. "In history class we talked about the war daddy fought in and in religious studies I learned about the three wise brothers who were the descendants of the Lord Creator and how one of them was meant to carry the light of good to fight off the devil. Did anyone see that happen?"

"The fight with the devil?" Caroline asked.

"Yeah," Mikey says. "The Moonshadow bible says it happened a few years ago."

"It happened around when you were born," Caroline said, but all I remember was a huge flash of white light. Someone wrote down the accounts of what they saw in that bible."

"The lights!" A woman yelled out loud. "The Nevada and New Mexico lights! There were visitors from another planet! I remember now!"

There was commotion around the school and two police officers came running to the woman who had apparently gone mad and was spitting out random words that made no sense.

"Ma'am we need you to calm down," One of the officers said.

The other office pulled out a thin silver rod that emitted a light and the woman's eyes went into a daze.

"Nothing to see here folks," The officer said. "She's having a mental breakdown.

"Maybe she used to be an Eye Opener," Caroline heard another parent say. "I hope they take her to jail."

"That was weird mommy," Mikey said.

"Yeah," Caroline said. "Some people have strange issues. Ok we need to go. It's a big dinner for Shane tonight."

"I did not tell the class that my mom knows the president," Mikey said. "I don't think they would have believed me."

Later that evening, Caroline arrived at the security gates at the White House. She was wearing a yellow evening gown, and Mikey was wearing a tuxedo. They walked up to the security guard who was scanning everyone that was walking through.

"Eye-D Please," The officer asked.

Caroline handed her and Mikey's Eye-D's to the guard who scanned them with a laser pointer then scanned both Caroline's and Mikey's eyes.

"All clear," The officer said into an earpiece. "Enjoy your evening ma'am."

"Thank you," Caroline said and they walked down a path into the newly remodeled White House, which was an exact replica of the one from the United States era.

"Caroline!" A woman called from the steps of the White House.

"Alice!" Caroline said with glee. "And Jesse! And little Kendra!"

"You look gorgeous," Alice told Caroline. "And look at you little Mikey. You look like an adult!"

"Kendra is growing up so fast too," Caroline said. "She looks just like a miniature version of you Alice. How old is she now?"

"She just turned five," Alice said. "She also looks like my sister too, who she was named after. God I miss her."

"I know babe," Caroline said brushing Alice's arms. "We lost so many people in that war. Shane did a great thing. Who would have thought he would have ditched becoming a photographer and join the armed forces?"

"The death of his mentor Derek in that car accident was hard on him," Alice said.

"Yeah and don't forget his parents died too," Jesse said. "Of natural causes, but the poor guy has lost so many people."

"Shane's friend Landon was also a victim of the war," Caroline said. "I never met the guy but he was good friends with Mike as well."

"I'm so glad America has been able to rebuild itself under Shane's leadership. He's done such an amazing job," Alice beamed. "To think I once dated the president."

"Ahem," Jesse cleared his throat.

"I love you dear," Alice said.

Caroline and Alice walked arm in arm chatting at each others' ear as if they had not talked in ages as they walked up the steps into the White House.

"Therapy is going well I take it?" Caroline whispered into Alice's ear.

"Yes," Alice blushed. "Jesse and I are doing better. No divorce for us."

Upstairs in the president's quarters, Shane Baker was tying his tie in front of a vanity mirror. His wife and First Lady, Penny Mills-Baker, walked into the room wearing a bright green dress that brought out the color of her eyes.

"You look beautiful," Shane said through the reflection of the mirror.

"And you are quite the perfect world leader yourself," Penny replied.

"Well only for tonight," Shane said. "I'm ready to retire. I'm thinking about building a beach house in Malibu in a private area. My parents once had a place there, but it burned down due to a gas leak. I miss that house. I used to live in it when I was in college."

"That would be nice," Penny said. "I know California is not well developed but we can make it work."

"We'll have everything taken care of for us," Shane said. "Just the perks of presidency."

"Your Aunt Pam is in the guest room," Penny said. "Should I walk her down to the dinner party?"

"Could you dear?" Shane said. "I need to have a quick meeting with Lockhart."

"Right, of course," Penny said and she gave Shane a kiss on the cheek and walked out of the room.

Shane put on his tie and adjusted it to his liking before he walked out of the room. Secret service was waiting for him outside.

"Sir, she is waiting for you in the Oval Office," The officer said.

"Thank you," Shane said. "I would like my meeting with her to be closed door and no interruptions under any circumstances. Is that clear?"

"Crystal clear," The officer said while grasping a replica of Shane's crystal that hung around his neck.

"Thank you," Shane smiled and he caressed his own necklace as he walked into the Oval Office.

A woman in a blue dress with auburn hair, who appeared to be younger than she was, even though she was in her sixties, smiled when Shane walked in.

"Miranda," Shane said. "You must be thrilled about tomorrow."

"I am," Miranda replied. "Going from Will William's Secretary of State to taking some time off from politics, then being asked by you to take your place—it has been a whirlwind of a year."

"You received the vote of the Reunited States," Shane said. "It was all you. How are you feeling?"

"About becoming the next president?" Miranda asked.

"No," Shane replied, "About getting your memories back. It must have felt like a rush when memories of your past came flying back to your mind."

"It was," Miranda said. "I cannot believe I was Mind Scrambled for almost a decade!"

"You understand why we had to do it, don't you?" Shane asked. "I mean everyone on Earth was Mind Scrambled. If anyone was to get memories of the past back, they are taken into custody until their minds have been altered back. Even my own wife Penny doesn't know the truth about her past or what she is. She thinks we met on a ranch that was owned by her mother. She thinks her brother died in the war. It's hard being the only one on Earth that knows the truth. It's a big responsibility."

"It must feel good to share it with me," Miranda replied.

"As acting president it is your duty to make sure that world order is kept as is. That our history books are written by our accounts of what we want society to think and that religion is kept so that the world knows that the Creator saved us from peril. We have the greater good now. They believe in a higher power and everyone behaves well. They are civil. This is my utopia. This is my Cosmos of Destiny. We are all equal and we treat each other with respect and love. As long as we continue the Reunited States of America this way and make sure our practices are exercised in other countries across the globe, then we will be just fine."

"Do you find it ironic that you created a world that is being lied to by the government," Miranda said. "A fact that caused the old United States era to fall apart?"

"It haunts me, yes," Shane admitted. "But I understand why it was done, and I'm doing it right, because the burden of the truth falls on the leader of the free world—us—you."

"What happens now?" Miranda asked.

"You Mind Scramble my memories," Shane said pulling out a thin silver rod. "I've dreamt of living a normal life. It is not important to me anymore to know that I was created by an extra-terrestrial race or that I'm a Humanoid. I do want to say my goodbyes to Manuel before you proceed, and I will introduce him to you."

Shane walked over to a cabinet shelf behind his desk. He pulled out a key from his pocket and unlocked the door. A silver cone was sitting on the shelf. Shane pulled it out and set it on top of the desk. He pressed the sides of the cone with his fingers and a hologram appeared over the tip.

"Shane!" Manuel's holographic face was floating over the tip of the coin. "It is time, is it not?"

"Yes," Shane said.

"Are you sure you do not want to come to Threa?" Manuel asked.

"I'm positive," Shane replied. "These are my people and I've led them well. Now I want to retire and live a quiet life with my wife. Miranda was part of the Noah's Ark Project and was the Secretary of State. She is well versed in the non-human relations."

"I will miss you dearly Shane," Manuel said emotionally.

"Me too, my friend," Shane said.

"I'm sure Derek will be watching over us," Manuel added. "And the Creator. They are making sure the universe always stays safe and restored. I will also give your best to Venus and the rest of her people. I'm due to send them a message soon."

"Thank you for everything Manuel," Shane said. "I can't believe this is really the end. It feels like I'm dying."

"Your memories and everything you worked so hard for are dying," Manuel said.

"Yes," Shane agreed, "but the actions of the memories are forever in full effect. Miranda will keep the tradition alive in passing down my memories and the story of the Moonshadow files forever on to the future presidents and one day she'll be removing these memories from her mind when she passes it on."

"It will be a pleasure to work with you and make sure that there is balance in our galaxies," Miranda said. "And I'm very excited that you have offered to replicate Territory 3 for us on Earth in the next few years as we continue to rebuild lost cities."

"The pleasure is all mine," Manuel said. "Our visits will not be frequent. We will only visit when it comes to improving and helping your technology so that your world may one day be one hundred percent up and running like it was before the Eye Openers' attack on New York City."

"I believe we will get there too," Miranda said.

"Manuel, tell the people of Threa I love them and that I am proud of how you all are thriving as a strong civilization. Be safe and Creator Bless you," Shane bowed to the image of Manuel's face.

"Best of luck in your new life," Manuel said, and he signed off.

"He'll be great to work with," Shane said to Miranda.

"Are you ready?" Miranda said while brandishing the Mind Scrambler.

"I am ready to put the past behind me and live my new present. I look forward to my future, which I have chosen. This is my destiny, because I made it so," Shane said, and he closed his eyes.

Miranda touched the top of Shane's head, and there was a white glow. Shane opened his eyes and had a dazed look.

The crowd was cheering, roaring, and whistling as Shane finished his final speech as President of the Reunited States of America. He looked over at his wife Penny who was seated next to his good friends Caroline, Alice, and Jesse. Their children Kendra and Mikey were there as well. A thought came to Shane's mind. Todd and Emily Baker, who were doctors in Beverly Hills, adopted him as a child. He made a mental note to tell Penny that he wanted to adopt a child or two after he left the office for good.

Shane took off his black crystal necklace and handed it to Miranda, as it was tradition for the president in office to wear the unique black crystal necklace that represented a new rebuilding from the darkness. The crowd cheered even louder and Shane waved his arms for them to quiet down so that he could say his last words as president.

"It has been an honor to serve you, my fellow citizens. The fight is over and the recovery commences, however, my job here is done."

About The Author

A.J. Mayers was born and raised in Laredo, TX. He is a true Texan by nature, however his passions and career brought him to Hollywood after he graduated from the University of Texas at Austin. He started off his career working for MTV, and then found a home at Paramount Pictures. As a kid, A.J. wanted to be an author. One day he sat down and decided to put together the Among Us Trilogy. Three years later, the three books were completed as A.J.'s first novel series. When he's not working on films or writing, A.J. is biking around Hollywood or taking his French Bulldog Dexter out for a walk.

Also by A.J. Mayers:

Among Us

Moonshadow

www.amongustrilogy.com

Made in the USA
Lexington, KY
12 November 2016